# Snake in the Grass:
## A Cobra McCoors Adventure

Michael Tumminio

COPYRIGHT

This is a work of fiction. Names, characters, places and
incidents are the product of the author's imagination. Any
resemblance to actual persons, living or dead, is purely
coincidental.

Snake in the Grass: A Cobra McCoors Adventure

cobramccoors.com
twitter: @cobramccoors

# DEDICATION

For Heather, who's always up for an adventure

*"I never knew of a morning in Africa when I woke up that I was not happy."*
…Ernest Hemingway

# ACKNOWLEDGMENTS

I'd like to thank Linda Friedman, Kathy Obbish, David Nganga, Nancy Karanja, James Morinte, Joseph Ngige, John Ngure, and the entire staff of Custom Safaris for making our safari dreams come true again and again.

# 24 HOURS FROM NOW
## 2007

"Oh no," whispered Delia, taking her eyes from her binoculars.

Automatic weapons fire, and the wet smacking sound of bullets against flesh. The monstrous roar of a titan in shock and pain. The panic and trampling of beasts trying to get away from an enemy they haven't seen.

There were five men in a vehicle thirty yards to the east of the herd, each with semi-automatic weapons, firing at the elephant nearest them, a big female. The other animals fled in confusion, and she tried to follow, but the bullets tore through her legs at the knees. It would be a slow death, as she was huge and the rounds couldn't penetrate far, until two of the men produced automatic shotguns and began blasting away at her temple.

"Do something!" screamed Delia.

"Everyone get down!" Cobra yelled back, an instant before they heard the sound of the glass of the headlights and windshield shattering and the pelting of bullets against metal. Everyone brought their heads down to their knees as if they were in a crashing airplane.

Cobra tried to reignite the engine, but it didn't respond.

"Jesus Christ!" yelled Mark. "Look out!"

1

Success… the engine turned over the second time and Cobra threw it in reverse, gunning it backwards about ten yards before the RPG hit the front of the Rover.

The car's hood blew to pieces of fiery wreckage as the vehicle catapulted up in the air, twisting around and throwing some of the guests out into the open. It crashed back to earth, slamming into a leadwood tree, upside-down with its tires still spinning.

Stunned, Cobra discovered he had been thrown about ten feet from the driver's seat, and he was alive. He no longer heard anything but a tinny ringing sound, and he felt heat from the fire behind him. He resisted the overwhelming urge to pass out and risked moving his head to look around.

The men in the car had stopped shooting at the elephant (which was down) and the Land Rover (which was totaled). Cobra saw a second car approach the first, and he witnessed a man with a black ponytail in the second car pull out a handgun and execute the driver of the first.

Cobra's vision blurred, and he was dizzy and delirious, but he knew what he had seen… *whom* he had seen.

*Black Tiger*, he thought, and he assumed those thoughts would be his last.

# PROLOGUE:
# MANY YEARS FROM NOW

Don't mind the smell; you're lucky to have stumbled into this place. I'm telling you, this is the best bar in Kathmandu, maybe even in the Himalayas. No, I haven't been to all of them. I'm working on it, though.

Oh, that empty seat? I'm meeting someone, but she won't be here for a while, so please, pull up a chair. This is my table. I always sit here, since it's closest to the fireplace. I like to look at the fire through my whiskey glass; it makes my drink really take on that amber color and the smoke really brings out the peat. Go ahead, order what you like. This place is fully stocked, with premium stuff. Don't ask me how they get it. This little baby is a nice Laphroaig ten year. They even have pretty good wings here, although I'm not sure they're chicken…

You've sure brought a lot of stuff. Let me guess… climbing Everest, right? Probably getting one last taste of civilization before the next month of freezing your ass off at 35,000 feet. Good for you! Khumbu Ice Falls and all that. You must be in dynamite shape. Oh, a little whiskey's not going to kill you. You've got to acclimatize anyway, I'm sure. You don't? Well, I don't know much about high altitude climbing, I guess, although I have seen Everest from the Tibetan side, many years ago.

Go ahead and take that call. Yes, you can even get cell service up here now, although that takes some of the fun out of an adventure, if you ask me. Many years ago, you walked into a place like this with a cell phone, and three people would fight each other to see who got the honor of robbing you. I'll bet you probably found this place on Trip Advisor or Yelp or Boozequest or some App, but I found it by staggering down just the right back alley in a horizontal snowstorm with a knife wound between ribs three and four. No, I'm not full of shit! I can show you the scar!

You know, you might want to put that thing down. I think that bearded Yeti-looking fucker over there with the five-times-broken nose is staring at you. He probably just wants to appropriate your wallet and passport, maybe commandeer that nice designer Polartek coat you're sporting. Don't worry too much about him; he's not the type who'll throw a punch in here.

Tell you what. Since I've got no place to go, why don't I tell you a story? I'll make it just long enough so that mutant will get loaded and pass out waiting for you to leave, and you can be on your merry way. Me? Oh, I have plenty of stories. After all, isn't that all we really want out of this ride? A few good stories to tell people around the fire before we die, like the cavemen before us? You're an adventurer; trust me, you're going to be into this one. And in my book, you can't beat one place for some of the best adventures: Africa.

# CHAPTER 1:
# NORTHWEST SOUTH AFRICA, NOW
# 2007

And just like that, there they were: the Middle of Nowhere, if Nowhere were sometime in the Triassic Period or some other primordial landscape lost to the ages. I suppose *just like that* doesn't really do justice to the four hours spent flying over vast wilderness in a 20-passenger propeller plane chartered from O.R. Tambo, especially if you were to add those four to the hours that many of them had already logged in traveling over the Atlantic.

After awkwardly stumbling down the fold-out steps onto the dirt landing strip, the travelers first saw him, leaning easily against a beaten-up, retro-fitted Land Rover, his arms crossed and his warm eyes just visible under the shade of his dusty old hat. He approached the plane with an unhurried pace and a confident smile, as if he'd done this a thousand times before, a knight in khaki.

"He looks like Crocodile Dundee mixed with Gaston from that cartoon," said Kevin Tsai, late twenties and tall.

"Down, boy," replied Xavier, about the same age, touching Kevin on the shoulder.

"Out of the way before I throw up," barked Andres, early fifties with a Teutonic accent, pushing past them.

"Rude much?" replied Kevin, whose protest could not be

5

heard over the din of the still-whirring propellers.

Andres bee-lined towards the man who had come to collect them. "It's ten degrees hotter than Hell in that flying coffin. Is this what passes for service in this third-world pit? I was told that our ranger would meet us here. I demand…"

"Pretty sure he *is* the ranger, Mister," called a dark-haired woman disembarking from the cabin, "so why don't you do us all a favor and take it down a notch?"

Andres couldn't reconcile this idea with the image of the dark-skinned man standing before him. "Oh. I didn't think our ranger would be, you know, I mean, this *is* South Africa."

"Call me McCoors," said the ranger, grinning at Andres' awkwardness. "And are we gonna have fun together."

"I still expect you to retrieve my belongings," Andres said, recovering his perpetually-irritated demeanor. "And be careful with the camera equipment. It's expensive."

"Of course," grinned McCoors. "Now go wait in the car."

The dark-haired woman, Delia, now stood on dirt, waiting for her friend Annie to climb down after her. She inhaled deeply, breathing in the smell of wild herbs and the minerals in the soil, and she was deeply happy. She turned to McCoors as he greeted the passengers.

"That guy is an asshole," she apologized. "He's been a jerk for the whole flight."

"I'm sure he just needs a stiff drink," said McCoors cordially. "And I'd be happy to oblige."

"What he needs is a stiff right cross to the nose," Delia replied. "And I'd be happy to oblige."

"Ouch! I like your spirit, but let me personally guarantee that there won't be any punching on this holiday," said McCoors.

"Did someone say stiff drink?" called out Annie, late twenties like her friend, from the plane. "My ears are burning!" And then, noticing McCoors, "Oh, my…"

Annie *tripped*, and you know why I said it like "*tripped*," and

6

fell into McCoors' arms. "Why, hello there, sir."

The other young woman leaving the plane after Annie, a pretty young girl with full features named Susan, shook her head derisively as she gathered her things. "I see the two-star review was hyperbole," she remarked, nose in the air.

From within the plane, a couple in their late sixties looked out and absorbed the vast panorama before them, and they took each other's hands as if they were in Heaven's Penthouse. "My God, it's perfect."

\*\*\*

The small plane ran down the dirt strip as though it were a fast car, rose above the tree line and then disappeared into the horizon. The sound of the propellers quickly faded, being replaced by birds calling, insects humming, and beyond that, the pure quiet found only in remote nature.

McCoors helped the older couple into the seats farthest back in the Land Rover, and they were surprisingly agile for people their age.

"You sure you don't mind sitting in the back?" asked McCoors.

"Do we mind?" responded the older woman, Hyacinth. "We're lucky to have it. You feel the bumps of the road more, but from up here, the view is the best!"

"You've done this before, have you?"

"Once or twice," said the older man, Mark, with a knowing smile that made him seem younger than he was.

As McCoors went to retrieve the last of the luggage to stow into the car, Annie turned around to Delia from the front passenger seat and said, "Did you hear the way he spoke? I think he's American!"

"Will you calm down already?" shushed Delia, who had seen this movie from Annie before. "Why don't you at least get to know him first?"

"What do you think I'm doing? That guy's a *M*an with a capital *M*. I agreed to come here with you to Jurassic Park instead of Paris; let me have a little fun."

"Oh, how I miss Paris," piped in young Susan with the kind of excessively heavy southern accent an actress from New Jersey would use in a movie, "although it can be so crowded this time of year."

"Can we please move it along?" complained Andres loudly as McCoors returned to the Land Rover full of vacationers and tossed the last bags within.

A bird gracefully glided onto the front hood of the car and snatched up a grasshopper.

"Look at that," said McCoors cheerfully. "First kill of the safari!"

Annie clapped, while Delia politely stopped herself from groaning. McCoors climbed into the driver's seat and turned to face the guests, reading from a folded piece of paper he produced from the pocket of his wrinkled, olive-green shirt.

"So, we have… Kevin Tsai, and Xavier Allison…"

"That's us," answered Kevin, happy to be there.

"Kansas City, eh? Good barbecue."

"I'm actually a vegan. That won't be a problem, will it?" asked Xavier.

"Is braised springbok vegan?"

"Uh, I don't think so…"

"Let me get back to you on that." Moving down the list, McCoors continued, "Susan Kaminsky, from Paris, France."

"*Oui*," sang Susan.

"Really? France?"

"By way of Savannah. I'm a travel writer. I write travel articles. That's what I do."

"Like, as a college intern, or professionally?"

"Professionally, of course. I only look twenty-one."

"You look seventeen; good for you. Remember to use sunscreen out here." Scanning down the list, he continued, "You must be Schenker, Andres, from…"

"Stuttgart, yes, yes. I must say, I'm disappointed in the level of service so far, Mr. McCoors. We've been sitting here for twenty minutes and we have yet to commence this game drive. We'll be losing the light soon and…"

McCoors opened up a small cooler next to the gear shift and threw a can of *Castle* beer at Andres, maybe a little harder than he was expecting.

"Relax, Andres! You're on holiday, so have a beer. We're a long way from camp and we'll have plenty of time for taking shots; I promise we'll be in a good spot when the golden hour hits."

"Fine," sulked Andres, opening the jostled beer to have suds spill out over his camera bag, to both his visible chagrin and the visible delight of the other guests. McCoors gently tossed beers out to the others to applause and catcalls.

"Let's see… Annie Herriot, San Francisco, and Delia…" McCoors paused.

"Go on, you can say it," said Delia, confidently.

"Wildhorse."

Childish laughing from the guests.

"Everyone wants a ride on the Wildhorse! Hey-oh!" joked Annie, throwing her hand up to Delia for an unreciprocated high-five.

"You're suuuch an idiot," said Delia, shaking her head.

McCoors didn't laugh, though. "Montana. Blackfoot?"

"I'm impressed," said Delia. "Crow, actually. Annie and I met in college. And what do we call you? First name, I mean, Mister McCoors?"

"Cobra," said McCoors as though that were as common a name as John or Joe. "Out here, I'm Cobra."

"Of course, you are!" purred Annie.

"No, your Christian name, Cobra," said Delia.

"Well, Anaconda, of course," he said.

Aside, Xavier whispered to Kevin, "That is the manliest man who ever manned. Seriously, if you squeezed one more drop of testosterone into that guy, he'd explode."

"I don't think he plays for our team," replied Kevin,

"Don't be so sure."

"What'll you bet?"

"Twenty bucks!"

"Done."

McCoors, *excuse me*, Cobra, came to the last two names. "And finally, Mark and Hyacinth Sarasota, Pasadena, Maryland. Mark, congratulations on your retirement, man."

Mark cracked open his beer and took a long gulp.

"Middle school gym teacher, you earned it. Hyacinth, you still work for the…" Cobra looked up from his manifest, "Hyacinth, are you a spy?"

"No, I just work in administration for the NSA. It's just a regular office."

"Right, right. Have you ever killed anyone?"

Hyacinth cracked open her beer and chugged. "Today?"

Clapping from everyone in the car.

"OK, so that's dark-haired Delia Wildhorse and her friend Annie, Andres the German photographer, young Susan from Savannah (by way of Paris) who writes travel articles, Kevin and Xavier from Kansas City, and recently-retired and not-quite-retired Mark and Hyacinth Sarasota, respectively. I'm terrible with names. Don't worry! You'll be surprised how fast I have them all down, but if I get confused at first, I'll know to refer right here to this page."

Cobra folded the paper and put it away. "Welcome to South Africa, and welcome to the bush. And merry Christmas, of course, in a few days! I'll be taking you through some of the property back to Rhino Horn ranch. Who's ready to have some fun?"

Raucous cheers from everyone, except Andres, uncomfortably checking his watch and noticing the height of the sun.

"Good! Now we have to all shut up."

Sudden quiet from the group.

"Just kidding! Although obviously, while we can have quiet conversation, loud noise frightens and irritates the animals, and you've all come to see our amazing wildlife, so keep it quiet and you'll see more. Now, what's the first rule of safari?"

"You don't have to out-run a lion, you only have to out-run the slowest person in our group," said Mark, reciting the oldest safari joke there is.

"You have done this before, haven't you? First rule is that you always, always, always follow the instructions of your ranger. That's me, for now, until we get to the ranch, and then you have the privilege of being guided by my boss, the best wildlife tracker I've ever met. Respect *our* experience, and you'll be safe and have a better experience of your own. What's rule number two?"

"Don't feed the animals?" asked Kevin.

"No, they all love Twizzlers for some reason. They can't get enough of them… impala, leopards, giraffe… We'll provide you with the Twizzlers of course, as part of your vacation package."

"Really?" asked Annie.

"No, not really. Of course, don't feed the animals. It's not a petting zoo. Rule number two is to stay inside the vehicle at all times. This is a custom-built Land Rover with an open-air roof to allow you better access to the environment around you. For the most part, the animals consider the car and everything within it to be sort of like out-of-bounds. It looks different, and the diesel makes it smell different. But step outside of the car, and suddenly, everything changes. You're in their world, and remember, this isn't the Kruger."

"The Kruger?" asked Xavier.

"Kruger Park," said Hyacinth.

"It's the big safari park in the East of South Africa, near Mozambique. Big tourist destination," said Mark. "It's beautiful, but it's like Yellowstone. Lots of cars, lots of lodges, lots of tourists."

"Very different over here. This is a private concession, in the North West, near Kgalagadi Transfrontier Park on the border of Botswana. There isn't another human being, not counting the occasional nomadic San, for two hundred miles of the camp in any direction, so if you get hurt, the best you've got is our first aid kit until we can arrange for a plane to airlift you out. So please, stay in the car. And the third and last rule?"

Crickets from the guests.

"Don't forget to tip your guides," said Cobra, turning the key in the ignition to hear the engine cough and do nothing.

"Here we go," he said, turning the key again, and again, not starting the engine.

"Totally normal!" laughed McCoors, trying a third time, the car like an obstinate thirty-year-old lawn mower.

"Hmm… did I remember to gas up before leaving camp?" Cobra said, appraising the nervous faces behind him before turning the key and hearing the engine roar to life, as though this were a show he put on for all new guests.

"Tip your guides," scoffed Andres.

\*\*\*

They drove for a while, more than an hour, and it seemed as though they made no progress. The wilderness seemed to crowd them in at every turn. This was not the majestic *Lion-King*, endless-grassland that typified the famous Serengeti of Tanzania, which was the image most Western tourists had in their heads when they thought of an African safari. Instead, it was dense, thorny, semi-arid scrubland, with stout, leafless bushes and gray leadwood trees looming overhead. Despite the vastness of the country and its great azure sky, the land had a claustrophobic quality.

The sun was slowly starting its descent, and it would soon hang low in the sky, blessing the dusty, brown landscape with golds, reds and oranges. It was beautiful in its austerity, but it was still pretty frigging hot.

"Probably around 85 degrees Fahrenheit right now," said Cobra. "It touched 97 around midday. The rains are late this year, very late. Sometimes you can see storm clouds way off on the horizon, but they disperse before they get here. It's like they're playing a joke on us."

"When do you expect them?" asked Mark.

"Could be tomorrow, could be two weeks from now, could be never, really. Sometimes nature can be a mercurial mistress."

Xavier mouthed the word "mercurial" to Kevin with an impish grin as if impressed by this outdoorsman's vocabulary.

"A joke is only seeing a Martial Eagle, a few dwarf mongooses and a bunch of bored impalas so far," complained, *surprise surprise*, Andres.

"Patience is the bushman's best friend," said Cobra. "You ready for another *bier*, Meisterburger?"

"I'll have you know…"

Cobra slammed on the break, sending Andres (and everyone else) lurching forward.

"What's the meaning of…" grunted Andres before Hyacinth quieted him. She, Kevin and Susan had already brought their cameras to their eyes, pointing at a graceful antelope who had crossed the dirt path not fifteen feet ahead of them. Mark went for his binoculars.

It was stately and regal, dark brown with a white and black muzzle and a pair of large horns that curved back in a dramatic scimitar shape.

"What's that?" asked Annie.

"That is…" said Cobra quietly, studying it carefully, "a

13

Roan antelope. Very, very rare here, or anywhere in Africa."

"Are you sure?" asked Delia.

"Of course," said Cobra, and then less confidently, "I mean, what else would it be?"

"Um, a Sable Antelope?" she replied.

"No way. There are even fewer…"

Cobra saw that Delia had a raised eyebrow.

"Well, now, let me check," said Cobra. He reached into the glove compartment and grabbed a thick field manual. He leafed through the pages, studied one in particular for a few seconds, and closed the book.

"Sable Antelope," he confirmed, impressed.

"Sable Antelope!" Mark whispered to Hyacinth with the same quiet enthusiasm he would have shown if they had found Jesus crossing the dirt path.

"Way to go, Professor," said Annie. "It's like you went to biology school or something."

"At least someone in this car did," muttered Susan under her breath, writing something in a notebook.

The only sound was the gentle breeze, some distant birds, the clicking of cameras, and the opening of the car door. Everyone's viewfinders suddenly revealed Andres sneaking up on the Roan, *excuse me*, Sable Antelope with his own camera as though he were at the Frankfurt Zoo.

"What the hell is he doing?" whispered Hyacinth.

"Hold still," said Andres, sidling up to the Sable, crouching on his knees and clicking away. The antelope snorted and then bolted into the bush, obscured at once by thorny branches and overgrowth.

Andres was brought back to his feet by Cobra, who had followed him out of the car and hoisted him up by his lapels. *Oohs* from the other guests.

"Get your hands off me," fired Andres.

"What was rule number one? Never get out of the

vehicle."

"I had to. The appropriate lens is still in my luggage, and I needed to get lower to the ground for a more dramatic photo," he explained indignantly.

"I said, never get out of the vehicle. Maybe I didn't emphasize the titanic importance of rule number one. It's for your safety."

"Oh, please. Did you think the big, bad antelope was going to bite me?"

"No. But *he* might," said Cobra, indicating the snake that had slithered out from underneath the vehicle and had stopped about two feet away from Andres. It reared up tensely. Nervous shifting from the guests; wide eyes from Andres.

"Boomslang, Professor?" called Cobra to Delia, who shook her head up and down furiously, confirming his identification.

Annie turned to Delia and accused, "You said no snakes."

"Boomslang's brutally poisonous. People die from boomslang bites in the Kruger, even with nearby medical centers. We have anti-venoms to some snakes back at the ranch, but not many, and we may as well be a thousand miles from the nearest hospital, so please, stay in the car."

\*\*\*

Cobra introduced the guests to the "African massage," which consisted of driving an old 4 x 4 over the millions of small, jagged rocks and pretending it was a road for half an hour, which lead to a *not-proverbial* happy ending: Cobra stopped at a clearing near a small watering hole and revealed a huge tree that looked as though it were upside-down, with roots for branches, which was strewn with multi-colored lights.

"Merry Christmas!" he declared, to the hoots and clapping of the guests. "Can anyone guess what kind of tree this is?"

"Douglas Fir?" asked Annie.

"Baobab!" blurted out Mark like the teacher's pet, and Hyacinth swatted him playfully.

"You are correct, sir! I know we're a few days early, but we're pretty festive here at the conservancy. The lights are solar, of course." He looked to the sun, which was now just touching the horizon line. "Hm. Do you know what time it is?"

Susan looked at her watch.

"Time for that most treasured of African traditions," explained Cobra. "The Sundowner."


After reassuring everyone that it was more or less safe to get out of the car if they stayed close by (which was met by more than a little skepticism after the boomslang encounter), Cobra assembled a portable table and produced a makeshift bar with all the trimmings. He explained that the secret to a perfect gin and tonic was both lime, lemon, THIS MUCH G and *this much t*. He provided the guests, already beer-buzzed, with drinks and snacks: traditional, air-dried South African jerky called *biltong*, nuts, and fried plantain strips.

It was impossible not to be impressed by the sun setting over the wild country, a feeling best enjoyed in Africa, perhaps appealing to our genetic sense-memory from our ancestral homeland. Gin and tonics were icing on the cake.

*Cobra, Annie, Delia:*

"The watering hole is actually man-made. The owner of this place had it bored to try to provide some relief to the animals in unusual drought, like now. It's a great spot to have a drink and take it all in," said McCoors.

"How do you get into this sort of work?" asked Annie. "Like, is there a school?"

"There are, here in South Africa, and up north in Botswana, to start. You have to undergo pretty rigorous training both in books and in the field to get licensed here."

"And you did?" asked Delia.

"Yeah, more or less," he said, and sensing some skepticism, added, "Both Sables and Roans are very, very rare. I've never actually seen one in the wild."

"I'm sure you're very qualified," slurred Annie.

"Like I said, I'm actually just picking you up. The owner and our tracker will be guiding you; they're both incredible."

"That's too bad," frowned Annie.

"I actually have the rest of Christmas week off. Looking forward to it."

"It must be tough, someone like you being a safari guide in post-apartheid South Africa," asked Delia.

"Why do you say that?"

"You know. It's only been thirteen years, you're Black, and you sound American on top of that."

"Believe it or not, I'm actually half-White."

"Really? Come on."

"As White as a Connecticut country club," declared Cobra.

*Kevin, Xavier, Susan:*

"I wonder how he works out," said Kevin.

"I bet he lifts elephant skulls or something." said Xavier.

"He seems like the kind of guy who kills his own food."

"I'm sure there's a fitness room back at the lodge; all the top safari hotels have them," said Susan, drinking. "This is good."

"Are you sure you're old enough to drink that?"

"Please. I've had champagne in a library in Barcelona, thirty-year-old whiskey at the Marriott in Taipei, and the finest Bordeaux at the Prime Minister's inauguration in Quebec."

"I thought Ottawa was the capital of Canada," said Kevin.

"Well, it isn't," said Susan.

*Hyacinth, Mark:*

"I can't believe we're here," grinned Mark, holding

Hyacinth with one hand and his scotch in the other.

"You always say that, every time."

"If this were the last time we went on safari, it'd be a good way to go out."

"Stop it. We've got a lot more time."

Mark took a deep breath and smiled.

"No. We don't."

She held his hand a little tighter.

After a moment, Mark said, "Look at that German guy, all alone, futzing with his camera. Do you think we ought to go talk to him?"

"Fuck that guy," said Hyacinth, prompting a belly laugh from Mark.

"I'm going to go talk to him."

Andres was adjusting his camera, pointing it at the watering hole.

"Whatcha shooting?"

"Nothing," grumbled Andres. "Too damn dark."

Hyacinth sauntered over and said, "I think that log in the pond is actually a crocodile."

"Good spot, hon!" said Mark.

Andres lowered his camera and squinted at the water. "You might be right. You have a sensible eye," he said, adding, "for a woman."

*Cobra, Delia, Annie:*

"Del!" chided Annie.

"I'm sorry, I'm being rude, and forward."

"No, I'm White, but I'm Black, too. Like that guy who's running for president."

"Barack Obama."

"I guess; I don't get much news out here. But my dad's Irish, and my mom's Jamaican. I can pass for a dark-skinned White guy, a light-skinned Black guy, a Puerto Rican guy, and I

18

always get mistaken for Middle Eastern at airports. I'd be the hardest guy to cast in a movie, but also maybe the easiest."

"I feel like you're having fun at my expense," said Delia.

"I am what I am," shrugged Cobra.

"Like Popeye? That's kind of a Taoist view of things."

"McCoors does sound Irish," said Annie.

Cobra explained, "I mean, if we're being honest, there is still a lot of... discrimination... here in South Africa. But the bush doesn't care what you are. It will reward you or punish you no matter what your heritage is. It doesn't discriminate."

The night-time frogs began their shift, and then the birds and insects, filling the air with their calls.

Quietly, tipsy Annie said, "bush doesn't discriminate."

\*\*\*

The sun was now gone, and in its place, the night sky of the Southern Hemisphere that covered the bare acacia tree canopy like a thick, heavy blanket. The Land Rover's lights cut through the darkness as Cobra drove through the bush, probably a little faster than he should have.

"How can you see? There's barely any road to follow," said Xavier.

"I've been out in the bush so long, my eyes have adapted to the point that they only need a little starlight, and I can see clear as day," answered Cobra.

"Really?"

"No, not really. This is actually somewhat dangerous, what with all the gnarly stuff underneath us. If we startled a buffalo, we'd be in trouble. But we're almost home."

"How can you even tell?" asked Annie.

"Look up ahead about one o'clock, and listen."

Some distance away (it was hard to tell how far) there was an orange light that grew larger as they approached. A fire - a big bonfire, blazing six feet up from a dug-out, stone pit - beckoned the guests with that most inviting scent of woodsmoke. As Cobra slowed down, they heard a high-pitched call almost like that of a wolf's howl but dropping off sharply in pitch at the end of each drawn-out note.

It was a man, standing behind the fire, calling out into the darkness. He was dressed in Cobra's khaki uniform, and he was ruggedly strong, but with an ancient face desiccated by years of sun and dust. Cobra turned off the ignition, and the guests absorbed the heat from the bonfire.

"That's Kotani. He's San. He'll be your tracker tomorrow," whispered Cobra as Kotani kept calling into the darkness, the firelight showing the glaucoma in his eyes.

Andres asked, "Why are we whisper…"

An answer came from the darkness: the same as Kotani's whooping call, but more primal, and more unearthly.

"Hyena," remarked Cobra. "And, we're here."

Behind Kotani and the fire were a few traditional rondavels - circular huts with thatched roofs - that had been updated with modern style and sensibility. Behind them stood a large visitor center made of wood and stone that could have been an old, colonial hunting lodge from a bygone era, and it overlooked a dry riverbed and some solar panels.

"No fences?" asked Annie.

"The outdoor dining area - what we call a *boma* in Swahili- has a barrier of thorny bushes surrounding it," said Cobra.

"Is that enough to keep out lions?"

"It's enough to, well, discourage them. And here's the man himself, the owner and operator of our humble little piece of Heaven. I give you my friend, my boss and my mentor, Wyatt Northside."

Northside stepped out of the visitor center with his assistant Katy in tow. If Cobra were physically impressive, Northside was almost mythic; in his late forties, he looked like he had either been carved out of marble or pulled out of a dumpster juuuuust in time for church on Sunday morning. If Annie were a cartoon, her eyes would have bulged out of her head and her jaw would have been in her lap.

"Welcome to Rhino Horn Ranch!" said Northside with an Australian accent.

"Isn't anyone actually from South Africa around here?" whispered Kevin to Xavier.

"Cobra and Kotani will get your bags, and Katy will show you all to your rooms. You must be hungry; *braai* in the boma in thirty minutes!"

\*\*\*

*Braai*, if you've never had the privilege of being in Southern Africa for dinner, is Afrikaans for "barbecue," traditionally prepared outdoors on wood or coals. After being settled into their rooms, the guests were served roasted bush venison at a long table outside in the cool air, the embers from the bonfire still smoldering nearby. Xavier stabbed at some greens.

"If you were vegetarian, I wish you would have told the travel booker, mate," said Northside at the head of the table.

"Vegan," corrected Xavier, before mumbling, "pretty sure I did."

"Stop complaining," nudged Kevin. "You have nothing to complain about."

Xavier opened his mouth to complain but stopped himself and said nothing.

"Well, at least it's organic," said Northside. "Katy grows most of our produce in the garden you see over here, and Kotani shot this impala about five hours ago."

"It's soooooo good," said Mark, who couldn't shovel it down fast enough.

"It's delicious," said Annie, sitting next to Northside and guzzling Pinotage.

"It's all right," said Susan. "I've actually had better venison at a restaurant in…"

"What a surprise; the young girl has an opinion," said Andres.

"Well, I never," said Susan indignantly, with her Southern accent turned up to eleven.

"Maybe you should," chortled Andres. "You still have spots, is that the expression?"

"That saying comes from the bush," interjected Northside. "Lions are actually born with spots, like their leopard cousins, and they lighten as they age."

"You know a lot about the bush," said Annie, touching Northside's arm, to an almost audible eye roll from Delia.

Hyacinth privately whispered to Mark, "Khaki fever is real."

Mark whispered back, "Hon, why do you think I'm wearing it?"

Noticing his absence, Delia asked, "Where's Mister Cobra?"


"Single or double, Cobra?" asked Kotani, reaching over the bar in the visitor center. Sweet smoke and old wood, like the smell of a two-hundred-year old museum, wafted over from the adjacent lounge, where embers still smoldered in the fireplace.

"Triple," said Cobra. "As of right now, I'm on vacation."

"Ha. Go ahead; kill yourself," Kotani said, retrieving a bottle of peaty Ardbeg.

"And I'm also buying. What're you having, Kotani?"

"I am not on vacation, Cobra. Early rise tomorrow, tracking with this new group." He poured heavily for Cobra, and seeing just a few drops remaining in the bottle, shrugged and took a swig.

"This ain't a bad bunch, as far as they go. You'll like them. The German's a pain in the ass, but Northside'll have his number quick. A few lovely ladies that may catch your eye, Kotani."

"Just what I need - more wives!"

"You're a legend, Kotani; I hope I'm half the man you are when I'm your age."

"The way you drink, I hope you live to be half my age, Cobra."

They clinked glasses, or bottle-to-glass, and drank.

"Merry Christmas, Kotani."

"Don't worry, Cobra. Santa Claus will find you, even all the way out here."

"Then you're confident you're on the Nice List," said Delia, strolling over to the bar with a glass of red.

Kotani threw the empty bottle in the bin and rose from his stool.

"We'll be up before dawn, so don't stay up too late, miss," said Kotani, leaving.

"Professor! Please," said Cobra, patting the empty seat.

"You don't have to call me that; I'm not through with my PhD yet."

"And then I *would* have to call you that?"

"Hell yeah, you would."

"Finished with dinner so soon?"

"Dinner was lovely, although the conversation was starting to turn a little sour. They're having dessert now. I thought I'd give Annie a little space to, you know, do her thing."

"You're a good friend, Professor."

"Yeah, I am. I don't think she's your problem anymore; she seems to have locked on to your boss. I'm glad; she's a little out of her element here and I wasn't sure she'd have any fun."

"And now, are you *my* new problem?"

23

"You wish, *Cobra*," she scoffed.

\*\*\*

Tableside, the conversation continued.

"The property is about forty square miles, none of it fenced in," explained Northside. "The visitor center was an old hunting lodge I bought a few years ago and refurbished. As you can see, we have to be pretty self-sufficient, because supply runs are so difficult. Everything runs on solar with a back-up, and after nine o'clock, power shuts down."

"What if there's an emergency?" asked Xavier.

"We have our radio. No phone lines here; no cell towers yet, which is the way I wanted it. We're in God's country now; best way to enjoy it is to be away from the rat race. Otherwise, you wouldn't have come here."

"But there's really nobody out here at all?"

"There could be some local Tsonga-Shangaan people way up north, maybe a few remaining San, like Kotani. They say there were Germans here way back in World War One, encroaching south from what's now Namibia, maybe. But for the next few days, it's you, me, Katy, Kotani, and the Holy Ghost, and that's about it."

"But you must get lonely out here," said Annie, eying up Northside *intently*, and that's the most polite way I can express *that*.

"Maybe," he said. "But when I found this place, I knew it was home. And frankly, if I weren't here, I'd be someplace somewhere else pretty much just like it."

"Like where?" asked Mark. "Mongolian steppe? Brazilian Pantanal?"

"Amarula?" Katy appeared, pouring a liquor into everyone's glasses.

"Thank you, Katy," said Northside. "It's made from the fruit of the Marula tree."

"How did everyone enjoy dinner?" Katy asked with

genuine hospitality as she finished topping everyone off.

"It was fantastic," declared Mark sincerely.

"Katy's our chef, head bookkeeper, head room stewardess..." bragged Northside.

"Groundskeeper, porter, maid, and reptile wrangler," bragged Katy.

"Reptile wrangler?" asked Hyacinth.

"When there's a mamba in your bathroom, I'm the one you call."

"Green *and* black?"

"Whichever you prefer!" Katy.

"Del said no snakes," repeated Annie to herself.

Northside deflected, "Katy prepared a wonderful dessert for us."

"I'm sure it is," said Susan, "and will more than make up for the lack of swimming pool, spa, and turndown service."

"I'm sorry, Ma'am," said Northside. "I don't believe we misrepresented ourselves in the ad."

"It's just that it seems standard in these safari places. My colleagues tell me that all of CCAfrica's properties in South and East Africa have them."

"Those places are tops," said Northside, "but we don't see them as competition. There must have been something about the remote charm of our humble operation that caught your fancy."

"Colleagues?" scoffed Andres. "Do you work for *Conde Nast?*"

"No."

"*National Geographic Traveler?*"

"Not really, no."

"*Frommers? Lonely Planet?*"

"I don't even know that one," she said indignantly.

"Then who do you write for?"

"I write a travel blog, if you must know."

Mark to Hyacinth: "What's that?"

Hyacinth to Mark: "It's like a website or something."

Mark to Hyacinth: "Like the Facebook?"

Hyacinth to Mark: "Yes, like the Facebook."

"Someone pays you to travel around the world and write on a website?" asked Kevin, while Xavier remained quiet.

"You could read it," said Susan, throwing her napkin down and following Katy to the kitchen in the Visitor Center, "if only this place had internet!"

Silence.

Kevin asked, "Do you?"

"Mate," Northside responded, "I'm not even sure we have a computer."

Finishing his triple Scotch, Cobra reached for a beer in the fridge behind the bar. Delia was still on her first glass.

"I'm sorry if I overstepped this afternoon, pushing you on that race stuff. Sometimes I come across a little forward."

"No problem at all," said Cobra. "I just don't think much about it, really."

"But isn't it a big part of who you are? Being bi-racial in a country torn apart by institutionalized racism? Being a foreigner?"

"Why are you so into this?"

"I'm Native American. I grew up on a reservation in south Montana on the Wyoming border, a community of 7,500 people. I respect them, I'm proud of who I am..."

"But you're tired of those people's expectations, of being who they want you to be, of doing what they want you to do."

"Well, maybe. Yes."

"So you left the reservation and made your life what you wanted, am I right?"

"I did. I left to get educated, but I always knew I had to return one day."

"Why?"

"Because I had to."

"Who said?"

"Those people are impoverished.  They're part of who I am.  I went to USC to study biology…"

"Where you met Annie, now drunk…"

"…so I could earn my grad degree, and now my doctorate…"

"…studying lizards in the Sonoran desert, you said."

"Not Sonoran, but close enough.  I wanted to one day go home to Montana…"

"Big Sky Country…"

"…and help my people in my own way, with land management, with wildlife management, with their heritage.  But even in California, people see my skin, they see my hair.  People see me and check the 'Native American' box first when they assess me.  It's the center of my identity…"

"I think you're blowing this a little out of proportion, Professor," said Cobra, tired but interested.

"It's just frustrating to hear you say that who you are means nothing to you when it's such a big deal to the world around you."

"But why can't I be Black when I need to be Black and White when I need to be White?  Why can't I just be whatever I want, whenever I want, and who cares what everybody else thinks?  And why can't you just be you, and you be in charge of who that is, not some anonymous machine called *society*?"

"But who are you?" she challenged.  "Who are you if who you are is only whoever you want to be at the moment?  Who is the real you?"

"That's the thing," said Cobra, chugging his beer.  "They're all the real me."

"Says who?"

"Says the only voice that counts."

"Yeah, sure.  You won't even tell us your real name, *Cobra*."

"What's that got to do with anything? What are you, a psychologist?"

"No, a wildlife biologist. And like any twelve-year old that watches Animal Planet, I can tell the difference between a Roan and a Sable."

"Well, then, Professor," said Cobra, finishing his beer, "you'll enjoy the rest of your vacation with Mr. Northside and Kotani, who are consummate professionals. I'll be at Mitchell's pub in Cape Town where all I need to know is the next single malt to order. Have a merry Christmas, if your identity allows it or whatever."

Cobra stood up to leave and fell over his barstool.

"Um," he said, "sorry."

Replacing the barstool, he turned and stumbled out into the African night.

Alone, Delia said to herself, "And this is why you have no friends," and finished her wine.

\***

In the kitchen, Katy washed dishes with water pumped from the well earlier. Susan, nibbling on a vanilla cookie, sat on a chair behind her.

"So, you pretty much run this place," said Susan.

"More or less," said Katy. "I have to radio the office in Praetoria to get the bookings done since there's no phone here, and I look after the day-to-day."

"It doesn't look so crowded here."

"No. Mr. Northside is pretty well-off, if you know what I mean. He doesn't really even need to keep this place open to tourists; he just does it because he likes it."

"How do I get to do your job?" asked Susan. "It doesn't seem so hard."

"You think so, do you?  Are you looking for work?"

"Maybe."

"Do you have any experience working in the bush?"

"I've worked with Robin Pope in South Luangua."

"Really?" asked Katy.  "I haven't heard from Robin in a few years.  Anywhere else?"

"Flatdogs Camp, in Zimbabwe.  Flatdog is slang for crocodile."

"I know," said Katy.  "Although unless they picked it up and moved it, Flatdogs is in Zambia."

\*\*\*

"It's all so silly, isn't it?" laughed Andres.  "I mean, how do you decide who does what?"

Xavier stood up from the table, his fists balled up.

"How could you possibly be such an asshole?"

"Calm down," said Kevin.

"Yes, calm down," mocked Andres with a smirk.  "I didn't mean anything by it."

"Easy, Mister Schenker," said Northside.  "You can spend tomorrow's game drive in your room if you can't be nice."

"I mean, do you flip a coin?  Who goes first?  I'm genuinely curious."

Kevin rose from the table.  "That's not a problem you have, I'd imagine.  No wonder you travel alone.  Good night, everyone."

Andres then turned to Annie, who preempted him by looking in his eyes and saying, "Fuck. You."

Northside helped Annie to her feet and said to Andres, "Stay up as late as you like, but keep to the visitor center or on the dirt path to your rondavel."

"Aren't you going to escort me to my room as well?  Or does this service only extend to pretty girls?"

"Right this way," said Northside, as Annie clearly mouthed the words "Fuck. You." to Andres.

Cobra's quarters weren't as, shall we say, *four-star* as those of the guests, but there was enough space to house a modest weight-bench and some sand-filled plates that might have been found in Gold's Gym in the actual seventies. U.S.-issued dog tags hung from the barbell, along with some laundry. A small, battery-powered lamp illuminated that the rest of the room was filled with books, piled high against all four walls.

He shut the door and threw Hemingway's *Green Hills of Africa* and Teddy Roosevelt's *African Game Trails* off the bed where they were lying, and then, burning through his buzz, searched through his library for a particular volume.

"Sable Antelope. Roan Antelope. Sable Antelope. Roan Antelope," he slurred, finding *Jonathan and Angela Scott's Safari Guide to East African Animals* and diving onto the bed with it. He furiously flipped through the pages.

"Ungulates: puku, hartebeest, kongoni, kudu, impala, sable… there's like fifty antelopes! Greater kudu, lesser kudu…"

His voice trailed off as he studied, tired and delirious, and if we're being honest, drunk.

"Go do… that kudu… that you do… so… zzzzzzzz."

Everyone was asleep for the night, except for Katy finishing up the dishes, and Hyacinth and Mark having a quiet whiskey on the comfortable couch by the still-glowing embers of the Visitor Center fireplace.

"We're not keeping you up, are we?" called Hyacinth to Katy.

"Nonsense. I have a little more to do, and then it's bedtime," she called back.

"How can it be that you and I out-drank all those kids and Marlboro Men?" asked Mark, arm around his wife.

"Because everybody sucks but us," she said in reply.

"True story," he agreed, touching glasses with hers.

"We should probably slow it down a little. Might interact with the medication."

Mark sipped. "Hon, do you honestly think it matters now? Let's just live."

"I was talking about the Malarone," said Hyacinth. "Vacation'll be a lot less fun with malaria."

"Eh, don't worry about it. Cobra said himself that the rains are late; there's so little standing water that I haven't even noticed any mosquitos."

"All right; you're a grown-up."

"And then some."

He inhaled deeply. "That fireplace smell always brings you right back, doesn't it? To me, it's like I'm way back to our first trip… how many…"

"Forty-one years ago."

"Forty-one years!" Mark kissed his wife. "All of them good ones."

"You get so sentimental on these vacations." She closed her eyes.

"Thank you. Thank you for this. I love you."

"Shut up," said Hyacinth, abruptly shushing him.

"Geez, just trying to be romantic…"

"Quiet… don't you hear that?"

Mark froze and listened, knowing that his wife was onto something, as always. He heard crickets, frogs, some birds, an occasional cracking from the fire, and a deep, resonant, low-pitched rumbling from outside, like a radio with the bass turned to *eleven* and everything else turned to *zero*.

Katy silently beckoned them from the kitchen, and they

quietly followed her outside, knowing the one thing on earth that could make that kind of sound:

A bull elephant stood about twenty yards from the Visitor Center, its footfalls counter-intuitively silent as it sauntered over to a nearby tree. It was old, fifty years or more, and it bent large branches around his left tusk with his trunk to snap them off. There wasn't much foliage or fruit, but he seemed content with his treasure and quietly moved on, a ghost of the savannah.

"Attenborough," said Katy. "He visits us from time to time."

"Hey," whispered Hyacinth to Mark, who was entranced.

"Have we ever been this close to an elephant before?" he said softly, not taking his eyes off the bull.

"Hey," she whispered again, more emphatically, until he met her eyes. "I love you too."

# CHAPTER 2:
# GAME DRIVE

Lions had roared throughout the night, and if you've ever been on a luxury vacation to sub-Saharan Africa, you'll know that there are only two ways that tourists interpret that unique soundscape. The first way is that the lions, along with the hyenas and hippos and dassies and night-time insects, create a sort of natural lullaby that, combined with a day of fresh air and a little alcohol, is more effective than three shots of Nyquil. That's how safari veterans like Mark and Hyacinth, for instance, reacted to it. The other is an abject terror, an insistence that the lions are *"right outside the tent, for God's sake,"* and an inability to procure even ten, let alone forty, winks.

To be fair, Delia fell somewhere in the middle of that scale. She slept rather well, but when she awoke before her cell-phone alarm sounded at 4:45, she looked across the room and saw Annie's turned-down bed *unslept-in* and initially choked back an instinctive scream.

Still in that Twilight Zone between dream and consciousness, she rapidly thought: *oh my god I brought my best friend to this place instead of Europe and she died and she got eaten by lions on her way back to the tent and it's all my fault and how am I going to explain this to her parents and...*

Moments later, finding her grasp on reality, she pursed her lips into a scowl. "Oh, Annie."

\*\*\*

"Do we have to do this now?" asked Kevin, brushing his teeth with bottled water *just in case*, like all the guidebooks said.

"There's never a good time, is there?" muttered Xavier, pulling on his underwear and trying to find his pants in the dimly lit tent.

"Why can't we just have a good time and enjoy ourselves? I don't want to fight about this now," spat Kevin, cleaning his brush.

"Yeah, right, Kevin. You always stonewall me with this conversation. It's not such a big deal, you know."

"Maybe not to you. It's a big deal to me," Kevin replied.

"Well my lease is almost up, and I have to give thirty days' notice."

"Everybody breaks leases."

"I won't have to if you'll just give me a straight answer," argued Xavier.

"I don't know, all right? I don't know," said Kevin.

"We've been together half a year. You've met my parents. What's the difference if I move in or not?"

"If there's no difference, why are you insisting on moving in right now?"

"So, you don't want me to move in."

"Don't do that. I didn't say that."

"Not in so many words, Kevin. But I get it."

"Do you? Do you really? Or are you just going to make me the bad guy again and then give me the silent treatment and ruin this vacation, like that weekend in New Orleans? Because if you want this relationship to succeed, you are not making a strong case for it right now."

"Oh, so there it is. It's me, it's my fault," said Xavier, rifling through some clothes in a big, burlap duffel. "Where are my goddamn pants?"

"Listen to you. I'm the villain, you're the martyr. Jesus, we're going to have fourteen hours to talk about anything and everything on the plane back home."

"Or you can tell me '*no, I don't want you to move in with me*' right now in under three seconds, and we'll be civil and move on with our lives."

"Is that it? Zero-sum game, nuclear option?" grumbled Kevin, lacing up his hiking boots that he bought specifically for this trip in which he'd be driven around in a car 90% of the time. "Your pants are on the bathroom counter. Don't forget sunscreen and bug-repellent. I'll be in the car waiting for you. Please don't carry on in front of the others." Kevin unzipped the tent and slid out.

Xavier, finding his pants on the counter, waited for Kevin to go beyond earshot before saying, "Asshole."

\*\*\*

The sun wasn't up yet, and there were still stars burning up above, but it was light enough that Delia easily found her way over the path bisecting the guests' quarters and leading to the Visitors' Center. She smelled coffee brewing from a kettle over the pit where last night's fire still smoldered. Katy was there, as if she never slept, as well as Kotani and a few of the guests. It looked like Mark and Hyacinth were there, indulging in some plain cookies, and Susan and Andres, too.

Delia turned the other way, however. She left the path and ventured farther into the property, past the inventory closets and backup generator and petrol pump, until she found the staff quarters. They were small and simple wooden buildings, utilitarian but not entirely Spartan.

Delia approached the first one and looked through the window… it was a mess, with no order to things. She knew right

35

away it was Cobra's.

"Books," she said out loud, surprised and a little ashamed at how she had pegged him for a brawny troglodyte, and then pleased with herself that she knew what a troglodyte was, and then back to surprised. Most of the clutter was from books. Cobra was a reader. She recognized *Jonathan and Angela Scott's Safari Guide to East African Animals* on the bed, as she had one of her own, and mentally took points away from Cobra's score since they were in southern Africa, not east Africa.

Still, this made her curious about him, and it instantly made her like him better. Too bad he was leaving today; she wanted to apologize (again) for being so forward with her line of questioning. She found his simplicity frustrating, but all these books made her second-guess her assessment of him. Either way, he wasn't there.

Delia thought for a moment that she heard a hyrax (or *dassie*, as South Africans called them): a small arboreal mammal that is a distant cousin of other proboscideans like elephants. Despite their size, they sometimes produced a chainsaw-like, grinding sound from their resting places in trees. Only, the sound wasn't coming from the trees.

She moved on to the next cabin: Wyatt Northside's. Sneaking a look through the window, she saw that he wasn't there, but of course, Annie was, and she was looking pretty damn comfortable under the thick, down blanket, her eyes closed and her mouth open. Any nature lover could be forgiven for confusing her snoring with the calls of a hyrax.

"Eaten by lions," said Delia through her teeth, shaking her head.

Clearly, Annie was planning on missing this morning's game drive, something Delia could remedy. She balled up her fist to pound on the door, but hesitated, thinking twice about rousing her best friend.

\*\*\*

"Come on, Wyatt, really?" asked Cobra, not happy to be up so early.

"Cobra, mate, I need this one. I really need this one," said Northside. "It's been so long since I've been with a woman like that. It's been…"

"Two weeks? Two and a half?"

"That's a long time for a bloke like me! My biological clock is ticking. I'm on overdrive. I'm in my sexual prime."

"You're 45, well-past your sexual prime. Didn't they have health class in Australia?"

"They did, but I missed them. I was too busy nailing Sheilas behind the bleachers."

"OK, even I don't think that's true."

"So I speak in hyperbole sometimes! Come on, be a pal. Be a team player."

"Wyatt, come on, man."

Cobra grabbed a bottle of water out of the Visitor's Center's unlocked refrigerator.

"Not to mention, I am your friend, your ally, your mentor, and not least of all…"

"Don't say it, Wyatt…"

"Your boss."

"You said it," sighed Cobra, crossing his arms in resignation.

"Look, mate," said Wyatt, putting his hand on Cobra's shoulder reassuringly. "It's only for today. I know you had plans for Christmas in Cape Town. I'll have your flight rebooked, and I'll give you a Christmas bonus."

"Come on, Wyatt. You know your money's no good here."

"That's because there's…" said Northside, and then they both said, "nowhere to spend it."

"Fine. Just today. You re-book my flight from the radio

this morning, and I'll do today's game drive."

"That's my mate! I love you, buddy. You'll be at Mitchell's in time for Christmas, I promise. And it's not so bad. I heard you found a Roan yesterday."

"Sable," corrected Cobra.

"What's the difference?" asked Northside. "A little salt, a little pepper… both just as good."

"Yeah, well, it matters to one of the guests. She's a biology student."

"Well, you see to her and the other guests, because I have to study the *biology* of her friend today."

"Ugh. You're the worst, *boss*."

"Merry Christmas, Cobra!"

"Merry Christmas, Wyatt."


Wyatt approached the fire, Cobra in tow, where the guests - Mark, Hyacinth, Kevin, Susan, and Andres - were warming with tea, coffee, and in Mark and Hyacinth's case, hot chocolate. The sun was still not ready to show, but the dawn chorus of birds and insects slowly welcomed the new day. The guests wrapped small blankets around themselves to fight the fifty-five degree chill as Katy gently set rubber bottles filled with hot water on the seats of the Land Rover. Kotani loaded lunches packed in foil and a cooler full of bottled water, beer and liquor into the back.

"Good morning everyone! Did you hear the lions last night?"

"Yes," said Andres in a way that could only be read as a complaint.

"How far away do you think they were? They sounded like they were right outside the tents," said Kevin.

"Oh, I bet they were closer to two, three hundred yards away," said Northside.

"That sounds about right," said Hyacinth, "although I slept through most of it."

Susan wrote something in her notebook and said, "the lodges outside Ranthambore in India are even closer to the wildlife. Tourists routinely see tigers from their balconies. At least, the four-star ones, anyway."

Mark whispered to Hyacinth, "*Bullshit.*"

"Aren't we missing a few people?" asked Northside.

"I'm sorry, I'm sorry," said Xavier, hurriedly shuffling down the path toward the group. He stood next to Susan and Hyacinth, separate from Kevin, who crossed his arms. "Ready to go."

"Glad to have you with us! There's one more, isn't there?"

"The Professor," mumbled Cobra.

"And her friend, right?" asked Kevin.

"Well, as it happens, she had a little too much of that local Pinotage last night and will not be joining you on this morning's game drive."

"Wait, aren't you taking us out this morning?" asked Andres, carefully assessing his lenses.

"Slight change of plans. I'll be taking you out tomorrow, for Christmas Eve. Cobra's going to be guiding you today, with Kotani tracking."

"Yeah, as it turns out, there was a problem with my flight this morning, and Wyatt's got some administrative stuff to do around the camp, so I'll be with you on your first official game drive," said Cobra, telling two generally harmless lies.

Mark and Hyacinth smiled, Andres and Susan frowned, and Kevin and Xavier looked away from each other.

"Hey Wyatt, is *Cobra McCoors* actually this guy's real name?" asked Mark.

"Yeah, it is," assured Northside with a smile.

"Like, is that what you put on his tax forms? His checks?"

"Sure, it is," said Northside. "Well, I guess, it would be more accurate to say that it would be if I didn't pay him in cash under the table."

Chuckles from Mark and Hyacinth, stone faces from the rest.

"He's too modest to tell you, so I will," said Northside.

"I'm gonna get in the car," said Cobra, outwardly embarrassed but inwardly loving that Northside told this story to literally every guest.

"People started calling him Cobra after he saved a guy from a Mozambique spitting cobra. You think Kotani over there has eyes like that because of glaucoma. Well, he does, but it's a lot worse because he once took a shot in the eyes from an MSC. See, those snakes don't just bite, although they can. No, an MSC can project deadly venom over six feet in the air to hit within an inch or two of their intended target. It hurts something awful, and if not properly rinsed and treated, it can cause permanent blindness. Scientists say that they hit right between the eyes something like nine out of ten times."

"Like the freaking Crocodile Hunter!" said Mark.

"Yes, sir. But unlike Steve Irwin, who's a legend to us Aussies, Cobra here didn't have any protective goggles or anything like that. He pushed this guy out of the way and shut his eyes, taking a full shot of venom right above the bridge of his nose. He then grabbed the snake from the front, not the back, completely blind, mind you, swung it over his head and threw it ten feet away like it was a pair of Bruce Lee *nun-chuck-oos*. And before you worry, don't: the snake was completely fine."

"I'm so sure," grumbled Andres.

"Was that here on the property?" asked Susan.

"Nope. At a party in Maun, Botswana. And if you want to know who Cobra saved, know that…" *and Cobra silently mouthed these words from the car as Northside said them,* "I was that guy."

"Is that really true?" asked Delia, sneaking up on Cobra and startling him from the side of the car.

"Professor, I personally vouch for the veracity of at least

sixty-five percent of that account," he said.

\*\*\*

The sunrises in Africa always deliver, and they are as spectacular as the sunsets. As Cobra quietly drove the guests into the wilderness, Kotani riding in front of the hood on a specially-mounted seat, rays of gold and yellow like early-season honey beamed through each branch of the tangled acacia forest surrounding them. That was, of course, from the east. In the skies to the north, clouds of deep indigo and purple oppressed the sunlight, and it looked like the descending criss-crossing of an old screen door underneath them.

"That's the rain," said McCoors. "Still far away, but finally where it should be. This country sure needs it."

"We are going to be drenched, then?" asked Andres, shivering.

"No. I doubt that will hit us until tomorrow, maybe even the next day."

"So, it won't be a white Christmas after all," said Susan.

"No, but maybe a green one. You'll start seeing a carpet of grass within hours of the first good soaking. Flowers bud on the trees. It's a spectacular transformation. Right now, many animals are getting their water from man-made dams and watering holes bored deep within the ground, but a lot of the reserve is actually a huge floodplain. Much of where we'll be driving will be under a few feet of water within days."

Kotani held up his hand from his seat at the front of the hood, and Cobra slowed down, pulling to the side of what passed for a road.

"*Ngala*," he said softly to Cobra. "*Nyathi*, too."

"Look below on the sand at those tracks," said Cobra. "Any guesses, people?"

Delia looked over the side and said, "After counting the

41

pugmarks and accounting for the size, I'm going to say that one's lion. Beside it, seeing twelve-centimeter bovine tracks, it has to be a cape buffalo. Am I close, *Cobra?*" she teased.

"I was looking for *panthera leo* and *syncerus caffer*, but since you don't have your doctorate yet, I'll begrudgingly accept that."

"Gee, thanks," she said. Clapping from the guests.

Kotani quickly shushed them, and the guests fell silent right away. The wind shifted, and there was the faint smell of rotting meat.

Cobra started the engine and slowly took the guests around some thick bush, obscuring a pride of lions feeding on a buffalo. The sight provoked some oohs and then religious silence.

Andres, sitting between Kevin and Xavier, pushed Xavier aside and began clicking away. Mark had a childlike smile plastered to his face, and seeing him, so did Hyacinth.

"I wasn't sure I'd ever see something like this again," he said to her.

There were two large males with black manes and dark noses a few yards away, and after briefly opening their eyes to assess the Land Rover, you'd have had to shake them to make sure they were still awake. Five mature lionesses laid closer to the buffalo, which had been completely eviscerated, leaving a huge, gory cavern under the ribcage where a few cubs with matted, red fur bounced and played.

"How far from camp would you say we are?" asked Susan, writing something in her notebook.

"About half a mile or so," said Cobra. "I bet they took this old retired general down around one in the morning last night. If you think the smell is strong now, come back at the end of the day when it's been exposed to the heat. You can see some of the stomach contents on the ground over there."

"Do you mind?" asked, really *said*, Xavier, pushing Andres' lens off his shoulder, ruining his shot.

"What's wrong with you guys, anyway?" Andres replied. "Trouble in the paradise?"

Kevin and Xavier both ignored and kept looking at the animals.

"Those are some big guys," remarked Hyacinth, taking pictures of her own.

"I bet the females did the job here. They do most of the hunting," remarked Delia.

"Not necessarily, *Professor*" said Cobra. "That's what most scientists believe, because most of the studies on lions were conducted in the open plains of Tanzania and Kenya, where that's largely true. Here, though, the slower but more powerful males have a lot more cover from the thick bushes, and they ambush large prey a lot of the time."

"Where'd you learn that? *Jonathan and Angela Scott's Safari Guide to East African Animals?*" she said, coyly.

"I think it was Jonathan Scott's *The Marsh Pride*," retorted Cobra, curious.

"Which was co-authored by Brian Jackman," she added, enjoying playing with him.

"These lions aren't doing anything. Can't you honk at them or something?" whined Andres, irritated.

"Lions sleep for up to twenty hours a day," said Cobra. "This is their natural behavior. Don't be misled by National Geographic, which are the best forty minutes taken from ten months of patient stakeouts."

"Are they related to sloths?" asked Susan.

"Hard no," said Cobra.

"Can't you at least move the car so I can get a better shot?" groaned Andres.

"I don't want to upset them, and I don't want to put Kotani too close. Be patient. Just like at the zoo, the more patient you are, the more you'll see. Put the high-paced mania of civilization behind you and try to accept the world on their terms, because although this car is our life raft, it *is* their world."

"Is Kotani in danger out there on that seat?" asked Kevin.

"Like us, he's relatively safe," said Cobra. "But he grew up out here. He knows how these animals behave, and he's sensitive to the signals they give off."

"You mean you're not scared, Kotani?" asked Hyacinth.

"Of course, I am," Kotani said quickly. "Can't you see? Those are fucking lions right there."

\*\*\*

It had been a very good morning game drive by any objective measure. If we're being honest, the sighting of the lions on a kill alone should have secured Cobra reasonable tips, but it was only ten thirty, and in the five-and-a-half hours since they'd been out, they had also seen a few impalas, some black-backed jackals, a few fleeting plains zebra and various birds, including the lilac-breasted roller and the superb starling. Not everyone thought this was so *superb*, however, and when there were opportunities to complain, Andres sought them out like a Ruppell's griffon vulture seeks carrion (which is to say, if you're not a wildlife expert, was as frequently as he could):

"Where are the cheetahs?"

"Why is my lens covered in dust?"

"Are you seeking out the rockiest sections of road on purpose?"

And so on.

Every once in a while, Susan would compare the experience to something better that she had allegedly experienced. I say *allegedly*, because just about nobody in the car believed she had experienced a fifth of what she had claimed, and also because nobody could figure out why the young know-it-all constantly attempted to impress everyone with her worldliness. Mark and

Hyacinth had a private game running where they made bets about how many times Susan would declare something they considered bullshit, and at the end of the day, the winner would get some, shall we say, *affection* of their choice back at the lodge if they guessed closest to the actual number.

"In the Amalfi Coast, the roads are smooth because the high taxes enable road crews to maintain them well, not like here," she said, and Mark tallied *one* with his finger.

"I flew first class to Cape Town from Kuala Lumpur, and you should always ask for first class, if you can, because it's noticeably better than business class," she said, and Hyacinth tallied *two* with hers.

"Prostitution is legal in Amsterdam, and the ladies there are famous for hand-jobs because they use a continental grip. They also tend to be better at both tennis and golf, and they dominate the local competition." Mark tallied *three*, and both he and Hyacinth rolled their eyes privately.

"That," said Andres *Tutonically*, "is true."

Mark and Hyacinth looked at one another, shrugged, and Mark brought his tally down to *two*.

They were about ten miles from camp when Kotani said, "Nhongo."

Away from the road, about twenty yards in the distance, stood the most striking antelope almost anyone in the car had ever seen, with regal horns spiraling backward out of its head and a thin, wispy strip of hair running down its throat.

"Kudu," said Cobra. "One of the largest antelope, behind eland. Very dangerous."

"What?" questioned Delia. "That's just plain false. Even male kudu are shy and elusive, from everything that I've read."

"Lesser kudu, maybe. This here's a Greater. I've heard stories of them impaling a grown woman on those horns, rearing back, and then using their bodies like punching bags for their front legs."

"Well, you must be a lesser guide, then. Kotani, come on, right?" she turned.

"You're right, Professor," Kotani said. "Cobra is just fucking with you."

Kevin laughed out loud, but Xavier folded his arms, and the kudu nibbled gently on some bushes.

"Thanks for nothing, Kotani," said Cobra. "But mark my words… I'd rather be faced with those lions than a male kudu if I were unlucky enough to be on-foot out here."

Susan said to Cobra privately, "Isn't Kotani worried about talking to the guests like that?"

"Like what?"

"You know, cursing? He said *'fuck'* twice in polite company."

"And he's still alive!" laughed Cobra.

"I can't imagine staff at a hotel in Paris speaking so casually with guests."

"One thing Wyatt Northside is, is loyal. He treats his people very well. If there's a problem with a guest objecting to his staff, he knows that in a few days, it's the guest who will be replaced, not the staff."

"Are you saying that we're all expendable?" asked Susan indignantly with Scarlett O'Hara-like inflection.

"I'm saying that the *business* is expendable, Northside is independently wealthy, and people should just treat each other like people, no pretense," he added simply.

"Are you saying people should just be who they are, and not imply that they are something they're not?" asked Delia, recalling last night's conversation.

"He's moving; want to follow?" redirected Cobra, starting the ignition and going off-road over the difficult, thorny landscape. "If we're pursuing an animal, we're allowed to follow."

Cobra drove slowly over tough, scrubby plants and rocks, and more than once did people on the edges of the Land Rover get whacked by stout branches. Hyacinth even took a thorn to the arm, but she didn't complain and just shrugged it off.

"This is some vehicle," remarked Hyacinth. "But what about the plants?"

"I know which I can drive over and which I can't," said Cobra. "What you've really got to watch out for is elephant dung. You see, even if it's dry, it still might contain three-inch acacia thorns that it's passed. Those can puncture even these tires."

"What would we do if something happened to the vehicle?" asked Kevin.

"I'd radio camp and then wait for Wyatt or Katy to come get us in the spare Jeep, no problem."

"And until then?"

"We'd be on our own," Cobra said matter-of-factly.

\*\*\*

"Don't get any ideas, boys," laughed Andres as he peed into the dirt, the kind of dehydrated urine that smells so offensive.

"OK, can I just tell you, you're such an asshole?" responded Kevin, zipping up.

"You can tell me. I just don't give a shit," said Andres, shaking it, zipping it up and wandering back towards the car.

"I wonder what that guy's problem is," said Kevin.

"Oh, so we're speaking again?" answered Xavier.

"I never stopped."

"Maybe he's just been alone so long, he's forgotten how to behave around people."

"Sometimes an asshole's just an asshole."

"I couldn't agree more," said Xavier, zipping up and walking away.

As it was past midday, Cobra had decided to give the group a bathroom break before finding a place to have tea and lunch, so he found a clearing in the bush near a cluster of old marula trees and checked for danger. It was hot enough now that most animals were probably retreating from the sun and would be less active anyway. Kevin, Xavier and Andres were just finishing up their business while Hyacinth went to photograph the trees with Mark and Susan.

Cobra was arranging some biscuits on the hood of the Land Rover while Kotani went to the back to retrieve thermoses full of coffee and hot water. Delia leaned against the car, finding its warmth against the back of her shirt a welcome sensation after the coldness of the morning.

"I'm sorry for last night," said Delia.

"For what?" asked Cobra. "Nothing wrong with a polite conversation."

"I think I was a little less than polite."

"Not much less. And all our lips get a little loose when we've had a few."

"I had one glass of wine; I was stone-cold sober."

"In that case, thank you for your honesty. I don't need anyone to bullshit me out here in the bush. And I was wrong about the Sable. Coffee?"

"No, thank you."

Cobra arranged some spoons with a few portable jars of sugar and artificial sweetener, pliable screens covering them to keep the bugs away.

"It's just that you frustrate me."

"Because you think I'm a fraud."

"No. Because I feel like you're not being honest with me."

"Because I don't conform to whom you assume I should be? This sounds like the kind of fight we should be having on, like, our fourth or fifth date."

"Ha! You wish."

"That's the second time you've said that! I'm blushing. Our relationship is strictly professional, Professor."

SNAKE IN THE GRASS

"Everyone thinks Annie's the fun one, but I'm nothing but fun. Most guys get intimidated because I have a few extra words in my vocabulary or because I spend my time in the desert studying reptiles."

"Well, that sounds like fun to me."

"You'd like it. Really. I mean, there's a lot of drudgery with the field notes and write-ups and stuff, but it's great being in nature all day long."

"You don't have to tell me about being outside all day, Professor. I have the best office in the world, and I meet a lot of interesting people."

"I bet that's your game, you and Northside. Every week, a new group of people come flying in, and the single ladies must flock to you two Super-Tarzan, alpha-male, Brawny-paper-towel he-men."

"You've got me figured out, Professor," said Cobra.

"But then, if that were true, why didn't you, well, treat Annie's *khaki-fever* yourself?"

"I guess we'll never know."

"Oh, I bet we will."


Hyacinth took a great shot from underneath a baobab tree, and the worm's-eye-perspective made it look gigantic, it's roots-in-the-air branches taking up the whole frame.

"I think there's a go-away bird up at the top," said Mark. "Did you get it?"

"I think that's just a branch," said Hyacinth.

"Go-away bird?" asked Susan. "Is that a real thing?"

"Yeah, it's like a turaco," said Mark. "When it calls, it sounds like it's saying 'go away.' We saw a bunch in Tsavo West fifteen years ago."

"Yeah, me too," said Susan, not keenly interested in ornithology. "So, what do you think about Wyatt?"

"Hm?" asked Hyacinth, focusing.

"Wyatt Northside?  The guy who runs this place?"

"You mean, who *owns* this place.  He seems like a good guy, for being so loaded."

"How do you think he came about that kind of money?  I mean, most people have never heard of him before."

"Maybe he robbed a bank," said Mark.  "He seems like the kind of guy who could rob a bank and get away with it."

"You are so weird," said Hyacinth, not taking her eye away from the viewfinder.

"Cobra said he was independently wealthy.  Do you think he inherited it?"

"Maybe he got the land cheaply."

"But like, could he have gotten his fortune suddenly?  Like, a good day at the stock market?" questioned Susan.

"I don't know.  It seems like that would be the sort of thing that would be all over the *Wall Street Journal*.  But I'm sure you've seen lots of folks just like him at fancy parties and stuff, what with your line of work."

"Yeah.  But nobody who would then come hide out in a place like this."

\*\*\*

After tea and coffee, Cobra packed up the Land Rover and drove another ten minutes with the guests before Delia noticed that nobody was riding in the front of the vehicle.

"Wait, where's Kotani?" she asked.

"He went on ahead, scouting."

"On foot?"

"On foot."

"Isn't that dangerous?"

"It is… to any of us.  The car is our life raft, our fortress. But Kotani grew up in this country, and he knows it better than any of us.  He's forgotten more about animal behavior than any

50

wildlife biologist with three doctorate degrees will ever know. And he's got the rifle."

"Wait," said Xavier. "*The* rifle?"

"*The* rifle."

"As in, we don't have one?" Xavier asked nervously.

"Although this reserve is private property, Mr. Northside is very serious about conservation. He doesn't like guns in his wilderness; as it is, that one rifle is really mostly for show and to occasionally procure dinner. It's an old, bolt-action that's probably been around since the British were here fighting the Germans in World War One."

Susan clutched at her purse.

"What's the matter? Afraid a honey badger will mug you?" chided Andres.

"Kotani saw some leopard tracks while we were having tea; they were probably half a day old, but if anyone could pick them up, it's him. If he's lucky enough to find it, he'll radio me and we'll meet him," said Cobra, slowing down and eventually stopping. "Besides, all that pea-shooter can really do now is make a loud noise, which could frighten away some animals, but it really wouldn't do much against something like that…"

And there they were, as if clouds had parted to reveal the sweet Hereafter: up in a dry riverbed about forty yards ahead was a herd of elephants, tearing up the desiccated grass with their trunks and kicking it loose with their massive feet. There were about fourteen in sight, from juveniles to the enormous matriarch, the true masters of the wilderness. Interspersed between them were cape buffalo, three of them, and at their feet were heron-like cattle egrets picking off the insects rustled out of the vegetation by the giants' footfalls.

"She's beautiful," said Hyacinth, readying a photograph. "Look at those eyelashes."

"I don't see any males," complained Andres, looking through his viewfinder. "I need a shot of a big tusker."

"Welcome to Africa," said Cobra.

"How big are they?" asked Kevin.

"The females can top out around 4,000 kg. Males can be even bigger, up to six."

Delia looked through binoculars, a contented smile on her lips.

"It's a matriarchal society. The females stay together their whole lives, transferring knowledge of their surroundings. Males leave when they come of age," Cobra explained.

"Do they never forget?" asked Xavier.

"That's not just an idiom; they remember where water wells up beneath the ground, even if they haven't been there in years. Like now, it's been very tough with the late rains for these ellies to find enough to eat, but pretty soon…"

"Oh no," whispered Delia, taking her eyes from her binoculars.

Automatic weapons fire, and the wet smacking sound of bullets against flesh. The monstrous roar of a titan in shock and pain. The panic and trampling of beasts trying to get away from an enemy they haven't seen.

There were five men in a vehicle thirty yards to the east of the herd, each with semi-automatic weapons, firing at the elephant nearest them, a big female. The other animals fled in confusion, and she tried to follow, but the bullets tore through her legs at the knees. It would be a slow death, as she was huge and the rounds couldn't penetrate far, until two of the men produced automatic shotguns and began blasting away at her temple.

"Do something!" screamed Delia.

"Everyone get down!" Cobra yelled back, an instant before they heard the sound of the glass of the headlights and windshield shattering and the pelting of bullets against metal. Everyone brought their heads down to their knees as if they were in a crashing airplane.

Cobra tried to reignite the engine, but it didn't respond.

"Jesus Christ!" yelled Mark. "Look out!"

Success… the engine turned over the second time and Cobra threw it in reverse, gunning it backwards about ten yards before the RPG hit the front of the Rover.

The car's hood blew to pieces of fiery wreckage as the vehicle catapulted up in the air, twisting around and throwing some of the guests out into the open. It crashed back to earth, slamming into a leadwood tree, upside-down with its tires still spinning.

Stunned, Cobra discovered he had been thrown about ten feet from the driver's seat, and he was alive. He no longer heard anything but a tinny ringing sound, and he felt heat from the fire behind him. He resisted the overwhelming urge to pass out and risked moving his head to look around.

The men in the car had stopped shooting at the elephant (which was down) and the Land Rover (which was totaled). Cobra saw a second car approach the first, and he witnessed a man with a black ponytail in the second car pull out a handgun and execute the driver of the first.

Cobra's vision blurred, and he was dizzy and delirious, but he knew what he had seen… *whom* he had seen.

*Black Tiger*, he thought, and he assumed those thoughts would be his last.

Now both cars drove slowly across the dry riverbed towards what was left of Cobra and his party, and Cobra saw men re-loading their weapons, but then the damndest thing happened:

The elephants rallied.

Once they had regrouped, they turned a hundred and eighty degrees and charged, trumpeting shrilly, thundering towards the two cars as they neared their felled sister. The matriarch bulldozed into the first car, slamming into the chassis with her lowered, 800-pound head.

Cobra heard tires squealing, men screaming, and the trumpeting of rampaging elephants, and then he heard nothing.

# CHAPTER 3:
# UNDECLARED
## SIX YEARS EARLIER

Sitting against a tree just outside the library at Stony Brook University was a rather scrawny nineteen-year-old kid with foam earphones around his head and a book in his hands.  I say *foam earphones* because that's what you listened to back then if you were a college kid in September of that year, waiting for the brand-spanking-new *iPod* to be released about a month later, if you could afford it, which this kid, incidentally, could not.  He was a light-skinned African American, or maybe a Caucasian kid with a deep tan, or possibly even Tunisian or something.

"*The Green Hills of Africa?*" called Screw-Up, his friend, alluding to the first kid's book.  (If you surmised that *Screw-Up* was not his Christian name but rather a moniker well-earned, then I'll only say that you're *prooooobably* right.)

"That's *Green Hills of Africa*.  There's no '*the*,'" said the first boy, removing his earphones.

"What's the difference, Campbell?" asked Screw-Up.

"The difference is Hemingway didn't write a '*the*.'"

"Why not?"

"Dude, I don't know.  I wasn't with him."

"So, they could be any hills in Africa?"

"He's writing about Tanzania, like, a hundred years ago.  He's super-dead now.  I think he ate a shotgun or something."

"Jesus, that's grim," said Screw-Up.

"It's actually pretty good, despite how dated the language is, and the brutal careless torturing of wildlife for fun, and the blatant racism, unashamed classism, and reckless colonialism that kept my people oppressed and in squalor for more than a century. Well, some of my people, I guess," said Campbell.

"Jesus, that's grim," repeated Screw-Up. "Want to buy some coke from those city kids and watch Monday Night Raw?"

"Nah. Don't think so."

"How about a pizza?"

Campbell and Screw-Up pooled together a five, two ones, and twelve quarters to procure their heat-lamp cheese pizza from the student union and had brought it home to their dorm room where Screw-Up tossed the box on his bed, since their table was already cluttered with various take-out boxes and empty PBR cans. Screw-Up grabbed a slice and made no attempt to find a plate, since the small kitchen space looked like a radioactive landscape after nuclear testing, with the sink being a watery graveyard of unwashed dishes.

Although cocaine-less, Screw-Up turned on the opening minutes of wrestling. Campbell tried to sit on his bed, but first he had to knock some of the many textbooks to the floor - the companions of diverse classes like *Ancient History*, *Intro to Arabic*, the *Eastern Philosophy*, and George Schaller's *The Serengeti Lion*.

The light on the phone's answering machine was blinking - that's the forerunner to voicemail, by the way - and Campbell picked up the phone and initiated the button sequence that enabled the tape-recorded message to play for him. In case you're unfamiliar, the device looked like the little rectangle in the middle of Darth Vader's chest, attached to a phone with a chord.

Beeeeeep: "Campbell! This is your bro. We just pulled into Tokyo. Wish you could see it. Hope you're having a blast; will try you again in a few days!"

Campbell looked over at a photo on his desk of a man in his early twenties in distinguished Navy whites, an officer, a man *doing something* with his life.

Beeeeeep: "Screw-Up, it's me," sounded a woman's voice. "Your car has been parked on the front lawn of our sorority for a week and a half now and everyone's blaming me. It smells. Come over and get it or I'll get my uncle, who's a mechanic in Port Jeff Station, to take it apart and bring it to you piece-by-piece."

"Hear that? It's a girl. She says something about your car..." said Campbell.

"Delete," said Screw-Up, raising the volume on the TV,

Beeeeeep: "Sweetie, it's your mom," said Campbell's mother with a subtle Caribbean accent. "Two things - are you coming home for Columbus Day Weekend in October? Because your aunt and uncle are coming to visit us in Mineola and..." Campbell zoned out, knowing that his mother usually opened with something trivial before getting to the real reason for the call. "Your father and I were wondering when you were going to declare a major. You've had a whole year to figure this out, and you're in your third semester. We don't want to pressure you, but as you know, college isn't free, even state school, and we think the time has come to make some decisions. Please call us back. Say *hi* to Screw-Up. Love you."

Campbell hastily hit delete, sighing heavily.

Beeeeeep: "Screw-Up," said another woman's voice, quaveringly, "My, um, *Aunt Flo* hasn't shown up, and it's been more than a week, so..."

"It's another girl, for you. I think it's..."

"Delete," said Screw-Up.

"Yeah, but I think it's..."

"Dude, I said 'delete.' I'm in the middle of something."

"Ooooookay," shrugged Campbell.

Campbell hung up the phone and took a slice, breaking etiquette and not taking one adjacent to the first missing piece, instead pulling a bigger one from the other pizza hemisphere. He jumped back on his bed, huffing sullenly.

"Who's that guy?" asked Campbell, alluding to one of the hulks in tights on the TV.

"That's Taz, Campbell."

"Like, he's named for the cartoon character?"

"So? I call you 'Campbell,' like you're a can of clam chowder or something."

"Well, that's my name."

"Is that who you want to be? Campbell? That guy was probably Fred or John or Kumquat or something, and he decided he wanted to be Taz, so that's what they call him now. We have got to find you a nickname."

"OK, *Screw-Up*."

"Geez, what did you hear on that machine that put you in such a bad mood all of a sudden?"

"Do you think I'm directionless, Screw-Up?"

"How about Lord Fuckingham?"

"What?"

"For your new nickname. I think it sends the right message. All the ladies will be lining up to kneel before Lord Fuckingham."

"You know what? Forget it," said Campbell.

"All right, stop being so pissy. What did you say?"

"I said, do you think I'm directionless? Like, wasting my time. Going through the motions."

"To tell you the truth, I'm not really the best guy to ask about this. I don't know what I'm doing from one day to the next. I'm not even sure where I am right now."

"Arnold called. He's on a ship, a destroyer. He's making a difference in the world, keeping people safe, helping people who need help."

"A woman in every port!"

"He's responsible for people's lives. He's seeing the world,

58

learning things, having adventure. What am I doing here?"

"You want to join the Navy?"

"No. That's not it."

"Navy guys do push-ups. They run miles. They swim, they learn to use technical equipment and stuff. I don't think that's for you."

"Why not?" asked Campbell. "I bet I could, if I tried."

"Do ten push-ups now."

"I've got a slice of pizza in my hands."

"Put it down and do ten push-ups. Do five."

"Anyway…" continued Campbell. "I've been here for a year, and I've gotten C plusses in most of my classes."

"You can speak some Arabic," said Screw-Up. "That's something, even if it's a dead language."

"It's not a dead language. Millions of people around the world speak it."

"I mean here in America. Speak Spanish or get out."

"Like, I'm interested in lots of things. I like being outside. But soon I'm going to pick a major, probably some boring, practical business degree. I'll graduate in four or five years…"

"Two years less than me!"

"And I'll get some job in the city. Commute back and forth from Mineola, work the grind for forty years, and then get ready to die."

"Wow, that's morbid. It's Monday for me too, you know."

"I'll get to see some far-away places, but like, on vacation every few years, and that's that. Is that who I am?"

"Well, who do you want to be?"

Campbell took a big bite of pizza.

"I don't know. Is that a crime?"

"Look, your brother is a man of action, and I understand feeling a little insecure after having to follow that guy," said Screw-Up sagaciously (for someone who was only a *little* high). "But maybe you should stick to what you're good at."

SNAKE IN THE GRASS

On the screen, Taz took a nasty fall, courtesy of a spear tackle from his opponent, Edge, and then the phone rang.

"I'm not getting that," said Screw-Up.

After five annoying rings, a voice projected from the phone's external speaker: "Dudes, where the hell are you? Party at Gino's, ASAP!"

Campbell looked at Screw-Up and said, "Really? On a Monday night?"

"Campbell McConnors," replied his roommate, shaking his head disappointedly, "I thought you said you wanted to be a man of action."

\*\*\*

Campbell was sitting on a couch in *someone's* living room, Gino's, I suppose, wondering what he was doing there as a party seemed to ensue both around him and in spite of him. Screw-Up was in the kitchen with some other people Campbell didn't know; they were building a tower out of Doritos and Bugles but never seemed to get higher than the first floor. Actually, that's a poor choice of words… they got plenty high.

The music was too loud, and it made Campbell feel all the more awkward, sometimes waving to strangers but not really engaging them, and always watching the TV. It made him feel socially safe; if someone asked him what he was doing there, he'd be able to say, "I'm watching this."

Nobody asked him what he was doing there.

He couldn't shake the existential questions that were, in truth, bothering him long before his brother and mother had called him. He felt like he needed to experience more from life, and yet, here he was with an opportunity to mingle with new people, and he just couldn't bring himself to do it. He was more looking *through* the TV than *at* it.

"Who are you?" asked some guy, a bruiser with a six-pack of light beer in his hands.

"Me?"

"Yeah, you," said the guy. "This is my house, and you're creeping me out."

"Lord Fuckingham," said Campbell.

"What did you say to me, asshole?"

"You must be a housemate of Gino's. I'm here with that guy," said Campbell, pointing to Screw-Up getting slapped in the kitchen by some girl. "You know what? Maybe I should leave."

He got up to go, but the bigger guy - whose name was Dan, although it doesn't really matter - stopped him.

"That's all you had to say, bro. Have a beer," said Dan.

"I'm not much of a drinker," said Campbell.

"Now you're just being rude. These are silver bullets," he said, taking a can off the plastic holder and thrusting it at Campbell. "It's not even drinking. Marathon runners drink this shit to *rehydrate*."

"Is that really true?"

"Fuck if I know. You running marathons right now?"

"I'm watching TV," said Campbell, the time finally right for his prepared line.

"Just drink it, man," said Dan. "Like the Nike slogan."

Campbell examined the can. "4.4% ABV," he mused. "Fine. What the hell."

\*\*\*

Campbell just had one beer and then walked back to his dorm, contemplating who he was and falling into a troubled sleep thinking about his future. That's what I *would* have told you if it were true, but of course, it's not.

Somewhere between beers seven and eight, Campbell had lost count, and he wondered if those life-changing experiences he sought would really count since he didn't expect to remember most of them in the morning. He marched to the kitchen, opened the refrigerator door and rummaged through like a foraging bear, not really noticing Screw-Up *not quite passed out*, ass on the linoleum and legs splayed out in either direction, one shoe missing.

"Sooo…" slurred Screw-Up, "How you doing?"

"Tapping the fucking Rockies, that's what."

"I said *how* you doing, not *what* you doing," replied Screw-Up. "At least, that's what I think I said."

Campbell emerged with his treasures, another beer and somebody's half-eaten carton of roast pork chow fun.

"Fantastic," said Campbell with no intonation.

Somewhere between beers eight and nine, Campbell found himself in a different room on a different couch talking to a pretty girl he did not know, in the middle of a conversation that he didn't remember beginning.

"Centuries of systematic slavery, Jim Crow, bombs in Birmingham… to many people, it's just Sociology class or History class or whatever, but to me…" he stammered.

"So, you *are* a Black guy," said the girl, fishing through his sentences. "Excuse me, *African-American*."

"Hells yeah, I am," he responded, inebriated but sincere. "I mean, I'm half White, but so what? All anyone sees when they look at me is Black, and everything that comes with it. Judgment complete, verdict in. How do you fight that? I bet I can't get a cab in the city fifty percent of the time."

"I never did it with a Black guy before," she said, touching his arm.

"Ha!" he chortled bitterly, spitting up a little beer. "Neither have I!"

The girl shook her head and moved on.

"I mostly take the subway," said Campbell, to nobody.

Somewhere between beers nine and ten Campbell threw up, but he was amused at how accurately he nailed the dead-center bull's-eye of the toilet bowl. At least, that was his perception, although the next party-goer to use the toilet might have begged to differ somewhat with his assessment, as would the next person to use the adjacent bathtub.

"And now," said Campbell, wiping his mouth on the bath towel, "Ham!"

Somewhere between beers ten and eleven, Campbell wasn't feeling so hot, but now he was on a compulsive mission to get to beer number twelve for his own satisfaction. If he hadn't been so hammered, he would have realized that his count was off and that he had already passed beer number twelve two beers ago.

The room was spinning around him, and closing his eyes only made it worse. The beer had helped him to further withdraw into his thoughts, not bring him closer to those around him. He felt sad, unfulfilled, and uncertain about his future, and he wasn't sure why those emotions seemed so clear to him as he braced himself against the stairs. Now that he considered it, this was the first time he had ever gotten knock-out drunk before.

"Experience," he said out loud, "Check."

*Now that I think about it*, he considered, *I've never even been in a fight before, unless you count that one time in the church parking lot.*

"What the hell?" roared Dan from the kitchen. "Where's my Chinese food? And where's my ham?"

"Experience," he repeated, "Check!"

\*\*\*

Campbell and Screw-Up had forgotten to close the shades when they miraculously made it back to their dorm, so the bright sun shined right into their eyes the next day. It was a beautiful morning, with only light clouds. If they weren't suffering tyrannical hangovers, it would have been a glorious start to the day.

"Uggggggggh," groaned Campbell, seeing 10:16 blazing in red electronic digits on his alarm clock. "How many beers?"

"Lots," said Screw-Up. "From now on, I dub thee Campbell McCoors."

Campbell touched his swollen eye and recoiled, and bits of dried blood from his nose crusted off as he stretched his mouth to yawn. He turned on the TV.

"Is it too early for Jerry Springer or too late for Montel?" he croaked, barely operating the remote.

There was news on the screen, however. And it was on every channel.

The first tower had just fallen.

"Find some cartoons," said Screw-Up, turning over in his bed, not seeing the horrible, black smoke billowing up over the New York City skyline on the live feed on the television. Not seeing the fires raging on the North Tower as the world prayed it would retain its integrity. Not seeing Campbell, suddenly stone-cold sober, his eyes narrowing and his hands tightening into fists.

# CHAPTER 4:
# POACHERS

From a void of comfortable darkness, Cobra felt an irritating, stinging sensation coming from what he approximated was his face. Like hearing a phone ringing at three in the morning, he simply decided not to answer it and continued indulging in a state of obliviousness.

He felt it again, this time more forceful, more annoying, and more difficult to ignore, despite his earnest attempts to disregard it. Finally, it happened yet again, hard enough that Cobra realized he was thinking in words and was thus too close to consciousness to ignore the fact that he'd just been slapped very hard three times across the face.

"*Hadha yulim*," he groaned instinctively.

"What?" came Delia's voice.

"That hurt," he translated, code-switching back to English from Arabic.

"Ladies and gentlemen, he's alive!" said Delia, helping him to his knees. Cobra had been lying face down, and he was covered in loose dirt, sand, and dried blood from underneath his lip.

"Fuuuuuuck," he declared, now feeling a dull, throbbing headache like a mild hangover combined with dizziness from a rush of blood to the head from sitting up.

"We were very lucky, Cobra," she said, pulling him up and letting him reorient. "We must have been thrown clear from car and landed in the soft sand of this dry embankment. You OK?"

Cobra assessed himself... he was banged up but not injured.

"Everything still seems to be where it should. You?"

"I think the crash may have readjusted my spine after sitting in planes all day yesterday, so thank you for that, good going."

"That was no crash," said Cobra, remembering. "That was a rocket-propelled grenade, and we don't get too many of them in these parts."

He looked ahead.

"They're mourning," he told Delia in a hushed tone, gesturing.

A hundred and fifty yards away, the elephant herd gathered in a concentric circle around the remains of the cow that had been shot and bled out. They indicated that they understood she was dead, not trying to rouse her as they might if they thought otherwise, but instead delicately touched her body with the tips of their trunks. The animals seemed to have an order in which they approached the dead cow, almost like a social hierarchy, but how it was arranged was difficult to conjecture. Even to Delia, an empirical scientist, it was clear that they were witnessing an elephant funeral.

She'd read about this phenomenon and had enough respect not to ask Cobra about it. "Poachers?" she asked.

Cobra rose to his feet, his eyes narrowing and his fingers clenching into fists.

"Poachers?" she repeated.

It was mid-afternoon and hot; everyone was alive, but not unharmed. The fire from the Land Rover had mostly subsided, but smoke still billowed upward to the sky, which at the very least, discouraged mosquitos and flies. The car was upside-down and lodged against a now-broken tree, its wheels no longer spinning, but otherwise in one piece. Everyone who had been in the vehicle had crawled out and had dragged themselves at some point to safety around it before collapsing.

"Mark, your hands…" cried Hyacinth.

The tops of Mark's hands had been burned and the skin looked like re-heated pizza.

"Second, maybe third degree," he groaned. "Probably second."

"Jesus, Mark," she said, "does it hurt?"

"Yes," he said emphatically.

"Do you think you can make it?"

"You know, I'm not sure. I think all the sunblock I put on this morning may have lessened the damage."

"Idiot," she laughed. "Help me up."

"Yes, ma'am!" he chuckled back. He tried to help her to her feet, but she cried out sharply and crumpled back down.

"It's my ankle," she gasped sharply.

On the other side, Kevin, Xavier and Susan sat inertly, groggily assessing themselves. Kevin's nose was swollen and bloody, and Xavier had a gash somewhere on his head above the temple.

"Thank God," said Xavier, hugging Kevin. "Are you all right?"

"My nose. I think it's broken," he said, and then surveying Xavier's blood-soaked hair, "What about you? Are you concussed?"

"I - I can't remember anything that happened after this morning. It's like I have amnesia."

"Don't stand up."

"Like, I vaguely remember we had some kind of serious conversation, but I can't
remember anything we said to one another."

"Oh my God, really?"

"Nope," smiled Xavier sardonically.

"Don't be a dick," said Kevin, pushing him playfully.

"No…" said Susan, next to Kevin, her voice panicked. "Where is it?"

"Susan, are you hurt?" asked Kevin.

"Where the hell is it?" she cried, crawling on her hands and knees.

"Girl, I think you're in shock," said Kevin, but Susan ignored him and moved through him and Xavier, to where her purse had been thrown about six yards away in a thorny bush, where a mob of curious banded mongooses was taking an interest in it. Eye level with the mongooses, they each stood bipedally to face her.

"Get away from that, you rats!" she hissed in *Southern*, as if it were a language of its own. "It's mine!"

They hissed back, *actually* hissing, but retreated a safe distance away as she reached for her property.

High up in the broken tree against which the car was leaning was Andres, folded over a branch like a garment bag.

"My coccyx," he whined.

"Your what?" called Cobra, approaching the vehicle with Delia.

"My tailbone," he repeated, and Cobra shrugged as if he'd never heard the word. "My ass, you moron, my ass!"

\*\*\*

"Cobra to Northside," spoke Cobra into the receiver of the radio, upside-down and attached to the dashboard of the car, also upside-down. There was no response - no static, no electric hum, no white noise. "Northside, this is Cobra," he repeated, knocking the radio with his boot but still getting no reaction.

"It's dead," announced Cobra to the group, stroking his chin and periodically keeping an eye on the elephant carcass up ahead in the dry riverbed.

"Dead," echoed Xavier, morose.

"My cell phone still has some charge," said Kevin.

"You're welcome to try, but I seriously doubt you'll get any service out here," replied Cobra. "It's like being on the moon."

"*My fucking lenses!*" muttered Andres in German and then repeating it loudly in English. His equipment was in dozens of pieces, trailing out of the Land Rover.

"Looks like my camera still works," said Hyacinth as Mark wrapped her ankle with some bandages from the first aid kit that had survived in the trunk.

"Can I..." began Andres.

"Not in a thousand years," declared Hyacinth.

"Well," said Mark, "I've seen enough broken legs in forty years of seventh-grade dodgeball to guess that you've probably only got a sprain."

"Is that your official medical prognosis, doctor?" she winced.

"Try to stand up."

With Mark, burnt hands also bandaged, helping her, Hyacinth bit through some pain and rose to her feet, heavily supported by Mark's shoulder and a tree.

"Now, tree pose. Broken table. Downward dog."

"Oh, shut up. Why don't you go play piano with those oven mitts on your hands?" she grunted back.

"What about you, little girl?" said Andres to Susan. "Got anything in that purse that can help us?"

"Not unless we're on the same cycle now, Andres," Susan spat back.

"Everyone relax," said Cobra. "Let's just take it easy."

"Well, that was the plan when we booked this vacation," said Xavier passive-aggressively (but mostly aggressively).

"If it weren't for Cobra, they would have hit us full-on," observed Delia.

"If it weren't for Cobra, we wouldn't have been here in the

first place!" said Xavier.

"That's not fair," said Kevin. "I don't think that's fair."

"You should have radioed home when you first saw those guys. You should have backed us away before they saw us," said Susan. "If we were at Governor's Camp…"

"Oh, blow it out your ass, Susan," said Hyacinth. "Let the grownups talk or we're cancelling Prom."

"Cobra, do we have any beers?" asked Mark.

"Oh, grandpa the safari expert wants a beer," shot back Susan in *Southern*. "Bad news: we won't be back in time for *Wheel of Fortune*. Why don't you take a nap?"

"You know, young lady," said Mark. "Not a terrible idea."

"What are we supposed to do now?" asked Xavier.

"Calm down," said Kevin.

"Where's Kotani?" asked Delia.

"No, you calm down. What are we supposed to do?"

Cobra ignored them and took two steps away from the group, watching the elephant carcass. The elephants had ceased mourning and had dispersed, traveling on. Up in the sky, Cobra saw the first vulture circling. With his finger, he tested the direction of the wind.

"God, it's hot," commented Kevin.

"We've got to go back," said Susan.

"We've got to get our *money* back," said Andres.

"Kotani's out there," mentioned Delia again. "What if *they* have him?"

Cobra turned his attention to the dead man lying face-down in the riverbed. He couldn't make out any features, or where he had been shot, but it reminded him of something he had seen, something he had done, a lifetime ago.

"Who?"

"Kotani," said Delia. "The tracker."

"Him? You're worried about that guy?" said Susan. "Cobra said he's like Tarzan. He's got the rifle. You're worried about him?"

"If the poachers found him," started Kevin.

"He's as good as dead," said Xavier. "Just liked us."

"Don't be naive," said Andres scornfully. "He's working with the poachers."

"Jesus, just shut the fuck up," said Hyacinth.

"I said *naive* out of courtesy. Perhaps I should have said *stupid*."

"Watch your coccyx," warned Mark.

"Please," explained Andres patronizingly. "He can make more money working with his countrymen to poach these animals. He leaves us just before they arrive, mowing down an elephant. He wasn't scouting for *us*, he was scouting big game for *them*, and he gets his cut. It's well-known that the best scouts are corrupt game rangers and wildlife officials."

"That is," said Kevin, considering, "kind of plausible."

"It's horse-shit," said Cobra, rejoining the conversation, his chin protruding slightly, indicating a ten percent increase in machismo.

Andres got "You, sir, are an idiot, and the worst…" out of his mouth before Cobra cut him off with:

"I am the worst at many things, *sir*… table tennis, Easter egg dying, maybe folding laundry," announced Cobra. "I'm the best, however, at knocking out stupid assholes who don't know enough to shut the fuck up."

"Are you implying…"

"I'm not *implying* anything. I'm explicitly saying that I'm going to knock your ass out and leave you for the jackals if you don't get silent as a wedding night fart, post haste. I'm saying you have a face that's just begging to be punched, and I'm just mentally deciding whether to hit the right side or the left side while the next words come out of your mouth. Go on. I'll wait."

Andres opened his mouth as if to say something, and then he backed off, crossing his arms.

71

"People, gather round," said Cobra. "We're close to twenty miles from home, and many of us are injured. We have no weapons, and we're in very treacherous terrain. You saw that lion pride. I wouldn't recommend hiking back to camp to even experienced survivalists, let alone a party suffering various debilitating injuries. We couldn't get through on the radio, but Northside or Katy will have seen the smoke from the explosion sooner or later and will come for us with the Jeep. Kotani, too… he's probably within a mile or two from us, and I'm sure he's seen it.

"As long as we stay close together and keep our distance from the carcass, I expect most of the scavengers will leave us alone. Lions don't need us when they have a few tons of fresh elephant waiting for them on a platter. We're going to stay here and hold out, nurse our wounds, and wait."

"What about the poachers?" asked Delia, eyebrow raised.

"I doubt they'll be back. This isn't the Kruger, and they weren't expecting us; I bet they were shocked to see anyone else out here. They're probably heading in the opposite direction," said Cobra, appearing as confident as possible telling this lie.

"Now, who remembers: what is the first rule of safari?" asked Cobra.

"Something about tipping your guides?" mumbled Xavier.

"Not the first rule," said Cobra, "although it still applies."

"*Ja*, good luck with that one," grumbled the only one who says things like *ja*.

"Always listen to your ranger," said Mark.

"That's right. Always listen to your ranger, right in front of '*always stay in the vehicle.*' Those rules are from the speech, which I gave to you when you landed, which I've given a hundred times to a hundred different guests who think they're at Disneyland. Now it's time for the other speech, and congratulations! You're the first ones on the business end of it," announced Cobra.

"Oh, good," said Delia, deadpan.

"This can be a magical experience for you, one you'll remember forever, or *you* can be a magical experience that your loved ones will remember forever. It's up to you. Follow my instructions explicitly, and we'll be just fine. You might even enjoy yourselves and learn a thing or two about the bush if you listen."

"I, for one, am having a blast," said Mark.

"We're going to die out here," said Xavier.

"No, just you," reprimanded Cobra, "if you have a bad attitude. Because I'm not working for tips anymore; I'm working to keep our casualties at zero, which I've done so far."

"Unless you count Kotani," said Delia.

"Unless you count Kotani," said Cobra, then retracting, "who is, I'm fairly certain, perfectly fine. I'm not trying to frighten you. It's just that our fortress, the car, is now a flaming death trap, and we're out in the open, on the ground, and at the mercy of nature, who is a cruel mistress."

"Wrap this up," said Delia.

"What I'm saying is, it'll probably only be a few hours until we're rescued, so stay close, keep your shit together, and relax… I'm Cobra M'fuckin Coors, and I'm here to keep you alive."

"Done?" asked Delia.

"Done."

"I feel like I should clap," said Delia, "except I'm not really that inspired."

"Do you think we'll have to get to the choppa next?" remarked Hyacinth to Mark.

"*You know where you are? You're in the jungle, baby,*" sang Mark to Hyacinth.

"We are all going to die," said Xavier.

"Fucking *schiza*," spat Andres.

"How about some lunch?" asked Cobra.

\*\*\*

Satisfied that the guests were comparatively safe, Cobra walked up the dry riverbed. He noted that there were about ten vultures and a few maribou storks on the elephant carcass, and he heard jackals' calls from far away. The skies of the distant north were an ominous indigo, dense and opaque.

Taking his hat off and wiping the sweat, dirt and blood from his brow, Cobra knelt beside the man that had been shot and unceremoniously thrown from the opposing car what seemed like hours ago, but in reality, was probably less than one.

He turned him over. The deceased was Caucasian, not a Shangaan, and had been shot neatly between the eyes at close range. Blood had soaked into the sand underneath him, but otherwise, he was clean and his appearance, unremarkable. Cobra checked him for any kind of identification - he had no wallet, although his boots were military issue of indeterminate nation. Beyond that, he was carrying nothing and had no weapon.

"They're all right back there," said Delia, sneaking up on Cobra for a second time and offering him a foil-wrapped sandwich. "Katy makes a good turkey sandwich."

"That's guinea fowl in that wrap, but yeah."

"They're shaken, but OK for now. They're eating and staying close to the car, like you told them. Mark made the most of that first aid kit."

"I did tell everyone to stay by the Land Rover, Professor."

"Did you? I didn't think you meant me."

"Why not?"

"Because I assumed you already figured out that nobody tells me what to do."

"Professor, you're starting to grow on me."

"What do you think happened?"

"I don't know. Maybe got a little overzealous, and the man in charge didn't suffer fools well."

"Please don't treat me like I'm an idiot."

Cobra rose, returning his hat to his head.

"Go on, then, Professor. Show your work."

"What poachers would carry an RPG with them? And if their goal were ivory, why would they use little AK-47s to slowly bleed out an elephant? Why would they pursue us after frightening us away?"

"To keep us from alerting the authorities."

"There are no SAN Parks patrols out here, and you said yourself that we're so remote, it financially wouldn't make sense to hunt a few elephants all the way out here without the means to transport them out commercially."

"All right, fine, but this stays between us," said Cobra. "I think this was a military outfit. A rogue military outfit, looking for something."

"What could they be looking for out here?"

"I don't know," he said, and quickly continued, "Some of the men were undisciplined and shot an elephant for, I don't know, spite, and it alerted us to them. The captain dispatched this poor slob for his carelessness."

"Thank you. You see stuff like this in the Army?" she probed.

"You've been spying on me, Professor."

"I spied on your room, looking for Annie. Those your dog tags?"

"Yes, right next to Jonathan Scott's book."

"I love being the smartest one in the room. It never gets old."

"Oh, good. Maybe you can think of a way out of this, because if those guys come back, we're Fucked with a capital F," said Cobra.

"I thought you were Cobra Mc Fucking Coors!"

"That's Cobra M'fucking Coors, thank you very much, and I was trying to calm everybody down, but come on. We're in no shape to hike back to the lodge. Two of them are in their seventies, for Christ's sake. Xavier has a head wound. Andres has a broken ass or something."

"You did lay it on a little thick, didn't you?"

"A little," he said, "but staying where we are is our only option right now. There's a very good chance that Wyatt's seen the smoke and is on his way already, if he's not too busy, um, studying your friend's biology or whatever."

"Gross. And if he didn't?"


"What the hell is this?" yelled Cobra upon returning to the Land Rover with Delia to find the group guzzling various forms of adult beverage.

"We finished our sandwiches, which were very good, by the way," said Mark, "and then we helped ourselves to a little… what would you call it on safari?"

"Mid-afternooner," chimed in Hyacinth.

"Mid-afternooner! As it turned out, all the booze survived the crash pretty much unscathed, although some of the limes were smashed."

"Which is what we're working on getting," said Hyacinth, ever supportive.

Xavier, Kevin, Andres - even Susan, *especially* Susan - were imbibing, coccyxes in the warm sand of the dry riverbed.

"Are you kidding? We could be out here for hours, maybe even overnight," said Cobra.

"Yeah, but we're still on vacation, aren't we?" said Mark, good-natured.

"Xavier could have a traumatic brain injury!"

"I agree, he *could* have a traumatic brain injury."

"I said lunch, not… mid-afternooners," repeated Cobra. "Don't you see? If we dehydrate now, we have limited access to fresh water. And if those guys come back to finish us off…"

"Which you personally assured us wouldn't happen…"

"Which I personally assured you wouldn't happen," remembered Cobra, turning to Delia for support but finding her already cracking into a beer and wiping the sweat off her forehead with the condensation on the bottle.

"Cobra, that cooler's incredible. There's still ice in it. How about a cold G&T to sharpen your senses, get you closer to nature?"

"Fuck yes," Cobra capitulated, figuring he'd projected enough responsibility to make the group at least consider that he was trying to do the right thing. "Although I'm not sure you understand how alcohol works."

While Mark went about fixing Cobra's cocktail, Hyacinth whispered to him, "It was my idea. He was asking for morphine twenty minutes ago for his burns. I figured this was a fair compromise."

"He'll be all right," said Cobra. "He's pretty stoic."

"When he has a cold, he carries on like a six-year-old watching someone light his Nintendo on fire," returned Hyacinth.


Later: the sun past its zenith in the sky, a Famous Grouse bottle still about half full… maybe four in the afternoon, no Kotani, no Northside.

Andres kept rubbing his arms gently, noting how bright red they had become. Susan sat a few feet from him, eyes transfixed on the macabre sight of a clan of nine mature hyena already pushing the vultures aside to take advantage of the huge windfall. They had smelled its death, its blood, from far away and gathered one at a time to commandeer this feast from the other scavengers. The elephant's skin was too thick for even their powerful jaws to make efficient work, so they started at the softest parts and worked from there: eyes, tip of trunk, bullet wounds on the legs. The belly would have to wait. Some were trying to bite and claw their way through the anus, which while unpleasant, made sense in Nature's cruel calculus.

"It's horrible," said Susan, holding her elbow, which had been banged up in the crash.

"It's just nature," said Andres. "Have you ever seen a hyena cub starve? They're like puppies. Equally unpleasant."

"Not the hyenas," corrected Susan. "Us. People. Massacre a beautiful creature like that, for what?"

"It's just nature," Andres repeated. "Human nature."

"They didn't even take the tusks."

"Be glad you didn't see that. They'd take a chainsaw and cut through the face."

"People are so greedy. They don't care what their greed does."

"Now, surely you can understand greed, can you not?" Andres answered. "A need to protect your own? Ensure your survival, your comforts?"

Susan shifted her purse and watched some of the hyenas chasing away the vultures and storks, who flew just out of reach and continued to wait patiently. They needed the hyenas anyway, to cut openings for them through which they could access the meat.

"Survival and comfort are not the same thing," she said.

"That depends on your perspective. Men who kill elephants do not live like kings; they risk everything and live just marginally better than their brothers who live in abject poverty. I'm sure you've come across this and more in all your *extensive* travels. When you were looking down from your Taj Mahals and your Eiffel Tower parties at the rest of the slime, how did you judge those beneath you?"

"You're rude, and an asshole," she said, getting up to move away from him. "That's your nature."

Andres kept watching the hyenas, imagining the photos he'd have been getting had his precious camera equipment not been smashed.

"*Schiza.*"

Still later: the sun descending, close to five, the whiskey bottle at about three-quarters drained, more empty beer cans than full ones in the cooler, no Kotani, no Northside. The hyenas were making steady progress.

"How are those hands?" asked Hyacinth.

"They hurt," said Mark, shivering a little. "I probably shouldn't have wrapped them so tightly. They're going to be a bitch to undo later."

"I'm worried about infection. You're going to need antibiotics."

"Well, got any?"

"Nope."

"OK, then," he said. "Can you stand up?"

"I've only had two beers, Mark, give me some credit."

"Your ankle, hon."

"I may have to cancel line-dancing at the Cancun Cantina when we get back next week…"

"That's the spirit, thinking we'll get back," he joked.

"You know me; glass is half-full, all right."

"Half-full, all right," he echoed. "Full of poison."

Cobra crawled past them to get to the cooler.

"Well, holy shit. There's still some ice," he said. "You guys all right?"

"We're gonna make it," said Hyacinth.

"I know you're gonna make it. I mean, do you want another beer while I'm up?"

"Beer me," grunted Mark. "You know, this actually reminds me of a time when we were in Kruger about fifteen years ago."

"Everything reminds you of something else," said Hyacinth.

"No, really. Our car broke down, just like this."

79

"It broke down in pieces of flaming wreckage?" asked Cobra.

"No, just some trouble with the alternator, actually. You know, now that you mention it, the two incidents aren't as similar as I thought."

"You ever guide in Kruger, Cobra?" asked Hyacinth.

"No, mostly just around here, although I visited Mala Mala once as a guest. Liked it a lot. Kruger deserves its reputation."

"For giving kids scary dreams and attaching knives to baseball gloves?" asked Delia, passing by.

"Different Kruger," said Cobra. "It's named for President Paul Kruger, colonial despot. I don't think they're related."

"Despot's probably a little harsh," said Hyacinth. "Although after the Boer War, they *did* run him out of the country."

"But he had a lovely singing voice," said Cobra. "Which of these bushes did we say was the bathroom again?"

Still *still* later: the sun was pretty low in the sky, around six-thirty, and the day's heat was starting to dissipate, much like the drop or two left over in the Famous Grouse bottle. No Kotani, no Northside. The sound of frogs coming out from the mud after the day's harshness ceased filled the air.

"You OK?" asked Kevin.

Xavier, worlds away, said nothing.

"We're gonna be OK," assured Kevin.

"It's been hours," said Xavier. "Why wouldn't Mr. Northside have come for us by now?"

"I don't know."

"He had to have seen us; the tracker, too. When we didn't come back, or even check in, someone at camp would have noticed."

"Maybe they're having trouble too. It's tough country; maybe it's slow getting out to us in the jeep."

"No," said Xavier. "They would have been here by now. Northside isn't coming, and neither is the tracker."

"How's your head?" asked Kevin.

"Hurts," said Xavier quietly. "I'm hungry."

Kevin pulled out two granola bars from his pants pocket and gave one to Xavier.

"We should go," said Xavier.

"On our own?"

"If we have to. Fuck everyone else. There's no point in staying here. Nobody's coming, and we have no supplies."

"You must have a concussion," said Kevin. "It'll be dark soon. It's twenty miles back to the lodge. Didn't you see those lions?"

"What about them?" Xavier said, gesturing to the hyenas chopping their way into the elephant's body. "We're going to sleep out here, a football field away from *that*?"

"Just relax, will you? There is just no way. At best, we'd have to set out in the morning when the sun comes up to hike home, and even then, it sounds impossible. Someone will help us."

"We're going to die out here," said Xavier, despondent.

A roar, deep and resonant and full of bass, like a jet engine.

"What was that?"

# CHAPTER 5:
# FLOOD

"Get on top of the car!  On top of the car!" yelled Cobra, helping Mark lift Hyacinth up to her feet.

"What are you blathering about?" protested Andres.

"Jesus Christ!" shrieked Xavier, skittering backward in the sand until he could stand.

Two lions trotted towards them from behind, following the dry riverbed like a road.  They were about fifty yards away and moving at an aggressive, determined pace.  They'd be on them in seconds.  They were males, and by the looks of their protruding ribs, hungry.

"Up!  Get up!" Cobra commanded.  The guests reacted as quickly as they could, but an afternoon of reckless boozing lowered their reaction time and diminished their motor skills.  To be fair, though, this was pretty sobering.

The Land Rover was still upside-down and leaning against the tree at about a sixty-degree angle, with the front bumper planted into the ground and the tail-light wedged into the branches above.  Underneath, the car's chassis made a triangular tunnel over the heated sand, highest at about five or six feet where the vehicle met the trunk.

Seconds, maybe four, and the lions had covered thirty yards.

"Ow!" cried Kevin, touching the underside (now the top) of

the Rover as he attempted to usher Xavier up. Although it was no longer flaming, the metal was still very hot from absorbing a full day's equatorial sun.

"Oh good, more burns," said Mark.

"Beats getting eaten!" barked Cobra, pushing Mark and Hyacinth up, and the lions were at a distance of ten yards.

Mark and Hyacinth were at the back of the car, the highest point, where it met the tree, and Andres was next, pushing past Kevin and Xavier but reaching out to help Susan. Kevin and Xavier were at the lowest point, about mid-way up the car, which shook as the guests jostled for space.

And just like that, the lions were upon them, flanking the car as Cobra and Delia, who hadn't had time to climb up, were stuck on the ground.

Wild screams from everyone above as Cobra, covered in automotive grease from helping everyone up, tackled Delia and slid underneath the car feet-first as if stealing home-plate. He felt her body shaking, but she was probably steadier than he was, trying not to piss his own pants as the lions slowed to investigate.

On Delia's side, a huge lion with tufts of hair covering his joints like the elbow pads of a tweed jacket sniffed curiously, and she instinctively recoiled in horror. On Cobra's, an animal of slighter build with a scraggly mane sprouting only above his head like a Mohawk padded forward, eyes focused ahead and paying little attention to Cobra and Delia. Let's call them Boss Tweed and Magua, respectfully and respectively.

"Sub-adults, a coalition," whispered Cobra.

"Do you know them?" responded Delia, doing a damn fine job trying to keep her shit together.

"No. They've probably just come of age. Brothers. Kicked out of their natal pride by their father, looking for a territory. Maybe expelled from this morning's pride."

Delia smelled the pungent stench of urine from underneath Boss Tweed's rear paws.

"What do you want to do?"

"They don't want us," whispered Cobra quickly. "They want the elephant. They must have smelled it, like the hyenas. Just be still for a minute."

"No problem."

Both Boss Tweed and Magua strode forward, and they marked the headlights of the car with urine. Delia saw the enormous footprints they left in the sand on the side of the vehicle. *Subadults*, she thought. *They look big enough to me.*

The hyenas had just noticed the lions, and they mounted an aggressive defense, standing on top of and around the carcass, all jaws pointed at them. It was intimidating, especially to these young lions who still hadn't reached full size and were green with inexperience, but they were desperate and could not pass up this opportunity.

Satisfied the car posed no threat, Tweed and Magua advanced together, and everyone let out a collective sigh of relief that they were no longer in immediate danger.

Until Susan carelessly let go of her purse, the strap slick with sweat and petrol, and it slid down off the undercarriage, just barely whacking the tip of Tweed's tail.

He instantly wheeled around in surprise, eyes narrowing in sudden rage, and he and Magua both rumbled from deep in their throats. Perhaps they had disregarded the big metal animal and the curious upright animals on its back too soon after all.

Everyone scrambled to jockey farther up the car's back; besides Cobra and Delia, Kevin and Xavier were closest to the lions, who trotted to either side again. The car shook, and Susan slid downward.

Tweed stood up on his hind legs, leaning his paws against the metal to gain more height. Level with Andres, Tweed stared piercingly into his eyes, and Andres quaked.

Magua took two steps onto the front of the car, not comfortable with the sensation of the hot metal and black grease on his paws, but curious enough to continue.

Hyacinth threw a beer can at Magua, which loudly *clang*ed next to him and compelled him to reconsider.

"No!" protested Mark, to which Hyacinth swiftly replied: "Don't worry. It was empty."

Tweed took a swipe at Andres, and two of his claws momentarily became stuck in the rubber of one of the tires. Andres was as-of-yet unharmed (in case you're rooting against him).

The whole car shook as Tweed tried to dislodge his claws from the tire, and it felt as though the car were going to fall from where it was leaning against the tree. Everyone braced as Tweed moved the Rover, and from underneath it, Cobra and Delia were forced to roll out into the open to avoid being crushed. Fortunately, Magua was still at the front and had sauntered around to where his brother was rocking the car, and Cobra and Delia hugged the opposite side.

It was then that some forest-green *thing* slithered from out under the rear wheel well where Tweed was clawing, and over Hyacinth's hand, down the car towards Kevin.

"Snake!" he exclaimed, consumed with primordial fear. Everyone jostled to get away, trying to cling to the edge of the car.

"No!" yelled Delia as Cobra reached for something back under the car. "Olive snake. Non-venomous. Non-venomous!"

Tweed cut free of the tire, leaving shreds of rubber hanging inertly from the hubcaps. Everyone tried to get out of the snake's way without falling, until another reptile - a beige, desert colored serpent - crawled upward from under the front axle, where it had been coiled in torpor.

"Cape Cobra!" yelled Delia. "Cape Cobra! Very venomous! Get off! Get off!"

Now everyone *really* freaked out, to be colloquial. People may be scared of lions, but they're *terrified* of snakes. Everyone rolled or jumped off the car as quickly as they could, lions or not, except for Andres, who ran up the car and back into the tree branch he had previously climbed out of. At once, the cape cobra entangled itself with the olive snake, biting it furiously as they knotted, the cobra attempting to devour its victim.

The car dislodged from the tree and crashed straight down like two and a half tons of old Birmingham steel. It frightened the lions just enough to force them to retreat two or three paces, just as Cobra managed to pull a five-foot metal roll bar from underneath it. He brandished it like a katana.

"Stop! Don't run!" howled Cobra, seeing people sprinting away from the vehicle, triggering the lions' chase instinct. "Don't run!"

Covered with sand, Cobra banged the side of the car with his impromptu weapon, steel on steel, to get the lions' attention. Magua wanted to follow Xavier and Kevin who ran as though they were possessed, but seeing that Tweed was now totally focused on Cobra, he, too, turned his attention to the man with the bar.

"That's right! Come to Cobra, boys. Fiesta time!" he said as they deliberately approached. He kept the bar straight, trying to keep them at maximum distance.

Tweed took one easy swipe and knocked the bar clean out of Cobra's hands as if he were a small child throwing a wiffle-ball bat. Cobra smelled Magua's breath when

AAAAAAAAAAAAAAAAAEEEEEEEEEEEEEEEeeeeeeeeee eeee....

Delia had thrust her leg through the cavity where the steering wheel was crushed under the car's weight, kicking the center and blaring the horn. Surprised and confused, the two brothers retreated a few yards, considering their options.

Picking up the elephant carcass' scent again, they evidently decided they could do better, and turned to continue their advance on the hyenas, who had not broken their formation.

Cobra helped Delia back up. "Now why didn't I think of that?"

"I don't know. Why didn't you?"

"Glad to have you around, Professor."

"Fiesta time? Were you implying you were going to hit them like piñatas?"

"Only implying. I mean, they *are* endangered."

"They didn't look so endangered from down here!"

"Come on, Professor, you're a scientist. I'm sure you've read that most big cats don't develop a taste for human flesh..."

On their way to the elephant, Tweed casually picked up the dead poacher by his head and Magua, by his leg, both pulling until lots of red gore and various unpleasant fluids pooled out beneath.

"...uuuuuuuuntil now."

From behind a termite mound, some big boulders, and a prickly bush, Mark, Hyacinth, Kevin and Andres tentatively watched the lions run towards their ancient rivals. Susan frantically dug through the sand near the car, finding her purse.

"I'm still up here!" yelled Andres indignantly, hanging from the branch and then unceremoniously falling straight down with a thud.

Cobra signaled to everyone to stay put as the following Animal-Planety, National-Geographical bush rumble commenced:

Boss Tweed and Magua dropped the human corpse and padded down the dry riverbed, criss-crossing twice, never taking their eyes off the bonanza they couldn't afford to lose. They both rumbled from deep within their throats, and it was Tweed who outright roared first, causing the hyenas to cackle and scatter in every direction, their muzzles wet with blood. The lions broke into a sprint and charged towards the massive carcass, now unattended. The vultures flapped back, but fearlessly, and only just out of range of the carnivores.

The hyenas would not wait long to counter-attack. Tweed and Magua, even as sub-adults, could easily handle one, two, even three or four hyenas, but ten? The spotted hyena matriarch, with what an anthropomorphist might conjecture was a hint of malice in her eye, waited for the lions to bury their faces into the carcass before rallying her clan to charge back, snapping at their heels and tails with the strongest bite-force of any terrestrial mammal. The lions wheeled around, surprisingly surprised, and swiped at thin air as the hyenas darted back and forth, evading their heavy paws.

Now it was high-stakes King of the Mountain as Tweed and Magua fought to defend their prize, and the hyenas sought to wrest it from them, encircling and overwhelming them, drawing them away from one another. Hyenas climbed the carcass, their high-pitched laughing cutting through the deep bass rumble of the lions' frenzied growling.

*HOLY SHIT*, mouthed Mark to Hyacinth, disbelieving that he was witnessing this spectacle but afraid to speak out loud. Hyacinth took a few shots and noticed through her viewfinder that the sky was very dark in the north beyond the melee. Cobra picked up his roll bar and backed up against the car.

"What are you gonna do with that?" asked Delia.

Cobra thought about it earnestly and said, "Um. Nothing?"

Tweed and Magua held their own and, if I may say so, acquitted themselves with honor. They knew this was worth fighting for, and possibly worth risking their lives over… it was just too much meat to pass up in a time when they were struggling to find enough scraps to get by. Like many bachelors evicted from their pride, they weren't doing well and had started to lose condition. Whatever fight they had in them, they sure brought to the hyenas, the taste of fresh blood reigniting their ferocity.

The hyenas, however, could not let this go either. There were cubs to be fed, and a growing clan requires a lot of protein. Their numbers advantage helped overcome their size deficit, and they played their strengths to the hilt. When Magua would come close to slashing one hyena, its sibling would snap at his rump; when Tweed thought he had cornered another, two more would appear from the side and cut at his underbelly. They were smart

and resourceful, and as fierce as any lion - they had to be, being
smaller.

Then something unexpected happened. A heavy rumble
thundered through the riverbed, but not from the lions. A minty,
musty smell permeated the air, which had started to take on some
humidity as the sun declined.

Delia clutched Cobra's arm and pointed. "Oh my God,
look at that!"

From the west charged in an elephant - a bull - with tree-
trunk legs and thick, weighty tusks.

"From last night!" Hyacinth shook Mark.

"Are you sure?"

"Yes! That's him! What did Katy call him again?"

"Attenborough," said Mark.

The bull - why don't we just call him Attenborough, too? -
crashed through the thorny bushes and into the sandy riverbed,
swinging his head madly from side-to-side, strafing at hyena and
lion alike with heavy ivory, his trunk like a massive mace and
chain. The hyenas ran for their lives up the west side of the bank,
their short tails in the air like radio antennae.

"Cobra did nearly get us killed," said Kevin to Xavier from
behind a termite mound, "but I think we actually do have to tip
this guy pretty well after this."

The lions weren't sure what to make of this. Even Tweed,
the dominant of the two, seemed uncertain how to take advantage
of this development. He decided to try to intimidate
Attenborough, taking a step towards him and roaring, but
Attenborough was having none of it. He trumpeted in a decibel
that had to be compared to an exploding artillery shell, and both
lions got the message, retreating quickly to the east side of the
bank.

Alone, Attenborough approached the carcass and sniffed
the air around it, and then reacted by touching his trunk against
the side of his mouth. He took a step backward, and then forward,

as if trying to figure out how to process this experience. The bull rumbled, but more quietly, more intimately, and placed his trunk on the dead animal's face.

"Do you…" asked Delia quietly, suddenly overwhelmed, "do you think he knew her?"

Cobra only nodded.

All eyes were magnetically locked on the elephants, so nobody was looking at Andres, but from behind the tree, his eyes welled up. He dried them before tears could fall and regained his composure.

The lions and hyenas watched intently, knowing Attenborough wouldn't stay forever and considering how to re-engage the battle before other scavengers arrived. They hardly noticed the water that trickled down the riverbed from the north, pooling behind the carcass and continuing towards the destroyed Land Rover.

"Hey," said Susan, noticing that her shoes were suddenly wet. No reactions.

"Hey!" she repeated more insistently, pointing to the ground below them, now a steady stream of water passing underneath them about an inch deep.

"Shit," said Cobra, adjusting his hat. "I thought we might have had another day or two."

"What's going on?" called Xavier.

"Everyone get to the bank!" commanded Cobra with his roll bar, holding it like Moses' staff. "Take what you can and go."

In moments, the river was six inches deep, flowing from the North, and then, up to Attenborough's knees. The tree was on the western bank of the riverbed, now a full-fledged river, with the upside-down Rover stuck in the current as it intensified. Kevin and Xavier struggled through the deepening channel to rejoin the others. Delia made it up, then Mark supporting Hyacinth.

Andres fell, face-first, and was gone. It was a flash flood, and the water was pushing forward hard now, about three feet deep.

"Andres!" yelled Cobra, splashing back into the muddy river after him. Frantically, Cobra thrust his hands into the raging water trying to grab him but came up empty.

"Behind you!" called Delia, pointing to six feet from Cobra's position, as Andres had already been carried away by the current. Cobra dove after him, the water now four feet and rushing quickly downstream, and he swam to intercept.

Andres got lucky: the water knocked him into the car, pinning him against it. Cobra splashed over to him and clutched him by the lapels, and he could have sworn he heard Andres cursing at him in German. Grasping Andres in one arm and his old hat in the other, Cobra pushed against the current and struggled up the muddy bank, Delia and Kevin waiting there to fish them out.

Where there had been none, there was now a river; where there had been a crashed, overturned car, there was only silty, brown water. Upstream, Attenborough was up to his shoulders, and he was forced to abandon the felled giant beneath him, surrendering her to the water. The vultures roosted in nearby trees.

Everyone had made it to the western bank, and they sat in silence, catching their breath, until Mark said:

"I'm sorry…"

"For what?" asked Susan.

"I only saved these two!" he said, producing a full bottle of vodka and an almost-full bottle of gin. "I mean, I can make martinis with this, but without a twist of lemon…" He shook his head, and Hyacinth pushed him playfully.

"Now what?" cried Xavier.

"This river sometimes overflows into the floodplain," said Cobra. "We're going to have to hike away from it, find some shelter, and hunker down for the night."

"Wait," said Kevin. "Where are the lions?"

They all looked to the water's edge; the lions were gone, and everyone felt their stomachs drop.

"I'm sure they're doing the same thing, looking for a little shelter," said Cobra.

"They're looking for a place to ambush and kill us all, you fool," said Andres, spitting up water.

"Trust me," said Cobra.

"Yeah, because you've been right about everything so far," said Susan.

"Will you listen to me? Night is coming soon, and they'll need shelter."

"I thought lions were mainly nocturnal hunters," said Mark.

"Shelter?" mused Delia. "Shelter from what?"

An ominous crack of thunder answered her question.


\*\*\*

Raining sideways; everybody, miserable.

They had marched sullenly east and north, their shoes getting stuck in the mud and, in the case of anyone without a hat, their eyes irritated by the constant deluge of water down their foreheads. Every few minutes a whiff of ozone followed seconds later by an angry flash of lightning sent the guests jumping and screaming, and then instinctively ducking, as if there were really any way to protect themselves anyway. They say if God wanted you dead, there was nothing you could do about it, although who knows who told *they* that.

"Back into single file," commanded Cobra from the front, leading this death march. "Everyone all right?"

"Fuck you!" cursed Andres.

"Glad to hear it! Positive attitude is everything!" yelled back Cobra.

"Cobra, he just said fuck you," clarified Delia, right behind him.

"What?" asked Cobra, genuinely surprised. "No! He said *thank you*."

"Pretty sure he didn't say that."

"Really?" asked Cobra again. "Andres, did you say…"

Cobra turned and saw Andres thrusting two middle fingers at him.

"Oh. Right. The bird."

"Did someone say bird?" asked Mark.

"No, hon, he said *the* bird," corrected Hyacinth, hobbling, supported by Mark's shoulder on one side and Cobra's roll bar on the other like a crutch.

"Are you sure? Because I could have sworn we just passed two Egyptian geese a minute ago," said Mark. "Cobra?"

"Yeah, sure, why not…" responded Cobra, scanning for potential threats.

"I knew it!" said Mark.

The rain was becoming lighter, and the lightning seemed to be more or less heading south, past them. While they were hot and uncomfortable all afternoon, now the group, drenched to capacity, were cold and shivering, sensitive to the gentlest breeze.

"At the World Cup in Germany last year," said Susan, "they provided rain slickers for the fans."

"There were ponchos in the Land Rover," said Andres. "Why don't you go back and get them?"

"Most people who live in South Africa could go their whole lives and see a venomous reptile twice, maybe three times," said Cobra to Delia. "You've seen two venomous and one non-venomous in two days, Professor."

"Maybe it's me," said Delia. "I guess snakes are just drawn to me."

"Are we talking about your personal life now, or strictly professional?"

"Six of one?"

"They must have slithered into the wheel wells because of the heat, maybe the narrow spaces," mused Cobra.

"Dizzy," said Xavier, leaning against a tree.

"Wait!" called out Kevin, steadying Xavier. "We've got to stop."

Susan helped Kevin lower Xavier to the mud.

"The bleeding's started again," said Hyacinth, noting the crimson liquid saturating Xavier's bandage and dripping freely down his cheek.

"How far are we?" asked Delia.

"Not far, if we're where I think we are," said Cobra. "Half a mile."

"What are the odds we are where you think we are?"

"Pretty good," and seeing the doubt on Delia's face, commented, "what, you want me to put a number on it?"

"Can you?" she asked sardonically. "Pretty pretty please?"

"I'm like, seventy-five percent sure. If that were a batting average, that'd be outrageously high."

The rain had mostly stopped, and now it was just spitting, but Cobra knew they didn't have much light remaining. He needed to get them to some kind of shelter before long to sit out the night. His eyes drifted to an object, metallic and glinting in the dwindling light, laying prone by a tree about ten yards ahead.

Cobra tentatively approached it, and when he picked it up, his stomach sank: Kotani's rifle, covered in mud. Delia came to investigate, leaving the others to see to Xavier.

"It's empty," said Cobra to Delia. "All shells gone."

"Has it been fired, or unloaded?"

"I don't know."

Cobra looked around, scanning the mud and earth.

"Whatever tracks there would have been are gone, washed away in the storm," he said.

"Like the vehicle tracks," said Delia. "You were trying to see if you could pick up the poacher's car, weren't you?"

94

"They went further north, hours ago, and now," said Cobra, upturning his hat and draining the water from the brim. "They could be anywhere."

"Unlike us. We're in the Middle of Nowhere."

"Not quite," said Cobra. "I'd say we're slightly Northeast of Nowhere."

Cobra turned to the rest of the group:

"People, I know we're not doing so hot right now, but we can't stay here. We can make camp about ten minutes from here if we don't encounter any surprises. How's Xavier?"

"We'll have to rebandage him," said Kevin.

"Can you walk?"

"Do I have a choice?" asked Xavier.

"I don't know, but I will say that it's hard to get a cab in this part of town."

"He'll walk," said Kevin.

\*\*\*

Cobra and Kevin supported Xavier from either side and at times, dragged him. They hiked as quickly as they could, racing the setting sun but pausing for a moment to take in the most beautiful, color-saturated African sunset any of them had yet experienced. Cobra insisted that they didn't miss it, and even in such a sorry state, all of the guests were humbled by how awesome it was. The violent weather had receded just in time to enhance the colors God had chosen for his palette, but the nanosecond the sun dipped below the horizon, Cobra demanded they continue.

"No sundowner?" called Mark from behind, helping Hyacinth trudge onward.

"Hey Cobra," wheezed Xavier into Cobra's ear.

"What is it, buddy?" answered Cobra. "Almost there."

"Kevin and I were wondering," slurred Xavier, a little delirious.

"Now?" asked Kevin, on the other side of Xavier.

"What's up?"

"Kevin and I have a bet about you," he smiled, demented like a ten-year-old about to tell a dirty joke.

"Now? Really?" asked Kevin.

"Do you, now?" asked Cobra.

"Yeah," wheezed Xavier. "Big, strong, super-macho masculine guy like you…"

"Don't," said Kevin, mortified. "It's the blood loss talking, Cobra."

"How do you stay in such great shape?" chuckled Xavier, enjoying a little fun at Kevin's expense, Kevin shaking his head.

"It's easy," declared Cobra, carefully setting Xavier on the ground. "Clean living and booze. And welcome to our humble abode for the evening."

They had come to the base of a gently sloping hill, and at the top was a huge baobab tree.

"We hiked all the way here to sleep on top of that thing?" asked Andres.

"Not on top," said Cobra. "Inside."

Upon closer inspection, they saw that the tree was hollow, with a massive eight-foot opening at its base.

"All it needs are some drapes," said Cobra.

"It's not exactly the Shangri-La," said Susan.

"I was here last week guiding the previous group. A pack of painted wolves had used it as a den, but I'm preeeeeetty sure they've moved on."

"Cue the painted wolves…" said Xavier, expecting the wild dogs to come bursting out any second.

"It should keep us relatively warm and dry," shrugged Delia. "If we create some sort of barrier at the opening. And, you know, chase the snakes out of it."

"It's perfect," said Mark.

"This sucks," said Susan. "It's unacceptable."

"Well, you better accept it," said Cobra. "Now, let's see if we can do something for Xavier's dressing."

"On it," said Kevin.

"Susan, you and Andres see if you can find some wood to make a fire."

"After that storm?" scoffed Andres. "How do you suppose we do that?"

"I don't know," said Cobra. "Maybe dry the wood with that wit of yours?"

"Does anyone else hear that?" asked Delia.

It started as a faint hum at first, but it grew steadily into the unmistakable sound of a small combustion engine. About half a mile away, a lone headlight moved due south with the sound and then stopped.

"Everyone," said Cobra calmly. "Go hide in the tree."

"What do they want?" asked Kevin.

"Maybe we should freeze," said Hyacinth. "We don't know he's seen us."

The headlight started moving again, course-correcting and making a beeline for Cobra.

"Go hide," repeated Cobra, marching down the hill.

"What are you going to do?" asked Mark.

"Nothing. Just going to have a little conversation. Don't worry about it."

The others didn't argue anymore; they retreated up the hill towards the tree, except for Delia (of course), who caught up to Cobra.

"You're not as good at conversation as you think," she said.

"I think I'm pretty not bad, actually, Professor."

"What are you going to say? You're a safari guide! You going to tell him the distinction between Grants' and Thomsons' gazelles?"

"Neither of which are endemic to this area, Professor," he said. "Let me handle this."

"Fine. I'll only get involved if I feel you say or do anything stupid," she said. "Actually, why don't we just save time and let me lead off?"

"Well, now it's a game between us, isn't it?"

The headlight cut through the darkness now enveloping this savage land, and Cobra and Delia could tell that it was a lone rider on some kind of small motorbike. As it came closer, the headlight blinded Cobra and Delia, who slowly put their hands in the air.

The rider skidded to a stop, clicked off the light, and dismounted, his AR-15 hanging loosely from a shoulder strap. There was just enough light for Cobra to see that it was a Black man with a neatly trimmed beard wearing a black beret, as well as a collared white shirt underneath a heavy, green military jacket. Sewn down the sleeves were many horizontal white stripes; Cobra couldn't place them, as they didn't look like any military ranking or badge system he'd ever heard of. He motioned with his weapon for Cobra and Delia to lower their hands.

"Easy, there. Are any of your people hurt?" he asked with a heavy central African accent.

"Some," replied Cobra. "My guess is a little dehydration, maybe some bad sunburn. Actually, now that you mention it, maybe it was the exploding rocket you fired at us that caused a few injuries. Are you offering medical assistance?"

"I can put them out of their suffering for you, if you like."

"Gonna pass on that. One of yours is dead, though."

"Yes. Probably the bullet in his cranium."

"I'm not a doctor, but probably, yes, that's what we were thinking," said Delia.

"I like her," said the man with the gun. "What's her name, *Cobra*?"

Cobra understood what he was implying, demonstrating that he knew his name, because there was only one way he could have.

"That's the Professor."

"I can speak for myself," said Delia. "But call me Professor."

"Zaire?" Cobra asked.

"D.R.C., since ninety-seven," said the man. "American?"

"Mineola, Long Island."

"Many half-breeds in Mineola, Long Island?"

"I'm all-man, pal."

"Jesus," groaned Delia with an eye-roll. "Let's move this along, boys. Who are you?"

"Call me Priest, Professor."

"Do we want to know the story behind that one?" she asked.

"Probably not. You can ask the clergy of the Kasongo Mission, if you like."

"Let me guess…" said Cobra. "In Hell?"

Priest smiled the kind of smile where your mouth curls upward, but your eyes don't change expression, just coldly stare. The white stripes on his sleeves, Cobra now understood, were obviously priests' collars.

"Well, Priest," continued Cobra. "This is a private concession, and we don't take kindly to wildlife crimes out here. You're trespassing."

"We apologize for the death of your elephant. As you can see, we've already disciplined our man."

"You also disciplined us, pretty severely," said Delia. "Why?"

"We had to. We thought you were SAN Parks out on anti-poacher patrol, which we were not expecting out here."

"You're not poachers, then."

"We were unaware of any tourist operation in this area. We were under the impression it was uninhabited."

Cobra said to Delia, "I told Katy we're not advertising properly."

Delia replied, "Me and Annie found it easily enough."

"It was our oversight," continued Priest. "If we knew of your presence, we would have dealt with you directly."

"I doubt management would have played ball with you," said Cobra.

"Your tracker - Kotani, is it? - is in our custody playing ball with us right now. He is," said Priest, searching for the right word, "uncomfortable."

Cobra fired back, "Well, now *you're* in *our* custody, and you better hope my friend is unhurt, or by tomorrow they're gonna start calling you Nun, because I'm gonna stuff your balls down your throat, and that's *before* I rip them off. That ain't even hyperbole."

Priest laughed, sincerely and deeply.

"Since we have your tracker, we don't really need you, but we don't need to kill you," said Priest. "Let's be civilized."

"You're not poachers, you're not tourists," cut in Delia. "Just what the hell do you want?"

"If you guide tourists in this area, you must have a unique knowledge of this land. We are searching for something very valuable."

"If you're looking for diamonds, there are no veins in this property. We're rich in wildlife, not precious stones. What else could you want? Timber?"

"Gold, obviously," said Priest.

"There are no mines here. If you're thinking of digging one, I'm not a geologist," said Cobra, who suddenly stopped, and he said quizzically, "Wait, you don't mean..."

"I do, of course."

"What?" asked Delia.

"You've got to be kidding," said Cobra. "That doesn't exist. And if it did, it'd be like a thousand miles from here in Mpumalanga."

"What is?" repeated Delia, frustrated.

"We believe it does exist. We believe it's here. And we believe you know where," said Priest coldly, taking the AR-15 off his shoulder.

"Come on, you're serious?" stammered Cobra. "That's ridiculous! Why not just look for Bigfoot while you're at it."

"Your tracker doesn't think so. After some - *conversation* - he indicated we were right. He hasn't revealed the location yet, but I hope to be there to help *influence* him to do so."

"I'm telling you, it's horse-shit. It's a fairy-tale!"

"You are an unconvincing liar, Cobra. I have instructions to bring only you back to our camp. Whether everyone else you're hiding here dies is up to you. Starting with the lovely Professor here."

"Is that so? And who gave you those instructions? Was it," he said, narrowing his eyes, "Black Tiger?"

That did it. Priest's demeanor changed immediately upon hearing those two words, and he pulled back the lever on his weapon, drawing it up to fire.

But blood burst from the bicep of his shooting arm, and the sound of three more shots rang out, snapping through the air. Delia hit the dirt, scanning for the shots' origin. Priest reflexively fired the AR-15, aimlessly, as Cobra pounced on him, knocking the rifle away from Priest with his left hand and clobbering him across the temple with his right.

The AR-15 landed in the dirt between them, and Priest immediately moved to recover it, giving Cobra an opportunity to plant a size eleven boot right between his eyes.

Cobra dove for the weapon, but a flash of steel from Priest's concealed knife slashed him across the torso.

"Sneaky fuck!" growled Cobra, rolling out of range. He grabbed a handful of sand and threw it into Priest's eyes, which, unlike every movie ever made, did absolutely nothing.

"You fight like a child," cursed Priest, turning the knife blade-in for more leverage with his next stroke.

Delia made a play for the rifle, though, and that did distract Priest. He had to deal with her. He thrust at her, his eyes wild and furious in the early moonlight. She backed out of the way.

Cobra threw himself at Priest again, securing his knife-arm and gut-punching him repeatedly, to which Priest responded with a solid head-butt.

Priest's head only caught Cobra's chin, though, and he rammed his elbow into Priest's throat in retaliation, crushing his windpipe. He dropped the knife.

Blood in the water, Cobra pressed his advantage, John-Wayneing Priest with four wild haymakers: ugly technique but very satisfying. Priest reeled backward and turned to run.

Delia picked up the knife.

Cobra picked up the rifle.

Priest threw himself on the bike and started the engine.

Cobra opened fire, jamming down on the trigger, blasting some guts out of Priest's right abdomen as he turned to speed off. Cobra kept shooting; Priest rode for his life.

A hundred yards away, Cobra and Delia saw Priest falling off the bike. Slowly, he somehow pulled himself back on and rode North, into the African night.

Cobra lowered the weapon, his heart pounding and his temples hot, some blood on his shirt from where he was slashed.

"Good conversation, Professor," said Cobra, the adrenaline still pulsing through his veins as he caught his breath.

"I told you, you should have let me lead," she said.

"And you, Susan," said Cobra, turning to see the guests who had come down from the hill, "you've been holding out on us."

Susan stood before them, a smoking Beretta in her trembling hands.

# CHAPTER 6:
# INSURGENTS
# 2003

"Forty-eight! Forty-nine! Fifty!" they all shouted in unison, and one of them added, "Both of these bastards are still going!"

About fifteen soldiers in light desert camo crowded around Specialist Campbell McConnors and Specialist Kurt Christian, both struggling to press a weighted barbell off their chest just *one more time* than the other, both laden with full combat armor down to the helmet. They weren't technically pumping iron, because the bars didn't support actual plates but instead buckets of sand on either end, and the benches were just that - benches, the kind a group of people would sit on to eat at a picnic table. Each bar probably only weighed about eighty pounds, but those reps sure added up quickly.

Also, they were outside and it was about a thousand degrees, and that's *barely* hyperbole. Their location was classified for security purposes, but I believe I am now authorized to reveal that it was in a country that rhymes with *Attack*.

It wasn't Norway.

Sweat waterfalled down Campbell's face, and he could feel his chest swelling with lactic acid buildup, but so could Kurt, and he wasn't about to quit this basically meaningless contest, even if it caused him a pectoral tear. Campbell knew Kurt, and he knew that he would never give up until he was physically incapacitated.

"Sixty-seven! Sixty-eight! Come on!" hollered the soldiers, one-dollar bills in their fists ready to change hands at the conclusion of this testosterone-wasting, dick-measuring challenge.

"One... more..." wheezed Campbell, his arms trembling wildly, concentrating everything he had into straightening his elbows with this final repetition.

Down the bar went, effectively pinning Campbell to the bench as definitively as a Honda Accord would. Two cheering soldiers immediately slid the buckets off Cobra's bar, and air once again rushed into his lungs. He discovered right away that A: he could no longer move his arms, and B: Kurt was still pumping, the soldiers counting up to seventy-five when he allowed them to remove the buckets.

Cheers and fist-bumping from the men and women.

When he finally could, Campbell sat up and removed his helmet, and he helped Kurt up from his bench.

"You son of a bitch!" said Campbell, shaking Kurt's hand. "What are you, a fuckin' cyborg?"

"How high did you get?" gasped Kurt.

"Sixty-nine!"

"You planned that!" said Kurt. "You better not have tanked it!"

"If I planned it, I would have stopped at seventy-six."

"Then I would have stopped at seventy-seven."

\*\*\*

"You know, two years ago, I could barely do a push-up," said Campbell, shoveling down some chicken fajitas.

"You should be proud of yourself," said Kurt, adjusting his glasses. "I'm proud of you."

The commissary was nice, like a mall food-court, not the burlap tents you'd imagine from movies. The base was almost comfortable, except for the heat, and it was relatively secure.

"I swear I'll never complain about the winters in Long Island again," said Campbell. "No cold will ever be too cold after this."

"No use complaining," said Kurt. "These people have lived here for thousands of years. For them, desert living is normal. They wouldn't know what to do in an upstate snowstorm."

"I don't mind complaining at all," said Campbell, taking a long drink of water. "No wonder this region produces so many terrorists. It's the heat. I'd blow myself up too if I were promised seventy-five virgins and central air conditioning."

"I don't think the Quran says anything about air conditioning."

"What are we doing here, Kurt?" asked Campbell. "I don't mean the United States in the Middle East or politics or whatever. I mean, you and me. Why'd you sign up?"

"I was in Union Square a few days after 9/11," said Kurt. "So many candles, so many have-you-seen-me flyers posted up. People who hadn't yet given up hope that their husbands or wives or brothers and sisters might still be alive. I guess I just wanted to help out."

"You're like Captain America or something," said Campbell.

"The more I see of these people, the more I see that they're *just* people. They just want to live, like us, only without the designer jeans and Classic Coke."

"Is that what we're fighting for? Our right to consume? I want my MTV?" asked Campbell, scratching his head.

"MTV doesn't even play videos anymore," said Kurt, impaling a potato with his fork. "What about you? Why did you sign up?"

"I don't know," he said. "At first, I thought I wanted some kind of revenge, but even then, I knew that wasn't true. I think I wanted to believe that I wanted some kind of adventure before I surrender to the machine, but look at me. I had one year of Arabic at college and now I'm an Army translator. I complain about the sunburn and the heat; I don't know if I'm really cut out for this either. At least you've been outside the wire a few times."

"You want to get out there and fight?"

"Fuck no," said Campbell quickly. "I thought I did, back when I had an ocean and a few gulfs separating me from actual combat. Now that I'm here, this is close enough. Because deep down, I'm starting to realize I'm not the kind of guy you can really count on in a place like this, and that depresses the shit out of me."

"At least you're honest," said Kurt. "Know thyself, and all that."

"Yeah," said Campbell. "At least I can do a few push-ups now. I should have just taken a yoga elective."

"Hey, isn't your twenty-first birthday coming up?" asked Kurt, trying to change the subject. "We should celebrate!"

"I don't know. I'm not much of a drinker."

\*\*\*

Campbell waited patiently, leaning against a brick wall, land-line phone resting between his ear and his shoulder. It rang (and rang, and rang…), and Campbell checked the piece of notebook paper in his hands to make sure he'd dialed correctly, until:

"This is Arn. Can't talk. Leave a message, please."

It felt so good to hear a familiar voice, even pre-recorded, that Campbell stammered into the mouthpiece. He hadn't really expected to get through.

"Hey. Hey! Hi!" he said, stuffing the paper into his pockets. "Hey bro. It's Campbell. How's it going? I don't know when you'll get to this message. I actually don't know where you are right now, but I bet you're probably as close to me as you've been in a few years. I bet they've got you in the Persian Gulf somewhere.  I don't know if you know this, but I'm deployed, so, um, want to hang out?"

That sounded stupid, out in the air.

"Just kidding.  Anyway, I wanted to let you know that I'm safe, and that I spend most of my time in the *Secured* War Zone, which beats the crap out of the *UN*secured War Zone.  I, um, just wanted to say that I hope you're OK too."

He felt stilted, like a too-old kid telling a mall Santa what he wanted, even though he no longer believed.  He put the receiver to his forehead and closed his eyes for a moment.  Then:

"I'm proud of you, bro.  Like, really proud of you.  I never appreciated what it must be like to be you, to do what you do, until now.  See you when I see you."

He hung up, and he felt very far from home, and very alone.

\*\*\*

"He says he's the only man of the house; it's just him, his mother and his sisters," translated Campbell, sitting under an awning next to a command center building.  A young boy, about thirteen, was speaking rapidly in Arabic, and a patient officer, Colonel Giese, sat across from him as Campbell tried to make sense of his words.  It was still god-awful hot.

"What's he yammering about now?" asked Giese, fanning himself with his hat (excuse me, military folks, *cover*).

"Zakaria says his father is dead, one of Saddam's political prisoners."

"Tell him we're sorry; we regret we couldn't have been here sooner to liberate his people."

Campbell did his best to convey Colonel Giese's message, although even with the supplementary training from the army after joining, one year of college Arabic was not nearly enough to speak like a native.  The boy shook his head and said something back.

"He says that's not our fault," translated Campbell. "What IS our fault is that during one of our airstrikes, a car overturned and destroyed part of the wall that penned in the family's goats."

Zakaria protested in Arabic, and Campbell nodded.

"I'm sorry. I think he said *sheep*, not goats."

"How does that matter?"

"It matters to him," said Campbell. "He's recovered all the animals, but he can't secure them anymore."

"Tell him we apologize, but materials are tight. We can give him some MREs and some bottled water, if it helps, but we can't risk sending people outside the wire to rebuild his family's wall."

The boy indignantly put his hands on his hips and kept talking.

"All right, all right," said Giese. "How would the *gentleman* like to be compensated?"

"He asks if we have Playstation 2."

\*\*\*


Campbell sat up on the hood of a troop transport, watching the sun descend into the endless sand outside the base's walls, and he was glad to be within them. The heat had broken, and now a gentle wind kissed him from time to time.

He read over a letter from his parents, one that had just come in today. He learned that they were both healthy, and that his dad was taking his mom out on the driving range and even letting her use his clubs. He learned that Aunt *Whoever* was pregnant, and that Cousin *So-and-So* got into Penn, and that one of his high-school friends got arrested for a DUI (but didn't hurt himself or anyone else, thank God). These words he read in his parents' voices, and at once he longed to be home and a part of their world and simultaneously felt utterly disconnected from it.

He felt stupid for enlisting, and naive. Yes, he'd put on a

little muscle and gotten a different perspective on the world, not to mention a righteous tan thanks to this miserable, unrelenting, *motherfucking* sun. This life seemed pointless and hollow, however, and he felt more like he was an actor playing a soldier than an actual soldier. He hadn't even allowed himself to get into the debate on whether or not this were a *just* war, if there such a thing even existed. Campbell wished he were home, accepting failure and the shackles of an ordinary life.

"Campbell," called Kurt, fixing his glasses. "Come on, they want us!"

"Us?" asked Campbell, turning around, knowing it was too late in the day for any scheduled meeting that would require his translation.

"You and me," he said. "Us!"

"Who wants us?"


Kurt led Campbell into a beige, brick building and through a hallway into a windowless debriefing room with a ceiling fan. Sitting at a conference table were four people - characters, really, like nobody Campbell had seen on base before, or in Iraq before, or even on Saturday morning cartoons before. They were each dressed in military fatigues, but that was the only thing they had in common, despite their very unusual name patches:

Red Scorpion: thick beard, a little older than the others, obviously the leader by the way everyone looked at him. He had an unusual eyepiece over his left eye, almost like a monocle, and he wore thin leather gloves.

Blue Viper: enormous, a mountain of muscle, ornate tattoos up and down his exposed arms (but Campbell knew enough not to stare at them now). He looked Asian. Campbell assumed he would have been decapitating his enemies, surrounded by harems of women on some endless steppe had he been born three thousand years ago.

Gray Shark: a woman, short hair dyed a deep burgundy, built like a triathlete. She had an intensity to her face, and when Campbell met her eyes, he felt like he would wither and melt. She was in the middle of field stripping a Desert Eagle, one of (if not *the*) most powerful handguns in the world, no matter what Dirty Harry might say about it.

And (wait for it):

Black Tiger: shoulder-length, jet-black hair pulled back into a neat ponytail. Campbell guessed he was Hispanic, maybe, and closest to Kurt and him in age. On his wrists were bracelets that each had some kind of fossilized bones - bear claws? - sewn onto them. Black Tiger quickly gathered some documents and maps and concealed them into a folder when Kurt and Campbell approached.

Campbell and Kurt stood at attention.

"This is the one?" asked Red Scorpion in a thick, European accent - Hungarian? Slavic? German?

"Yes, Baron. Specialist E-4 Campbell McConnors, U.S. Army translator," said Black Tiger in almost perfect, non-regional English, although Campbell could have sworn he heard the *tiniest* trace of Bronx hiding underneath.

*Baron?* mouthed Campbell to Kurt, who continued to stand at attention and utterly ignored him.

"Did I say something funny, specialist?" asked, or really, *said* Black Tiger.

"No sir," quickly recovered Campbell. It just then occurred to him that he had no idea of what their ranks were.

"They'll have to do," said Red Scorpion, or the Baron.

"At ease. Have a seat, gentlemen," said Black Tiger.

As Campbell and Kurt tentatively sat at the table, Blue Viper reached into a cabinet behind them. He came back with a bottle of Ararat - an Armenian brandy - and six glasses, which he placed in front of everyone at the table, including Campbell and Kurt. He poured, starting with Red Scorpion.

110

"We would ordinarily use our own people, but an opportunity has presented itself and we must move quickly," explained Black Tiger.

Campbell picked up his glass and brought it to his lips until Grey Shark shot him a look. If looks could kill, not only would Campbell be dead, but so would his whole nuclear family. He quickly put the glass down and waited.

Red Scorpion picked up the glass, swished the maroon liquid in a clockwise direction, closed his eyes and sipped. The others followed, and Campbell and Kurt only watched.

"Not to your liking, boys?" asked Grey Shark, and it surprised Campbell to detect an obvious Irish brogue. He quickly took a gulp.

Kurt, however, did not touch the glass.

"Not while I'm on-duty, ma'am," he said simply.

"We're not cops," Campbell quickly whispered to him. "Drink the damn wine."

Kurt refused. "Thank you, ma'am," was all he said.

"McConnors, our information says that you are fluent in Arabic. Is that accurate?" continued Black Tiger.

"*Qualilanaan*," he said.

"Yes or no, Specialist."

"Somewhat," Campbell translated. "Yes. Yes."

"And Specialist Christian, you are rated to drive the armored Humvee?"

"Yes, sir," said Kurt.

"How much combat experience?"

"About six months, sir."

"We need your talents. You've been conscripted for a very delicate and crucially vital operation that engages tomorrow at oh-four-hundred hours."

"Outside the wire?" gasped Campbell.

"Obviously," said Black Tiger. "Is that a problem?"

"No, no sir," lied Campbell, immediately feeling uneasy in

his bowels.

"We won't let you down," said Kurt.

"What - what's the op?" asked Campbell.

Black Tiger looked to Red Scorpion, who nodded.

"We've recently encountered a contact who has provided us with a lead on a secret munitions cache - *the* secret munitions cache. Recent bombing has unearthed it, and based on details from the contact, we think it's legit."

"You mean - you don't mean…"

"The big one, the justification for the war."

The words echoed in Campbell's head. If it were true, this was huge. And if it were true, this mission would be outrageously dangerous.

"We're going to destroy it?" Campbell stammered.

"No. Just document it. A tactical strike later will make sure it's properly contained in the case of hazardous chemicals. We'll reconnoiter tomorrow at oh-four-hundred, so don't be late. I think that's about all you need to know for right now. As you can imagine, this is very sensitive intelligence, and you are forbidden to share anything you've learned here tonight with anyone. If you do so, the penalty will be severe."

The word *severe* echoed in Campbell's mind like iron bars shutting in a super-max prison.

"Now, if you're not going to finish those…"

Campbell shot-gunned his brandy, and then slammed down Kurt's too, the fiery alcohol burning his throat.

"…you are dismissed."

They stood at attention and saluted. As they turned to leave, Black Tiger added, "Get a good night's sleep, gentlemen. Tomorrow, we make history."

It seemed peculiar to Campbell that all four soldiers were smiling, as if Black Tiger had said something entirely amusing.

***

"Duuuuuuude…" said Campbell to Kurt as they walked back to the barracks. The night sky had replaced the harsh sun, and the dry desert air made the stars appear brighter than they were at home.

"Wow," said Kurt.

"Wow? Holy shit! Did you get a load of those guys?"

"Those guys were Deltas, I bet. Deltas can have beards and long hair and tattoos and stuff, and nobody really gives a crap."

"Deltas?" repeated Campbell. "Deltas my ass! Those guys were G.I. Joes! Black Scorpion? Blue Dragon, or whatever? I mean, come on!"

"They were pretty intimidating; I'll give you that."

"Have you ever even seen them on base before?" asked Campbell.

"No. Maybe they just arrived. What if they're with the C.I.A.? Some special unit?"

"I don't know if they're even American! Did you hear the way the head guy spoke? What was that, Ukrainian or some shit?"

"I guess if Schwarzenegger can be Governor," mused Kurt.

"And there was a woman!"

"In W's army? I wouldn't be so surprised; liberal Hollywood's given you the wrong idea," said Kurt.

"She could have been on American Gladiators. They all look like they were from the A-Team or something, and they want us? Us?"

"Campbell, they were talking about Saddam's hidden chemical weapons plant. The WMDs. Do you understand what a big deal this could be?"

"It's a conservative fantasy. Do you think it's really possible?" wondered Campbell.

"I guess we'll find out tomorrow."

"But…"

"Are you going to be OK?" asked Kurt.

"But what if those guys aren't, like, for real? We don't know anything about them."

"What do you expect, our orders printed out and bound with brass fasteners? An email? The nature of this kind of op requires no paper trail, right?" said Kurt.

"But if this is the real deal…"

"You said today that you wanted to make a difference, outside the wire," said Kurt.

"I said the opposite! I said I didn't want to be in the unsecured war zone!"

"Campbell," said Kurt, stopping him and looking him in the eye, "I'm going to make sure nothing happens to you out there. It's my job. You're going to be safe. I promise."

Campbell looked up at the crystal-clear night sky, so familiar and yet so different from home.

# CHAPTER 7:
# SOUTHERN CROSS

Cobra pointed up into the night sky at two very bright stars, and Delia, sitting with him on one of the baobab's big, flat branches, followed his hand.

"See those two stars? Look slightly to the right of them, and you'll find it."

"I don't have them," she said, but suddenly she smiled, "There it is!"

"And that's how you spot the Southern Cross. If you draw a line in the sky that connects the two stars, and you'll see where it bisects a line from the vertical axis of the Southern Cross. It'll point due South, every time."

"Like the North Star back home," she said.

"It's not Big Sky Country, but we like it, Professor."

They heard the crickets and night-time insects, and every now and then the whooping of distant hyenas.

"They should be on the other side of the river; I doubt they'll give us any trouble. And they can't climb."

"Just the same," she said, stretching out on the broad branch as if it were the palm of some giant. "I don't mind if they keep a little personal space."

"Leopards, on the other hand…"

"Kinda more concerned about lions," said Delia.

"Oh, those two? They've probably gone off to chase some

zebra or bushbuck or something.  Lions are generally sort of befuddled by bipedal prey."

"Befuddled?  That's how I'd describe an English gentleman in some Jane Austen novel.  Did they look befuddled to you today?"

"Anyway, they don't have the wrist joint that allows for good climbing, like leopards."

"So, you're telling me they can't climb?"

"I'm telling you they can't climb *well*."

Delia scoffed, folding her hands behind her head.

"You did OK today, Cobra."

"I mean, I think I could have done worse," beamed Cobra. "And if I didn't thank you for saving my life…"

"You did not."

"Well, thank you, Professor.  Quick thinking, hitting the horn."

"I told you, you don't have to keep calling me that.  I haven't defended a thesis yet."

"Do you really want me to stop calling you that?"

Delia smiled.

"No."

Cobra stretched out on his side of the branch and saw that the bonfire guarding the entrance to the tree hollow below, where the others were hopefully sleeping, was still burning brightly.  He closed his eyes.

"So," said the Professor.  "You're really not going to make a move?"

He opened his eyes.


\*\*\*

One hour before this cutesy, possibly-romantic interlude, however, it was a little less *storybook* and a little more *crime novel*.  To recapitulate:

Cobra lowered the rifle, his heart pounding and his temples hot, some blood on his shirt from where he was slashed.

"Good conversation, Professor," said Cobra, the adrenaline still pulsing through his veins as he caught his breath.

"I told you, you should have let me lead," she said.

"And you, Susan," said Cobra, turning to see the guests who had come down from the hill, "you've been holding out on us."

Susan stood before them, a smoking Beretta in her trembling hands.

"Maybe you want to lower that gun, Susan," said Cobra, bleeding from his torso. Hands unsteady, she pointed the weapon down.

"Holy shit!" yelled Xavier. "You've had that the whole time?"

"I knew there was more to our *fraulein* than she led us to believe," smirked Andres.

"Why would someone need a gun on vacation?" asked Mark.

"Susan," Cobra said calmly and steadily, "let me have that, please."

She shook her head, hot and euphoric, barely containing the rush.

"Susan, honey…"

"Don't you *honey* me, Cobra. I just saved your life," she said, words returning to her.

"You did, and I thank you for that. But I need that gun. Please let me have it."

"Why should I listen to you? I'm the one with the gun."

"Because I'm the *grownup* with the *other* gun. Let's not make this a thing, huh? Just relax and hand it over."

"No. Not happening."

"Just give him the gun, Susan," said Xavier.

"She doesn't have to," said Andres.

"What? Of course she does!" said Kevin.

"He's not a police officer. This is not a crime scene," said Andres plainly.

"Shut up, you," cut in Hyacinth.

"What do you need a gun for?" asked Mark directly.

"Come on, Susan," asked Cobra. He took a step in her direction and she reflexively fired a shot near his feet, eliciting screams from everyone. He stumbled back.

"OK, too much," he said.

"Sorry. I didn't mean to do that."

"Susan, would you at least put safety on and put the gun back in your purse?" asked Delia (excuse me, *the Professor*, as she secretly likes to be called). "You can keep it, but just put it away so it doesn't frighten people."

"OK," she said, and as she did so, people saw that she had at least one thick stack of some kind of currency which only Andres recognized as Euros.

"All right, good conflict resolution, Professor. Let's all calm down," said Cobra.

"I totally assumed you were going to tackle her and take it after she put it in her purse," the Professor replied.

"Really?"

"I did," said Kevin.

"Me too," said, well, pretty much everyone else.

"Should I now?"

"I think the moment's passed," said the Professor.

"I would have locked it up, but there was no safe in my room," said Susan. "Unlike literally every other hotel in the entire world."

"Where did you get that thing? How did you get it on the plane?" asked Mark.

"I bought it in Joburg. Don't worry about how I got it on the plane."

"Get into lots of high-octane gunfights as a travel writer?"

asked Hyacinth.

"Well, uh, a girl can't be too careful, especially traveling alone."

"Not buying it," said Hyacinth.

"Leave her alone. She just saved Cobra and Delia's lives. Maybe ours too," said Andres.

"Look, it's mine, I need it because I need it, and that's it. I'm not going to kill anyone."

"Have you? Killed someone?" asked Kevin.

"Of course not," she lied. "And I obviously didn't bring a handgun to poach rhinos."

"What did the poacher say, Cobra?" asked Hyacinth.

"Hm?"

"Before you did all that jiujitsu and shooting and all that. What did he want?"

"Oh, him. He mostly wanted to make sure we weren't going to turn his party over to the authorities. Now that he confirmed we have no radio, we aren't really a problem for them."

"But why'd he try to shoot you, then?"

"Kind of a miscommunication," said Cobra quickly. "I told him I wouldn't get involved, and he didn't believe me, and there you go."

"Really?" asked Hyacinth, raising an eyebrow and turning to the Professor, who stood still for a moment before replying:

"Yup!"


Somehow, Kevin managed to find enough dry wood and parched grass, even after that sudden storm, for Cobra to start a big bonfire outside of the baobab tree's hollow. It was the Professor who had actually checked the inside for snakes, and to her slight disappointment, found none (although, *surprise!* plenty of insects). It barely smelled of mold. The earth within was soft but not mushy or wet, and it was approaching being bearable if you could find a spot without a big root protruding from underneath. It was actually more spacious than a four-person tent; it was a shame that there were eight of them.

Although everyone was very famished, most were so exhausted that they surrendered pretty quickly to a deep sleep despite the events of the day. Xavier wasn't feeling any swelling from his head wound, which was a very auspicious sign that there probably wasn't any fluid building up; Kevin tried his best to keep it clean. Andres, grumbling, tried to sleep on his side, keeping pressure off his bruised tailbone. Surprisingly close to him was Susan, who slept sitting up with her knees to her chest and her head down.

Mark, however, had a hard time falling off. The pain from the burns on his hand had returned, and he was shivering. That didn't make it any easier for Hyacinth to rest, either, and she kept her worries about his open skin getting infected to herself. She at least tried to clean his wounds with some of the alcohol he had saved. Both of them had medications they were supposed to be taking, too, but neither complained because, hey, they were in Africa and it was their favorite place in the world.

It being crowded, Cobra and Delia volunteered to sleep up in the branches, and, where were we?

Cobra stretched out on his side of the branch and saw that the bonfire guarding the entrance to the tree hollow below, where the others were hopefully sleeping, was still burning brightly. He closed his eyes.

"So," said the Professor. "You're really not going to make a move?"

He opened his eyes.

"You say something, Professor?"

"Nope."

"Because I could have sworn you just said…"

"Nope; didn't."

"Oh."

The two listened to the chorus of nocturnal insects, of dassies and of faraway jackals, calling out into the lonely night.

"Cobra, you've known Wyatt Northside a long time, right?"

"About four years."

"You don't think he'd have left us out to dry like this intentionally, do you?"

"Wyatt? No way. He's a good guy."

"Then why do you think he hasn't come out to get us?"

"By the time he realized we didn't make it back, there was a river separating us that wasn't there in the morning. He'd have to go a lot further south to find a place shallow enough to fjord it in the jeep, and by then, it would have been too dark to safely get to us."

"You don't think those military guys got to the lodge… got to where Annie is…"

"I really, really don't think so, no. For one, Priest only mentioned Kotani; if they were at the lodge, he'd have said so. And two, they were travelling further north, in the direction of Botswana. The river would be too powerful at that point."

"I guess that makes sense."

"Don't worry about your friend. Wyatt's the real deal. He's the toughest, most resourceful guy I've ever met. If he weren't here, he'd be boxing kangaroos in Sydney or arm-wrestling sumo masters in Kyoto or crossing the Gobi Desert on a dromedary or something."

"He's like you, is what you're saying."

"Like me," said Cobra, but adding, "but legit."

"You were legit enough to keep us all alive today. I had you wrong, Cobra."

"It's Campbell."

"What is?"

"My name. It's Campbell. Don't spread it around, please."

"Like the soup? Geez, I can see why you go by Cobra."

"It's funny; in my head, that's the name I call myself now. *Cobra* feels more genuine to me. Like, I've become Cobra. It's really who I am."

"So, like, if you were to meet a new girlfriend's parents, you'd introduce yourself as Cobra?"

"One hundred percent."

"Ha! One hundred percent bullshit."

"I want you to remember you said that when you introduce me to Mr. and Mrs. Wildhorse one day."

"Wow! Are you making some kind of prediction there?"

"I thought it might be a good segue to making a move."

"You wish!" she laughed. "Now, you've got to earn it."

"Wait…" he said. "Listen…"

In the distance, maybe miles away, they heard the unmistakable sound of lions roaring, cutting through the nocturnal symphony. They overlapped one another, a duet.

"Are those…"

"Our boys? I think so. Probably trying to avoid other males, stronger prides, so they don't wander into a fight and get killed."

"It really goes straight through you. I can feel the reverberation as much as I can hear it," she admitted.

"That's because they have an ossified hyoid bone in their throats. It's part of their voice box. Only the big cats - lions and leopards here in Africa, and jaguars and tigers - can roar. It's what separates genus Panthera from genus Felidae."

"*Felis.* Feli*dae* is a family, isn't it? In the order carnivora."

"Excuse me, Professor."

"Lions, leopards, jaguars, tigers…" she repeated, almost musically, and then asked, "What is Black Tiger?"

# CHAPTER 8:
# LAMASSU
# 2003

Even dark, at four AM (excuse me, *oh-four-hundred-hours*), wearing full armor and a helmet still brought Campbell to the edge of perspiration. Kurt made sure the Humvee had a full tank and stood next to the driver's side door with Campbell, who was fidgeting with a thick, laminated book of Arabic translations. Both had rifles slung by their sides. They smelled the sand and clay beneath them, an earthy scent that rose from the ground as the day began to heat.

"Are we early?" asked Campbell.

"Right on time."

"Maybe I should go use the bathroom again. Think there's time?"

"Campbell, just chill out."

"I'm fine, I'm fine… I just, what if I have to use the bathroom out there?"

"Don't worry about it."

"But what if…"

"You have the runs?"

"No! But it's not like we can take an exit off the Jersey Turnpike and go at a McDonald's or something."

Kurt turned to Campbell and steadied him by his shoulders.

"First time out there's a little scary. Everyone gets scared. We're going to be fine. Trust me. Just keep breathing, and stay hydrated. Humvee is very protected. Just do your job."

"Are we interrupting, boys?" asked Gray Shark, who approached from the yard with Red Scorpion, Blue Viper, and Black Tiger. With the watch lights above them, they looked imposing and ominous, like the cover of *Queen II*, if that means anything to you.

"No. No, ma'am," stammered Campbell.

"Don't ask, don't tell," she laughed, abruptly shoving a canvas bag into his arms. Kurt opened the doors and climbed into the driver's seat.

Blue Viper dropped two heavy, hard-plastic cases at his feet.

"Load these up," he grunted.

"What's in these?" asked Campbell, suddenly feeling overwhelmed.

"Not your concern, Specialist McConnors," said Black Tiger, checking the magazine on his rifle. "Just stow them in the back."

"But, like, are they explosive?"

"McConnors, are you unfamiliar with the concept of taking orders?"

"No, sir. It's just…"

"This isn't Westbury out there. We give orders, you execute. Copy?"

"Mineola, sir."

"What?"

"I'm from Mineola, not Westbury."

"Thanks for clarifying; now we know where to send your dogtags."

"Wasting time," said Red Scorpion, adjusting his eyepiece

for some purpose… accommodating low light, maybe?  The others responded to his simple two words without delay, boarding the vehicle.

It took a lot of effort for Campbell to muscle the two cases into the storage area, and he couldn't believe that Blue Viper had lugged them both out to the car, one in each hand.  He felt his whole body shaking, like a child about to ride his first roller coaster on a dare, and already he was covered in sweat.  It barely even occurred to him that Black Tiger had either read his personnel file, or he was a native New Yorker himself, able to pin down his home town by accent.

Campbell climbed in; Red Scorpion was riding shotgun.  "Where should I…"

Withering stares from Blue Viper and Gray Shark made it clear he wasn't sitting with them.

"Oooooo-k," concluded Campbell, making his way to the back, where the only available seat was next to Black Tiger.

He felt claustrophobic right away, as though he were locked inside some space shuttle about to go to the moon.  Kurt started the engine, and the air conditioning gunned to life on max, but it would be a long time before the vehicle felt cool enough to breathe comfortably.  The recycled air made Campbell want to vomit.

They drove to the gate, Red Scorpion handed some papers to the guard on duty, and they were off, outside the proverbial wire.  Campbell hoped they would make it home for dinner; hell, he hoped they'd make it back at all.  He wouldn't know until much later that he'd never see *inside* the wire again.

\*\*\*

Being in an unsecured war zone, as they termed it, made Campbell feel like the Humvee's walls were made of cardboard.  It wasn't a tank, after all.  He had seen what an IED could do to one of these things.  Once, they towed in the wreck of one of these basically souped-up SUVs, and he had remarked how it looked like a beige and brown pinata after a child's birthday party. The unlucky soldiers that had been riding within at the time were blown to pieces, as in, arms over here and legs waaaaaay the hell over there, and those were the ones who weren't trapped inside the flaming hulk, being barbecued alive.

He'd never been out here; when he entered the country, he had been flown right onto base. It was an island: a huge, fortified hotel. Now, as they drove through the dusty streets, he saw actual hotels, in big piles of smoking rubble. They hadn't driven more than a few miles from base, and it was getting pretty real, pretty quickly.

It wasn't exactly what he expected, not completely, anyway. He thought it would look like the future from *Terminator*, with the roads paved with skulls and only two walls standing from every building. Instead, only one or two buildings on each block were smoldering craters, and the smoke from the fires was thin enough that you had better visibility here than while swimming in the Long Island Sound.

The sun had risen, and Campbell heard the *adhan* – the call to prayer - echoing from sepulcher loudspeakers through every alley and street. He had heard it many times on-base, but it sounded different being out here among the people, more beautiful, but more alien, both alluring and threatening, even though he had once been forced to memorize all the words to it in a basic Arabic class in what already felt like another lifetime ago.

People lived here, going about their business, doing the mundane chores of everyday life, despite the chaos of the nightly shellings and the suicide attacks and the occupation. Campbell saw women and children at marketplaces and men in tea houses. He wondered what they were thinking of him, driving through their streets in an expensive armored car, changing their regime or whatever; he wondered how many deaths they had caused to do so.

And then he saw a woman staring at the car - no, staring at *him*, locking eyes - from the corner. *Why was she doing that?* he wondered. *Why is she so interested in...*

A loud BANG, and the vehicle lurched upward violently. Campbell screamed a falsetto, kicked-in-the-beans scream, sharp and loud.

All eyes in the car laser-beamed onto Campbell clutching his rifle in one hand and his book in the other, as though the book could be used as some kind of anti-shrapnel shield.

"Just a pothole, amigo," called Kurt from the front.

"Black Tiger, double-check to make sure his safety's on," said Gray Shark.

"God-damned baby," murmured Blue Viper, tearing off some tough beef jerky with his teeth.

Red Scorpion - the Baron, as they had called him last night - looked on dispassionately, continuing to indicate direction to Kurt with simple commands.

"First time in combat, Specialist?" stated, rather than asked, Black Tiger.

"Look, I can speak the language, but I can't interpret sciencey stuff in Arabic. I don't know if I can do what you want."

"Science? What would you need to know about science for?"

"You know, chemistry? Bio-hazards? Pressure gages and the like?"

"What?"

"Like, in the lab?" asked Campbell, confused. "Aren't we raiding a secret WMD factory? Why else would you need a linguist?"

"Listen, Specialist. You aren't going to be in the line of fire, if you catch my drift. All you'll have to do is have a few simple conversations with our contact. Think you can handle that?"

"I think I can handle that. I mean, I think I can handle that, *sir.*"

Black Tiger turned away. Apparently, the conversation was finished.

"Mets or Yanks?" asked Campbell.

"We don't have to talk, Specialist."

"Yanks, I bet," continued Campbell. "Bronx Bombers."

"Fine. Sure. Yankees."

There seemed to be something so secure, so confident about Black Tiger, and about all of them, really. Campbell knew there were men and women like this, people with nerves of steel who were tough as nails and all that, but there was something else about Black Tiger. Campbell almost couldn't believe he were real. Black Tiger didn't seem like an actual person; he seemed more like he stepped off an assembly line in some Detroit weapons factory, programmed to give people *twenty seconds to comply*. No, he was from the Bronx, Campbell hypothesized, which meant he was likely tough, but not some machine.

"Pelham, right?" pushed Campbell. "Near the zoo?"

"Specialist McConnors," turned Black Tiger, giving him his full attention now. "Yes, I am from the Bronx. Yes, I root for the Yankees. Yes, they will always be superior to the Mets in every quantifiable way. No, you don't need your nose to execute your role in this operation, and yes, I will break yours if you continue to fraternize with me."

"Aw, Black Tiger made a new friend," taunted Gray Shark, to Black Tiger's disgust.

Campbell wanted to ask about the animal claw bracelets on Tiger's wrists but thought better of it and looked away.

The sun was still low in the sky when the vehicle broke free from what many would consider civilization and into the fringes of wild, Arabian desert. There was sand, and lots of it, but also large expanses of rocky plains and plateaus. Roads still existed and showed evidence of having been maintained decently during

Saddam's time, before the war, although there was obviously evidence of shelling and heavy ordinance even out here.

"Can we open a window? Little stuffy back here," called Campbell, obviously out of turn by the reaction he got from Blue Viper.

"That's a negative, McConnors," replied Kurt from the front, trying to diffuse tension. "May I remind you that we are still in an…"

"…unsecured war zone, yes, thank you for reminding me."

They continued, cutting through the expanse, the cloudless sky a bright azure. Campbell surveyed the vehicle's occupants: everyone was in their own worlds, preparing, he supposed, for all the life-or-death that should be happening any minute now. Campbell still had no idea what they were really doing out here. He felt vastly unprepared; it was good that this was apparently a need-to-know affair, because he sure didn't know.

Everybody's stillness made him uncomfortable.

"Still, it's not like the windows are bulletproof anyway, are they?"

He saw Gray Shark turn the dial on her iPod clockwise.

"Not getting enough AC back there?" called Kurt.

"No, it's fine. Nice and cool, thanks. Just covered head-to-toe in this stuff. Not complaining," he said, tapering off, "I'm fine."

The truth was that the farther away they got from the city, the more relaxed he became. He liked the wilderness, and he liked being outdoors. His sense-memory brought him back to when he was young, maybe fourteen, when his parents took him and his brother on a family vacation to Canyonlands National Park. It looked a lot like this; maybe it was friendlier on the surface, but he had gotten separated from his family and had to survive for a night on his own out there before a park ranger found him the next morning. It was one of the most terrifying, though formative, experiences of his life, and it taught him a love of the solitude of nature. The Utah desert would have killed him just as indifferently as the Arabian. Maybe, he thought, he should have pursued working for the park service. The pay was modest, but at least he could spend his days outside in the sun and not worry about roadside bombs.

Red Scorpion instructed Kurt to navigate through some sparse villages, and Campbell's education continued. Buildings were rectangular, and generally only one story, as if it were constructed by Tetris bricks. It was a very spartan aesthetic out of necessity, like some Adobe settlement out in the American West. Small boys wearing white and covered in dust tended small flocks of sheep. Campbell still saw smoke from the wreckages in the city behind them.

"Black Tiger, huh," remarked Campbell. "That a call sign? Like, are you a pilot?"

Black Tiger icily turned to Campbell and threw him a sardonic glance.

"Excuse me," corrected Campbell. "*Naval Aviator?*"

"Yes. That's why I'm out here driving through the desert."

"Well, that is impressive. Permission to buzz the tower? Negative, Black Tiger, the pattern is full. Bet you've never left your wingman."

In spite of himself, the side of Black Tiger's lip curled into the beginnings of a smile. Seeing a crack in the dam, Campbell continued.

"I figured you probably weren't."

"What gave it away?"

"Well, the ponytail, for one. I dig it, though. Very Steven Seagal, *Out for Justice*. Is that regulation?"

"Keep it up, Specialist," said Black Tiger, suppressing his smile. He could almost feel the judgment from his peers, and being the new man, he needed their respect.

"You got the best combination, if you don't mind me saying. Black and tiger. I don't think Purple Tiger would have worked. I don't think Yellow Tiger would have worked. It's like a cartoon animal, like Snagglepuss or something. But Black Tiger, that's a cologne. That's a body spray you can sell to teenage boys."

"Can it, Specialist."

"Are you saying that because I'm named after soup?"

The vehicle came to a sudden stop.

"Oh my God, I'll shut up. Please don't leave me out here."

"Translator," said Red Scorpion, looking at Campbell through the rear-view mirror, "you're up."


Campbell stepped out of the car and immediately felt a sense of extreme vulnerability coupled with paranoia; the car was, after all, the fortress. His legs locked up when his boots hit the dusty earth below him, unwilling to take him farther from the Humvee and expose him to threats from a full 360 degrees.

He was hit by a wall of dry heat; he hadn't realized how much work the air conditioner had been doing to control his personal climate. Campbell wondered how people could live like this, subjected to so much constant arid, hot weather.

*Get a grip*, he commanded himself. *Earn yourself some margaritas tonight.*

It was an unremarkable village, a white and tawny maze of near-colorless brick covered by a thin layer of ubiquitous dust, with a central road bisecting it and a dozen side streets on either flank. It was kind of like a cowboy town in some old Western. The people, however - men leaning against walls, women with children - looked upon him with what he hoped was just suspicion, if not outright hostility.

Campbell flinched when another pair of boots hit the ground next to him.

"Don't make eye contact," warned Black Tiger. "They'll take it as an insult."

"It's rude? Learned that the hard way here?"

"Learned it the hard way in the South Bronx, McConnors. Let's go."

Black Tiger took the lead, striding confidently ahead and holding his rifle loosely, pointed down. Campbell followed closely, tense from head to toe, clutching his book like an industrial compactor. They turned a corner, and eyes followed.

Black Tiger knelt abruptly, and Campbell nearly bumped into him.

"Insurgents," said Black Tiger quietly, holding up some spent shell casings.

"I kind of feel like we're the insurgents."

"Potato, potahto," said Black Tiger, casually tossing the shells to the side. "Just semantics out here."

"You really think it doesn't make a difference?"

"Why don't you debate it with *them*, Specialist?"

A group of boys, probably around ten years old, had curiously approached, and it bothered Campbell how easily they had snuck up on them.

"*Sabah alkhyr*," said Campbell.

"*Ah salaam alaikum*," the tallest one replied, and he gently touched the muzzle of Campbell's rifle.

"Don't touch that," he said, and then immediately *translated*:

"*Where are you from?*" a boy asked.

"*A place called Long Island, far away in America.*"

"*Are you here to shoot someone?*"

"*No, of course not.*"

"*Are you a Muslim?*"

Campbell paused; he could probably get away with it.

"*Yes. Yes I am.*"

"*Don't they kill Muslims in America?*"

"*No. That's not true.*"

"*My father says Christians kill Muslims in America.*"

"What are they saying?" asked Black Tiger, as more children surrounded them, and as more adults had come off the main road into the alley to get a better look at them.

"*Is he a Muslim?*" asked one boy, pointing at Black Tiger.

"They want to know if you're a Muslim; I'm going to tell them yes."

"Do that."

"*Yes, my friend is a Muslim, just like me.*"

"*He doesn't look like a Muslim,*" said another.

"*If you are not a Muslim…*"

"*He is, he is.*"

"*…my father says that American soldiers are evil.*"

"*American bombs killed my cousin.*"

"*My friend.*"

"*My grandmother.*"

This was getting out of hand quickly.

"Do something," commanded Black Tiger, touching the safety on his rifle. They were now effectively trapped by these children.

From deeper in the alley, an older child strode towards them purposefully, and Black Tiger aimed his rifle at him; the kids screamed in unison, and the adults from the road advanced.

"What the hell are you doing?" stammered Campbell, reaching for Tiger's rifle.

Black Tiger hit Campbell hard in the face and took aim again, but the boy had disappeared. He clutched Campbell by the lapels and slammed him against the nearest wall; the kids scattered.

"Don't do that again," he seethed.

But Campbell's fear had instantly turned to an adrenaline-fueled anger.

"I'm here to translate words, not shoot children!"

"And if that kid had C4 strapped to his chest, we'd both be dead and all these children with us!" he roared. "You, with zero combat experience, want to take responsibility for that?"

Campbell stood in silence, dumbfounded. He hadn't even considered that possibility.

133

"No shoot, no shoot," came a voice from behind a pen with sheep, a makeshift wall that must have been repaired hastily after an errant explosive destroyed it.

Tentatively, the older boy who Black Tiger almost ventilated a moment ago, came out from behind his cover with his hands up.

"*You are here for me?*" he said in Arabic.

Black Tiger lowered his rifle again and got a better look at him, as did Campbell, who was more confused than ever.

"*That's* our contact?" asked Campbell. "Zakaria, you're our contact?"

\*\*\*

They continued further into the desert in the car, where there were few landmarks Campbell could really make note of. It was a plain, really, a chalky sort of flat land that looked white when the sun powered down onto it. A desiccated tree here, a rock there, maybe a small human settlement came and went to break up the monotony. At least there was a road - one road, as far as Campbell could tell.

"*Turn left here,*" said Zakaria, squished between Blue Viper and Grey Shark.

"He says left turn here," yelled Campbell from the back, behind him.

Kurt slowed the vehicle and turned back to face them. "There's no road here; is he sure?"

"That's what he said."

"Listen to the child," said Red Scorpion, and the matter was settled. Kurt took the Humvee into the expanse, toward a horizon that looked a thousand miles away.

"*How's that Playstation 2 working out for you?*" asked Campbell.

"*I like the FIFA 2004. I'm the best in the village,*" replied Zakaria.

*"Then you have electricity?"*

*"Some men gave us a portable generator."*

*"Pretty lucky. What men?"*

"Stop talking in Arabic," commanded Black Tiger.

"I thought that's why I was brought here."

"You were brought here to follow orders."

"Yeah, well, I wasn't the one who almost shot our contact, so don't take it out on me."

"Looks like someone found your place," teased Gray Shark, "and put your ass there, Santana."

Black Tiger did not like that Gray Shark had used his real name instead of his handle, and Campbell knew it. *Santana*, he thought. *Santana from the Bronx.* Campbell was also figuring out the dynamic here: Black Tiger was not just the youngest: he was the new guy, the lowest rung on the ladder, and Campbell was embarrassing him.

Zakaria said something in Arabic.

"Am I allowed to translate that, Santana?"

"Go on."

"He says there is a group of two trees about three kilometers away."

Zakaria protested in Arabic.

"That's three trees, two kilometers away."

"I'm glad we brought the expert," spat Black Tiger.

"About two o'clock," continued Campbell.

"I see them," said Kurt, turning slightly to beeline towards it.

*"How did you get mixed up with these men, Zakaria?"* asked Campbell.

"I said stop talking in Arabic," growled Black Tiger.

"I'm clarifying his instruction," said Campbell, turning back to Zakaria. *"What did these people tell you?"*

*"I have some family out in the desert,"* answered Zakaria. *"They discovered a special place when a bomb fell out there. I tell the other American*

*translator, and these four are very interested."*

*"Other translator? Who?"*

"What are you yammering about?" asked Black Tiger impatiently.

"He says we're going the right way."

"Good. Now shut..."

The vehicle's radio crackled to life.

"Come in, Specialist Christian," came a voice through the speaker.

"Go for Christian," spoke Kurt into the mic.

"I have Colonel Giese for you."

"Put him through."

"Christian, where the hell are you? Is McConnors with you?" grinded Giese through the speaker.

"Yes, sir. What is it?"

"Turn around immediately!" he grunted. "You two are officially A.W.O.L. You wouldn't know anything about a dead..."

Red Scorpion abruptly powered off the radio.

"Sir?" asked Kurt, confused.

"Don't worry about it, Specialist," said Red Scorpion. "It will make sense in a few moments."

"Wait, hang on," called Campbell from the back. "What is going on here?"

"Just shut the fuck up," growled Black Tiger to Campbell menacingly. He grabbed Campbell's shoulder.

"No, you shut the fuck up, Santana," said Campbell, and he pushed Black Tiger off. "He said we were A.W.O.L. Why would he say that, *Mister Scorpion*? Why would you turn the radio off?"

"Is this how you address a superior officer?" asked Red Scorpion from the front, amused by Campbell's brashness.

"*Are* you a superior officer? I don't even know what rank you are. I don't know *who* any of you are."

"Let's calm down, McConnors," said Kurt, trying to ease

the tension.

"Yes. Let's," said Black Tiger as his right arm slithered around Campbell's neck and constricted, with his left arm chicken-winging Campbell's nearest appendage. Air flow ceased immediately.

"*We're here*," said Zakaria.

\*\*\*

Campbell hit the dirt hard when Black Tiger pushed him out of the vehicle, but at least he was breathing again. Black Tiger stood over him, shaking his head derisively until Kurt ran around the Humvee and got between them.

"You don't belong out here. You're not even a man trying to play soldier; you're a boy trying to play man," said Black Tiger.

Catching his breath, Campbell said, "Gee, thanks, Dad. I won't let you down again."

Black Tiger casually pushed Kurt to the side and then stepped on Campbell's hand, pinning his fingers to the hot earth.

"I know you won't," said Black Tiger.

"That's enough of that," said Red Scorpion, stepping out of the Humvee, and Black Tiger relented immediately.

"Gentlemen, let's be honest," said Red Scorpion. "Due to the sensitive nature of this operation, we have disseminated our intelligence to as few individuals as possible, and even your Colonel Giese is unaware of our presence for the time being."

"Wait, are you saying we've stolen a Humvee and deserted the base?"

"Only on the surface, and only for now. It has to be this way. My people and I report directly to the CIA."

"Are you mercenaries, then?" asked Kurt.

"No, we are fully commissioned, and I assure you that our operation is legitimate. By the end of the day, you will be fully exonerated heroes of the Coalition. I'm sorry that I cannot allay your fears further, but we have a job to do and we require you to continue to do your best. Can you handle that?"

"I guess so," said Campbell, rising.

"Excuse me?"

"Yes, sir," they both replied.

"Excellent. I know we can count on you," said Red Scorpion, his European accent sharp. "Just the same, however…"

Black Tiger took both of their rifles from them and followed Blue Viper and Gray Shark. Red Scorpion strode ahead, and Campbell looked at his friend, trying to say *"this is all wrong"* with his eyes.


The three barren trees led Campbell, Kurt and the soldiers to an even smaller, more remote outpost in the brutal desert, and beyond, more wilderness. A few animals shepherded by young kids picked at dry grass. Men stayed in what passed for shade out here, but the sun was almost directly overhead. There must have been women too, but Campbell didn't see any. Campbell felt like he had stepped back in time, as if he were a character in the Old Testament.

"Here we are," said Red Scorpion, seeing who-knows-what through his high-tech eyepiece.

Zakaria emerged from a small, one-story brick shack with a bearded man carrying a tray with glasses filled with tea. He spoke in Arabic, and Campbell translated:

"Welcome. Tea; please drink as a sign of our friendship."

Zakaria distributed the tea to each of them.

Black Tiger took the lead.

"Ask him where it is," he said, and Campbell translated, and the bearded man spoke again.

"He says be mindful of our…" and Campbell flipped through his book, finding the right words, "arrangement. Deal."

Black Tiger turned to Red Scorpion, who nodded

unceremoniously, and Black Tiger took a huge bundle of U.S. dollars from one of his pockets and placed it neatly on the bearded man's empty tray.

"The first half now, the rest when we have it," said Black Tiger, and Campbell translated. "Use it to fund your holy war, or build a school for your children. It's your choice."

"You really want me to say that?" asked Campbell. "Who are these people?"

"Just ask him where it is."

Campbell did so, and the bearded man responded.

"He says there is a small canyon about five hundred meters to the west, and in the canyon's..." Campbell searched in the book. "...wall? Rockface? In the canyon's wall there is a felled tree."

The man continued, and Campbell continued.

"Behind the tree there is a," more book searching, "tear in the earth. Cave. A cave!"

"Tell him we'll take his grandson," said Black Tiger.

Campbell did so, and the man agreed, adding in Arabic: "*Beware false idols. Allah forbids them.*"


Kurt moved the vehicle to the place the old man described: a shallow canyon about a half a kilometer from the village. It looked like a narrow depression in the plain that was probably somewhere around twenty-five feet deep and thirty yards wide, stretching lengthwise for at least a football field or more. The wind whistled through, and it felt like the canyon was struggling to breathe in the tyrannical heat.

Actually, now that Campbell thought about it, the wind was really starting to pick up.

Gray Shark and Blue Viper went to unload their huge, heavy boxes from the storage compartment; Zakaria hopped out and shaded his eyes from the sun.

"No wonder the U.N. never found this place," said Kurt to Campbell, climbing out of the vehicle. "It really is in the middle of the desert. How would a satellite find chemical weapons buried all the way out here?"

"Yeah, it's like there's no military presence here at all, no infrastructure. It's like," and Campbell looked Kurt right in the eyes when he said this, "there is no way an industrial weapons complex could be hidden here." When Black Tiger came around the Humvee, Campbell returned to his normal speech pattern: "It's brilliant. There isn't a thing to draw attention to it."

"Keep the car parked here, out of the canyon; you two help with the equipment," he commanded.

"Yes, sir!" said Campbell, over-the-top.

"Keep that shit to a minimum. We're almost through with you."

Zakaria took the group down into the canyon, the earth beneath their feet parched and hard, and just like the old man said, they came upon a downed tree near the steep, western face of the canyon's wall.

The wind pushed through, and it chilled the sweat on Campbell's face, even as it replaced the perspiration with a thin layer of dust.

"Pay up," said Gray Shark. "One thousand, in my hand, now."

"Not yet. Not until we have it," said Blue Viper.

They stood over a small hole in the rock - a cave, or more accurately, an opening that seemed to lead vertically into the earth. It was narrow, perhaps two and a half feet in diameter, but it was open and unobstructed.

"Take a look, McConnors," instructed Black Tiger.

"Is there something down there you need me to convert to English?"

"Are you saying your usefulness on this mission has come to an end?"

"My pleasure," said Campbell, dropping to his knees and bracing on his hands, sticking his head into the chasm for a few moments before coming back up to his knees. "It's dark. I can't see very far."

Black Tiger nodded to Blue Viper, who handed Campbell a large flashlight, as Red Scorpion looked on.

"*Watch out*," said Zakaria.

"*Don't worry; I'm fine. It's just…*"

The biggest scorpion Campbell had ever seen crawled out of the hole and scrambled between his hands on the parched earth. Campbell jumped backwards in shock, and the rest of the group laughed.

"I'd say that's a good omen, considering your namesake," said Gray Shark, but Red Scorpion dispassionately crushed it beneath his boot.

"Let's not be sentimental," he said.

"Yeah, I don't think that's your problem," said Campbell, shaken. He crawled back to the edge of the hole and shined the light down.

"It's hollow. I can't see the floor. I think it widens out the farther down it goes."

"Out of the way," said Black Tiger. He motioned to Gray Shark, who lowered a small, hand-held electronic device down the shaft on a long rope. She waited a few minutes, her red hair dancing in the increasing wind, and then pulled it back up.

"$CO_2$ is present, but tolerable," she said, looking at the device. "There's a little methane, but I don't think it'll be a problem."

They all looked to Red Scorpion, hungry with anticipation.

"Green light."

\*\*\*

Blue Viper had opened the case and, with Gray Shark's help, had taken some of its contents and assembled them into some mechanical winch, which he was now in the process of bolting to the hard earth. They were spooling a long metallic cable around it.

Campbell and Kurt stood with Zakaria about ten feet away, and they spoke as quietly as they could. The others were busy and seemed to be focused on their task, but they were still within listening range.

"This is all wrong," whispered Campbell.

"It's irregular, at least."

"Geez, you think?"

"Well, what do *you* think? They're imposters? How'd they get on base, then?"

"Doesn't it bother you that Colonel Giese thinks we're deserters? That we stole a hummer and took it for a joyride?"

"What if they're telling the truth?"

"Come on, if that's a chemical weapons depot, then I'm Hugh Hefner."

"Who's Hugh Hefner?"

"The *Playboy* guy! You don't know the *Playboy* guy?"

"Well, excuse me! I guess I don't read as much porn as you!" he whispered loudly, and Blue Viper turned to look at them. They both smiled innocently and lowered their voices.

"It doesn't matter. All I know for sure is that they're lying to us," Campbell said. He added, "I think they're going to kill us."

"What do you want to do?"

"Zakaria," said Campbell. "*These are bad men. I think they're going to...*" Campbell flipped through the pages, and it took a few seconds before he found the right words, "*double-cross your people.*"

"*What should I do?*" he asked. "*I'm not giving back my Playstation.*"

"*Run. Go. Hide somewhere. Quickly.*"

Zakaria bolted, running away from the canyon.

"Where's he going?" yelled Black Tiger. "Nobody said he could leave."

He raised his rifle, training it on the boy.

"I asked for some water. Is that not allowed?" Campbell replied.

Black Tiger's rifle followed Zakaria.

"No. It isn't."

"What's wrong with you, you twisted fuck?" hollered Campbell, and he rushed towards Black Tiger, who swung the barrel towards him. Campbell stopped in his tracks.

"It seems our translator has some courage," said Red Scorpion, lowering Black Tiger's weapon. "Let's see how much."

\*\*\*


It only took a few minutes to lock Campbell into the harness, which was securely attached to the metal cable spooled out of the winch into the hole. Behind him, Black Tiger was securing himself into a similar contraption. Blue Viper and Gray Shark stood facing opposite ends, scanning either side of the canyon, and Red Scorpion watched from a few paces away, lighting an old-fashioned tobacco pipe, of all things. Kurt helped secure Campbell into his harness.

"I've never been spelunking," said Kurt, "but this looks like it'll keep you in business. Just hold tight, and we'll lower you right down."

"Why am I going?" protested Campbell.

"*Somebody* has to take the first hit," said Black Tiger nonchalantly.

"I'll go," volunteered Kurt.

"No," said Black Tiger. "This one will do just fine."

"What am I supposed to be looking for?"

"If there's any danger, just let us know."

"Yeah, but what am I supposed to be looking for? Chemical drums? Warheads? Sticks of dynamite?"

The wind picked up again, and it blew dust and sand over the edge of the canyon like waves crashing against a rocky beach head.

"Well, let's start by looking for the floor," said Black Tiger, pushing Campbell over the hole in the ground, the metallic cable going taught and suspending him in mid-air. Campbell instinctively clutched the cable, holding on for dear life, and accidentally dropping his book of Arabic words and phrases below him. It was a few seconds before he heard it hit rock bottom.

"I wouldn't hold onto that without gloves," warned Black Tiger. "The metal will shred your hands to pieces. And don't touch anything until I get there."

"If you insist," said Campbell, shaking.

Blue Viper took his eyes off the canyon ledge and cranked down on a lever, and the power winch slowly lowered Campbell down into the darkness. It was only moments before the blackness enveloped him, and he felt like a worm on a hook about to be swallowed up by whatever was down here. He heard the gear above grinding away, groaning against his weight.

"You all right down there?" called Kurt, and though Campbell had only descended about ten feet, Kurt's voice sounded distant and faint.

"So far," called Campbell, hearing his own voice echo as he inched down, and then added to himself, "so good."

It was stuffy and hard to breathe; he hoped Gray Shark had read that thing right, whatever it was. He felt claustrophobic, as the diameter of the shaft hadn't opened up an inch. He had a flashlight, but it was attached to his belt and he couldn't reach it.

The cable stopped suddenly, and he bobbed up and down like a piece of cork on the sea. It occurred to him that if something went wrong, there'd be almost no way to climb back out, and he felt his heart rate accelerating.

"Everything OK?" he called, to which he heard no reply.

He was starting to freak out a little now, and he imagined some nightmarish, cavern-dwelling monstrosity reaching up from below and gnawing off his legs.

"I said, is everything…"

He started moving again, dropping deeper down into the inky blackness, until the shaft began to angle both down and sideways. His feet hit slippery rock, and with the continuing slack from the cable, he slid farther down.

The shaft opened up into what he perceived as a wider, empty space when the cable reached its end, suspending him above open air.

"Is that all we have?" he yelled back up, and it occurred to him that if there were people stationed down here, if this were some kind of military installation, they now knew he was both here and helpless. Something told him that it wasn't, that it couldn't be… that this place was something different, and that nobody had been here for a long time.

Now he could get a hold of his flashlight. He clicked it on, and he discovered that he was only two feet above a solid floor, and that he was at the beginning of a horizontal tunnel that bored deeper into this Subterranea. Campbell undid himself from the carabiners, and he dropped down onto his feet.

"I'm down!" he called.

It wouldn't be long before Black Tiger were down here with him; luckily, the shaft was only wide enough for one man at a time. *This was all wrong*, he thought. *These guys are not who they seem.* Whatever was down here, he had to find it first. Maybe he could use it as leverage, if he needed it.

Cautiously, he inched forward through the cave. He couldn't make out any features on either wall. He thought, *it would have been gneiss if I had studied a little geology*, and he might have even smiled a little.

He touched the cave wall, expecting something rough and maybe with spider webs, but he found it to be smooth and flat. Maybe it was man-made. Maybe this place was even some kind of tomb. What could the Baron want down here?

Knowing there were scorpions, he was diligent about scanning around with his flashlight. So far, there wasn't much, just wall, wall, wall…

Human skull!

Campbell stumbled back and checked to make sure he hadn't shit himself (and, if we're keeping score, he hadn't, although he might have needed a little extra Clorox in his next underwear wash). Catching his breath, he angled the light back up.

It wasn't a human skull at all; it was a human face, and it wasn't real, it was carved out of solid stone, with impressions of a curly beard flowing down from his chin. It was an enormous stone statue, with a bull's body, the resting wings of an eagle, and lions' feet. Campbell guessed that it may have been seven feet tall at the shoulder and at least ten or twelve feet long, resting on a horizontal base. The thing was massive, with an inert heaviness, and it looked as if it had been untouched for thousands of years.

Moreover, a quick sweep of the flashlight revealed that Campbell had ventured into a larger room, a chamber of some kind, with three of these mighty manimal statues flanking either side of the pathway. He had seen things like these before in a museum, no, a textbook.

The most amazing thing in that room was small, however, and waiting patiently at the end on a modest pedestal. It looked like the six statues in the room, with three notable exceptions: One, it was small, about twelve inches long and six inches tall. Two, while it had the features of eagles' wings, lions' feet, and bovine body, the face was that of a beautiful, Persian woman staring upward regally, like a queen. And three (and probably the most significant), it was made of what looked like solid gold and bejeweled from top to bottom.

Campbell slowly approached the pedestal. It was even more magnificent up close, with the flashlight refracting off the precious stones radiating color in all directions. It was mesmerizing, hypnotic… and the only thing that broke him out of that trance was a foul smell.

There was a sulfur vein cracking through the wall behind it, the element creeping out in yellow, crystalline form.

He put his hands on it, and it dawned on him that his were likely the first hands on this thing in thousands of years. The bearded man had warned him to beware false idols, and he wasn't kidding…

"I wouldn't touch that without gloves," came Black Tiger's voice, from behind. "When Howard Carter first excavated King Tut's tomb a hundred years ago, people said it was cursed. A few of his crew mysteriously died shortly thereafter, the eternal boy king striking at vandals from beyond the grave. We now know there was bacteria on the sarcophagus."

"You did say we were looking for deadly weapons; this wasn't what I had in mind."

"Turn around, slowly, and keep your flashlight on, pointed at the ground."

Campbell complied, and he saw that Black Tiger was wearing night-vision glasses, extremely sensitive to light. He pointed a small firearm at Campbell.

"Just who the hell are you?"

"A self-made man who just leveled up. I *earned* my handle," he said, tapping the claw bracelets on his arms. "You don't think the old boy just handed me these."

"Not the zoo."

"India. Now, that golden lady there is mine."

"It's a lamassu," said Campbell, remembering from that time, whenever.

"They teach you that back in Mineola? Assyrian, three, maybe four thousand years old. Those people didn't work in gold like this back then, and not with gems. This lady is special."

"Why do you want it?"

"Because *they* want it."

"I see," said Campbell. "This is your coming-out party, isn't it? Your confirmation. Your first run with the big dogs."

"It wasn't easy getting an introduction with these three; they're elite, and they don't consort with just anyone."

"Not some punk from the South Bronx."

"Santana's long dead, Specialist McConnors, and it was a long, painful path to killing him. You, on the other hand…"

"Just hang on. Nobody has to die over this."

"They already have."

"Colonel Giese on the radio…"

"Our original translator; he proved unreliable, untrustworthy. That's why we needed you, a last-minute replacement."

"And Kurt."

"A pair of car keys to us," Black Tiger said, cocking the hammer on his gun. "Now, if you don't have any other bright ideas…"

"Just one."

Campbell slammed his flashlight against the sulfur vein hard, and it ignited like a roadside flare. The sudden bright flash seared Black Tiger's retinas, and he threw the night vision goggles off, squeezing the trigger and blasting one shot in Campbell's direction. The report echoed through the chamber, ringing in both their ears.

In the split-second he had, Campbell grabbed the lamassu and hammered Black Tiger's cranium with it, hitting him hard enough to dislodge one of its jewels. Black Tiger dropped like a bunch of broccoli.

Using his flashlight, Campbell saw that he was out cold. He took Black Tiger's gun and trained it on him. White hot with fear and anger, he justified all the reasons for blowing this bastard away - threatening to kill Zakaria, manipulating him and Kurt, being a Yankees fan - but couldn't do it.

He stuffed the lamassu into his backpack and jammed the gun in his pocket, where the handle stuck out awkwardly. The tip of the barrel was still hot; why did guys on TV always casually slide guns into their pants? Lastly, he took Black Tiger's gloves and left him with just about nothing else before running back towards the winch cable.

"Back so soon?" greeted Gray Shark as the Campbell emerged from the pit. He stumbled awkwardly forward, unhooking himself from the harness and feeling hot wind push against his face. It felt like a hurricane was approaching; he'd never felt winds like that in this country before.

"You were right. Missiles stacked up high, weapons-grade uranium… the works. It's a good thing we found this place."

"This kid's funny!" laughed Gray Shark, and even Blue Viper smiled. "Your friend is funny, Christian!"

Campbell saw that Kurt wasn't laughing, because he was on his knees with the business end of a rifle - his own rifle - pressed squarely against his head by Red Scorpion. He was bleeding from his nose, and his eyes were blackened.

"Kurt…"

"You should be proud of your friend," said Red Scorpion. "He tried to do the right thing."

"He always does," said Campbell.

"It's all right, Campbell," said Kurt, spitting blood. "It's all right."

"Now," continued Red Scorpion. "Where is it?"

"Down there. He has it."

"If he had it, you wouldn't have come up here," said Red Scorpion.

Speaking into a satellite phone, Blue Viper said, "Ready for extraction, on our coordinates…"

"You're just plunderers. Looters."

"Don't do it," whispered Kurt. "Don't give them anything."

"I feel as though you aren't taking me seriously," said the Baron, and he fired into Kurt's head, spraying red onto the parched earth.

Tears instantly welled up in Campbell's eyes as he drew the gun from his pocket and aimed it squarely at Red Scorpion. Everyone else pointed their weapons at him.

"Let's not be sentimental," said Red Scorpion.

"You fuck! You miserable fuck!" cried Campbell. "He was a good person! He was here to help people! Not like you! You're a bunch of fucking thieves, pillaging this country, financing insurgents!"

"Oh, but you, you're in a lot of trouble, Specialist McConnors. First, you murdered an enlisted man, another translator, yesterday back on the base. Then you stole a Humvee and went A.W.O.L. before killing your own friend out here in the desert. And now, you're about to go and massacre a whole village of noncombatants so nobody can tell of what you found out here. Looks like your only chance now is to hand over the idol that we know is in your pack and see how far you can run. That desert doesn't take prisoners, but it's better than nothing."

Campbell took off his pack and held it above the empty chasm.

"Let's see how priceless this thing is after a forty-foot vertical drop."

"Suicide it is," concluded Red Scorpion. "I do have to admit, I'll remember you. You've got more guts than we gave you credit for."

"No, Baron. You've got guts," said Campbell, shaking with anger. "And one day, I'll stand over you, cleaning them off the street. Oh, look: non-combatants!"

The sound of automatic weapons fire resonated through the canyon and everyone hit the dirt, scrambling to find cover - behind a tree, next to a rock, wherever - as the rounds kicked up the dust at their feet. It was the bearded man and half a dozen men or more, each sniping down from the top of both sides of the canyon ridge.

Campbell threw himself over Kurt's body as if to shield it. He knew he had to make a break for it, but it felt vile to just leave his friend here. He deserved better than that.

These plunderers, as Campbell called them, were no easy targets, however. You *could* call them proverbial sitting ducks, but only if those ducks were brilliant marksmen, armed with semi-automatic rifles and grenade launchers, and had ice in their veins. Despite having been ambushed, they were only at a disadvantage for seconds before Gray Shark nailed one of the villagers in the guts.

Then Blue Viper got the bearded man right in the throat, and he tumbled over the side of the canyon, drowning in his own blood.

Another for Gray Shark, and another for Gray Shark, and one for Red Scorpion, although his was just a graze, but still a good shot considering the now-fierce winds.

Blue Viper got dinged in the arm, but it barely slowed him down; he switched rifle hands and kept blasting away from the hip.

In the chaos, Campbell frantically searched Kurt's pockets for the keys to the Humvee, his only ticket out of here.

"I'm sorry, Kurt," he said.

He couldn't find them. Snapping his dog-tags off his neck, Campbell rose to his feet, only to see Zakaria running through the canyon towards him.

"*Tueal maei! Tueal maei!*" he shouted over the guns and wind. *Come with me! Come with me!*

"No! Get out of here! *Akhraj min huna! Akhraj min...*" Campbell screamed to him, but it was too late.

Zakaria touched his abdomen, almost surprised, and saw that he had been shot perfectly through the heart. There wasn't even any pain. He simply dropped to his knees as though praying, and then fell forward, face-first on the ground.

Campbell swung around and fired blindly three times, all misses, and saw Red Scorpion pointing his own M-16 at him.

"Looks like we have no further need of a translator," he said callously. "Good-bye."

At that point, Campbell assumed what he was experiencing was the Wrath of Satan or something cataclysmic, even biblical. A wall of sand powered over the eastern edge of the canyon like a tsunami of particulate matter; tons of dirt and dust rushed over the land and into the small valley like a furious god erasing some terrible mistake. The sky overhead darkened, and a glacier of dust and sand towered fifty feet in the air as it marched over the barren landscape.

Campbell covered his mouth and nose as best he could, shutting his eyes and firing three, four, five more times in the direction he last saw Red Scorpion.

In turn, he faintly heard bullets snapping past his ears, and he instinctively thought that the childhood mornings he thought were wasted at Sunday School must have been just barely enough for God to spare him from Red Scorpion's bullets, because he couldn't think of any other reason he was still standing.

He bolted, running away through the canyon as the sandstorm raged around him, feeling the bullets from Scorpion and the insurgents alike passing juuuuust by him. He couldn't see a goddamn thing, and each step felt heavy, leaden with sand as the wind manhandled him.

There was nowhere to go anyway. The desert was just about certain death, but it looked like certain death was his best bet now.

# CHAPTER 9:
# LIKE CHRISTMAS (EVE) MORNING

There's nothing in the world like morning in the African bush. Even when it's overcast, like this morning was, there would still be the dawn chorus of birds to gently rouse you from your peaceful slumber, even if you were cradled by the thick branches of a tall baobab tree overnight. And if that didn't do it, four deafening gunshots shattering the tranquility of nature would probably be enough to get you going.

"What the hell?" blurted Cobra, awoken from a dead sleep and now barely hanging onto the branch that was his bed last evening.

"Look at those razor-sharp senses," yawned the Professor, still fully clothed (for those of you who might be interested in that sort of thing). "Cat-like reflexes."

Cobra scrambled to get back on the branch, his legs spinning like egg-beaters in the open air.

"Don't worry, Professor," he panted. "I'm sure it's not those terrorists coming back to kill us this morning or anything."

"Not. Before. Coffee," she yawned again, rubbing the sleepiness from her eyes.

"Sure, let me just call room service," grunted Cobra as he pulled himself back up. He took up Priest's rifle and surveyed the veldt, stretching endlessly in all directions.

"Breakfast is served!" called Hyacinth from below.

154

"You were saying?" asked the Professor dryly.

"Hey. It's Christmas Eve. Merry Christmas, Professor."

"Merry Christmas, Cobra."


It wasn't easy climbing down from the tree, and if you're asking how they managed to climb up in the first place, I'll just say it was a hell of a lot more difficult than climbing down and leave it at that. The bonfire was out, but the embers were still smoldering; Xavier, Hyacinth and Mark were each huddled around it as Kevin fed it some sticks and twigs.

"Hey *Professor*," said teased Hyacinth. "I think your bra fell down from the tree last night."

*Oohs* from the group.

"Yeah, no," Professor said. "If anything happened last night, trust me, you all would know."

More *oohs*.

"What's going on? Who's shooting at us? Why aren't you all running in terror?" asked Cobra.

"That was just me, you know, saving us again," said Susan, her handgun smoking. Andres was beside her, and he was holding two dead helmeted guinea fowl from their rubbery necks.

"Did they attack you?" asked the Professor, sardonically.

"There was a whole school of them over there," Susan started.

"Flock," corrected Professor.

"And they were making noise this morning, and they look just like chickens. I thought we could use something to eat, seeing as how we went to bed without supper."

"Susan, how many more rounds do you have?" asked Cobra.

"Rounds of what?"

"Bullets, Susan, bullets."

"However many are in a clip, minus..."

"Magazine."

"Well, however many are in a *magazine*," she said in *Southern*, "minus three shots yesterday, and four shots this morning."

"Susan, listen to me," said Cobra. "You are not to shoot any more animals."

"Oh, come off your high zebra, Cobra," said Andres, birds dangling. "It's not like they're even endangered or anything."

"And it's not like you're about to get us breakfast," added Susan.

"Well, shit," concluded Cobra, seeing the hungry faces on all the guests. "Let's get that fire going, then. But Susan, no more shooting animals, understand?"

"No problem," she said. "What about people?"

\*\*\*

Cobra spearheaded the *defeathering the birds* initiative, since he had held onto Priest's knife and already had some experience.

"Survival course?" Mark had asked.

"Cooking class," Cobra had answered.

"Geez, is there anything this guy can't do?"

"Ask my ex-girlfriend that one day."

Soon, Kevin had stoked the fire to something that could barbecue the guinea fowls, and Cobra allowed Hyacinth and him to impale the birds on sticks and apply some direct heat.

"Not too closely," Cobra warned.

"I'm going for some caramelization here," answered Hyacinth, and to Mark: "Want to try for a while?"

"Think I've had enough fire for a little while," he said, reaching into his bag for a sketchbook and some pencils. "Are you at all concerned that those poachers will see our fires and come after us?"

"It burned brightly last night for a long time, and they didn't show. That guy…" answered Cobra.

"Priest," said the Professor.

"He was a priest?" asked Kevin.

"No, that's his name," said the Professor.

"Priest managed to find us even before the fire, and if he managed to make it back to their camp, they'd all know our location for sure. And if he didn't make it back…" said Cobra.

"Then you killed him," said Xavier.

"Let's not jump to conclusions…"

"Doesn't that bother you? That you might have killed someone?"

"It would have bothered me more if he'd have killed me, to be honest. Or one of you. Or all of you."

"I suppose you've killed dozens of people before," said Xavier. "You were probably some mercenary or something."

"He strikes me more as a lumberjack," said Kevin.

"Rugby player," said Mark.

"Army medic," said Hyacinth.

"Disgraced English Nobleman," said Susan, adding, "who's good with accents."

"Trash collector," said Andres.

"Please, people. I'm just some guy who really loves animals," said Cobra, before noting, "Give those birds a turn; you want to make sure you really roast the hearts."


It took about half an hour before Cobra felt that the guinea fowl were well-done enough to consume; Andres complained that they were tough and burnt, but Cobra insisted.

"You'll be happy we played it safe. We've seen some exotic wildlife, but between the stress, the alcohol, and the dehydration, we're lucky none of us have come across any wild ass yet," he said.

"Is that some kind of extinct zebra?" Mark asked. "Like

Przewalski's Horse? Or the Quagga?"

"No, it's the polite way of saying when a safari-goer has the shits. Speaking of, how is everyone feeling this morning?"

"Great," Andres said in a tone that suggested that he was, in fact, *not* great. "For one thing, we didn't all die of carbon monoxide poisoning every time the wind shifted the smoke from the bonfire into the tree hollow last night."

"Sorry about that, but it did keep the hyenas away. Might have kept you safe from the mosquitoes and the flies, too."

"Speak for yourself," said the Professor, scratching some bug bites on her arm.

"Don't worry; if you have malaria, you won't feel the symptoms until two or three weeks from now when you're back home. Xavier and Kevin?"

"Tired, irritable," said Xavier. "Didn't sleep so great."

"Sounds like home," Kevin muttered.

"I think the swelling's gone down."

"What about you, Mark?" asked Cobra.

"My hands don't hurt at all," he said cheerfully.

"It's probably because all the nerves have been burnt," said Hyacinth. "Like this guinea fowl."

"Let me say how delicious it is!" said Mark, tearing a piece off with his teeth. "Anyway, the pain'll come back later, but I can still hold a pencil, so it can't be that bad."

"Hyacinth?"

Hyacinth spit out a bullet.

"Ankle hurts, but if I can use that roll bar you brought as a walking stick, I shouldn't slow us down. What is the plan, if you don't mind me asking?"

"Glad you asked. Since it looks like everyone is on the mend, and since we have a lot of daylight, we're going to start hiking back toward the direction of camp."

"Wait, what?" asked Susan. "I thought you said we were twenty miles away!"

"We don't have to make it all the way back; just far enough that we can cross the river safely and get to a rendezvous point where Wyatt can come get us, about ten miles. Easy hike at a slow, deliberate pace."

"Why can't he just come get us now?" asked Xavier.

"The river's current is too strong. I know of a foot-bridge that we can use; a car wouldn't make it over. He wouldn't know where to look for us over here anyhow."

"That's looney-toons," said Andres. "Either he's coming for us or he isn't. Why do you think Wyatt's looking for us now? Why didn't he come last night?"

"Too dark, too dangerous, and he trusted me with you."

"We trusted you, and look where we are!"

"Still breathing, for better or worse," said Cobra. "Besides, I'd like to put some more distance between us and those poachers."

"I thought they weren't interested in us," said Kevin.

"They're not, but do you want to chance it? Look, people. The Cobra Express pulls out of Baobab Station in twenty minutes. You can either stretch out so you don't blow a hamstring and follow me, a guy who knows this country as well as anyone, or stay here and wait for some*one* or some*thing* to shoot you or to eat you. I mean, Susan *does* have a gun and eight bullets."

The Professor eyed Cobra skeptically but said nothing.

"What about Kotani?" asked Hyacinth. "Those men have him, don't they?"

Cobra paused, looking up at the cloudy sky that fully obscured the sunrise.

"I don't know, Hyacinth. I'm working on it."


After breakfast, the Professor kicked some dirt on the fire, extinguishing it with a minimum of billowing. Everyone went to neutral corners around the big baobab to prepare for the arduous trek ahead. While waiting, Mark sat on a rock, delicately sketching a torpid agama lizard trying to heat up for the day. Hyacinth, in turn, quietly took pictures of Mark without him noticing, a bittersweet smile on her lips.

"That's not bad," remarked Cobra. "I thought you were a gym teacher, not art."

"Oh, this? This is just for fun, a little creative outlet, nothing more. Hyacinth's got the real talent."

"No, it's a good likeness," said Cobra. "I read that Paul Kruger was fond of these lizards. I heard he even kept a few as pets when the British forced him out of South Africa a little over a hundred years ago in like, 1901 or 02 or something."

"Yeah, along with some two million British pounds of the country's treasury," added Hyacinth, getting one more click in.

"Good for him, planning for retirement," said the Professor, admiring Mark's drawing.

"Not quite," said Hyacinth. "It all disappeared, like it never existed. Some say it was buried somewhere in the Blyde River area of Mpumalanga, not too far from where Kruger park is today, and Kruger never managed to reacquire it."

"You know your history, Hyacinth," said Cobra. "That story is local legend around here. People still look for that gold, like chasing for Bigfoot or El Dorado."

"Well, as long as we're not doing anything…" suggested the Professor. "I've got student loans that I'm planning on defaulting, but it'd be nice to pay some of them back…"

"Mpumalanga is hundreds of miles from here, Professor."

"Do you think anyone will ever find it?" asked Mark.

"I'm a hundred percent certain that they won't."

"Pretty confident," said Mark. "Why do you think so?"

"Because it doesn't exist."

"You don't believe in Kruger's gold?"

"I didn't say that; I said it doesn't exist," said Cobra, getting to his feet. "Which bush did we say the bathroom was again?"

\*\*\*

Kevin touched Xavier's chin, gently turning his head to get a better look at his wound.

"I said I'm fine," said Xavier, moving his hand away.

The two of them stood on the other side of the tree, gathering what few things they still had with them.

"This again?"

"You just called me irritable in front of the others," said Xavier.

"I did not. You called yourself that, and I was trying to make a little joke," protested Kevin.

"Ha ha, very funny. I'm glad you can at least commit to a gag."

"I'm not committed? I just dragged you across two miles of jungle while it looked like you were about to die!"

"Now who's being dramatic."

Kevin turned away, and Xavier reached out to him.

"I'm sorry," he said. "I am tired. I'm hungry, scared, and I don't feel well."

Kevin turned back to him. "Well, what do you want to do? Do you want to stay here and wait to be rescued? Because I'll stay with you, if you want. You know I will."

"How much faith do you have in our guide?"

"Some. I don't know. Why?"

"What if we had Susan's gun?"

\*\*\*

"I think Hyacinth's catching on," said the Professor, as she and Cobra did one last sweep through baobab tree to make sure they'd left nothing. "She's really smart, and very perceptive."

161

"Catching on to what?"

"To the fact that you're not really planning on taking us back toward the lodge."

Cobra stood, facing her.

"This baobab didn't seem so bad. Probably a little crowded, but if it rained again last night, we'd have been the ones who got soaked."

"Cobra…"

"Look," he whispered to her. "We'd never make it back to the lodge. It's just too damn far, and we're walking wounded. Also, there's a big pride of lions between us and home. What we really need is a vehicle, and there's only one way we can get one of those now."

"Why don't you leave these people here then and go off on your own? You have a gun, and apparently, so do they."

"I can't. It'd be riskier to leave them on their own. They're kind of lovable, but they're a bunch of idiots, and they don't like each other. The animals are too dangerous, and there is the possibility that those people come back. I mean, maybe *you* want to stay with them, make sure they're safe, while I go on alone."

"Uh-uh, nope," she said quickly.

"No, really, Professor. You know a thing or two about wildlife, and you've shown you can take care of yourself."

"Aw, that's sweet, but hard pass. You know, you still never told me what Black Tiger is."

"Didn't I?"

"Didn't."

"You sure?"

"Sure."

"Just a guy I worked with a long time ago; not really germane to our current situation."

"Fine, don't tell me. Don't tell any of them what your plan really is. But I hope you understand that you're gambling with all of their lives, and you better be up to the task here. Your cavalier attitude and macho swagger may fool them, but not me."

"You know, I see what you're doing here, adding on the responsibility, but what you don't realize is that I actually perform my best under pressure," he said.

"Well, where was that attitude last night in the tree?"

"What?"

"Nothing."

Andres took a good, long piss on the edge of a thicket of dense acacia bushes, and it was far and away the best thing about his morning so far. Internally, he noted that the so-called *golden hour* (as photographers called it) had passed, even though it was dark and cloudy. Not that it mattered; he cursed his camera's misfortune.

He didn't really notice a small bachelor herd of impala, a kind of antelope analogous to a white-tailed deer of the bush, quietly nibbling away at some buds and leaves, their modest black horns turning upward from the base of their skulls.

"Hey," said Susan, approaching him from behind and startling him enough to suffer a modest backsplash.

"Men's room, *fraulein*, men's room."

"Thank you for sticking up for me last night."

"I did nothing of the kind. You were right, they were wrong, and that's all." He zipped up and wiped his fingertips on his filthy khaki shorts.

"Well, thanks for not treating me like a child, like everyone else, then. At least, with the gun and all."

"Anyone who can fire a gun at a complete stranger with no hesitation deserves at least some consideration, I think, be they child or adult."

"I'm nineteen," she said. "Swear to God."

"I believe you," he said. "I'm forty-nine, if it matters to

you."

"You know Michel Merle?"

"From the news? Yes. Personally? No."

"Well, I do. Personally," she paused, and then said, "Intimately."

"How can that be?"

"He likes his women young, and two years ago, I was just young enough," she said. "I met him at a party in Provence. I had run away from home with the money my parents had saved for college."

"But come, now. You must have recognized him, didn't you?"

"I didn't watch the news when I was in high school, Andres. All I knew was that I needed to get away from Georgia, to travel, to see the world. My parents and I didn't, well, see eye to eye."

"But you did see eye-to-eye with the head of the most notorious Parisian crime syndicate in twenty years? How could you not know of his reputation?"

"To a kid in Savannah, everything about Michel seemed extraordinary, larger-than-life, high-society. I wouldn't learn of his... cruelty until later."

"I don't imagine Michel Merle is the type to let his women come and go freely," said Andres.

"I knew I had to get out. I had tried twice and failed, and he punished me. Severely. But there wasn't a snowball's chance in hell that I was going to let him do to me what he'd done to the other girls."

"So you escaped."

"I did, with a shit-ton of his money, which I both needed and felt he owed me. But he didn't just let me go. He's been after me, his men dogging me all over Europe. I may not really be a travel writer, but I have been here and there. It's a good enough cover."

"And now, you've found your perfect hiding place, in the middle of nowhere, out of even Michel Merle's reach."

"I did come here, looking for a place to stay. I was hopeful I could beg for a job at the lodge, stay off the grid for a long time. Maybe he'd give up on me. But when those poachers attacked us, I…"

"…assumed it was your pursuers, after you, somehow finding you."

"I think I blew it. I'm not supposed to have this gun, and if we get back, Cobra's going to tell Mr. Northside, and they'll kick me out."

"Maybe not. You did save his life. You are quite resourceful, really," said Andres. "I wonder if you could even help do me a favor."

"Like what?"

"I wonder if you might help me *borrow* Hyacinth's camera. Just for a little while."

Susan raised an eyebrow and just said, "Hm."

"I like you, Susan," said Andres. "You're a survivor. Just stay close to me, and you'll be safe from harm."

"Soooooo…" said Cobra softly, tip-toeing up to Susan and Andres very slowly. "I don't know if you're aware, so I'll go ahead and tell you, that you're standing about ten feet from a white rhinoceros, the second-heaviest land animal on Earth."

"You," barked Andres, not really listening. "Can't I even relieve myself in peace on this cursed holiday?"

"Sh," said Cobra, slowly pointing to the five-thousand-pound beast quietly ambling through the thicket, his head low as his wide lips vacuumed up the grass underneath it. The big rhinoceros snapped through branches without paying them the slightest attention.

Andres and Susan's eyes grew wide. Susan slowly reached into her purse for her gun, but Cobra shook his head, careful not to make any sudden movements.

"Don't," he whispered. "Couldn't kill him with that pop-gun anyway, not even with a perfect shot through the eye."

Still, the rhino seemed all but oblivious to the three of them, grazing peacefully. It was close enough that Susan saw the cracks on his dry skin and the tiny hairs inside his swiveling ears. It smelled musty.

"Be still," instructed Cobra. "His eyesight is very poor. He may just walk right on by."

"That's the plan? Do nothing?" whispered Andres.

Cobra scanned the immediate vicinity, quickly finding what he was looking for.

"See that jackalberry tree about twenty feet from here?"

"I don't know the names of the trees!" Andres whined.

"The tree. That tree. The only tree, over there behind me."

They both nodded.

"If our friend here gets…"

Suddenly, the rhinoceros froze, its enormous grayish white body tense. He snorted, blowing out from his big, open nostrils on either side above his upper lip. At once, he raised his head like the front end of a bulldozer, inhaling deeply, and the three of them got a good look at its four-foot, scimitar-shaped horn, impressive even by pre-poaching era standards. He could shish-kabob all three of them and still have room for tomatoes, onions and peppers.

"Run," Cobra said quietly.

"Did you say…"

With a grunt, the rhino came crashing through the thicket, busting through the thorny vegetation which offered him all the resistance of popcorn. Andres squealed and bolted toward the tree, Susan right behind him. The rhino galloped after them at a speed that looked impossible for a creature so huge.

It was as though Andres had wings; he was up that tree so quickly he couldn't have gotten that high faster if he had an escalator.

"Don't look back!" coached Cobra, running the other direction and waving his hands frantically.

Susan looked back and saw the R-train throttling towards her, kicking up a cloud of dust and dirt; she threw herself upon the trunk and tried to shimmy upwards, until Andres reached for her hand and helped heave her up.

The rhino rammed into the tree, shaking it free of dry leaves and nearly dislodging Andres and Susan, clutching the branches for dear life. The beast furiously scraped his horn on the tree's trunk as if he were a butcher sharpening his cleaver.

"Rhinoceros!" yelled Cobra, about thirty yards away, jumping up and down and making an awful ruckus. "Are you looking for something in particular, or are you just browsing?"

"Are you serious?" screamed Andres. "How is that funny?!"

"You're right!" called Cobra. "White rhinos are grazers, not browsers. It doesn't really work, zoologically speaking!"

"Do something!" shrieked Susan.

The rhino was still butting into the tree, frantically thrusting its horn up and down like a kid trying to get his kite unstuck from a tall branch. Andres felt the tree's limb straining under the weight even as Susan detected a faint snapping sound near the trunk.

"Rhinoceros!" yelled Cobra again. "Come and get me!"

But the rhino was fixated on Andres and Susan, as if they had personally besmirched him.

"Jesus, did you say something about his mother?" Cobra asked, walking a few steps closer to him. He picked up a small rock and threw it, pelting the rhino in the shoulder.

That did it. The rhino turned around and saw Cobra on foot, and sure enough, took off like a rocket. Cobra had accomplished phase one of his plan at the exact moment he realized that he did not have a phase two. He bolted back towards the thicket and the dense, tangled thorn bushes.

He'd never outrun him, and he knew it. Only a distraction could save him now. Or, perhaps, his recollection of his surroundings.

Cobra sprinted towards the group of impala - the small antelope herd that had been anxiously watching the scene unfold - as the rhino quickly gained ground behind him. He suddenly baseball slid to the right into an acacia bush, and the rhino came so close to trampling him that he felt the sting of the little rocks and pebbles the animal kicked up.

The rhino kept running, now locked onto the impala, which darted out in every direction. They were easily fleet-footed enough to avoid the big bruiser, who, frustrated, gave out a great snort and gave up the pursuit. Annoyed, he ambled back into the thicket and resumed his breakfast.

Cobra stood up, his clothes covered in dirt and his face and arms replete with thin, bloody scrapes from the thorns. Impressed with himself, he only now did the calculation that there was probably only a thirty percent chance the rhino would have followed the antelope and not him.

The branch broke, and Andres and Susan both fell straight down, landing hard on the ground below.

"My coccyx," cried Andres (again).

Susan stumbled awkwardly to her feet and offered him a hand.

"Aw, who says Chivalry's not dead?" said Cobra. "Let's not make falling out of trees a habit. You've just met the critically endangered white rhinoceros, *rhino* meaning nose, and *ceros* meaning horn. They have poor eyesight, but a remarkable sense of smell, and are actually not as bad-tempered as their black rhino cousins."

Andres angrily pushed Cobra's hand away.

"I thought you said whatever you do, don't run! Wasn't that one of your precious rules?"

"What I meant was, don't run from *predators*."

# CHAPTER 10:
# MUDSLIDE

"I survived a rhino charge by my quick thinking and ingenuity alone," boasted Susan, while Andres' simultaneous account of the incident was different, but equally succinct: "That miserable Cobra almost got me killed yet again."

"Please, people," smiled Cobra, taking a perverse joy in Susan's and Andres' struggling. "You're both wrong."

The party had moved out and pressed on in single file, with Cobra in the front and the rest in tow, spread out about ten yards. Where yesterday the landscape was parched and brown and choking for want of moisture, today it was transformed into a green paradise. After only one hard rain, grass began to probe tentatively from the ground below, and trees began to blossom brilliantly. Hornbills and drongos swooped in from above, taking advantage of the insects and other invertebrates the moisture had encouraged out of their subterranean slumber.

It was not a nice day, though. Thick clouds effectively blocked the light, and if you hadn't been looking for the sunrise peeking above the horizon at dawn, you might not have known east from west.

"How do you know we're going the right way if you can't tell which direction we're going?" asked Xavier.

"Who says I don't know what direction we're going?" Cobra replied.

"Well? Which direction?"

Cobra kept marching, offering only: "straight ahead, of course."

A light rain fell, and everyone hoped it would not get worse but knew that it probably would. In the far distance, the Professor saw lightning. She kept it to herself.

They were, it seemed, following the river from up above the bank. The ground was muddy and wet, and where possible, Cobra lead them away from the water.

"Let's not get too close. The dirt is pretty soft, and we don't want to go for another swim."

"Because of the crocodiles, right?" called out Mark.

"Yes, like those guys down there," Cobra said, indicating three large females laying torpid on the opposite bank, charcoal-colored with armored scutes rising from their backs like small sails. Hyacinth snapped a few pictures, to Andres' visible disgust.

"They'll be inactive for a little while until it heats up and regulates their temperatures. They could even have clutches of eggs nearby that they'd defend very aggressively. I don't need to tell you about the death roll and all that."

"Nope," said Xavier, pretending to know that the death roll was a crocodile's preferred method of killing prey. Since their jaws don't really have the capacity to chew, the croc bites down and locks onto its victim and barrel-rolls violently until chunks of flesh, sometimes whole appendages, are torn off by the massive force into swallowable pieces. Sometimes other crocs helped to expedite this process; it was often after the reptile submerged and drowned the struggling animal. Honestly, Xavier was probably better off not knowing any of that, especially when Cobra offered this next nugget of wisdom:

"To tell you the God's honest truth, though, I'm less concerned about crocs than I am about hippos. They kill way more people in Africa. You see, they spend most of the day submerged in the water to protect themselves from the sun, but the males, they'll fight each other over territory. They have enormous tusks that they sometimes even kill each other with when they spar."

"Well, let's not spar with hippos then, check," said Kevin.

"Of course, because that'd be crazy. But what you have to worry about is getting between a hippo and the water. You see, they sometimes leave the rivers and watering holes at night to go look for vegetation. They might even go out on a cloudy, rainy day when they don't have to worry about sun damage, but when they come back, if you're between them and the water, guess what?"

"They quietly wait for you to pass and then tip-toe back home?" answered the Professor sardonically.

"They dance ballet in a tutu," said Kevin.

"Sure, if that tutu is made of human skin, I suppose. A hippo can open its mouth almost four feet wide, maybe a hundred and fifty degrees. While charging, hippos have been known to bite people cleanly in half, like a tyrannosaurus rex or something. You'd see your legs up in a tree somewhere before you realized you just got killed."

"Fuck," said Xavier. "And then what?"

"You die," said Cobra, confused. "Blood loss? Shock? A bright light and angels?"

"Jesus, Cobra," said the Professor, shaking her head. "These stories work in the car, but not on foot."

"I'm only trying to emphasize how important it is to be careful, that's all."

"It's *your* job to be careful, Cobra," reminded the Professor.

"And it's *everybody's* job to listen to me. Don't get too close to the water."


It seemed like they were on the move for hours, but in reality, they'd only been trekking behind Cobra for about thirty-five minutes. The light rain was irritating, and their clothes chafed, but it beat the sunburn that would have been their reward for slogging through the bush with no protection this morning. Knowing that there were animals out there just out of sight created a tension that made some, like Xavier, Susan, and Andres, uneasy, but in others, like Hyacinth, Mark and Kevin, heightened a long-lost connection with nature that had been dulled by so many years of civilization. And the Professor was fine, in her element and well within her comfort zone. This day would soon push the limits of that comfort zone.

Hyacinth would stop briefly to click a few shots - the crocs in the river, a moth on a tree branch - as she hobbled forward, her injured ankle slowing her down as she supported herself on the metal bar from the Land Rover. Susan sidled up to her.

"Hurt much?" she asked.

"It's talking to me a little."

"You're really tough, Hyacinth. I hope I'm in as good condition when I'm your age one day."

"Gee, thanks."

"You know, a long, long time from now."

"Yeah, I got it."

"Are you a photographer?"

"Well, you see me here with this here camera and these zoom lenses and this bag of film, so obviously, I bake cakes," said Hyacinth, shielding her camera from the rain with a plastic cover.

"Like, professionally, though?"

"I've won a few contests," Hyacinth admitted.

"I'd like to see your stuff. Maybe I could use your pictures in my travel blog. Make you some money, get you some exposure."

"Oh, would you? That would be so swell," smirked Hyacinth.

"I mean, I'd make sure you were paid under the table. I know you can only have so much income when you're dependent on Social Security before taxes become a problem."

"Sure. I'd even be happy to shoot your *quinceañera*, if you'd like."

"You see? You're cool, you're hip for your age, even if that comment was mildly racist, but as I'm not Mexican, I take no offense. I once enjoyed the *quinceañera* of the daughter of Mexico City's mayor, and it was one of the most splendid affairs I ever had the distinction of attending."

"I'm sure it was. Could you move? You're standing in my light."

"You want me to carry some of your stuff for you? It must be hard enough marching through this muck on that broken ankle as it is."

"It's not broken; barely a sprain, I bet."

"Come on, let's get some of the weight off you. I'll even carry your camera and hand it to you when you need it, like an assistant."

"Sure, if you let me carry your gun and bag full of money."

"Thanks, but I must politely decline."

"You sure? I don't mind at all. I'm a licensed **NRA** member, which you can be too, in a few years."

"I don't think that's in the spirit of what I was suggesting, Hyacinth."

"Then please stay out of my light."

Behind Hyacinth and Susan walked Xavier, who stumbled on a tree root until the Professor took him by the arm.

"Thanks," he said.

"No problem. I'm glad it was a tree and not another snake."

"Cobra said the chances that we'll even see another snake are remote."

"He's right. Statistically, it's wildly improbable that we've already seen so many."

"You don't have to placate me; I'm not a child."

"Seriously. There have been times when I've been in Saguaro National Park actively looking for coachwhips and black-tailed rattlers and not come across one for days. Generally, they avoid us."

They resumed the march.

"So, snakes, huh?"

"Yup. It's not exactly Jane Goodall and the chimps, but one of my professors hooked me up with a scientist at WCS who needed someone for a project studying reptiles in the desert, and I couldn't refuse. Once I have my doctorate, I'll use the experience to start my own research project back home, maybe pronghorns or something."

"Do you like it? Snakes, working in the desert, that sort of thing?"

"I love it. It's a little lonely, and most of the time it's just typing data into a computer, but I get plenty of fresh air and I sleep like a baby every night."

"I used to sleep like a baby every night. I'd wake up every forty-five minutes and cry. A little Xanax and a lot of therapy later, and here I am."

"And here you are. Why Africa? Why not Bora Bora or Copenhagen or something?"

"Do I seem a little *fish-out-of-water* to you?"

"No. It's just that it's a long way from home, and it's not the kind of vacation most people settle on, especially for what it costs."

"Kevin and I were going through some brochures - India, Thailand - and this looked kind of fun." He leaned closer to her and whispered playfully, "don't tell anyone, but we're actually *gay*."

They both laughed.

"We both work in finance, boring suit-and-tie jobs. This seemed so exotic, so different. I was hoping that maybe a radical change of scenery might, I don't know..."

He looked up ahead at Kevin, who was having a conversation with Mark.

"...kind of make or break us, I guess. It's silly, now that I say it out loud."

"I don't know about that," answered the Professor, looking ahead to Cobra and Andres at the front of the caravan. "There's definitely a magic to this place."

"Magic," laughed Xavier. "So, what do you think our chances really are?"

"Chances of what?"

"Surviving."

"One hundred percent. They say that one of the biggest factors that go into surviving a crisis is having a positive attitude. That, and this is still my vacation, and I'm not going to die before I get all the days that I paid for."

"I'll take those odds. Still, I'd feel a lot better if I were armed…"

"Honestly, I think you might be a little harsh," said Mark, brushing the back of his hand against a tree by accident and recoiling in pain.

"He does this all the time, making a scene and forcing the issue," said Kevin. He was keeping a close eye not to get too close to the edge by the river.

"To be fair, this isn't like a long line at the Louvre or a breakdown on Space Mountain. This is a pretty extreme vacation obstacle, and considering the head trauma, I think he's hanging pretty tightly."

"He *can* be very charming…"

"But…"

"Yes, he also has a really amazing butt, and this conversation just took a turn I didn't expect."

"No, I mean, you were saying he can be very charming,

*however…"*

"Oh. I don't know, it's just that I don't know if we're really clicking. It's been almost half a year."

"How'd you meet?"

"We were both on a soccer league. Did you know there are adult clubs for just about every sport? Soccer, lacrosse, softball… even ultimate frisbee, whatever that is."

"I'm a retired gym teacher," said Mark. "I get enough sports. You were on the same team?"

"The opposite, actually. He literally knocked me right off my feet. I hope this isn't, you know, making you uncomfortable."

"Why?"

"Sometimes people aren't cool with, you know…"

"Because I have a little extra mileage on me? You don't think they had gay people in the seventies? I think they invented them back then."

"You and Hyacinth seem like you've got it together. How many years are you married?"

"A lot. A whole lot of them. The days are long and the years are short. One day you wake up, and all of sudden, your hair is gray and you're old. Might as well be gray and old with someone you love."

"I thought I heard you say you've been to Africa a few times."

"We got engaged in Tanzania, married in Kenya, anniversaries in Zambia and Botswana, back to Kenya a few times," said Mark, going through a rolodex of memories in his head as they continued marching forward.

"Why here? Why do you love Africa so much?"

Mark smiled. "At first, it was just a dream of mine, to see the endless plains of Kenya. When we were young, I discovered it was a dream of Hyacinth's too. They say once you've been to Africa, it stays with you, that you have to return. It gets in your blood."

"Like malaria."

"Yes! Like malaria," laughed Mark. "But you can feel it, can't you? There's something really special about this place, like you can't believe places like this can even still exist anymore, that there can still be lands where lions roam and elephants march over the savannah. Like, how can it be that mankind hasn't extinguished it, snuffed it out, like we have all over the supposedly civilized world? That it's still here, just hanging on? I've emptied my pockets many times over just to be here, to feel free and young like when the world was new, far away from all the made-up problems and conventions and responsibilities that society chains us down with. Does that make sense to you?"

"Yeah, Mark. I think it does."

"And to be able to share that feeling with the love of your life, throughout your life, well… there's a life well-spent, even if I was just a teacher for most of it."

"I really envy you, Mark," said Kevin. "The way you and Hyacinth are. Anyone'd be lucky to spend their 'forever' with someone they're so devoted to."

"Well," said Mark, smiling softly. "*Nothing* lasts forever."


Up at the front, Cobra was careful not to set too fast a pace. It was all too easy for the leader to go too quickly and have his party not keep up, fanning out a quarter mile behind as they struggled to follow. Then, not seeming to be part of a large group, they'd be easy pickings for any of the many capable killers that could be stalking them now.

He looked downward as his boots pushed through the mud, trying to avoid getting too close to the edge of the embankment. He hadn't seen *it* for a quarter mile, and he feared that the rain that helped create *it* may have now washed *it* away, but he found *it* again: a long, three-inch-wide track that blazed forward in a straight line as though a large snake had slithered through the wet ground without undulating left and right.

"What is it now?" asked Andres, right behind him.

"Nothing. Just some spoor."

"Shit? You're looking at shit?"

"That's *scat*; *spoor* means tracks."

"I don't see anything."

"Of course, you don't. You don't have a specially-trained eye to look for these sorts of things."

"I know what a damn animal track looks like, man. They're all more or less the same, with big circles in the middle and three or four little ones in the front."

"Unless it's a rock python that has no feet."

"Then why the hell are we following it?"

"Relax, Andres. This track is old. This fellow may have passed by here more than a day ago," said Cobra as he continued, occasionally keeping his eye on the *motorcycle* track he was actually chasing.

"I don't need you talking down to me, Cobra. You may have fooled the others, but not me."

"Go on, Andres. You've been so hopeful and encouraging so far; let's see what your brilliant deduction is."

"You talk like some big roughneck, an expert survivalist, but in reality, you'd be more qualified to drive a taxicab than a safari vehicle. You want us to trust you with our lives, but what are you, twenty-nine years old?"

"Twenty-five."

"You're just like all the other meatheads who can do a few pushups and expect all the ladies to throw themselves at you. You're barely out of college, if you even attended university at all. So what that you have twenty-inch biceps and can ride a zebra to work every day. So far, every decision you've made has put us only further and further into harm's way. And with your ego, you don't even care."

"Is that what this is? Did the jocks pick on little Andres in school?"

"No, all the cool kids were obviously into photography," spat Andres.

"I'm sorry you broke your camera. I'm sorry you don't like the food at the lodge. I'm sorry it was a bumpy flight from Johannesburg. I am, however, responsible for none of these things," said Cobra.

"You are, however, responsible for having our vehicle destroyed and your guests injured. For me almost being swept away by a flash flood. For setting up a picnic where two hungry lions attacked us. For having no backup plan for getting us safely back or communicating with the lodge. I blame you for all of this, and I will hold you accountable for every scrape any of us suffers on this fiasco."

"The poachers destroyed our car and hurt the guests. I saved you from a flash flood. I got us away from the lions with no casualties," retorted Cobra.

Cobra continued marching, glancing back at the people lagging behind, and wiping the rain from his face.

"You're right, though. I didn't have a backup plan to communicate with Wyatt and Katy. That's on me; that's my fault. And if anyone gets hurt, that's entirely my fault too. Whatever happened to Kotani is also completely my fault. You're a glass-empty kind of guy, Andres, and I can see you're kind of a loner. I can respect that. I hope I can change your opinion of me by the end of this experience, whether you admit it or not. And if not, I'll still have all of this," Cobra said, gesturing to the vast wild landscape surrounding them. "And you'll still have..."

Cobra looked at Andres, and he couldn't make out the expression on Andres' face. There was something expectant about it, as if he were assuming Cobra would say *'and you'll still have nothing,'* and then feel familiar pity and disdain. Cobra sensed a profound loneliness.

"And you'll still have a new camera. I'll have Wyatt replace it."

Andres' lip quivered almost imperceptibly, and he replied, "Good. I expect nothing less."

Cobra took his hat off and drained some of the rainwater that had been pooling up within. He thought he heard the shrieks of some Sykes' monkeys or vervets to the east, which would be a concern if they had spotted a predator. Cobra wondered if there even were Sykes' monkeys in South Africa.

"Have you ever read Bernhard Grzimek?" asked Andres.

"Sure. *Serengeti Must Not Die.* A must-read for anyone considering a career in the bush. He and his son Michael did a lot of pioneering conservation in Tanzania, made a film about it I've never seen. Countrymen of yours, I believe."

"I'm told Bernhard was a distant cousin of mine. I never knew him."

"You're shitting me. Is that true?"

"Who knows," shrugged Andres. "It's a family legend that persists. Michael famously died in a plane crash in the Serengeti towards the end of the project, and all his father could do was weep."

"I know," said Cobra. "They buried him out there, so he could be with those animals he loved so much all his life, in that place he loved with his father. And his father did more than weep; he dedicated his life to conserving the wild places his son thought were important. Could do worse."

"It's probably bullshit," said Andres. "I bet it's just..."

Andres' left boot sunk into the muddy embankment, and it gave way beneath him. He slid downward and accelerated into a roll, tumbling towards the river below. The other guests froze.

"Everyone stay still; nobody go down there!" commanded Cobra.

"No problem!"

"You got it."

"Whatever you say!"

"Yeah, now they listen," Cobra muttered to himself.

Cobra turned his boots sideways against the muddy slope and leaned into the embankment, attempting to control his descent as best he could. His fingers clutched at the mud, and if nothing else, at least his hands would be exfoliated by the time this was done.

"Cobra! Why didn't you warn me about..." barked Andres, lying belly-down on a small patch of mud next to the flowing water, his appendages splayed out in a crawl.

"Sh," warned Cobra for the second time this morning (and probably not the last).

"Oh," said Andres, now alert to the fact that there were two motionless crocodiles lying on either side of him. Their mouths were both open wide revealing dinosaurian smiles, although as Cobra internally noted, *crocodiles and dinosaurs aren't particularly closely related*.

"Are those real tears, or crocodile ones?" asked Cobra quietly.

"You bastard," whispered Andres. "You miserable bastard."

"Females. It's still kind of cold. They're torpid for now, or they..."

One of them flicked her tail, and Cobra fell backwards on his ass. Andres suppressed a guffaw.

"You laugh, we're gonna die," said Cobra as quietly as he could while still conveying his irritation. Cobra slowly, deliberately rose to his feet and extended an arm to Andres. He helped him up and they cautiously retreated to the embankment. Both of them were covered in clay and mud.

"Don't worry; you look beautiful."

Andres slapped Cobra's hand away.

"We're really lucky, Andres. An hour later, and these ladies would have been ready for brunch."

"We just say late breakfast or early lunch, and go to Hell. I'm making a mental note of this incident."

"Fine, but keep it mental. If we're too loud, it could rouse even these slow reptiles."

"Oh my God!" screeched Xavier from up above, and the crocs opened their eyes, their protective membranes sliding horizontally like theater curtains being drawn.

"Shall we?" asked Andres, terrified once again.

"After you."

They scurried up the embankment as quickly as possible, struggling against the slippery mud wall, and found everyone thirty yards from the edge, inland, facing away from them.

Cobra dashed towards the group and saw that one was missing.

"What now? Where's…?"

"Right over there," said the Professor. "You can handle this, can't you?"

Kevin was a few yards away in a small clearing in the trees, surrounded by chacma baboons, including one particularly large fellow encircling him, shrieking like some kind of off-key air horn. Now, if you don't know anything about chacma, or cape, baboons, here're the crib notes: they can be almost four feet tall if standing erect, have frighteningly accurate memories that can even recall specific humans, can weigh up to a hundred pounds and have canine teeth larger than a leopard's (with whom they regularly fight, and often win). There can be upwards of fifty animals in a troop, and by the looks of it, there were at least twenty here, running around Kevin.

"Now how the hell did *this* happen?"

"I don't know," cried Xavier. "One minute, we were watching you and the crocs, and the next, well, these apes must have chased him away from us!"

"Technically, monkeys," corrected Cobra. "Most apes have no tails, and as you can see, these guys have long tails."

"See? That's what I've been trying to tell everyone," said the Professor.

"Gorilla's an ape," said Mark. "Chimp's an ape."

"Orangutan," offered Hyacinth.

"Orangutan," confirmed the Professor. "What about gibbons?"

"Bonobos, of course," said Cobra, "although most people just confuse them with the chimps."

"Oh my God, what is wrong with you fucking people?" howled Xavier.

Kevin was curled up in a fetal position with his head down on the ground as the apes, excuse me, *monkeys* kept running around him in circles, the massive patriarch standing on Kevin's back, baring his fangs.

"Use your karate," suggested Andres.

"You racist ass," cursed Xavier, "although he *does* have a red belt in tae kwon do."

"Listen to me," called Cobra. "Don't use your tae kwon do. I repeat, do *not* use your tae kwon do."

Kevin did not reply but stayed his current course of curling up and pretending this wasn't happening.

"Good," said Cobra. "You guys all stay here, and don't move."

"No problem!"

"You got it."

"Whatever you say!"

And with that, like Jesus walking on water, Cobra waded into the baboon circle and they flowed around him like a mountain stream around a boulder. Comparing Cobra to *Our Lord and Savior* might seem a little inflated, but it was both pretty impressive and totally awesome. He kept his shoulders back, his chest out, and his chin up as he radiated total confidence. If John Wayne shot himself up with HGH and then drank half a bottle of bourbon, he would have been approaching this level of manliness.

"That's amazing," gasped Mark.

"He's insane," cried Susan.

"Eh, he's all right," downplayed the Professor, but even she wore a big, dopey grin observing this spectacle.

The big one, the patriarch, roughed up Kevin, rifling through his clothes, tearing and shredding as necessary. He came up with a bag of chips that Kevin had squirreled away in one of his cargo pockets. The baboon held his treasure up to the sky and lorded it over his subjects, ripping it open and raining chips downward onto his coarse fur. The others hooted and squealed back in submission.

Cobra approached to within five feet of Kevin, still paralyzed with fear from this mugging, and the baboon. The big monkey made eye contact and exposed his fangs threateningly.

"You have a machine gun, you know," called Xavier.

"Shut up," hissed Cobra, not breaking eye contact with the animal, and not unslinging his semi-automatic rifle from his shoulder.

Cobra narrowed his eyes.

The baboon cocked his head like a Staffordshire terrier.

Cobra lowered his forehead.

The baboon tilted his neck the other way.

Cobra folded his arms.

The baboon brought his lips together, sheathing his canines.

"Holy shit," remarked Mark quietly.

"He's telepathic!" whispered Susan.

"He really is like Crocodile Dun…" said Xavier, when the baboon suddenly shrieked like it had been kicked in the nuts and launched itself onto Cobra, knocking him down on his back.

"Everybody RUN!" screamed Cobra as he furiously fought to avoid being bitten, baboon drool and potato chip crumbs showering down upon his face in equal measure.

It took zero encouragement.  Everyone, even the Professor, bolted back towards the river embankment and then in whichever direction they could find space, screaming like seven-year-olds watching *Halloween* for the first time.  The baboons ran around wildly, some chasing the people, some chasing each other.

Kevin picked his head up, tentatively opening one eye.  "Is it safe now?"

# CHAPTER 11: BUSHFIRE

"I thought you said, *'whatever you do, don't run!'*" cursed Andres.

"That's still true," said Cobra, his face covered in baboon scratches, but thankfully and improbably, no bites. "Except for rhinos, and now, baboons."

"Is that list comprehensive?" asked the Professor sardonically.

"Yes," said Cobra. "As of *now*."

It had taken ten minutes for the group to reassemble after that (*I'm sorry - I have to say it*) monkey business. Most of the baboons weren't genuinely interested in the people, whom they saw as dangerous and not worth the trouble. The patriarch had given up on Cobra when he was satisfied that A) he was carrying no food, and that B) he, himself, was not food. Cobra had heard stories of people killed by baboons even at tourist stops like the Cape of Good Hope, in the parking lot, and worse stories of baboons perforating people's faces clean off, and *still even worse* stories of baboons biting men's genitals and spitting them out like used chewing gum. For the ordeal, Cobra looked a mess, dirty and scratched and eyes slightly sunken from fatigue and stress which, let's be honest about it, only added to his roguish good looks.

The rain let up, although it was still cloudy, and Cobra took the group farther away from the river now. The vegetation was breaking down a little, and there was more open space, transitioning from savannah woodland to semi-arid desert. Peach-fuzz grass had begun to spring up, but the ground was still largely pink and ochre sand. It reminded Cobra of *another desert*, one that was just as unforgiving and even more difficult to forget.

It was mid-morning and God had cranked up the heat, sucking out the moisture endowed by the rain efficiently and quickly.

"I see you looking for tracks, Cobra," said Mark. "Anything we should worry about?"

"He said it's a rock python," interjected Andres. "Hell if it is, though."

"Well, it sure ain't a triceratops," said Cobra. "Either way, I don't have it anymore."

"What the..." said Hyacinth suddenly, searching through her bag when she noticed the familiar strap around her neck was missing. "Mark, do you have my camera?"

"No, hon."

"Well, that's odd. I don't have it. Are you sure you don't have it?"

"I'm sure. It's gotta be in your bag. Where else could it be?"

She double-checked, and then triple-checked, and then a frustrated, despondent expression overtook her face.

"It's gone. I must have put it down when Andres slid down the hill and forgotten about it," she said fretfully. "I mean, where else could it be?"

"That's terrible," said Andres insincerely. "From one photographer to another, I know what it's like to be in a once-in-a-lifetime location and not have your camera."

Susan looked at a configuration of trees in the distance, pretending to see some birds or something.

Mark said, "Cobra, do you mind if we backtrack a little? Just for half an hour or so?"

188

"I'm sorry, Mark. We're at least half a mile from that spot, and pretty soon we're going to be in the heat of the day. If Hyacinth left her camera there by mistake, there's a good chance one of those baboons ran off with it anyway," said Cobra.

"Damn it," cursed Hyacinth. "How could I have been so careless? I've never let that thing out of my sight."

"Don't beat yourself up over it, hon. You still have six or seven rolls you've already shot in your bag. I don't think we're going to forget this vacation, photos or not."

"I guess," she stammered, still not entirely willing to concede that she had overlooked this most prized possession. "I just... fine. Fine. Let's just go."

"You can use mine if you like, Hyacinth," offered Kevin. "It's just a simple point-and-click, but I just loaded this roll before the apes."

"Or mine," said the Professor. "I'm barely using it."

"Thank you, both of you. You're both very kind. I'm all right, just a little disappointed. Let's get on with the show."

They continued forward, and Andres muttered, "Nobody offered to lend me a camera when mine got smashed."

"Because you've been a prick to everybody, and nobody likes an asshole," muttered Xavier, just out of earshot.


Cobra held up his hand, indicating that everyone should stop, but since he didn't explicitly teach them that signal, everyone kept walking past him anyway.

"You're dead, and you're dead, and so are you and you, and all of you," said Cobra, shaking his head. "You continued walking when I wanted you to stop, and now a pride of lions hiding in the tall grass has killed you, vacation over, life over."

"You have died of dysentery," said the Professor, referencing an old computer game, and laughing at him.

"You didn't tell us to stop," said Susan. "Why didn't you

tell us to stop if you wanted us to stop?"

"Because sometimes, it's important to be silent, so we don't alert our presence to nearby danger."

"Is there nearby danger?" asked Xavier.

"Well, no."

"Then why didn't you just tell us to stop?" asked Xavier.

"All right, from now on, when my hand goes up like that, it means *stop*. Cease. Desist. Become inert. Got it?"

Everyone nodded.

"Now, stop for a moment and check this out," said Cobra, pointing to a large boulder. The Professor was the first to see it.

"Oh my God," she said, in awe. "It's rock art."

Painted on the boulder was the effigy of an of antelope, stylized but recognizable, with long, curved horns spiraling behind it: a kudu. The colors were muted by who-knows-how-many years of exposure to wind, sun and sand, but it persisted here anyway.

"Khomani San, or Bushmen as they're sometimes called by Westerners," explained Cobra. "Ancient, nomadic desert people."

"Can I... can I touch it?" asked the Professor, entranced.

"I think so. This could be thirty, forty thousand years old. If it's withstood all that weathering, I doubt a little oil from your skin is going to make much difference."

She delicately placed the very tips of her fingers on the boulder and closed her eyes, trying to reach across the dozens of centuries that separated her from the artist.

"A relic from a bygone age," commented Mark, in awe.

"Not entirely, Mark," explained Cobra. "The San may have genetic markers from the same people who left Africa to colonize the rest of the planet some two hundred thousand years ago - in a very real sense, they are the ancestors of us all, if you subscribe to what anthropologists call the Out-of-Africa premise. But they're still here, out in the bush, up in the Kalahari trying their best to hang on."

"You mean people still live like cavemen out here?" asked

Susan.

The Professor opened her eyes. "Show a little respect, Susan."

"I just mean to say that I find it hard to believe that there are humans out here in this wilderness shooting animals with bows and arrows and absorbing the sun with no clothes."

"The world is full of things that you would find hard to believe," said Cobra.

"Especially for someone who purports to have traveled the world," added the Professor.

"She has," said Andres. "But high society is not ancient society. You wouldn't know about such things, Cobra."

"I clean up real nice, Andres. And if you don't believe me about the San, look around. We're standing on the site of a settlement that I'd say was abandoned maybe a week ago."

"I see it now," said Xavier. There were some sticks scattered about in a concentric circle on top of a faint pile of ash. "Someone made a fire here."

"Good eye, X," said Kevin, clapping him on the back.

"And over there," Xavier noticed, excited that he was making these discoveries. "An animal skull."

"Oryx!" identified Mark, gleefully.

"We call them gemsbok down here, but yes," said Cobra, allowing the guests the wonder of finding archaeological evidence. "I bet if we sifted through the dirt and sand, we might even find an arrowhead or two."

Hyacinth was noticeably upset that she couldn't photograph the painting. Mark sensed her unhappiness and took her hand.

"Come on, let's find a spear-tip. You'll be like Mary Leakey," he said.

"Why don't you look over there," suggested Cobra, pointing to a few patches of dry grass protruding from the dirt.

Mark helped Hyacinth to her hands and knees and rooted

around where Cobra had indicated. The dull pain left her ankle now that she was no longer standing, and when she pulled gently on some of the grass, it displaced the dirt. It was lightly packed, even after the rain.

"What's this?"

"Hold the grass and carefully part the sand around it," instructed Cobra. The Professor watched intently, suspecting that Cobra knew exactly what was just beneath the dirt.

Mark helped, and Hyacinth came up with a large, white, oblong object with some dry grass protruding from the top: an ostrich egg.

"That's how these people survive. Those ostrich eggs are pretty much watertight. If it weren't for people like the San, and their imagination and ability to innovate, the human race may have gone extinct literal millennia ago," said Cobra.

"Yeah, OK, it's just a water bottle," said Andres, taking it from Hyacinth, ripping the grass out of it and taking a long drink, liquid dripping wastefully down his chin.

"What the hell!?" scolded Cobra. "You can't do that!"

"*Can't* is a word for people like *you*," said Andres. "A little minerally, but it suffices."

Cobra snatched the egg from Andres' hands and glared at him angrily.

"These people depend on these caches of water. They'll return and find it missing. We have no water to replace it!"

"There's still some in there if anybody wants. Come, now. You expect us to believe that you knew exactly where this campsite was, that you zeroed in on it with some sixth sense? You obviously planted this here to administer this children's history lesson."

"You're such a piece of shit, Andres," said the Professor, grinding the words through her teeth, until Cobra resumed:

"Well, then, let me just continue with the history lesson, if you like. The San, like many peoples across the world, were decimated by disease and programs of organized genocide perpetrated by those like you and me. Us Westerners worked pretty hard to wipe them out, and when that didn't succeed, we marginalized them politically and hoped pushing them out to the harshest environments would do the rest."

"Where have I heard this story before," said the Professor.

"The San were displaced off public lands in the thirties here in southern Africa, but I assure you, they still survive and they are very real, and we've committed a serious offense by using their stores of water."

"I didn't kill anyone, I didn't push anyone off their reservation, and I didn't take away anyone's right to vote. I just had a drink of water. I'm sure these supposed Bushmen will understand," said Andres.

"I hope so," said Cobra. "Because I think they've been watching us for a while now."

Xavier became tense and agitated, scanning panoramically for people that might be hiding in the grass, behind trees, wherever.

"Mark, we're going to need that bottle," said Cobra.

"I guess it's the least we can do," Mark replied, forking over the liquor he'd salvaged from the Land Rover. "It's not exactly Gatorade, but I'd rather find this than nothing if I were thirsty."

Cobra carefully buried the alcohol in the same position the ostrich egg was found and marked it with the tall grasses, burying it under shallow sand.

"These are Kotani's people," said Cobra. "Bottoms-up, if you're out there."

"Cobra, I think I found something," said Kevin.

"Arrowhead? Let's just leave it where we found it."

"Not unless San bows fire bullets," said Kevin, holding up old, discolored shell casings that had been hiding in the sand.

Cobra examined them.

"The poachers," said Susan.

"No. These are spent rounds, from World War Two

rifles," said Cobra.

"You're wrong," said Andres, swiping them and holding them up to the light. "The Great War. World War One. These are German, I bet, from a Gewehr 88. Real antiques."

"Horseshit," said the Professor. "How do you know that?"

"Superior education, *professor*, not like your rubbish American system that requires you to earn two post-graduate degrees for the same knowledge of four quality years of European university."

"But the Germans were active in Namibia back then," protested Mark.

"German Southwest Africa," corrected Andres.

"What I mean is, South Africa was still imperialist British back then, with the Germans being North and West of here," continued Mark.

"The Germans and the British had some *disagreements* in this part of the world a hundred years ago. I'm sure if we had the time, we might find some English shell casings around here as well. Do we?" asked Andres.

"We do not. Break's over, people. Let's get moving," declared Cobra.

They all got to their feet, some more sluggishly than others, and continued going wherever Cobra was taking them. The Professor lingered for a moment, absorbing the significance of this place. She touched the sand beneath her feet reverently and then reached out to the rock painting, struggling once more to make a connection before catching up with the group.

As the party trekked farther away, nobody noticed that Andres had gone back to the San campsite. That is, nobody noticed but Susan, who alone heard the click-click-clicking of a camera.

"Here comes the sun, doo-doo-doodoo-doo," sang Mark to

Hyacinth, pointing to a break in the clouds.

"It's all right," she answered.  She looked up and said, "Hm.  That's funny, don't you think?"

"What is?"

"Well, the sun is on the right."

"So?"

"So," she continued.  "It's still morning, right?"

"I don't remember having lunch, so I'm going to say it is."

"That means the sun is still rising, east, on our right."

"Oh," said Mark, understanding.  "We've been going North all morning."

"More or less.  I couldn't see before with the clouds and rain, but now…"

"The lodge is south," said Mark.  "We're marching away from it, not towards."

"There must be something on our guide's mind, something he doesn't want to tell us.  Something he thinks we can't handle," she concluded.

"Like what?"

"I have a suspicion.  Let's keep it between us for now," she said quietly.

"Sure.  Want to play a game?"

"OK.  How many more times do you think Delia will flirt with Cobra before sundown today before he realizes she's into him?" she asked.

"Five.  Usual stakes?"

"You're on.  And don't forget, I won the last one.  You better pay up tonight, even with those bum hands," she said.

"I always do!" he said, taking her by the hand again, trying not to wince.  They watched Cobra and the Professor at the front of the line, passing through the scrubland.  "You know, they kind of remind me of us when we were younger, hon."

"You wish," Hyacinth said.

"Delia says that!" Mark said.

They walked past some tall jackalberry trees on the left, leaves just beginning to bud, with sandy scrubland on the right. Xavier stopped and leaned against a tree.

"I need a rest," he said, touching his head.

"Let's not fall behind," said Kevin. "I hope it's not some kind of cranial edema."

"No, Doctor House, and incidentally, I know you made that term up just now. I'm just tired."

"All right. Catch your breath. I think you're dehydrated," said Kevin.

"Hey, did we get a gift for Miley?"

"What?"

"We said we're going to my cousin's baby's first birthday party in two weeks; did we get her a book or a teddy bear or something?"

"Are you seriously worried about that right now?"

"Just thinking ahead."

They paused, starting to sweat again and wishing they were at their local Kansas City watering hole.

"Teddy bear," recalled Kevin. "We got her a teddy bear."

"Did you pick it out, or did I?"

"I did. Me not introducing you to my family means we only have one stupid set of relatives to have to waste our Sundays on," said Kevin.

"I'd go to your cousin's daughter's birthday party," said Xavier. "And I wouldn't complain about it, either."

"Well, you're just fantastic, aren't…"

Kevin's sunglasses rose from the bridge of his nose as though gravity had reversed itself. Startled, he and Xavier pushed away from the tree as a small, grey, black and white monkey scampered up its trunk, carrying Kevin's glasses, where he joined five more that looked just like him.

"What the hell? Those are UV filtered!" complained

Kevin.

The caravan stopped and watched.

"Cobra, can you do something about this?" Kevin asked.

"Nope. You only get one monkey-pass per safari," Cobra called.

"Seriously?"

"What, do you want me to shoot him?"

"Can you?"

"No. Those are vervet monkeys," explained Cobra. "Pretty harmless, but they've got busy hands. They can be bold about lifting your stuff. Curious little guys; I think you better kiss your shades good-bye."

"Aw," said Kevin, disappointed. "That's twenty-five bucks down the drain."

"Don't you mean *up a tree?*" asked Xavier.

"This is kind of your fault," snapped Kevin. "We stopped here because of you."

"Think of it this way. Your outlook just got a lot brighter."


Cobra was hungry, and he knew that if he were hungry, his group must be starving too. People didn't perform well with nothing in their bellies; I think Napoleon said something about an army traveling on its breakfast or something. Two guinea fowl weren't much for a group of eight people to go hiking on for a full day, especially when one was a vegan and did not partake.

"I think we have to slow down," said the Professor. "Hyacinth, Xavier, Mark, Susan… they're starting to lag."

"I know. We've got another two hours, and I might have a little surprise for our happy campers. Can you hang in there, Professor?"

"Are you saying you're going to make me a happy camper?"

"What?"

"Nothing."

About five yards behind, Hyacinth, who still had perfect hearing, added *one* to her tally.

Quieter, the Professor continued, "You know, last night, Priest said something about looking for gold. This morning around Mark and Hyacinth, I pretended I never heard anything about it."

"I'm guessing there's a point here."

"As a matter of fact, there is. Those men are looking for Kruger's lost gold, which you say is hundreds of miles east, if it exists at all…"

"…which it doesn't…" said Cobra.

"Those guys certainly think it does. They've invested considerable resources into finding it, and they're willing to kill to prevent anyone from getting in their way. We're hiking farther away from the lodge. Could it be that, besides rescuing Kotani and getting us a car, we are actually looking for this lost treasure too?"

"Lost treasure?" Susan asked.

It seems the Professor had been speaking a little more loudly than she had intended.

"That's a negative, Professor," said Cobra decisively.

"Wait, I thought I heard Delia say the words *lost* and *treasure*," Susan repeated.

Cobra held up his hand, and to his genuine surprise, the caravan stopped.

"The thing about lost treasure is that it's lost. It's gone. It's not findable."

"We're looking for Kruger's Lost Gold!" Mark exclaimed. "I knew it!"

"No, we're not," said Cobra emphatically.

"That's why we've been walking away from the lodge!" Mark said.

"*Away* from the lodge?" Xavier said, feeling queasy at that thought.

"We are not walking away from the lodge. We may be taking sort of a roundabout route, but our goal - our *only* goal - is reaching the lodge, where there is food, water, showers, beds and medical care, which we all desperately need. Now, who's with me?" redirected Cobra.

"Are we treasure hunters now?" asked Kevin.

"*Away* from the lodge!" Xavier repeated, angry.

Susan said, "Cobra, if there are riches out in this wilderness, and we're out here anyway…"

"There aren't, and even if there were, the secret, underground bunker Wyatt told me about where there was supposedly millions of rand worth of buried gold is more than twenty-five miles of wild savannah away from here."

Everyone gasped.

"That's not what I meant," backpedaled Cobra.

"Let's find it! Let's get it before the poachers do!" said Mark.

"You know where it is, don't you?" Susan accused, her eyes lit up like diamonds.

"We'll need a vehicle," said Hyacinth. "Maybe we can take the Jeep once we get back to the lodge."

"People, calm down. Don't you think that if I knew where the treasure were, I would have gone after it myself years ago? Believe me, I've been on an actual treasure hunt before and these things don't always end up with a pot of gold or the Holy Grail. Now, maybe Wyatt's told me a few campfire stories about Kruger's gold after a few shots, and if we make it back…"

"*When*, Cobra, *when* we make it back," corrected the Professor.

"*When* we make it back, Wyatt can tell you those same stories while I'm on a plane to Cape Town, Merry Christmas, thank you and good night."

Susan asked, "Who is Kruger?"

"Do you smell something?"

199

Far away, on the eastern horizon, a wide wave of color stretched across the scrubland like a ribbon, with black smoke stretching upwards.

"Bushfire," said Cobra, and everyone tried to process the scale of how large the fire was based on how far away they were. "That could be thirty miles to the east."

"Lightning strike?" asked Mark.

"Maybe. Could be a controlled burn from those *imaginary* San Bushmen. Could be our new friends from yesterday. Fire's a normal part of nature here; it actually encourages new growth. We shouldn't have to worry about it for a few days," said Cobra. "Unless the wind shifts, of course."

Cobra stared at the wide, burning swath rising up, eating through dead vegetation. It reminded him of another lifetime ago when he saw sand and dust rise up to the sky, swallowing him, assimilating him into an endless desert.

# CHAPTER 12:
# HOT IN THE SHADE
# 2003

Before we begin, you should know that the chapter's title is somewhat misleading for two reasons. One, to say that it was merely hot does little to convey how brutally, oppressively, tyrannically, hyperbolically scorching it actually was out there in the Arabian Desert. Two, there was no shade; it's just idiomatic speech.

Like a corpse rising from a shallow grave, Campbell pushed himself upward from total submersion in the sand. He gasped for air, an infant taking his first breath of life, the oxygen flooding his lungs even as the sand flowed from his nose, his ears, and the sockets of his eyes. Coughing uncontrollably, Campbell felt burning pain in his chest from inhaling so much dust, which indicated to him that he was still alive.

He crawled to his knees, and then his feet. Behind him, thirty or forty miles away, the sandstorm continued to sweep across the flat, endless plateau. Campbell saw no glimmer of where he'd been at all - not the canyon, not the village, no grouping of trees and no vehicle. He couldn't even estimate how far he'd gotten; maybe two miles, maybe only a hundred yards.

If he survived, he knew, those mercenaries could have as well. With that understanding, Campbell knew he couldn't stay and wait, and he began his long, lonely march into what was surely an infinite desert.

At least the storm had covered his tracks. The more he thought about it, the more certain he was that Red Scorpion and the others had made it through and would be after him. He opened his backpack and drained the extra sand from it, lightening his burden, and he got his first good look at it, this thing that was worth so many lives:

The lamassu was a little dusty, but otherwise it looked brand new, right off the old Assyrian assembly line. In the bright sun, her face looked powerful and severe, both terrible and hypnotic, like some desert siren. She glittered brilliantly. Her golden skin reflected the heat, and the myriad of jewels shined in every direction.

Campbell noticed she was missing a jewel; a prominent place in the center of her neck was bare with a small dent where some sapphire or ruby probably sat for thousands of years. He smiled; it had come off when he hit Black Tiger with it. *There's your consolation prize, asshole*, he thought. *Go bring it to your bosses.*

Stowing it in his backpack again, he walked in the direction of the sun - west, if it were past midday - and tossed his helmet into the sand, burying it. Black Tiger was right about one thing: this object was definitely cursed. People killed for it, died for it, and why? What could it have been worth? A million dollars? Ten million? Thanks to this little gold statue, Campbell was now a deserter, a thief, even a murderer. If he returned to base, if Colonel Giese got his hands on him, he'd have to go before a military tribunal; he'd be executed for treason. That's if the Americans were even looking for him at all.

And Kurt. This was a man he admired, looked up to. He replayed Kurt's death in his head with each step, watching it over and over like some kind of snuff film, remembering how he'd done nothing to help him. Campbell thought about how even now his body was still lying there, buried by sand as though he never existed at all. It was his inexperience, his indecision, his *cowardice* that pulled the trigger, not Red Scorpion. He couldn't even tell Kurt's parents the truth of what happened. These unbearable thoughts spiraled through his mind, searing themselves into his conscience, and he remembered Black Tiger's words: *you are a boy playing at being a man.*

And on top of that, in his heart, he knew he was going to die out here, alone and mourned by no one. But at least he wouldn't freeze to death, he thought. *Bright side, Campbell, bright side.*

\*\*\*

Two hours of walking later and Campbell wasn't certain he'd gone anywhere at all, except closer to the sun, if that were even possible, because magically it had somehow gotten even hotter than before. He was saturated in perspiration. Campbell felt his own hot breath on his lips and thought they were cracking in real time even as the idea occurred to him.

He thanked his mother's Caribbean blood for his dark complexion, helping him to bear the sun's punishing rays. He remembered his dad's marshmallow-white Irish skin and thanked Jesus he hadn't inherited it, just his Irish alcohol tolerance, or so he convinced himself. *A Coors Light would really hit the spot right now*, he thought.

"Yeah," he said out loud as if he were engaged in a full conversation with some invisible person. "I'd love a beer, thank you."

He shed his body armor and tried to cover it under a thick, dried-out bush.

"That works," he said, again, to nobody. Encouraged by the sensation, he threw off his thick, collared shirt, exposing his sweaty arms to the air. His tee shirt looked as if he'd been swimming in it.

He thought he heard whispers, voices. Someone was just

behind that dune, around that bend, right behind him. Campbell spun around, waving his sidearm wildly at the emptiness around him, and saw nobody. The heat exhaustion was making him delusional.

"Don't fucking follow me!" he roared into the desert, and it struck him how uncannily silent it had been this whole time except for his own footfalls and heavy breathing. A brief echo, and then it was quiet once more.

Suddenly, he saw that he was not alone. On the ridge, about a hundred and fifty yards away, there was an animal. It had four legs and scimitar-shaped horns. He didn't know that it was called an Arabian Oryx and that they barely persisted out here in the desert; he only knew he was ravenously hungry.

Without a plan for how he would skin it, butcher it and cook it, Campbell fired four shots at it, but the antelope was so far out of range that it didn't even run. Sand flowered up where the bullets had each struck, the farthest one probably fifty yards away.

"Never mind," he said, and then to his imaginary companion, "Sure, I'd like some ice with that."

The oryx suddenly bolted, spooked. Campbell heard a sound approaching from the northeast: a helicopter. He dove under a small sand bank and covered himself as best he could: the mercenaries, the Americans, even the insurgents… any of them would be his demise as certainly as the wilderness itself.

It flew right over him, quickly, and Campbell could not get a good look at whose chopper it was. It didn't really matter.

"You're gonna wish you let those guys pick you up and kill you," he said to himself. "Mark my words."

"We'll just see about that," he replied, again, to himself.

"You don't even have a plan, do you?"

"Do you? If you're not going to be helpful, then go fuck off."

"I just will, then. Good-bye."

"Good-bye," he said, picking himself up and continuing his

march west, not noticing the venomous snake he had just shared the sand bank with.

\*\*\*

Finally, eventually, at long last, the sun ultimately decided to quit torturing Campbell and set. Campbell collapsed, laying back onto the sand as though it were a California king mattress in a four-star hotel. He looked straight up now that the sky had earnestly begun its transition from light blue to the color of the tar on the Northern State Parkway back home. One by one, the stars peeked through the blanket of night.

He was thoroughly exhausted, utterly dehydrated, and completely famished, but there was nothing to do and nowhere to go, which was in a way, good, because he hadn't the energy to do anything or go anywhere anyway.

The temperature began to drop, and Campbell felt a peaceful calm overtake him. Sleep came easily now; the total fatigue had dissolved the anxiety that he would probably be dead in the next thirty-six hours. He wasn't even worried about the scorpions that were crawling around out here. Some of the madness and delusion was still there, but not enough to keep him from forty winks.

\*\*\*

It was sometime in the middle of the night, and Campbell was *fucking freezing*. He hadn't even gotten twenty winks. His teeth chattered like he was a cartoon Tasmanian devil dropped into an icy pond, and he couldn't possibly remember why he had abandoned his jacket miles and miles ago. Curled up in the sand, he thought, no, *knew* that people were out there watching him. *Maybe they have a blanket and some Nyquil*, he thought, and resumed his march toward hypothermia.

\*\*\*

The second day was just like the first, but worse.

\*\*\*

The second night was just like the first, but worse.

\*\*\*

It was the third day, and Campbell was still alive, but really only in a strictly medical sense. He hadn't had a drop of water or a morsel of food in something like forty consecutive hours, and the desert sun had been actively trying to exterminate him as though he were some kind of pest that had crawled out of a crack in the old caulk in the wall.

He couldn't remember if his mother actually were Jamaican or not anymore, since his own skin was now pallid, cracked, severely burned and peeling right off. In fact, he couldn't remember much of anything... his pants had a modern camouflage pattern on it, so he must have been a soldier, but he sure didn't feel like it. He had stopped sweating early this morning and figured that probably wasn't a good thing.

He was no longer thinking in sentences, just impulses, and he obeyed only the compulsion to walk to that next rock or to that bunch of pebbles or to that next withered old tree. Campbell was like some kind of vampire now, a lurching zombie, one that had apparently lost significant weight over the last God-knows-how-many miles.

There was an image that sometimes flashed before him, like a presidential address interrupting your regularly scheduled program: Black Tiger. Campbell could barely remember his name - Satana or something - but from time to time, his face appeared before him, taunting him. *You are not a man*, he had said. *You are a boy playing at being a man.* When Campbell lost his balance, these words seemed to broadcast through his mind, and he'd grind his teeth and continue. *You are a boy. You are a boy. You are a boy.*

Campbell didn't use words in his mind, but innately, he had an understanding: one day, he'd see them again - Scorpion, Tiger, Shark, Viper - and he was going to *fuck their shit up in a very profound way.* To do that, he'd have to live. To live, he'd need water.

To get water, he'd have to walk to that trough he saw twenty feet away from him, where the camels were drinking.

Like Moses - well, not really the *actual* Moses, but Charleton Heston *playing* Moses in that old movie - Campbell had fought through the wilderness and threw himself into the water, gulping it down and paying no mind to the big, Bactrian camels also tanking up. The water had a lot of camel backwash in it, but Campbell felt strongly that he'd be dead from dehydration in sixty seconds if he didn't imbibe immediately. Two of the camels seemed confused, and one seemed offended.

"*Madha tafeal!*" called a voice that Campbell either didn't hear over his own splashing or just blatantly disregarded.

"*Alaibtiead ean hunak!*" called the voice again, and Campbell wheeled around this time, drawing his gun on him.

It was Zakaria.

"What the fuck is this?!" Campbell screamed, his gun shaking.

"*Raja,*" he said, and again, "*Raja, la.*"

A moment of clarity returned to Campbell, who remembered *raja, la*: please, no.

Zakaria's face became blurry and distorted, and Campbell realized he was actually looking at some woman just trying to survive.

Her young husband stepped out from behind a camel and chastised in Arabic, "*You never steal water from someone in the desert.*

*Water is life.*" Campbell mostly understood and was deeply ashamed.

"I am sorry," he said, then translating, "*Ana asaf. I need it.*"

"*We would have given you water if you had only asked, even in that uniform,*" the man continued. He filled up a small canteen and tossed it at Campbell's feet. "*Take what you want and go. Don't hurt us.*"

Campbell picked up the canteen and, still holding the gun on the couple, filled a bag with some unleavened bread and dried fruit from the nearby table.

"*Which way to the river,*" Campbell demanded.

The man pointed west and added, "*It is many miles.*"

"*Thank you,*" said Campbell, and he dunked his head back under the trough and resumed his impossible journey.

# CHAPTER 13:
# COLOURED

Cobra continued the journey through tough, semi-arid scrubland. Grass had sprouted and added some more color to the tapestry of the plains, but it was still hot and dry. Clouds continued to dominate the horizon, but at least it kept the sun out of their eyes.

The Professor walked in stride with him, occasionally walking ahead of him.

"Hey, down in front," he said.

"Well, if you can't keep up…"

"Professor, didn't you just tell me to slow down a few minutes ago? For the sake of our injured friends?"

"That's right, I told *you* to slow down, Cobra. I'm trying to enjoy this hike; I'm still on vacation, you know."

"I'm the leader of this little expedition, Professor. Walk with me, or behind me."

"Leaders lead, Cobra."

"Well, thank you so much for volunteering to be first in line for when a predator ambushes us. I appreciate you taking the first hit for me," he said. "You kind of deserve it, blabbing about some insane treasure hunt."

"Kind of makes it more fun, doesn't it? Look what it's done for morale," she said, looking back and seeing the strung-out faces on the rest of the group.

"Yeah, OK. Just remember, *you're* not working for tips. And the wilderness is not some kind of playground. It's no place to screw around."

"Ha! You wish," she said.

"Men looking for El Dorado in the Amazon came to call that place Green Hell. If you lose focus on nature, she punishes you for it."

"I like that you referred to nature as a *she*. It's very forward thinking of you."

"I'm good like that. And as long as you insist on walking *ahead*, at least take the gun. You know how to fire a semi-automatic?"

"Only from every movie ever," she said, accepting the weapon. "Putting a lot of trust in a complete stranger, Cobra, really rolling the dice. I'm impressed."

"I've got a good feeling about you."

"Look at me, I'm blushing!" she joked. "You know, I read in a book before coming here that the San don't use arrowheads. Did you know that? Or were you just having the gang sifting through the dirt for nothing?"

"Your book is only half-right. They don't traditionally use metal arrowheads; they're usually made from organic materials, like bone. They dip them in poison secreted by beetles. So there."

"Now *I'm* impressed," she said.

"You sure seemed interested in the San back there; you took it personally when Andres was talking smack about them," remarked Cobra.

"I was going to say the same thing about you."

"Kotani's a San. When people imply that there are no cultures like that out here in the bush, it really rubs me the wrong way, like yahoos who don't believe the Holocaust happened, or that the twin towers collapsed from bombs detonated from inside in some bat shit conspiracy. It's disrespectful."

"Yes, Kotani's a San, but he lives like a Westerner," said

the Professor. "Hundreds of years of Colonialism and decades of Apartheid took a man who was born into one of the most significant cultures still existing on Earth and turned him into a guy who does bushcraft tricks for tourists."

"That's a pretty superior attitude, don't you think?"

"Why, thank you," she said.

"No, I mean *smug*."

"I know what you meant."

"Wyatt pays Kotani more than me. Because of this safari lodge, Kotani can feed his family, offer his children medical care and schooling. He's sharing his culture with you because he's proud of it. He's not submissive to some Christian mission. Kotani has the right to live how he chooses and to take advantage of whatever opportunities that come across him. If he wants to live in the bush and hunt gemsbok, he can, but if he wants to get a bachelor's degree, he can do that too."

"That's an illusion, a simplification," she countered. "People on my reservation are told they have a choice, that they can be anything they want."

"Like you, Professor."

"But that's only after centuries of forced relocation by the government, after the Crow have already been thoroughly pacified. Most people think Native Americans are just bad guys in cowboy movies, that we're already extinct. We're just like the San."

"So why study biology? Why not become a lawyer, an activist, a teacher, if that's what's so important to you?"

"The land and the animals are our natural heritage, too. It's an aspect of life on the Montana/Wyoming border people forget about. That's how I'll help my people."

"Or," said Cobra, "you just like animals. You *do* like animals, don't you?"

"Of course, I do," she replied, stepping over some deadfall. "Less so, when they try to eat me, but yes. I love animals."

"I think you're doing what you love, what you want to do, because that's what *you* want to do, and you've found some way to reverse-engineer that into a career that satisfies what your people - your family, folks on the reservation - want and expect from you."

"Don't diminish what I do. *I* don't work for tips, Cobra. And you, you're part African, and you downplay your own heritage, like it doesn't mean anything to you. I don't get you."

"It's only been a day and a half; it takes about three days before someone really knows everything about me."

They kept walking, the Professor in the lead. A small, furry thing darted in front of them and then scampered behind a bush, taking refuge.

"Scrub hare?" she asked.

"Genet cat, I think."

Cobra picked up the motorcycle track again and said nothing; the Professor was already going the right way. He checked behind and did a quick headcount; everyone else was slogging along.

"I like to golf," said the Professor.

"Really?"

"Eighteen holes; one of my favorite things to do. Bet you didn't expect that."

"Got your own clubs and everything?"

"Of course. My family hates it. It makes me look like some kind of snob or something, but I don't care. I just like it, so I keep playing."

Cobra laughed.

"You don't seem like the kind who lets anyone tell her what to do."

"I hope that was a compliment."

"It was," he said. "It's a big compliment."

She slowed ever so slightly and walked beside him.

"Coloured. With a *U*. That's the name for bi-racial people here in South Africa," said Cobra.

"Coloured? That's like something a slightly racist grandma would say."

"I have to say, people were always cool to me growing up; nobody in high school really gave me a hard time about being coloured, mixed race. I'm sure they talked about me, about my parents, behind my back, but for the most part, I had a good childhood."

"You're very lucky, Cobra."

"I know. But when I was in college…"

"You went to college?"

"Only freshman year, and about a month of my sophomore year. Everyone always had an opinion about who I should be. Some of my Black friends thought I should *fight the power*, play up that side of me, like you. That I should be more active in the struggle, that I wasn't doing enough, like an Uncle Tom."

"I actually have a literal Uncle Tom," she said. "True story."

"But some of my White friends kept telling me to play towards my Caucasian side."

"Whatever that means," Professor said.

"Or they saw me as some kind of novelty. I could be the Black friend they said they had whenever they prefaced some kind of racial statement. Everybody had no problem telling me I was too Black, not Black enough, not White enough, this, that. My own identity got kind of lost. I needed to find out who I was, not who people thought I should be."

"And you thought you should be Cobra McCoors."

"When I was in the army, they told me exactly who I was: how I should dress, how I should cut my hair, how to walk. I was a soldier. Only, who they decided I was really wasn't me either."

"How long were you in the army?"

"Not long. Maybe two years, if you count basic."

"Is that all the commitment the army signs you up for when you enlist?"

"No. No, it isn't."

"What happened?"

"That's a long story, and I can't tell it without at least three pints in me."

"I'm sorry," she said. "I'm sorry I don't have three pints."

"But even after my time as a soldier ended, I couldn't figure out who the hell I was, only what other people wanted me to be. I needed ownership of who I was. And that's how I became Cobra McCoors. I made myself into who I am. It wasn't easy, and it didn't happen overnight, but when I looked inside, I found myself lacking, so I took steps to make myself into who I wanted to be."

"You're a self-made man, is what you're saying. Like Wyatt Northside?"

"A little, yes."

"And like Black Tiger?"

Cobra paused. "A lot like Black Tiger."

"Whoever he is, I hope I meet him some day."

Cobra shook his head. "God, I hope you don't."

The Professor held up her hand, nobody stopped.

"Hand up! Hand up!" she whispered loudly.

"I thought that was only when Cobra did it," said Kevin, behind them.

"What? Do traffic lights only apply to Hyundais? That's ridiculous," she said.

"Good spot, Professor," said Cobra. "It's an ostrich nest."

Sure enough, sandwiched between a cozy cul-de-sac of mopane trees was a clutch of dozens of football-sized ostrich eggs, each like the one the San had filled with water and buried.

"It's a dump nest, like an ostrich daycare center. Many females lay in one spot so they're easier to guard, since they can't build nests in the trees," explained Cobra.

"Bad move," said Xavier.

"I'm simply ravenous!" said Susan, rushing towards the nest.

"Hold on a minute," said Cobra. "This is not a buffet. We can't just…"

"Oh, here comes the ostrich police," moaned Andres.

"We're not supposed to…"

"What, now it's all right to shoot guinea fowl but not make a few little omelets?" asked Xavier. "We're going to die out here, aren't we? This is an emergency, isn't it?"

"I thought you were a vegan," remembered Cobra.

"And the Bushmen can have ostrich eggs, but not us? Why? They don't even pay taxes!" complained Andres.

"Come on, Cobra," said Susan. "Don't they farm these things anyway?"

Cobra looked to the Professor, who shrugged. "I don't think they're endangered. Two or three couldn't hurt, could it?"

Mark said, "Don't look at me. I hate eggs."

"It's a victimless crime!" said Susan.

"All right," Cobra relented. "Only three. We'll be like the unseen hand of natural selection."

"You don't have to rationalize everything, Cobra," said the Professor.

"Be my guest, Susan," said Cobra, standing out of her way.

Susan knelt down in front of the nest like a kid on Easter Sunday, carefully choosing the biggest, best colored eggs to extract from the pile.

"If only we had some flour and some butter; I'd make the best Georgia biscuits to sop these up with…"

Heavy, rapid footfalls getting louder.

Susan fell backward onto her keister, and the eggs rolled out of her arms, not even cracking. Cobra grabbed her by the shoulders and pulled her back across the dirt as an eight-foot-tall, black and white bird ran squawking back to the nest through the trees. He splayed his wings out, flapping them madly, and kicking at the dirt with his huge, three-toed claws. This bird was pissed.

Everyone took a big step backward.

215

"Looks like you were almost a victim of this victimless crime," said Cobra, slowly pulling her farther away. "One of those kicks and your intestines would be in those trees like tinsel; merry Christmas."

The ostrich strutted around the nest in a circle and continued hissing and snapping at Susan and Cobra, its flapping wings sounding like a rattlesnake's tail and producing the same effect.

"Easy, fella, we got the message," he said, and to Susan, "that's called a threat display."

"Duh, why do they call it that?" snapped Susan.

"It's like a dinosaur," said Kevin.

"It *is* a dinosaur," said Hyacinth.

"She's right," said Mark. "Same lineage, direct descendant of small theropods. All birds are dinosaurs."

"Even penguins?" asked Kevin.

"Every Thanksgiving, you're having dinosaur with mashed potatoes and brussels sprouts," said Mark.

"I hate brussels sprouts," said Andres.

"Why don't we just shoot it?" whined Xavier.

"We're just going to relax and calmly back up. No sudden moves, no shooting, no running," said Cobra quietly, and then with a tilt of his hat, mused, "Mitchell's pub actually does make a delicious ostrich burger. More like beef than chicken. No, we…"

Two lions bounded out from behind the mopane trees, bringing the ostrich straight down as if its legs were immediately broken at the knees. Everyone screamed and fell backward.

"No! Don't run!" warned Cobra. "Don't run."

"Ohmygodohmygodohmygod…." chanted Xavier.

*Click click* from Andres, but nobody noticed, their eyes locked on this grisly, bloody assassination.

Susan reached for her purse, but Cobra physically blocked her.

"No, Susan," he whispered.

"Cobra," said the Professor, pointing the assault rifle at the lions.

"No, Professor," he said emphatically.

"Cobra," she said again, the barrel trembling slightly.

"Delia, no," he said again. "Just stand up and quietly walk backward."

It was Boss Tweed and Magua. Tweed had his jaws almost *hermetically* sealed around the ostrich's hose-shaped neck, practically decapitating him. Death came almost mercifully, instantaneously. Magua, his scruffy mohawk mane matted and coarse, sat upon the ostrich's back, weighing the lifeless bird down. Both of them growled gutturally, like a motorcycle engine revving. When Magua got too close, Tweed clipped at him with his paw, relegating him to the ostrich's rump.

Both were emaciated. They obviously hadn't eaten since they'd gotten a few bloody mouthfuls at the elephant carcass. This ostrich was a very lucky break for them both. Gore dripping from their stout muzzles, they locked eyes with the Professor.

It felt as though time had stopped; she was no longer aware whether or not she was still breathing. She was terrified beyond measure, but hypnotized as well, as though she could feel their wildness, their willingness to do anything to survive. For a second, she felt as though they had shared a piece of the hunt with her. Later, she would downplay this primal instinct as if she were crazy and rationalize that it was just her imagination, but deep down, she knew better. It humbled her, it impassioned her, and it revitalized her.

She lowered the gun, and the lions broke their stare, resuming the consumption of their kill. Emotion then flowed freely from her, eyes welling with tears from the intensity of the moment.

Cobra softly took her hand and led her away from the lions, and everyone else as well.

"I think maybe we should take a little detour," he concluded, and nobody disagreed.

# CHAPTER 14:
# JUST AN ASSHOLE

The little detour was more than just a *little* detour, but since nobody but Cobra had any idea where they were actually going, it didn't seem to matter much to the group. Tweed and Magua sure as hell weren't moving out of Cobra's planned route for a while, so there wasn't a whole lot of choice anyway. Cobra had explained that they'd have to circumvent that mopane forest by swinging a little east, through a canyon that fissured through some tall rocks.

Standing before this canyon gave Cobra flashbacks to a time some four years ago when he stood before another *desert* path flanked by high walls of earth and sand, and it was not a pleasant memory. You know the one I'm talking about.

This one was different, though. For one, the canyon walls were both taller and steeper, making it really impossible for anyone to climb up or down, unless they were a klipspringer, I suppose. For another, nobody was shooting at him.

"We've got to go through that?" asked Xavier.

"We don't *have* to, I suppose, but it takes us the least out of our way. When the sun's all the way up, we're going to want to find a place to rest," answered Cobra.

"You mean the sun's not even all the way up?"

Cobra looked at his watch.

"Almost."

Xavier wilted at the thought of it getting even hotter, and

the rest weren't all that enthused, either.

"Cobra, I've got to be honest, I'm getting a little fatigued. The spirit is willing, you know…" said Mark, and Cobra saw that dehydration and pain was bringing out his age.

"I know, Mark. We're all tired, and you guys have done really great so far. This canyon's only about a half a mile long. Once we get through it, I promise, we'll rest through the heat of the day. I might even have a surprise waiting for you."

"Oh good, more surprises," grumbled Andres.

"Can you?" asked Hyacinth to her husband.

Mark smiled, packing away his discomfort. "Fuck yeah, I can."

"Good man," said Cobra. "Like I said, it's getting hot, so most of the animals should be finding places to rest. We shouldn't have to worry about wildlife."

"Excellent," said the Professor, "because it looks like there are only two ways in or out of that canyon."

A tower of giraffes - tall, stately, aloof - galloped out of the canyon, a wash of muted brick and tan color as their necks undulated in odd rhythms, like oil rigs pumping up and down. Six, seven, eight of them ran out, turning stage left at the canyon's entrance and narrowly avoiding the party.

The professor looked to Cobra, her eyebrow raised.

"Like I said, it's getting hot, so most of the animals should be finding places to rest. We shouldn't have to worry about *predators*," Cobra corrected.

"I see," she said. "All right, then, let's tread carefully. Cobra said it's twenty minutes until we rest."

Xavier dropped his bag.

"No."

Kevin tilted his head. "Come on, X. We've got to move."

"No," he repeated emphatically, touching his head again as if experiencing a migraine. "I think I'm not going anywhere. Not with this guy, not anymore."

"Who, me?" asked Cobra.

"You're trying to get us all killed. Can't you see we're a mess? I mean, can't everybody see that?"

"Xavier, we can rest now if you can't…"

"No! You're lying to us about getting us back to the lodge. You said we're going north, but the lodge is south! That doesn't make any sense! Doesn't anybody else have a problem with this? Why are you doing this?"

Cobra said, "Trust me, Xavier, it's…"

"Trust you? Trusting you has gotten us here!"

"That's right, it has," said the Professor. "Alive."

"That's easy for you to say! You have the freaking gun!" he yelled. "Why does she get to have the gun? She's not an employee of Rhino Horn Lodge. Like, now you're his girlfriend, so you get to be Assistant Commandant on this Bataan Fucking Death March to the Seventh Circle of Hell?"

"Oooh…" said Susan.

"Shut up, Susan!" he turned. "I don't know why you get to have a gun, either. Like, it's not a major felony to carry and conceal a weapon in South Africa? What is this, Texas?"

"Buddy," said Mark, "I think you may have taken a harder hit to the head than we realized. Maybe you've got pressure building up in there…"

"Thanks, Coach! You've clearly wasted your life as a gym teacher when you should have been raking in cash as a surgeon."

"That is enough out of you," scolded Hyacinth. "You're not so old that I can't give you five fingers across your face."

Kevin pleaded, "Xavier, get a hold of yourself," but Xavier kept on rolling.

"Don't break your hand, grandma. How come when I want to stop, it's '*nooooooo, onward Christian soldier, we're making good time, so let's go jogging with jaguars,*' but when Hyacinth or Mark want to rest, it's '*let me fetch your slippers for you?*'"

"We *are* a little older than you, son," said Mark.

220

SNAKE IN THE GRASS

"Jaguars are native to the Americas," said Cobra. "Their best analog here would be leopards."

"And before you say anything, Andres, just shut the fuck up. Whether Kev and I *take turns* is none of your fucking business, all right? You're the only one here with nobody. That's no surprise to anyone, because who could tolerate a piece of sub-human dogshit like you for more than three consecutive minutes if they're not trying to win a bar bet?"

"Words hurt," laughed Andres heartily. "You wound me so."

"What are you trying to say, Xavier?" asked Cobra.

"I don't know what it is you think you're doing, whether you're trying to find some lost treasure, if you're going after your tracker friend, or if you're just morbidly curious to see which of us drops dead first. You said there wouldn't be animals in the canyon and before we even step foot in there, ten of them come charging out."

"Cape giraffe, one of seven debated subspecies..."

"Don't care! There's only more mayhem that way, and I don't have confidence that we're going to make it through if we keep following you. Something's going to get us... a poacher, a lion, a freaking space alien."

"So then, what do you want to do?"

"We turn around and go back the way we came. We can get to the tree we slept in last night if we walk later when the sun goes down, and we swim across the river and make our way back to the lodge, since Mr. Northside is definitely not coming."

Everyone shook their heads.

Cobra said, "Xavier, I don't think you know what you're saying. It'd be a hard push to get back where we started. Then we'd have to find a place to cross the river where the current were slow enough that we didn't drown, which would mean it'd be an ideal habitat for crocs. And then it's two, maybe even three days' walk to the lodge. I'm taking us up and around, not backward,

221

where I know it's safe to cross, and if we have no major setbacks, we'll be opening presents there tomorrow on Christmas morning."

"Bullshit," Xavier protested. "Who wants to go back, and who wants to keep following this maniac to the whatever's behind Door Number Three?"

"That's a pretty tough sell," said Susan.

"Xavier, this isn't going to help," said the Professor.

"After all the kind words you've had for me?" laughed Andres.

"Blow it out your ass," said Hyacinth. "I've got a broken ankle and you don't hear me complaining."

"I thought you said it was barely sprained?" asked Mark.

"Whatever."

"Fine," said Xavier, touching his bandage and finding some blood seeping through. "Then just let me and Kevin have a gun and we'll be on our way."

"X," said Kevin, genuinely sorry. "I'm not going back."

"What do you..." yelled Xavier, and then softly, "oh."

Xavier slumped to the ground and put his head between his knees. Kevin sat beside him and put his arm around his shoulder.

"What I mean is, *we're* not going back. *We'd* never make it. I'm not leaving you. Don't leave me."

"Just," sighed Xavier, dejected, gently pushing him away, "just skip it, Kevin."

"So, it's settled, then," said Cobra cheerfully. "Into the canyon we go!"

\*\*\*

At least they had a little shade in the canyon. The clouds still dominated the African sky, but whenever the sun peaked through, the canyon walls blocked at least some of it if you walked close to the right side.

Kevin re-dressed Xavier's wound, and Mark was satisfied

that there still probably wasn't any fluid buildup, but like Kevin astutely pointed out, Mark was not a doctor. Kevin worked to assure everyone that Xavier's outburst was a result of a combination of blood loss, head trauma, dehydration and exhaustion, which was *mostly* all true. The fact that Xavier wasn't even all that embarrassed after collecting himself was probably a sign of something, but nobody was sure if that something was good or bad. Although some didn't care, Cobra actually did, because he knew he'd have to get Xavier - get *everyone* - back home safely, somehow.

There was a small creek running through the canyon, around which were grass and small plants. Mark ran his hands through it, bandages and all, recoiling in sharp pain at first but forcing them to stay submerged.

"Got to clean the burn," Mark explained. "Doesn't even hurt!" he lied, and Hyacinth frowned.

"Do you think it's safe to drink?" asked Susan.

"Maybe," mused Cobra. "It goes underground and then joins the river later. The animals probably drink from it. I mean, drink running waters, avoid still, as they say."

"I wouldn't," suggested the Professor. "If you don't know where its source is, unless you're about to die, you probably want to avoid it if you can. I once drank from a stream in Arizona that the locals said was clean, but I didn't realize a horse had died a half a mile upstream and was decomposing in it."

"I bet you punished that toilet," said Susan.

"Frankly, Annie's done worse in Cancun, but it was not a fun experience," concluded the Professor.

"Well? Are we about to die?" asked Kevin.

"I am," said Andres. "From listening to your disgusting anecdotes. I am embarrassed for you."

"You never miss an opportunity to say something mean," said Hyacinth. "Settle a bet for us, will you, Andres? Mark thinks there must be a reason why you're such a piece of trash, that some

223

horrible experience ruined your life and made you this way. I, like Kevin and Xavier before, said that sometimes people are just assholes. Come on, Andres, which is it?"

"I don't have to reveal myself to complete strangers; I owe you nothing."

"I guess I win, then," said Hyacinth.

They turned to leave, and Andres rubbed his eyes together and stopped.

"I come from a close-knit family in Germany," he began, and Susan listened curiously. "My father was a local businessman and philanthropist, well-respected in our suburb about twenty kilometers from Stuttgart. My mother was the apple of his eye, a good and kind woman who always had time for all the neighborhood children, and for all the elderly in our church.

"I was very close with her. You see, I was a sickly child with severe asthma. I couldn't run and play with the other kids without experiencing coughing fits. Often, I was forced to stay indoors. My mother helped me, encouraged me. She bought me my first camera and took me outside. She said if I could not run and play, I could photograph the trees and butterflies and deer and birds. That camera was everything to me. My mother had boundless love for me, so it was hard for me to believe that doctors said she had a weak heart. She was my whole world, until I met Alice."

"Your girlfriend?" asked Susan.

"My wife," he smiled, and then the smile faded. "For a time. Alice was beautiful and strong, witty and smart. We fell in love instantly; our courtship was short and we were married inside of a year."

"You're a romantic," said the Professor.

"We were expecting our first child, a daughter, whom we would name after Alice. I don't know if you believe in God; I'm not sure I do anymore, but I do believe in the Devil. My wife's pregnancy was difficult, full of complications. The doctors weren't sure she could take our baby to term, but Alice was a fighter. She delivered our daughter," he said, and then added, "though not without cost.

"The doctors called it Bright's Disease, a terrible kidney ailment. I knew, knew in my heart that she would make it, and we'd begin to raise our little girl together. It's funny the things you swear you believe and turn out to be mistaken. I said good-bye to my beautiful Alice on a cold February morning."

"Oh, my God," said Kevin, hand over his mouth.

"But she would not be the only light to fade. My mother had contracted typhoid…"

"Typhoid?!" gasped Cobra, in disbelief that anyone still could have suffered from typhoid in the latter half of the twentieth century in the civilized world.

"Yes, typhoid. She left me on the very same day as my Alice, only hours apart. It was… what is your holiday in America, with the cards and chocolate?"

"They both died on Valentine's Day?" gasped the Professor.

"February fourteenth, yes. The irony was not lost on me. Broken, I left my home. I couldn't understand why my life had suddenly become so dark. But, I still had my camera," he exhaled, before adding, "that's something, I suppose."

Susan was practically in tears, and Kevin and Xavier stood in stunned silence.

And then Mark and Hyacinth burst out laughing.

"How dare you? I bared my soul to you! Don't you doubt my story!"

"Oh, it's a true story, all right," laughed Hyacinth. "Just not yours!"

"I worked at a school for decades, you don't think I read a book or two?" said Mark, doubled over. "That's Teddy Roosevelt. His wife and mother both died on Valentine's Day, his mother of typhoid, and his wife of kidney failure after giving birth. You had me until typhoid!"

"The camera was a nice add," Hyacinth admitted. "And I win! Sometimes a person is just an asshole, and that's that."

Even Andres could not resist a smirk at manipulating everyone's emotions.

"You are a bunch of idiots! I'm surprised any of you even knew about your own country's history," he chortled.

"Jackass," said Kevin, shaking his head.

"You miserable..." trailed off the Professor.

"I actually thought that was kind of funny," admitted Cobra.

They continued through the canyon, but Susan stopped Andres.

"It was something, wasn't it?" she said. "You don't have to tell me. But you don't always have to put up the wall, with your insults and your meanness."

He smiled. "*Liebchen*, that's a pain I choose to carry alone."

"Lucky break!" said Cobra about halfway through the fissure.

He ushered them to a tall tree growing next to the stream.

"It a marula tree," he explained. "The fruit is usually ripe in January or February, but since it's been so dry, they might be edible now."

"I'm so hungry I would chew on that tree's bark," said Kevin.

"Don't do that when we have these," replied Cobra. He picked up a piece of fruit that had fallen from the tree and tucked in. "These'll do."

Everyone rushed to pick some up from the ground, and they tore into them without abandon.

Andres spit his out. "Mine has a worm in it!"

"It's probably a mopane worm," said Cobra, mouth full.

"Also edible."

The Professor ate without abandon, and Cobra found himself staring at her as the juice ran down her chin. There was something very attractive about that.

"What?"

"Nothing, Professor," he smiled, and then pantomimed touching his lip. "You've got a little something…"

"I must have left my napkin in my evening gown," she said, wiping it off with the back of her arm.

"They use these to make that liquor you may have had after dinner two nights ago," Cobra said to the group.

"Is it true that elephants eat these fruits after they ferment on the ground for a few weeks and get drunk?" asked Mark.

"Local legend, and totally bullshit," he answered. "They do eat them, but the quantity of fermented fruit it would take to even buzz a six-ton elephant would be more than an elephant could really forage without losing said buzz."

Mark tried to fill his pockets with them. "What about a two-hundred-and-twenty-pound adult human?"

"Plausible!"

"These aren't even ripe, hon," said Hyacinth, "let alone fermented."

"They're worth keeping as snacks, though," Cobra instructed. "Just don't let the vervets catch you with them. Or baboons."

They picked up a few extras for the road and stowed them in their bags and pockets. When Susan opened her purse, Xavier casually peaked inside, seeing the gun and money without making it seem as though he were paying any attention.

"Something I can help you with?" asked Andres.

"Just a little dizzy," Xavier answered quickly and moved on.

"Go be dizzy over there."

"You're a real peach, Andres."

"Am I the only one who hears that?" asked the Professor.

A soft bleating sound, like that of a goat, gently echoed through the canyon.

"That sounds like an animal in distress," said Hyacinth.

"Wait here, backs against the canyon wall," instructed Cobra. "If we could hear that, then so might *other* things."

"You see?" whispered Xavier to Kevin. "This is what I'm talking about."

Cobra tentatively walked forward about twenty yards and looked around the bend. He stood very still, and heard footsteps following him. It could only be the Professor.

"You know, I wanted you to stay with the others. You're the one with the weapon," he said.

"Susan's got a gun; they're fine."

"And before you say anything, obviously I know you're *not* my girlfriend."

"You wish," she said, before seeing what Cobra was seeing and then remarking simply, "Oh."

Cobra silently motioned for the rest to follow, and some of them gasped in wonder as they saw an exhausted giraffe peeling the afterbirth from a small copy of herself laying between her long legs. The baby was wet and confused as though she were seeing the world for the first time, because she was.

"I think she just gave birth about fifteen, twenty minutes ago," Cobra whispered. "This is a nice, secluded spot."

"She's beautiful," remarked Susan, obviously touched.

Andres tried to surreptitiously reach into his bag to take a photo, but stopped when Hyacinth said, "God, I wish I had my camera."

"I've never seen anything like this in all our trips to Africa," said Mark. "Thank you, Cobra."

"How long before she can stand?" asked Kevin.

"Within the hour, if she's healthy."

"We shouldn't be here," said Xavier, shaking his head.

"Jesus, just relax," said Susan.

"No, he's right. The mother's not going to want us around; giraffes sometimes kill lions with their hooves. And predators could smell the afterbirth. Let's give them as much space as we can and quietly move around them. Follow me," Cobra said quietly.

With their backs against the other canyon wall, they slowly shimmied around the giraffe, and she eyed them distrustfully. She took a few steps toward Hyacinth.

"Easy there, hon," she said calmly. With Hyacinth's eyes very distracted, Andres snapped a quick shot of the baby.

Xavier, however, could have sworn he saw Andres with a camera.

"Be still," commanded Cobra quietly.

The giraffe clipped down with her hooves, kicking up the dust, and Hyacinth flinched.

Cobra clapped his hands, trying to divert the giraffe's attention, but for some reason, she was totally focused on Hyacinth. She kicked down again, about three feet from her.

"That giraffe really hates the shit out of you, hon," said Mark.

A chittering sound, almost like squeaking birds, came from the direction they entered, and the giraffe bolted back to her calf.

"Dogs!"

A pack of fifteen adult African wild dogs, their tawny coats painted with individual patches of black and white, flooded the canyon and circled the mother and calf.

Two of them, their great big radar dish ears stiff, loped toward the group.

"No," commanded the Professor, authoritatively. "I said *no*!"

The Doberman-sized dogs slowed, but continued to approach, curious.

"That usually works at home!" she said.

"I don't think they've been to obedience school," said

Cobra.

"Hyacinth, throw your roll bar!" said Mark.

She tossed it over their heads, and sure enough, they went after it.

"Let's get out of here, people," said Cobra, motioning them onward.

The dogs kept testing the giraffe, nipping at her heels as she kept kicking downward at them, scattering them momentarily. She was smart, experienced: she would not be drawn away from her calf, whom she kept centered below her four post-like legs. The dogs were persistent, nipping and retreating, goading the mother away as the baby shook like a leaf, trying to balance on her spindly little legs. They all kicked up so much dust, it obscured the dogs from view.

"Can't we help them?" asked Susan.

"We can't," said Cobra as he ushered them out of the canyon, the animals fighting for life behind.

"Sure, we can! Just fire a few shots in the air, scare them off. Do something."

"I'm sorry, Susan. Nature can be cruel, but it doesn't take sides, and we can't either."

# CHAPTER 15:
# WATERING HOLE

"I feel like your solution to all wildlife situations is *'don't move,'*" said Kevin.

"Don't forget *'back away slowly'* or *'climb a tree,'*" answered Cobra.

"And they pay you for this?" asked Susan, shaking her head.

"I also work for tips, and since we're all still *mostly* alive, I expect you guys to pony up at the end of this vacation."

"I assumed *not dying* was inclusive of the vacation package," said the Professor.

"Then clearly, you didn't read the brochure."

They made it out of the canyon and into what looked like, for the first time, open grassland speckled with a few trees here and there. It was flat and offered an unobstructed view of the sky, very much the idealized impression most people have of the African panorama. A few small springbok looked up from the grass, and seeing no threat, resumed ruminating (that's *ruminating* as in *chewing regurgitated cud from their first stomachs*, not *thinking intensely*, although who the hell really knows what issues antelopes might think about).

The group could still hear the clashing of the giraffe and the wild dogs echoing out of the canyon behind them, and Susan was unhappy that they had done so little to ensure the survival of the baby.

"How could you be so cruel, Cobra?" she asked.

"We have to respect the economy of nature, Susan. Unless people directly contribute to the suffering of an animal, like catching an animal's leg in a wire snare or hitting a wildebeest with a car, we have to let nature take its course."

"Don't you even care? What would have been the difference if we saved one baby giraffe?"

"You only say that because you sympathize with the giraffe, but tell me, have you ever seen a starving puppy before?"

"I have not."

"You don't hate puppies, do you?"

"God, no. I'm not a monster," she said.

"Wild dog pups are, as their name implies, puppies. They're every bit as cute as your little rescue lab or shepherd pup back home. Now, let's say the mother giraffe fights off those dogs and her calf lives. The pups back at the den don't eat, they get weaker, maybe some of them starve to death. You want to be responsible for that?"

"All right, Cobra, I get it. I understand. It just felt so, so cold."

"What do you think the giraffe's chances are?" asked Mark.

"Pretty good, I'd say. I think it's pretty unlikely they'd be able to get at that baby unless the mother is very inexperienced. If I had to put money down, I'd bet on the giraffe, but I'm comfortable not knowing," he said. "And here we are."

About fifty yards ahead was a large pond - a watering hole - with a few trees on the fringes.

"That's amazing," gasped Hyacinth, blown away by the panoply of life around the watering hole. Gnus romped and played, sparring with their modest little Viking horns. Zebra stallions, rejuvenated by the rains, bucked and kicked each other for herd dominance. Toilet-seat-rumped waterbuck and shaggy striped nyalas grazed the short growth, and nervous impalas took turns delicately sipping from the pool.

"It's like Paradise," said Mark.

"Let's get a little closer, shall we?" smiled Cobra, and he led them on.

In the back of the line, Andres muttered, "I hate puppies."

Cobra brought them to a small group of trees that offered some shade from the midday sun which peaked intermittently through those obstinate clouds, and after checking for snakes, motioned that it was safe to sit down and rest.

"This watering hole probably wasn't here two days ago," he remarked. "These animals are out here even in the heat of the day; this could be the first time they've been here since last season's rains."

"Look at that, over there," said the Professor, pointing to an antelope with dramatic horns curving backward at an almost ninety-degree angle.

"Sable," he smiled, and then said, "No, roan, no sable. Definitely sable."

"It's a roan," she said, sitting and shaking her head derisively.

Cobra knelt by some dry grass protruding from the ground in little patches, much like the ostrich eggs the San had left at their encampment.

"Did I get the *antelope* part right at least, professor?" he asked, pulling at the grass.

"No, it's a roan *polar bear*."

"Ah, here we are," Cobra said, ignoring her.

From just a few feet underground, Cobra unearthed not an ostrich egg, but an airtight container, which he dusted off and opened.

"Anyone hungry?"

Everyone gathered around him as he passed out sealed bags of dried fruits, granola bars, and biltong. He distributed metal bottles filled with water, and best of all…

"That's a bottle of gin!" Mark exclaimed. Cobra broke the seal on a bottle of tonic and began mixing.

"Free with the tour," Cobra declared. "Although, I apologize in advance for the lack of limes and lemons."

"We're going to have to make some sacrifices, I suppose," said Hyacinth, and remembering Cobra's recipe, added, "THIS much G, this much t, please."

Susan asked, "Is that Bushmen property, Cobra?"

"Nope. Bushmen actually make a kind of booze called Karrie out of honey and bee stingers; this gin was made in a factory outside London somewhere. I actually buried this cooler here a long time ago; it's sometimes a fun little moment on safari that surprises and impresses guests."

"I'm both of those things," said Mark, bringing his cup to his lips, his hands shaking. "Surprised and impressed."

"This is as good a spot as any for a little siesta," said Cobra. "Why don't we stop here until it cools a little?"

Even Xavier ate the biltong, throwing his veganism out the window, and Kevin gulped down his gin and tonic as though he had been crawling through a desert all day, which he kind of had been.

"Let's be careful not to leave anything behind. Monkeys would love to get their hands on these snacks," Cobra mentioned.

"Yeah, you don't say," said Kevin, and he smiled at Xavier, who turned away.

For the first time in a while, the group seemed content to be still, to sit in the grass. As all the animals ran and drank and played by the watering hole, they all felt the power of this wild country, the allure of the African bush that makes it difficult to leave and even harder not to return.

"Leopard," said Andres nonchalantly, and everyone stiffened up.

"Where?" asked Susan.

"In that tree, about seventy-five meters away, next to the bank. Look for the tail, dangling over the branch."

"Great spot," said Cobra, squinting.

"You don't see him, do you?"

"Of course, I do. He's right by, you know…"

"One o'clock, midway up the trunk," whispered the Professor.

"One o'clock!" said Cobra, "midway up the trunk! And if you look carefully, you can see half a warthog carcass dangling from the branch. Could have killed it two days ago, maybe."

Some of the antelopes snorted and stomped their hooves, looking in the leopard's direction as if Andres had tipped them off to it.

"I think we're OK for now. He's got a good lunch, and he's not going to come down from there now that all the antelopes and zebra see him."

"What if hyenas smell the carcass?" the Professor asked.

"Jesus, can't we just rest for one single second?" asked Susan.

"We're fine, for now. Let's just keep an eye on him," said Cobra. "You're pretty lucky. Some people come to Africa three, four times and don't see a leopard. Thing about a leopard is that you don't see him unless he wants to be seen."

"I bet you wish you had a camera now, Andres," said Xavier, bluntly.

"I've found a way to move on," he smiled.

"I *know* you have."


As the afternoon passed, most of the group closed their eyes at least once, being both exhausted and a little buzzed. They each knew they'd probably have to start moving again soon, but nobody wanted to be the first to suggest it. For once, everybody tacitly agreed to wait for Cobra's instructions and then complain about resuming the trek later.

Mark sat still, his eyes squinting, as a young nyala touched his muzzle to the water's surface, ripples echoing forth in concentric circles. He tried to draw it, but as he secured his sketchbook in his lap, his pencil hand would not stop shaking no matter how he tried to stabilize it.

Turning to Hyacinth sadly, he said, "I… I don't think I can anymore."

Hyacinth gave him a tired, warm, knowing smile. "That's all right, hon."

"It just, it's just that it hurts."

"You don't have to draw this. Close your eyes and capture it in your memory and remember it as it was when you need to smile one day."

He closed the sketchbook, and she took his arm. They breathed deeply together.

"If you had your camera, I'd have you take a few shots. Maybe I'd draw it later."

"You'll do just fine from memory."

Susan looked elsewhere, guilty, and if Xavier had heat vision, he'd have burned a hole through Andres with his stare. Kevin touched his knee, breaking his stare.

"How are you feeling?" he asked, quietly.

"Alone," replied Xavier.

"I'm here. We're here."

"Why didn't you back me up before?"

"Don't do that."

"I haven't gone crazy, you know. I know we probably wouldn't have gotten far, that we would have had to get back to the group…"

"But now we have a little food, a little water. We're safe. We made the right choice," said Kevin.

"No, *you* made the right choice, which was leaving me."

"X, I never would have left you. I would have knocked you

out and carried you on my back if I had to."

"I'm sorry I had a meltdown. I just wanted your support. I wanted you to say, 'fuck everyone else,'" said Xavier. "Does this... do we... does it just not work?"

"I think it can."

"It *can*, right?"

"Yeah. It can," said Kevin, and he took Xavier's hand. In the distance, looking like ants in a line on the horizon, a herd of big cattle-like animals slowly marched toward the watering hole.

"Cape Buffalo," said Cobra to the Professor. "They can be really cranky. They probably kill more people in Africa than any of the Big Five, way more than lions or elephants."

"About 200 a year," she said, "according to the guidebook."

"Haha. You don't have to be right about everything, Professor."

"I know I don't have to be. It just happens that I usually am."

"Things are looking up for them. The dry season favors the predators, because the browsers and the grazers are stressed out with less vegetation available. There are fewer places to drink, and the lions know that the herbivores are dependent on what few permanent water sources remain. To them, it's like salsa and chips at a Mexican restaurant... sooner or later, whether you've ordered or not, those chips are going to be on your table. You just have to wait."

"Don't tease me with chips and salsa."

"But when the rains come, there's plenty of grass, and more water sources. They can go anywhere, and the lions have to work to hunt them. The balance swings in their favor."

"And when do you think the balance will swing in your favor?"

Cobra smiled at her. He suddenly noticed that the rougher she looked, the more beautiful she was. This was a woman who belonged out here in the wild: rugged, strong, confident. Watching the two of them briefly, Hyacinth quietly tallied another point.

"OK, Professor. I bet I can still surprise you."

"Really? What do I get if I win?"

"What do you want?"

"I would love a shower," she said.

"Good choice! You really stink, Professor," he replied, and she punched him playfully in the shoulder. "Look at this."

Cobra grabbed a small grass seed from the ground and held it in his hand. He applied a few drops of water from his bottle to it.

"You're right; that is truly spectacular," she said.

"Just wait for it."

Within thirty seconds, the seed sprouted roots from within and began *moving* itself on Cobra's palm as though it were a tiny animal.

"That's how quickly life returns after the rains," he said, placing it tenderly in the dirt. "All it required was the right circumstances."

"Cobra McCoors, you have surprised me."

"Sometimes all we need is the right push, and we can change everything about ourselves."

# CHAPTER 16:
# A BAR IN TANGIERS
# 2003

It was a pit: a filthy, disgusting pit, the sort of place where you should have checked twice to make sure your tetanus inoculation was up to date before sitting at a table. It did, however, A) have beer, B) have *cold* beer, and C) provide a location where no questions were asked. To call it a dive bar doesn't seem fair to legitimate dive bars, because at least *those* establishments had to have licenses and health-code inspections; here, if they used soap to scrub the dried blood off the tables, it was a good day. Again, though... cold beer, so there's that.

This was the sort of place that was made specifically for a man like Wyatt Northside, who strode through the door with a woman on each arm, and when he did, all the bar's pirates and cutthroats and (I'm pretty sure) one of the *actual* Thugee Guards from *Temple of Doom* put down their whiskeys to mentally size him up. If they had protractors, they could have measured the right angles of his Dick Tracy square jaw at nearly perfect ninety-degrees. Swarthy stubble, luxurious hair on his massive chest visible through the open buttons on his shirt, crow's feet lines cut into either side of his eyes... this was a guy who *must* have just led some expedition across the Sahara on camelback, or was the lone survivor of a gunfight with a bunch of horse thieves, or discovered some hidden chamber buried deep beneath the Valley of Kings.

"Don't get up on my account," he said with an impossibly thick Australian accent, and then repeated it in French as he and his companions headed straight for the bar.

All the other drinkers, rogues themselves, went back to the business of inebriation, keeping tabs on Wyatt from the corner of their eyes. Wyatt, meanwhile, had his eyes on one man - a little on the younger side, thin, wearing desert camo pants and with dog tags dangling from his neck - slowly sipping water at his table alone, eyes down.

"*This place is like a sewer, but with worse air quality*," said one of the two women with Wyatt, in Portuguese.

"You're right," admitted Wyatt. "Why don't you two go back to your hotel? It's been a fun twenty-four hours, ladies, but maybe this is where we part ways."

He gave them money for a cab, flashing more cash than he should have in a place like this, and they each kissed him on the cheek.

"*Thanks, Wyatt. You're a true gentleman. The other girls won't believe us about you.*"

"Don't join a convent, *senhoras*; you'd break too many hearts."

He made sure they left the bar unaccosted and bellied up, surveying the dusty bottles on the shelf, and he wondered why there were several patches of tiny, grouped holes in the ceiling above the bar.

"Bartender…" he called, and a young African woman with tightly cropped hair and the kind of face that could sell anything from Cheerios to hemorrhoid cream if she were pictured on a TV commercial appeared as if by magic.

"What can I get you?"

"What an accent, ma'am! Are you Kenyan?" asked Wyatt.

"Yes, sir, Kikuyu. Been there?"

"I consulted for the KWS in Meru when they were trying

to repopulate the park. Lovely, lovely country."

"That it is," she said. "You're a long way from home, mister."

"We both are. Please call me Wyatt."

"My name is Florence. Welcome to Morocco, Wyatt."

"How about a double of your least watered-down whiskey?"

"I've got a Jack Daniels bottle, not even opened. I'd skip the rocks, unless you've got three days to spend within ten feet of a water closet."

"Jack it is, Florence," he said.

"Right away."

As Florence wiped out a glass to make it at least appear clean, Wyatt turned and looked at the forlorn man with the now-empty glass of water.

"Florence, what's the story with that guy?"

"Him? This is the third day he's been here. He says he has no money, and he only orders water. I slip him some bread when nobody's looking."

"Why do you do that?"

"It's a Muslim country, and their Muhammad says to give alms to the poor."

She poured Wyatt's Jack Daniels, and he gave her three times the cash that it was worth.

"Do me a favor, Florence. Get that man a beer and some proper food; keep the rest for yourself. Don't tell him it's from me."

"That's very generous, Wyatt. May I ask why?"

"He's a soldier," Wyatt said solemnly. "No soldier's going to drink water and go hungry if I'm in the same bar as him."

It didn't take long for Wyatt to bring his whiskey to a table where five others had been playing cards, and it also didn't take

long for him to piss them off. This motley assortment of shifty
characters included a guy with an eyepatch, a woman smoking
from a long, thin cigarette holder, an ogre with a long, braided
beard, a twitchy fellow wearing a karate-kid-style headband, and a
young gentleman dressed in - no joke - a full tuxedo.

"How can I be cheating you if I don't understand the
fucking rules?" asked Wyatt.

Eyepatch said something rapidly in some language Wyatt
didn't understand, and Beard pounded the table in agreement.

"I'm barely ahead of you cocksuckers, honestly! No
offense, Cigarette."

"Lots offense," said Cigarette. "Lots offense!"

Karate Kid explained, "He said, in Arabic, that if you don't
give back his money, he will pay what he has left to the rest of us to
take it back from you."

"That was not Arabic. I don't know what the fuck voodoo
language that was. People, let's be civilized, shall we?" asked
Wyatt.

Eyepatch said something to Tuxedo in what was *supposedly*
Arabic, and Tuxedo nodded gravely as though Eyepatch had just
relayed that Wyatt had told him to go fuck his mother.

"Jesus, now what's he want?" asked Wyatt.

In a French accent, Beard said, "He wants his money back,
and because you are stealing, he wants your hand as well."

"Now you're just fucking with me. What is this, Conan the
Barbarian times? And how would you even expect me to cut my
hand off for you?"

Tuxedo stood up from the table and drew what looked like
an eighteenth-century British cavalry sword, and everyone in the
bar pushed back from their chairs to watch.

Eyepatch again launched curses and swears in some
language, gesticulating threateningly to Wyatt, who stood up slowly
and raised his hands in the air.

"Look, people, I think there's been some

miscommunication. Karate Kid, please translate for me. What I mean to say is," said Wyatt calmly, stuffing his money into his pockets. "Why don't you go fuck your mother?"

Eyepatch whipped out a revolver and cocked the hammer, when a glass bottle shattered over his head. Scalp bleeding (but revolver dropped), Eyepatch turned around to see the thin soldier - Campbell McConnors, of course - very much regretting having done that.

"Thanks, mate!" said Wyatt, and he overturned the table, knocking Beard on the chin with it and sending him crashing backwards. Everyone leapt to their feet, and Tuxedo dashed towards Wyatt, swinging like the propellers of a prop plane.

Campbell had the sense to kick the revolver across the floor before Eyepatch threw himself upon him, securing his hands tightly around Campbell's throat. They both collided with the adjacent table, sending empty bottles flying and giving the other drinkers an excuse to join the fray and get their free hits in.

As Wyatt tried to fence Tuxedo with an overturned chair, Cigarette pulled a heavy chain from her purse and Karate Kid wrapped his hands with strips of canvas as if preparing for twelve sanctioned rounds. Cigarette kicked the still-unconscious Beard for no apparent reason, and then they both went after Wyatt.

Campbell went for Eyepatch's nuts, but Eyepatch had been in a scrap or two before and knew to turn his knees at a slight angle to keep his jewels safe. Campbell felt the life draining from him, his carotid arteries compressed and his eyes about to pop out of their sockets. He punched Eyepatch in the nose, and he felt a satisfying crunch of busting cartilage, but this only served to irritate him further.

Instinctively remembering a judo move from Basic, Campbell secured Eyepatch's wrist, pivoted, and turned his own hips perpendicularly to gain instant leverage and toss Eyepatch onto a nearby table, breaking more glasses. The move mostly worked, but Eyepatch held onto Campbell, dragging him down too.

Tuxedo committed to a killing thrust, throwing all his weight behind it, allowing Wyatt to side-step him like a toreador and splinter the chair over his head.

"Have a seat!" he said, pleased with himself, a split-second before Cigarette's chain bore down upon him, wrapping up his arm and securing him in place. Karate Kid glided right into Tuxedo's spot and blessed Wyatt with a blur of quick jabs and crosses to the mid-section, saving the uppercut for last.

Now Eyepatch's nuts were fair game, and since Campbell was pinning him to the table anyway, he drove his elbow into Eyepatch's groin. If you've ever been hit in the nether regions with so much as a wiffle-ball, you'll appreciate that Eyepatch had no physiological option but to release his grip on Campbell's throat. Fortunately for Eyepatch, four of the other bar dwellers whose tables had been overturned in the rumble were happy to take his place, kicking and punching Campbell indiscriminately.

Wyatt, nonplussed that Karate Kid had possibly knocked one of his fillings lose, grabbed the chain and pulled with all his strength, turning Cigarette into the club of a medieval morning star, swinging her into Karate Kid. He then used Beard's (still-) unconscious body as a stepladder to climb onto one of the tables that had somehow not yet been overturned and then dove off of it, rocketing downward like a meteor upon both Cigarette and Karate Kid.

Campbell scrambled to get to his feet, but he was now like the pinata at a child's birthday party, except that the *children* were, in fact, vicious, drunk adults, nobody was blindfolded, and nobody took turns. Eyepatch, crumpled in the fetal position on the floor, thought about nothing but the powerful, throbbing pain in his groin, but as luck would have it, he had landed right next to his revolver.

Struggling to his feet and still bent over, Eyepatch took aim at Campbell.

244

Boom! Shotgun blast, into the air, right above the bar. Dust rained down from buckshot, adding a new grouping of holes into the ceiling. Florence aimed out into the crowd, and everyone stopped.

"I have two more hours in my shift," she called. "Now knock this shit off until the next girl comes."

Eyepatch shook his head and said something in *maybe Arabic*, but then Campbell answered in the same *maybe Arabic*. They had entered into a terse, brief conversation.

"What's he saying? That's no Arabic I've ever heard," said Wyatt.

"It's *Hassaniya* Arabic," said Campbell. "It's like one of ten languages they speak here."

"Well, what's he want?"

"He says you skipped his turn."

"That's…" said Wyatt, considering. "You know what? I think I did."

Eyepatch looked at Wyatt, and then looked at Campbell, confused. Campbell translated.

"Tell him I'll give him his money back. And this round's on me."

\*\*\*

Campbell thought that he was now in some kind of Bizarroworld. He was sitting at a table next to Eyepatch, whose arm was around him as if they were long lost pals even as the bag of ice sitting on his groin was starting to melt. Tuxedo had fixed his tie, Cigarette lit another, well, cigarette, and Beard was just finally coming to. Karate Kid was telling some story in an English so broken you'd need a degree in linguistics to decipher it, but here was Wyatt, laughing riotously at the punchline.

"Killed by a snake?" Wyatt roared. "That's hysterical!"

"No - impaled by a rake," corrected Karate Kid. "A rake!"

245

SNAKE IN THE GRASS

But it didn't matter. Soon everyone at the table, including Karate Kid, was cheering, "Snake! Snake! Snake!"

"This guy gets it," said Wyatt as he clapped Beard on the back, setting everyone up with another shot. "May we all live until we die."

In a bar full of loud, drunk scoundrels, their table was the loudest, the drunkest, and dare I say it, the *warmest*, despite the fact that they had all resolved to murder one another only a few short minutes ago. Campbell considered how quickly fortunes could change. He wasn't sure what his place in all this was, but Wyatt just nodded to him from across the table and was glad to have a friend for the first time in what seemed like a hundred years.


Hours later, after Florence had left and another bartender had replaced her, Campbell sat with Wyatt alone at a dimly lit table near the corner. They each had full plates of lamb, some kind of fragrant couscous, and some dried fruits. Wyatt had to make sure Campbell didn't choke, as he couldn't eat fast enough. The baby roach that crawled out from underneath his plate didn't slow him down in the least.

"Thanks for helping me with Eyepatch," said Wyatt. "He was acting like a real pain in the dick."

"Don't you mean pain in the *ass*?"

"I do not. Which sounds worse to you? A pain in the ass or a pain in the dick?"

"Dick sounds much worse," Campbell admitted.

"It is, mate, it is. And remember: anyone can be a pain in the ass, but it takes a man to endure a pain in the dick. Free wisdom, from me to you."

"Thank you for that. And for the beer before. Florence told me it was you."

"I hope you drank it before you broke it over that guy's head. Anyway, it was the least I could do. Thank *you* for your service."

"You're American?"

"No. But I respect all soldiers. I've never had the balls to put my life in someone else's hands. And fuck Saddam Hussein, while we're at it. Just war or not, he was a piece of shit and he made a lot of people suffer. So, thanks for that, soldier."

"To tell you the truth, Wyatt, I don't really think I qualify as a soldier anymore," said Campbell, poking at the couscous and tucking his dog tags beneath his shirt.

So, Campbell proceeded to tell Wyatt, nearly a complete stranger, his whole story. He told him about his listlessness at college, about his flawless, ass-kicking brother, about his complicity in mowing down a whole town's worth of Iraqi insurgents (including a fourteen-year-old boy), and about Kurt's lifeless body bleeding out into indifferent dust and sand. Having nothing left to lose, Campbell regaled Wyatt with the tale of stealing the lamassu from Black Tiger, of the wrath of the sandstorm, and of nearly dying ten different ways in his aimless trek through the Arabian Desert. He finished by explaining how he somehow made it to the river and traded his gun to a sailor in exchange for stowing him away on a freighter out of the country, all the way through what he *assumed* was the Persian Gulf, Arabian Sea, and Suez Canal (but didn't actually *know* because he was hiding below deck).

"And here you are," punctuated Wyatt.

"In a bar in Tangiers. I can't go home; I'm a deserter and a traitor. If I'm lucky, the army told my family that I'm dead. Can't get a job here with no papers, and I have no money. All that's left of me are the stinking clothes I'm wearing."

Wyatt said, "I wasn't going to say anything. You do smell somewhat less than fresh."

"But the worst of it is, I can't go to Kurt's family and tell his mother how he really died. He deserved at least that much."

"That all sucks on ice, mate. You are Fucked with a capital *F*."

"All I wanted was to have a little adventure, to have a little action before I died. See the world! But I'm not that kind of guy. I know that now. I'm just not meant for that kind of life. Black Tiger even said I was just a boy playing at being a man, and I see what he means now. I should have just kept reading National Geographics, took the cookie-cutter finance career waiting for me, and left the heroics to guys like you and my brother," said Campbell, morose.

Wyatt laughed sincerely, deeply.

"Not really the reaction I was expecting, but hey, whatever."

Wyatt leaned in and said, "With only one year of college and some basic training in *Arabic*, you fought off a consortium of trained mercenaries, stole from them a priceless treasure, survived a forty-foot tall sandstorm, and suffered through at least seven days in a hostile desert wilderness with neither food nor water, and *you're telling me* that you aren't cut out for a life of adventure?"

Campbell had never thought of it like that. Hearing someone recount his feats like that out loud made them sound all the more like fiction, and yet, all those exploits were true.

"Sometimes we try to push our comfort zones to prove to ourselves we're capable of being more than who we believe ourselves to be," said Wyatt, drawing from his own experience. "And then, after we jump from that plane or take that job in Seattle or put our in-laws in their places, we think we've accomplished something totally out of character. But here's the funny thing about that idea, and my whole point: those actions really *were* in character, and they were always in character all along. We just didn't choose to go looking for that stuff."

"What are you saying, Wyatt? Even guys who read can kick some ass when they get lucky?" asked Campbell.

"What I'm saying is, if you want to be a stockbroker, go do it if it makes you happy. But if you want to be a race car driver, get out there and race some fucking cars, and don't worry if people don't see you as the kind of guy who drives three hundred miles per hour at Monaco."

"What if I have no idea how to race cars?"

"Figure it out, man! Read a book, rent a Mazda and redline it at two in the morning. Hang out with some mechanics and learn. How hard can it be?"

"Yeah," wondered Campbell. "How hard could it be? I read books."

"Books are great, and I really, really mean that. You can't ever read enough books. But that's only a starting point. You've got to get out there and do it at some point, because we only get one go-around on this ride. Don't ever let someone else tell you how to live your life, and more importantly, don't ever let anyone else decide for you *who you should be*."

Campbell finished his water. Even cloudy with particulates and at room temperature, he was happy to have it.

"OK, Wyatt, I'm inspired. But I'm still homeless and penniless in a foreign country with one set of clothes. Any practical suggestions?"

"First, you're going to write a letter to that guy's family. I'll loan you postage."

Campbell's eyes would have welled with sudden emotion, but his body politely reminded him that it couldn't spare the moisture to manufacture tears.

"Thank you, Wyatt."

"And then," he said. "And then. Do you still have it?"

It took Campbell a moment to figure out what Wyatt was talking about, *and then*:

"I was going to pawn it off at the local museum, see if I could get a few... whatever they spend in this country. Moroccan pesos or whatever."

"You know what *Hassaniya Arabic* is but you don't know about Moroccan *dirhams*?" asked Wyatt.

"Anyway," said Campbell. He carefully removed the

lamassu from his dusty, distressed backpack and placed it reverently on the table, guarding it from prying eyes with his arms. Even in this filthy hole, the gold was still dazzling. Wyatt touched it, feeling its antiquity, its uniqueness.

"It's missing a jewel from when I hit that guy, but even still, it's a few thousand years old and unlike most other Assyrian effigies of its time. I'll sell it to you, if you want, for cheap. I can't exactly pay for a pizza with it if I were starving, which I am, so…"

Wyatt leaned backward and interlaced his fingers behind his head.

"I don't think I'll buy it, no."

"Thanks anyway. And thanks for dinner, and well, for the fist fight."

"Because you're going to give it to me."

"Come again?"

"You are going to give me that thing, that piece of metal and gems that basically does you no good anymore anyway," said Wyatt.

"Um, wait. Are you about to rob me?"

"Rob you? Mate, I'm going to train you!"

"Train me? To do what?"

"In exchange for that pilfered hunk of cultural heritage, I'm going to bankroll you, provide you with food, clothing, lodging, and most importantly, experience."

"Like Yoda."

Wyatt said, "Yoda was trying to make Luke a *Jedi Master*, not give him a Master*card*, but that's the idea. Stick with me for three months, and I will personally turn you from a homeless drifter marooned on the Island of Misfit Fucking Toys into the ass-kicking adventure-seeker you've always wanted to be."

"How?"

"I've recently come into a little bit of money, mate," said Wyatt. "Let me pay it forward, so to speak. Africa is the greatest classroom there is. Come on, it'll be like our little summer project!"

"Just to be clear," said Campbell, "and because I really have no other options - you're not, like, hitting on me, are you?"

"To be clear, no."

"Because, again, to be clear, since I have no other options, in that case I'd have to insist that I'd be *pitching* in exchange for your generosity."

"To be clear *again*, no, I'm not, and no, you would be *catching*."

"Then thank you, Wyatt," said Campbell, extending his hand. "We have a deal."

"Excellent, Campbell!" said Wyatt with a firm grip. "The first thing we have to do is work on that name."

# CHAPTER 17:
# BUFFALO HIDE

Cobra stretched out against the tree and yawned; he was confident that the growing number of cape buffalos steadily approaching the water hole were far enough to the west that he needn't worry about them yet, and he was also content that the leopard was still lazing away in the tree with his prize. The afternoon African sun was enough to sap even the most ferocious of motivations, be they stalking unsuspecting prey below or hiking to safety after being dealt the business end of a rocket-propelled grenade.

Andres kept eyeing up that leopard, though. It was too good a shot *not* to take, but he wasn't ready to give back the camera just yet. He stifled his impulses and watched on in silence, mentally willing the leopard not to move until the others were looking the other way or something.

"So, if we wanted, in theory, to look for Kruger's lost gold…" began Susan.

"Are you still on this? It's a dead end. Even if you had a fully funded archaeological expedition at your disposal, and many people have, there's just no substance to it," said Cobra.

"But if you still wanted to, not on this ill-fated three-hour-tour," half-sang Susan, persisting, "but on a totally separate trip, where would you start?"

"You would start by booking a flight to Hoedspruit, easily

done via Cape Town or Joburg, and you'd start surveying up and down to Mpumalanga and back, over and over by car, on the western edge of Kruger Park. You'd need permission from the various private concessions like the exclusive ones in the Sabi Sands, who would no doubt ask for a rand or two to compensate for ruining their lucrative safari businesses while digging through their property. A helicopter might help, also, not free. Finally, you'd need to work it out with the hundreds of farms and townships along that path. That's if you're sticking to the prevailing school of thought that Kruger hid his stuff, and that it's undisturbed, somewhere near the park that bears his name, let alone in the park itself. But hey, if you think you can get further than all the geologists, historians and archaeologists who've spent small fortunes themselves looking for this gold over the last hundred years, be my guest," said Cobra.

"That's if we're sticking to the *prevailing* school of thought," said the Professor. "What's the other school?"

Cobra tilted his hat over his eyes and yawned once more. Usually telling this story was good for tips; it sprinkled a little intrigue to the safari and added to the guests' sense of adventure. Now that there were people who were actually out there willing to kill for this treasure, it made it a little less fun.

"Don't get excited, people. Wyatt once told me that he heard a story in one of his many travels to far-away places with fabulous people. He said that an old man running a curio shop in Zimbabwe, near Hwange, informed him that the treasure had been looted a long time ago."

"How long ago? Are we talking Reagan time, or Clinton time, or what?" asked Susan.

"When did we get so old?" asked Hyacinth.

"Three or four weeks ago, I think," said Mark.

"We're talking Woodrow Wilson time, people. The short version is that soldiers from German Southwest Africa conducted a raid across the border into British-supported South Africa, all the way from northwest to northeast, with cars and trucks. They had obtained a map that divulged the location of Kruger's gold, and they quietly made a play for it in the middle of the night."

"So, it's in German Southwest Africa," said Kevin.

"Namibia now, and no, not if you believe what the guy in Hwange told Wyatt. Apparently, the British caught on. They alerted their troops by the border and cut the Germans off, preventing their escape. The Germans fought bitterly, but they couldn't get out. The British managed to defeat the Germans, who were killed to the very last man."

"So, it's in some bank in London," said Hyacinth.

Buffalo had now taken over the watering hole, their deep, guttural grunts intimidating all but the most intrepid antelope away from the water's edge. There were close to fifty of them, with more streaming in from the horizon each minute.

"No. The British found no treasure at all, and with no Germans to interrogate, there was no way of knowing if the Germans had simply failed to find anything in the first place or abandoned it, hiding it somewhere along the way."

"We did find World War I bullets before at the San settlement," said Kevin.

"That only confirms that the Germans were there at one point, not that there is any gold buried anywhere within a forty-mile radius of Rhino Horn Ranch. It could be that the British did find it and kept it from the South Africans," said Cobra. "But if I really did believe it were still out there, I'd have spent every waking moment searching for it, not leading tourists around the bush. I mean, you're all lovely people, but come on."

"*Still* out there," said the Professor. "Curious choice of words, Cobra."

"Hyacinth," whispered Xavier, who gestured with his head towards Andres, who was extending the zoom lens on Hyacinth's camera to focus in on the leopard.

"What the hell?"

Hyacinth got to her feet, sprained ankle and all, and marched up to Andres like someone who'd been waiting at the DMV for five hours. She clutched him by the shoulder and spun him around to face her.

"What?"

"What do you mean, *what*? What are you doing with my camera?"

"Obviously, I'm photographing that magnificent cat, but unless that cloud moves in front of the sun, the light will be far too harsh for a proper exposure."

"I'm going to properly expose all the blood in your thick skull when I break your goddamn face! See how harsh you think *that* is!"

"Please, woman. There's no need to threaten violence, especially if you haven't had your osteoporosis supplements today."

Mark stood up, not to hurt Andres but to keep Hyacinth from fulfilling her promise to bust him up.

"You son of a bitch! You've had her camera the entire time?" he accused.

"Obviously I was going to give it back sooner or later; I was just pushing for *later*. I'm surprised it took you *that* long to find me with it. I will pay you for the roll that I used, and I'll make you copies of my photographs for free," he said, utterly unapologetic. He clicked the button to rewind the film, and the camera's little internal gears whirred to life.

"You stole my camera! I can't believe you stole my camera!" fumed Hyacinth, turning red. "These were once-in-a-lifetime moments that I missed, and you took them from me!"

"Let's be honest, Hyacinth. There were two of us photographers and only one camera between us. Naturally, the more gifted photographer should have been entitled to the equipment. I always intended to give you copies of my photographs."

"Oh my God. Now you're actually justifying stealing my

camera!'"

"Technically," Andres said, "Susan stole it for me."

"Oh shit," Susan whispered, and then stood to face Hyacinth, Mark and Andres.

"Sooooooo…" Susan began, "that's not true. I saw the camera near the riverbank when Andres slid down, and then when I picked it up, everyone was running after Kevin and the baboons. I swear I was going to give it to you, Hyacinth. Andres must have taken it when the monkeys started chasing us."

"That sounds like monkey shit," said Hyacinth. "Why didn't you tell me that when I realized it was lost? I almost went back to the crocodile river to look for it!"

"Now, don't soak your Depends, grandma. I was trying to help, no thanks to you."

"Talk to me like that again and I'm going to slap the disrespect out of you. You can blog about that, and then I'll cyber-bully you again in the comments section," said Hyacinth.

"Ooh! Someone's grandkids taught Hyacinth how to turn on a computer! Next you'll be sending text messages on your portable cellular telephone! I just hope someone's there the next time you've fallen and you can't get up!" jeered Susan.

Andres ejected the film roll from the camera and secured it in his pocket. By now, Cobra, Professor and Kevin were watching, and you'd have gotten the impression that Cobra was now doing a mental checklist to see if he'd forgotten a second buried cooler with some popcorn in it.

"Maybe you should do something?" asked the Professor.

"They're all grownups," said Cobra. "At least, three of them are, I'm pretty sure. Let them sort it out."

"But Susan has a gun!"

"So do you, Professor. Let's see how it plays out."

Andres extended the camera to Hyacinth as though it were an olive branch.

"Here, Hyacinth. Thank you for being so gracious."

When Hyacinth reached for it, however, Andres dropped it, and the lens attachment shattered into pieces of glass and plastic.

There was a moment of silence, as if even the animals couldn't believe what had just happened.

Hyacinth planted both her feet in the ground and punched Andres squarely in his left eye; it was the sort of punch trainers would have complimented her for during a cardio kickboxing class, fully transferring her weight from hip to hip. Andres staggered backward, and if he were in a cartoon, there would have been literal fires ignited in his eyes. He marched forward to retaliate.

But he didn't hit Hyacinth; he instead hit Mark, who had pulled his wife out of the way. Mark stumbled backward into Susan, bumping her in the forehead, and now she was seeing little canaries - I mean, *lilac-breasted rollers*, since we're in Africa - orbiting her head.

Dazed, Susan threw a blind kick - a fifty-yard field goal kick - forward, and it connected with Mark's gut, doubling him over.

Hyacinth obviously wasn't having any of that, and she tackled Susan to the ground below, mounting her and slapping the disrespect out of her repeatedly, as she had promised. Grasping for anything, Susan threw a handful of sand into Hyacinth's eyes, which did absolutely nothing to slow her down.

Mark and Andres scrapped a little, but Mark couldn't really do much with his burned hands, and in truth, Andres really didn't want to hurt him. Mark went for a single-leg takedown, a wrestling move he'd taught literally thousands of times over the years on a cushy, foam mat, but it didn't knock Andres off his feet. Mark just awkwardly clung to Andres' hip like a dog going to town on some poor bastard's leg, and Andres kept slapping the crown of Mark's head like an old bongo.

When enough was finally enough, Cobra carefully extricated Andres from Mark, and it took both the Professor and Kevin to manage prying Hyacinth off Susan.

"I was wrong about you, Hyacinth," said Andres. "You

don't hit like an old lady after all."

"You reptile," seethed Hyacinth. "And as for you, Cupcake…"

"Check to make sure neither of your hips is broken before finishing that sentence, granny," said Susan in *extra* Southern.

"All right, that's enough of that," said Cobra.

"Why? I was just getting started," said Mark.

"Oh, maybe because of that…"

Cobra pointed to the buffalo herd at the water hole's edge who had obviously taken notice of the fight and were looking in their direction.

"Really?" asked the Professor. "Because I thought you meant because of *that*."

Cobra looked to the north and west, where the Professor was pointing, and said, "Well. Fuck."

A vehicle was speeding across the horizon, probably three miles to the west but perfectly visible. It looked like a Toyota Land Cruiser, or some other rugged four-by-four, and it was ejecting a trail of dust six feet high from behind its rear tires.

"Could it be another safari…" started Kevin, but Cobra cut him off:

"It's them."

Cobra knew that if they had binoculars and the inclination to look in their direction, the people in that car very well could have spotted them already. There was too much distance to go back to the giraffe canyon, and their bipedal profiles would give them away for certain. There was really only one option available.

"All right, people, follow me," said Cobra.

"Wait," said Xavier. "Follow you where?"

"We're going to have to hide behind the buffalo herd."

"What? You just told us how dangerous they are, that they kill more people in Africa than lions! That they're aggressive and bad-tempered!"

Kevin said, "Xavier, I don't think we have a choice."

"Yes," said Xavier, pulling Susan's gun out from underneath his shirt, "we do."

Everyone took a step back.

"Hey! You stole my gun!" cursed Susan.

"Oh, now you don't like it when someone steals *your* things, huh, princess?" jabbed Hyacinth.

He waved it around at everyone, even Kevin.

"This has gone on long enough. We're never going to make it back alive. Let's go turn ourselves in and see what happens."

"Xavier, no!" pleaded Kevin. "They killed their own freaking guy, remember?"

"We don't know what they want! We only know we're going to die out here, and I refuse to get gored or trampled or eaten by one of those things!"

"Well, I personally guarantee they won't eat you," said Cobra. "They are one hundred percent fully herbivorous."

"Please don't do this," said Kevin.

"Look, Xavier, buddy... we don't have time for this," said Cobra, and when he took a step forward, Xavier pointed the gun straight up and fired, twice.

The car stopped.

The buffalos lowered their heads menacingly, and some of the juveniles ran behind their mothers for protection.

Xavier himself seemed shocked by the noise, as if he had never heard a gun before. The Professor raised the rifle and aimed it at him. Kevin threw himself in front of Xavier and put his hands up.

"Don't," said Kevin, but the Professor kept the barrel locked on the two of them now. Kevin turned to Xavier. "X, you mean too much to me, and maybe there's a world where we might have a future together..."

Kevin suddenly slapped the gun out of Xavier's hand.

"...but I am not about to let you go get yourself killed."

The Professor lowered the rifle, and Kevin clutched Xavier by the shirt, dragging him along. With a delirious grin, Xavier said, "Tae kwon do. Haha."

"Quickly, quietly," said Cobra, taking the lead. Everyone followed behind him, single file as he had instructed. Mark picked up Hyacinth's camera, leaving the shattered lens behind.

The buffalo were even more imposing up close. These weren't some cows at a petting zoo; they expressed their displeasure at the party's presence by snorting loudly, kicking up dust with their hooves and sending the ever-present cattle egrets at their feet to a safe distance away. Cobra tried to do the mental math, finding a distance close enough to the buffalo that their huge numbers and massive bulk would provide a blind against their antagonists, but far enough away that they would not incite a stampede. Twenty yards away from the bovine wall seemed the crazy answer to a totally insane question.

Cobra motioned for the group to crouch down low, and even as he did so, he knew they were way too close to these powerful animals. The group felt as much as heard the sound of their clump-clump-clumping hooves pounding against the earth, and the sound of the constant ripping of grass from the dirt by a dozen mouths at once seemed terrifyingly near.

"See?" whispered Cobra. "They barely even notice us."

"I'd have that carved on your tombstone," said the Professor, "except that nobody's going to bury us out here."

"Who has specs?" he asked, and Mark handed over his binoculars.

Through the hundreds of legs in front of him, Cobra looked out across the watering hole and at the horizon. The car started up again and was driving towards them. It was about two miles away and closing.

"Well?" asked Hyacinth.

"I wonder if it's too late to turn ourselves over to them," said Cobra.

"What?" whispered Xavier.

"Joking. Totally joking," he replied, and then to himself, "Not joking." He turned to the Professor and asked, "Have you ever killed anyone?"

"Of course not," she said, adding, "You mean, like, have I ever killed anyone *today*?"

"Atta girl. I hope you're a better shot than I am."

At a mile and a half out, the car stopped again. Cobra looked through the specs and saw three tough guys in desert camouflage, and *him*: "Black Fucking Tiger."

"Is that Black Tiger?" asked the Professor, and Cobra held the binoculars in front of her eyes.

"*That* is Black Tiger. Mercenary, looter of cultural artifacts, stone-cold murderer."

Cobra got a good look at him. He had a small scar on his forehead now from some acute blunt trauma, the memory of which made Cobra smile, and now a dazzling green gemstone hung loosely from his neck. Otherwise, there was no mistaking him, although he'd put on some more muscle in the last five years: black ponytail, tiger claws tied around his wrists... Santana, the Black Tiger. *What the fuck was he doing out here?*

"I'm going to have to ventilate this sucker, aren't I?" asked the Professor.

"What are you, a twenties gangster? While you're at it, why don't you keep the change, you filthy animal?"

That was an obscure reference Cobra dusted off for the Professor, but before having to explain it, Black Tiger and his men started up the Land Cruiser and headed south, almost parallel to the path Cobra and the party had taken. They drove another mile or so to a cluster of large rocks and stopped again.

"Cobra," said Mark, alluding to the tons and tons of beef ambling ever closer to their position.

"Yeah, yeah, in a minute," dismissed Cobra. "I don't think they've seen us."

Black Tiger and his men got out of the car, and three of them retrieved a large device that resembled a lawnmower from the trunk. One of them connected it via cable to what was probably a laptop computer. Cobra saw that Black Tiger was giving orders, and the men began pushing the thing around over the grass and dirt.

"It looks like they're cutting the grass," said Susan.

"I think it's a ground penetrating radar, or maybe a magnetometer," said Cobra.

"Did you just make up those words?"

"No, he is correct," said Andres. "They look for anomalies under the ground, disturbances that could indicate the presence of man-made objects or structures."

"They're metal detecting," said Kevin.

"They're treasure hunting," said Susan. "They're looking for it."

"Maybe they know something we don't know," said Hyacinth.

"Hey, guys…" said Mark, insistently.

"Just a sec," responded Cobra, focused on Black Tiger and his prospecting.

"But, um, Cobra…"

"I'm sorry, Mark, what is it?"

What Mark had realized (but everyone else had not) was that the buffalos had decided not to cooperate any longer. As a unified front, a wall of muscle and horns advanced as one, pushing in on the intruders. It was like Pamplona, but with much larger animals, many more of them, no doors and windows for jumping to safety, and no tapas at the bar afterwards, if there even *were* an afterwards.

"Stay cool!" commanded Cobra. "Don't provoke a charge!"

"Why doesn't anyone ever listen to me?" whined Xavier.

"Keep low and crawl backwards. Give them space."

The group backstroked on a sea of short grass as the buffalos followed, swinging their huge, heavy heads side-to-side. The buffalos closed the gap... fifteen yards, ten, nine...

"Now what?" asked the Professor.

Cobra quickly scanned the surroundings. Black Tiger hadn't taken notice of them; on the other side of the watering hole, to the west, were some thick trees.

"We'll have to get to that miombo forest about a quarter mile. Stay low, and be calm."

"I don't know the names of the trees!" complained Susan.

"Those trees! The only trees! Those trees over there!" clarified Cobra.

Andres looked up at the trees asked, "Where is the leopard?"

The leopard leaped clear over Xavier's head, pouncing on a two-hundred-pound Cape Buffalo calf. The little buff tried to shake the leopard off his back as the cat tried to tear through his not-quite-impenetrable skin, but he wasn't strong enough. The calf's mother thrust her snout underneath the leopard's belly and catapulted the predator off the calf and through the air.

With a crash, the startled cat landed on Cobra. In a frenzy, she tried to right herself, regaining her equilibrium in milliseconds as she found her footing on Cobra's torso. Her rear claws slipped on either side of Cobra, slicing through his pantlegs, and in a panic, the leopard snapped her jaws near Cobra's face again and again.

The Professor charged in and swung the rifle like a club, convincing the leopard to launch herself off Cobra and back into the herd to stir up as much commotion as possible among the buffalos. Cobra now had eight small punctures on his chest, and a lot of leopard saliva on his face.

"Come on," the Professor said, helping him to his knees.

"Free tattoo!" gasped Cobra, clutching his chest and sucking wind.

They had lost the leopard in the undulating buffalo herd, and on their hands and knees, they made a play for the miombo forest (which, if you didn't know like Susan, is a colloquial name for the genus *brachystegia*, a common tree in savannah woodland).

# CHAPTER 18:
# GREATER KUDU (THAT YOU DO)

The buffalos behind, many of the group were starting to take their survival for granted instead of realizing how close to death they really had been. Cobra's hubris at bringing a group of wounded tourists on foot to within a stone's throw of a herd of buffalo had reached dizzying heights. It had been touch-and-go for a while, but the buffalos seemed more concerned about the marauding leopard than the foolish humans, and if Black Tiger had detected them, he didn't show it. When close enough to the cover of the miombo forest, Cobra signaled that it was probably safe to stand. Crawling on hands and knees to the forest for a quarter of a mile did Mark's hands no favors. Likewise, it did little to alleviate the swelling in Hyacinth's sprained ankle nor to prevent the throbbing in Xavier's head from worsening. Andres' coccyx was fine.

The forest was thick, and Cobra blazed his own trail through it. The forest canopy sheltered them from the sun but did not stifle the heat. Hyacinth, straying momentarily from single file formation, walked through a spider web four feet wide but said nothing, refusing to complain. They marched north, parallel to the river, which they were close enough to hear but not to see.

"Keep an eye out for leopards; this is good ambush territory," said Cobra.

"What are the odds of encountering another leopard in

such proximity to the one that just used you as a scratching post?" asked Mark.

"Up until today, I'd have said pretty rare. If we were seeing all this wildlife from the car, I'd have said this was the most amazing safari of all time. I'd have written to National Geographic about it if I thought they'd have believed me."

"You should probably have those leopard cuts cleaned out; don't want them to get infected," said Mark.

"Anyone have any water?" asked Cobra.

"No," said everybody in unison.

"Anyone have any disinfectant?"

"No," said everybody, again.

"How about bandages? Anyone have those?"

"No," said everybody, again.

"All right, then. Moving on."

Hyacinth asked, "Don't they hurt?"

"No, not really. I'm pretty lucky she didn't go for my throat. She was just as scared as I was, and all that."

Hyacinth persisted, "Really?"

"Christ on a bike, they hurt so much. I hope I haven't contracted rabies from her right paw and feline AIDS from her left. It's like someone left eight pennies in the sun in Death Valley and then superglued them to my chest. Anyone have any painkillers?"

"No," said everybody, again.

"All right, then. Moving on," said Cobra, making the best of it. "Thanks for saving my life, Professor."

"Oh, did I do that?" she asked, wiping sweat from her forehead. "I mean, did I do that *again*?"

"Let's not get carried away, Professor. I just needed a little momentum to throw her off."

"Whatever, Cobra. Pretty soon, you're going to owe *me* a tip at the end of this safari."

"I think you've earned more than just the tip, Professor,"

jousted Cobra, and in the back, Hyacinth added another to her tally. "I appreciate you not accidentally *ventilating* me, too."

"I wouldn't have fired. For one, I might have *accidentally* hit the leopard. Two, with those guys out of the car, I don't think there's any way they wouldn't have heard a second round of gunshots."

"Speaking of," remembered Cobra, "Susan, did you retrieve your gun?"

"Nope, and I'm sure your company will reimburse me for that, won't they?" Susan grumbled.

"Of course, we will. Right after we prosecute you for bringing a concealed weapon onto our property."

"With the evidence you have from where?"

"Xavier? Did you grab it?"

"If I had," said Xavier, dizzy and supported by Kevin, "I'd have shot you by now."

"Oh, that's just the hematoma talking. Anyone? Did we just leave a loaded gun behind?"

"We were in such a rush to get away, I don't think anyone picked it up," said Mark.

"Some baboon could find it," scoffed Andres. "Take over his troop with it."

"Maybe poachers would think twice if they knew the animals could shoot back," said Hyacinth. "On the plus side, I think my camera still works."

"Typical American, using violence to solve everything," said Andres.

"You're right, you Germans are known worldwide for your sensitivity. You did break a six hundred dollar zoom lens, and I expect dollars, not euros."

There was a rustling in the dense trees ahead, and Cobra held up his hand. Everyone froze. Something big was coming through the bushes.

"Jesus, what's next?" cried Xavier.

From behind the trees sauntered a huge antelope with a wispy beard and regal, spiral horns reaching extravagantly behind him. Beautiful blacks, grays and creams painted this extraordinary creature's coat, and dark, ebony eyes made him seem like the monarch of the forest.

"Greater Kudu," said Cobra, taking a step backward and readying his knife.

"Cobra, come on," teased the Professor. "We talked about this, remember? Kudus are shy, elusive animals that are notoriously skittish."

"And I told you, those are lesser kudus, not greater kudus," he whispered.

The kudu bull, even bigger than the one from yesterday, stood still, curiously judging the group.

"You just wrestled a leopard, and now you're telling me you're afraid of what's basically a deer?" she laughed, and quickly added, "Yes, I know it's an antelope and not literally a deer."

Cobra motioned for everyone to give the kudu some space. It wasn't a predator, but it did have powerful muscles in its neck and shoulders, and there was no doubt an errant kick could probably do some damage. The Professor, though, held her ground, slowly removed the rifle from her shoulder, and passed it back to Cobra.

The kudu slowly approached the Professor, cautiously placing one delicate hoof in front of the other. For her part, the Professor kept her hands down and her head low, trying to appear as non-threatening as she could. Closer and closer the bull antelope came to her, and he lifted his head up high as if he were a king at a coronation, sharply drawing in air through his nostrils. She was prepared to step back if the kudu wanted to initiate actual physical contact, because she didn't want him to become too accustomed to humans, but when he was about two yards away, he stomped his front right hoof onto the leaf litter below.

It sounded as though a dinosaur had smashed through the

forest.

Puzzled and frightened, the Professor skittered to the closest tree, and the kudu took off like a bolt of lightning. An enormous elephant - a bull with heavy tusks - thundered through from the east, flapping his ears and trumpeting.

"Attenborough!" recognized Hyacinth.

Attenborough broke any trees that might have constrained him as easily as stalks of celery, snapping them with his titanic bulk. He turned to the Professor and the others and ran forward, kicking up dust and dirt as though he were riding on a cloud of fire, and then stopped short of grinding them into paste beneath his feet.

As Cobra rounded up the Professor, Attenborough walked backward, a steam shovel in reverse. He flapped his ears back and forth as though he were trying to create gusts of wind with them.

"That wasn't so bad, was it?" remarked Cobra with a wry smile, almost as if to give Attenborough his cue. The elephant crashed forward a second time, splintering more trees, and halting even closer to the screaming, cowering group.

"Fire, you idiot!" yelled Andres, and Cobra realized that he was holding the rifle. "Make some noise!"

Cobra hid the rifle behind him, trying desperately to keep it out of sight, and Attenborough stood still, letting out a deep rumble from his throat. He was still furious, but his demeanor changed in a subtle way that seemed to suggest that with the rifle out of sight, Attenborough's rage could at least begin to subside.

The elephant hoisted his trunk up, culling diverse scents from the air, and after a moment, turned his whole head to face Mark and Hyacinth.

"Do you think he…" whispered Mark.

"Shh," whispered back Hyacinth.

The tip of Attenborough's trunk was so close to Mark and Hyacinth that they clearly made out the two prehensile fingers framing the nostrils, and they felt the air being pulled from in front of them as the elephant acquired their scent.

With a blast of hot air from his trunk, Attenborough turned and resumed his march west through the forest, toward the river. It seemed like an eternity before anyone knew it was OK to move, and when they did, Mark and Hyacinth hugged each other. Each was quivering like a leaf, but they had permanent smiles chiseled into their faces.

"Come on," said Cobra, following Attenborough to the western edge of the forest. The elephant had made it to a shallow bend in the river where the bank was flat on either side. The current was slow and meandering, and the water only came up to Attenborough's belly.

"We can cross here!" declared Susan, but Cobra stopped her from going any farther.

"You first," he said, and at a second glance, she saw the crocodiles submerged just beneath the surface, waiting for fish to just jump into their mouths.

Cobra turned to the Professor. "Are you all right?"

"Yeah. Yes. I think so."

"It wouldn't kill you to admit that you maybe don't know every little everything. I mean, Jesus, Professor, that was stupid, especially for a trained wildlife biologist. Next time, please just do as I ask."

"You've got some nerve! What was I wrong about? I said the kudu was safe, and it was."

"Why can't you ever just listen to anyone? If you've got nothing to learn, why did you even come here in the first place?"

"I have plenty to learn, *Campbell McConnors*." Everybody reacted to that name. "Starting with learning who I should put my trust in. I went along with you because I thought, despite my better judgment, that there was something special about you. But these people are right. You're just making this all up as you go along."

"Of course I am! And it's hard enough when suddenly everybody has a goddamn degree in bush craft all of a sudden.

You think I want anyone's else's death on my hands?"

"What are you saying, Cobra? You've gotten someone *else* killed with your three-part bravado, one-part experience cocktail you've been so drunk on all this time?"

"Yes! I have! And I've been living in the bush a thousand miles from civilization for the last four years to hide from that reality! Except, it wasn't my bravado that got those people killed. It was my indecision."

"And now, you're making all the decisions," she said, thrusting the rifle into his arms.

"I am, because that's my job now. Keep people safe in the African wilderness. That's what I've been trying to do this whole time, *Delia*."

"No, *Campbell*," she said. "What you've been trying to do this whole time is catch up to Black Tiger and his gang, because you're trying to free Kotani, and you're using all of our lives as collateral. We're not headed home, and we never were."

"Wait, what?" asked Kevin. "We're really not headed home?"

Andres laughed. "Of course, we are not."

Mark said, "Cobra, are you lying to us?"

"Don't handle us," said Hyacinth. "Tell us the truth."

"The truth is that I am trying to do both. I can't do one without the other. I don't know if Wyatt is hurt, if these men have taken him and Annie and Katy, but I do know that if we're all going to survive, we need to get back to the lodge. To do that, we need a vehicle, one that can carry us all. The only way we can get one of those is by taking one from the poachers, who, since you've already figured this out, are not trading in ivory or rhino horn at all. Since Wyatt cancelled my flight out of here today, there is no plane coming in on the airstrip, or I would have guided you all there. This is it."

"But we could have turned ourselves in back at the watering hole, if that was your plan," said Mark.

"We didn't have any leverage, and that's what we've been tracking all this time," explained Cobra.

"Priest," said the Professor. "You've been trying to find Priest, to see if you could trade his life for Kotani's."

"Priest would know where their camp is, and if Kotani is still alive, I'd use Priest to negotiate for Kotani. In return for a vehicle to take us back to camp, I'd give them what it is they're really looking for."

"Jesus," said Hyacinth. "You do know where Kruger's gold is."

"More or less," said Cobra. "Yes and no."

"But what if you can't find Priest? What if he already made it back to their camp?" asked Mark.

"What if he's dead?" asked Susan.

"Then I'll have to go back to the watering hole and track that car directly, and take my chances," said Cobra. "Listen, everyone. I know you're exhausted, and I know you can't go much farther. I'm sorry that I strung you along, and that now some of you don't think you can trust me."

"I never trusted you!" cursed Andres.

"But you do trust her," said Cobra, and he thrust the rifle back in the Professor's arms. "I need to leave you here for a little while. With luck, I should be back here in an hour with a car and you'll all be back at the lodge in time to watch the Grinch on the TV in the visitor's center."

"Campbell," said the Professor, "I mean, Cobra... Are you sure you want to do this? How will you pick up on Priest's trail?"

Cobra looked up at the sky through a break in the trees and said, "I think I've already got it. Don't go near the river, and don't start shooting at anyone or anything."

Cobra began walking east through the forest, and suddenly the group felt profoundly alone out in the wilderness without him. Kevin took two steps towards him and said:

"Cobra, just wait a..."

Kevin screamed and then doubled over in white-hot, intense pain.

"Kevin!" yelled Xavier, cradling him.

Cobra ran back and saw that Kevin's pantleg had two big shreds in it just behind his right knee. With his knife, he hacked the khaki fabric away, revealing an ugly, weeping snakebite.

"Did anybody see what it was?"

"I didn't get a clear view," said the Professor. "I think it was a puff adder."

"You think, or you know?"

"Think," she said.

"Oh fuck," whimpered Kevin. "Oh fuck oh fuck oh fuck oh fuck."

The Professor took the strip of clothing Cobra had just cut away and tied it tightly around his knee.

"It looks like a big bite, both fangs delivered," said the Professor.

"It's not lethal, is it?" asked Xavier.

"No. It's painful, but not lethal," she said to Xavier, before taking Cobra aside and saying privately, "It's lethal. It can be, anyway, if it's a puff adder. Cytotoxic venom; causes necrosis, deep tissue damage. Do you have antivenom for it at the lodge?"

"We should," said Cobra. "How much time does he have?"

"Better go get that car, Cobra. Better not stop for coffee."

# CHAPTER 19:
# DARK MANE

Cobra rested briefly against a tree on the edge of the woodland and looked out onto the plains. With everyone in banged-up shape back by the river, and now with venom poisoning the flesh of Kevin's leg, he knew he didn't have the luxury of being tired. Just the same, he could use a three-hour nap in an air-conditioned room, one or two of those ostrich burgers he was supposed to be having right about now at Mitchell's Pub, and a tall, frosty glass of *anything*.

He looked up again and saw them, high in the updrafts: vultures circling, probably a quarter mile northeast. Although he hadn't seen the motorcycle track for a few hours now, he intuited that Priest was lying somewhere beneath those aerial scavengers. Whether he was still alive or already rotting was another story. He really hoped that if Priest were dead, at the very least, his bike was still functioning.

Cobra tilted his hat backward and started across the flat lands. The sun was mostly at his back now and the walking was easy, relatively speaking. A small dazzle of zebra speckled the grasslands with their black and white barcodes; otherwise, besides the remnants of the buffalo herd to the far south, the plains were pretty much empty, at least to the naked eye. There was no sign of Black Tiger, who must have returned to wherever he came from or ventured farther south with his contraption.

At long last, the vultures - Lappet-faced, Cape, and

Hooded - were nearly overhead, and Cobra finally saw the motorcycle laying on its side on the tawny grass. It was still intact. Cobra stood the thing up and steadied it with the kickstand.

"That is still mine," came a weak voice from underneath a nearby, thorny bush, "as long as I am still alive."

Cobra could see him now. Priest's dark skin, though scorched by the African sun all day, was pale and colorless as though much of the blood had been drained from it. He was covered in dust and had wide bloodstains on the right side of his stomach and from his right bicep. Priest made no attempt to get up, or even to move.

"I could change that for you, Priest."

"You are here… to finish me off?"

"No. To rob those vultures of their early-bird special. I see your friends didn't come looking for you."

"Where is… my rifle?" Priest's speech was slow and labored.

"With the Professor."

"My knife?"

"Well, it's my knife now. I'm keeping it, since you dropped it and didn't go back for it, and also, because you slashed me across the stomach with it. I think that's fair. Now let's get up. We've got things to do and places to go."

"Just let me… die… in peace."

"You see, I would. I mean, I'm sure you let those missionaries die in peace back in DRC. But I need you to take me to Black Tiger."

Priest started to laugh but choked on some blood. "For what?"

"To have a conversation, work out our misunderstandings. Maybe he's got a bottle of Gatorade and some Band-Aids for you."

Cobra tried to bring Priest to his feet, but he was dead weight, offering no help.

"You know… his name. However… your paths… have

crossed, you must… know what… kind of man he is."

"I know he's smart, and if he's reasonable, maybe we can work something out, assuming my friend is still alive. And if Kotani isn't, then our conversation will take a very different turn."

"He is… a killer. He came from nothing… tortured himself, tortured others… to be what he is now. He has… traveled the world… bleeding it out to make himself stronger, deadlier… in every way he can. He did not send someone… to find me… That was his mercy… not killing me himself."

"We all have our problems today, I guess," said Cobra, hoisting Priest up throwing him across the bike. "I'm sorry if that hurts. Not very sorry, but, you know, a little bit contrite."

Cobra straddled the motorcycle and saw that the key was still in the ignition. It looked like there was still fuel in the tank.

"Do you think you can stay up?" Cobra asked. "Don't grab my waist too tightly, now."

"You… are just another colonist… taking this continent and… selling it to the Europeans and the Americans."

"I'm not the one looking to dig up millions of rands' worth of South African treasure to fund… whatever it is you guys do. And I'm bi-racial. Mixed race. Coloured."

"You are… not. You are White."

He tried to start the bike up, but there was no reaction.

"I'll have you know that I identify as both Black and White. A little bit of coffee, a little bit of creamer."

"You are… no African. You are not one of us."

Cobra tried again to start the bike, and again, nothing.

"It's too bad you tried to kill the Professor. I think you two would have enjoyed arguing about this."

Third time, as usual, was the charm. The bike coughed to life. It wasn't exactly a chopper, but it was burning gas, and maybe it could get the two of them wherever it was Cobra needed to go.

"That treasure… was amassed… on the backs of Africans suffering. It's only right… I get my share of it."

"You'll die before you see one cent of it, I guarantee. But please, don't die yet; I still need you. Now, where are you fellas hiding out?"

\*\*\*

They rode for ten miles through patchwork savannah, going in and out of dense forest. Priest became so weak he stopped giving verbal directions and instead pointed this way or that. Finally, they came through a clearing in the trees that gave way to an elevated, rocky outcrop, and there was the unmistakable stain of a large-scale human enterprise operating on sacred wilderness.

At a casual glance, this was what a poacher's camp looked like: portable canvas tents, 4x4 vehicles with large drums of fuel stacked on top of one another, and racks of bushmeat drying in the African sun with all the flies that go with them. Cobra made out skins of zebra, leopard, even what looked like cheetah, with blood still pooling underneath them. To Cobra, this was beyond obscene.

There were also many men, each working at some prescribed task, each of whom stopped their work to point their semi-automatic rifles at Cobra and Priest as they rode into the center of the camp. Cobra shut off the motor and dismounted; without Cobra, Priest toppled off the seat.

"Take it easy, gentlemen," announced Cobra, lifting Priest off the ground and holding him up by his collar. "I believe this is yours."

"It is," said a Caucasian man with thinning hair, muscular arms and a healthy beer gut. He spoke with some kind of African accent. "What do you want?"

"I'm here to see Black Tiger. I have some information he might find useful."

"Is he expecting you, then?"

"Does he have a secretary? I would have called."

"You can think of me as his secretary, if you like."

"Zambian?"

"Zimbabwean. My name is Maiden."

"Ask him why... he is called that..." wheezed Priest.

"I'd rather skip that story for now," said Cobra, and then to Maiden, "Did we come at a bad time?"

The men surrounding them still had all their guns pointed at Cobra's head.

"Maybe yes, maybe no. Mister Hernandez Santana has had a run of bad luck, you see. I do hope you can cheer him up, because if he's in a sour mood, he'll make it known to you. Why don't you come with me?"

Cobra dragged Priest across the floor, hyper-aware of all the weapons around him with direct lines to his heart, lungs and brain. He followed Maiden past the canvas tents to the outskirts of the camp.

"First Priest, now Maiden," said Cobra. "Who's next? Megadeth?"

"No Megadeth. In all likelihood, just yours."


Maiden led Cobra, with Priest dragging behind him, to the grasslands behind the camp, where Black Tiger stood with a high-powered rifle. Cobra's physiological response to seeing Black Tiger for the first time in four years was immediate: his heart pounded, the muscles in his chest tightened, and his teeth clenched down like a vice. Seeing him on binoculars from a few miles out was one thing; he never thought he'd be this close to one of the four people who'd destroyed his life. Cobra wasn't a vengeful man, but he had to fight hard to resist the urge to plunge Priest's knife into Black Tiger's throat.

"Mister Santana, I present to you... what's your name, man?"

"Cobra McCoors."

"Yeah, why not," laughed Maiden. "Cobra McCoors."

"Wait," said Black Tiger, not even turning around. He was staring out across the plains, the short grass undulating in the light breeze, at a powerful male lion with an uncanny black mane about two hundred yards away. His nose was dark with years of maturity, and the dry season had apparently been kind to him, for he was muscular and fit.

Black Tiger rested the rifle against his shoulder and looked out through the scope for four, five, six seconds before taking the shot, the report echoing across the open air. The lion ran in circles frantically, confused and in pain, looking for his assailant. Black Tiger pulled the trigger again, and this time the lion went down, convulsing in the grass.

"He'll bleed out in a few minutes," said Black Tiger, and then he turned. "Now who is this?"

"I'm not sure if you know that killing a male lion in his prime has severe consequences for the pride," said Cobra, working overtime to conceal his disgust. "Other males could move in and kill all the cubs, kill any juvenile males."

"Then it seems I'm an agent of change."

"It's murder."

Maiden was surprised at Cobra's audacity and took a step backward. Two men had followed them and still had their guns aimed at Cobra.

"I provided an opportunity, then. And I can't very well conduct my business with those things running around out there. Now, Mr. McCoors... are you here to offer me an opportunity?"

It suddenly occurred to Cobra that Black Tiger hadn't recognized him and had no idea who he was. Cobra was older than when they'd last met; he was bigger, stronger, had some facial hair, and wore a hat. He hadn't counted on that and would use that to his advantage.

"Yes, I am. First of all, I returned your man to you. Feed him, give him water, treat his wounds, blow his brains out. I figure it's your business, but I brought him as a sign of respect."

Cobra released Priest and let him slump to the ground.

"Priest, I figured you for a coward, good enough for killing men of the cloth and innocent nuns, but you've impressed me, surviving the last twenty-four hours with those injuries."

Priest would not beg, but his lip was quivering, and Black Tiger pointed the rifle at his head.

"But, a bunch of tourists on holiday inflicted those wounds on you, so what does that say about your effectiveness?"

Black Tiger nudged him over with the rifle point.

"Maiden, give him a bottle of water and see if he lives through the night. If he does, we'll talk about sewing him up and giving him some antibiotics."

"You heard the man; let's take this poor bastard away," said Maiden, and one of the men lowered his weapon and dragged Priest away with him.

"You too; we're fine here," said Black Tiger to the other man. He joined Maiden and the other, leaving Black Tiger alone with Cobra and the open steppe.

"You, on the other hand, look like hell. I see big cat claw marks near your clavicle. You must have some guts to make it through an encounter like that."

"Leopard."

"I respect that. I once had a close confrontation with a big cat myself."

"I know," said Cobra. "Bengal tiger claws on your wrists."

"That's very impressive, for a safari driver. I assume that's who you are, no? From the vehicle we hit yesterday, near the elephant? Most people would assume the claws are lion, us being in Africa. Only a very perceptive man might tell the difference."

"That's some jewelry," said Cobra.

"One of my first hunts, in my early twenties, in India. I didn't use a gun, and he didn't just give them to me."

*This bastard really doesn't recognize me*, thought Cobra.

"I mean your other jewelry."

Black Tiger touched the brilliant green gem hanging from his neck. "Oh, this. This is just a memento from another lifetime. Now, I hope you're not here for revenge for yesterday, because if you are, that isn't going to work out the way you hoped."

"If we're being honest, revenge would be optimal, but I was thinking more along the lines of working out a deal," said Cobra.

"I assume you're bartering for your own life, which, if we're being honest, isn't much capital."

"Lives, actually, as in plural. We have wounded, including a man suffering from a nasty snakebite."

"That's audacious, Mr. McCoors. Lives are expensive, and I can't really afford all of your surviving guests to know that we're operating here, outside the auspices of the law."

"You sent Priest to retrieve me because you've hit a dead end. You're looking for a certain depository of British gold, and your leads haven't panned out. All this, and you're empty-handed."

"And now I suppose you are going to tell me you've known where it is all along and you're going to inform me, in return for sparing your lives," said Black Tiger.

"In return for sparing our lives - all our lives - and the use of one of your four-by-four vehicles to get these people safely to our lodge."

"A vehicle! A four-by-four, at that. Maybe you can pick out the model and we'll have it all gassed up for you out front. Again, very audacious."

"You think I'm bullshitting you. I get it. You think I'm stalling to buy time. I get that too. But the fact is that I've been exploring this region for years, and I know precisely where Kruger's gold has been sitting for the last hundred years."

"You're saying you've discovered the location of millions of dollars' worth of gold and you haven't already cleaned it out, content to shuttle tourists around the jungle."

"I may have helped myself to a little, here and there, but the people who own this property have been kind to me, and I don't betray my friends. Do you betray your friends, Mr. Santana?"

"No. But I don't have any friends, only associates."

"With that charming personality? I'm shocked."

"All right, Mr. McCoors. Take me to the gold, and afterwards, I'll provide you with a vehicle and provisions to bring your people back to your lodge."

"No. I'll tell you the gold's location. I need to get to my party immediately before my guest dies of puff adder venom. Once I'm in the car, I radio you where to go. Otherwise, you get nothing. You kill me, you get nothing. You mow down my guests, you get nothing. And if my friend Kotani is already dead, you get nothing. Because right now, you have nothing. What do you have to lose?"

"Only my patience. You negotiate like a man, Mr. McCoors. I'll give you a vehicle, but Maiden will escort you. If you've lied to me, I will radio him to torture and kill you and each and every one of your guests in ways that will make you wish you were only envenomated by puff adders. What do you have to lose?"

"Not a damn thing, Black Tiger. Catchy name, by the way; I'd like to hear the story one day."

"I'm quite sure you won't."

"And Kotani comes with me."

"No. We will return your tracker to you when we collect our car, assuming we've been successful in retrieving the gold. Otherwise, consider him our property now," said Black Tiger.

"Considering an African your property is pretty ugly, Black Tiger. You speak like a highly educated man, like you've been to an exclusive finishing school or something. I didn't know they had those in the South Bronx."

Black Tiger froze, and then smiled. "Now I'm very

impressed, Mr. McCoors. You're both a zoologist and a linguist. I've been trying to extinguish any trace of that accent for years. Now come with me, and we'll get you on your way."

Black Tiger led Cobra back through the camp, around the canvas tents and tall, metal racks of slaughtered animals.

"Wait here," said Black Tiger. He summoned Maiden, who was eating a piece of very rare, well, let's call it *venison*, and two other men dressed in desert fatigues. They spoke for a moment, and then Maiden threw the leftover fat and skin onto the ground, approaching Cobra with a smile.

"I'll go start her up. We'll go just now," he said.

"Yeah, go do that," said Cobra.

Black Tiger beckoned Cobra over to one of the meat racks, which smelled awful and was crawling with flies.

"I know you find this distasteful, but an army travels on its stomach. You look hungry; want a little something to tide you over before you get to your lodge?"

"I'm going to pass on that, Tiger."

"I have a very good feeling that with your help, the gold is finally within my reach. Now that we're friends, I know you won't try to go back on our deal."

"That's right, Black Tiger," said Cobra. "We're like Jeter and A-Rod."

Black Tiger took Cobra around to the opposite side of the meat rack.

"Are you sure I can't offer you anything for the road?"

Between two bloody, drying zebra carcasses hung Kotani, completely naked. It looked like he was unconscious, but every few moments, his body would shudder and convulse as the flies landed on his eyes, nose and lips.

"He gave us a few leads," said Black Tiger, "But it seems either he doesn't know how to use a map, or his memory isn't quite as sharp as he'd like. We're still checking a few of the locations he suggested. Between the two of you, I feel very optimistic that it will be a very merry Christmas for us all."

Cobra's face contorted at the sight of his friend like this. He choked back his impulses; there were just too many guns on him right now.

"It will be for me, at least, Black Tiger," said Cobra. "Because I know for a fact that I'm getting exactly what I want this year."

# CHAPTER 20:
# AMBUSH

They even let Cobra drive, as though this were all some joke, and that sooner or later, he would be the punchline. Maiden sat in the passenger seat, two handguns holstered underneath his shoulders as though he were a cop in a retro, 'eighties action movie. Behind them sat two super-bushwacker, just-as-soon-kill-you-as-look-at-you, tough-guy mercenaries, each armed with AR-15s. A shovel rested between them.

Cobra drove two hundred yards away from camp into the flat grasslands and saw three adult lionesses pawing at something in the grass. They were agitated, restless. The male that Black Tiger had shot earlier was lying dead between them, his eyes still open and staring lifelessly at the afternoon sun.

"Circle of life, eh?" said Maiden.

"Your boss holds life very cheaply."

"And yet, you're still alive, aren't you? Let's keep it that way, shall we?"

Maiden took the radio speaker from the console and clicked it, speaking into it: "Our boy here has something to say to you. Over." He thrust it into Cobra's face.

Black Tiger's voice came through, tinny and muted: "Surprise me and tell me the truth, Mr. McCoors. Over."

Cobra spoke into the speaker. "You're a contemptible bastard. Over."

"On that, we agree, Mr. McCoors. I'd like to be rich as well, and I'd like to cut your friend down. I'm growing tired of him begging me to end his life. Over."

Through the driver's side mirror, Cobra saw a faint flash of light, and he understood that it was the sun reflecting off the scope on Black Tiger's rifle back at camp, aimed at him. A portable radio was being held by one of his men to his ear.

"There is an escarpment about six miles due north and west of your camp; it's the base of some steep hills that go from what should now be the river for about nine miles east. Over."

"We know it," said Black Tiger.

"There is a small, subterranean bunker at the base of the escarpment. It's one hundred paces from the river and dug right out of the hill. It's covered with loose dirt, but the Germans hastily built an aluminum door that recedes slightly into the hill's face. Over."

"Thank you, Mr. McCoors. You'll hear from us in about an hour when we've searched it out. If you've been disingenuous with us, you'll hear from us sooner. Over."

"I'll wait by the phone," said Cobra. "Over."

The driver's side mirror exploded into shards of tiny glass, shot to pieces by Black Tiger from two football fields away. The lionesses scattered, running back towards a thicket of umbrella-shaped acacia tortilis trees, and Cobra brushed the glass fragments away from his shirt.

"Guess he hung up," said Maiden.

\*\*\*

On the edge of the grasslands, where the plains met the miombo woodland, Cobra abruptly stopped, putting the vehicle in neutral. The tough guys in the back looked at one another, and then up at Cobra, distrustfully.

"What is it?" asked Maiden.

"Shut up, quiet…" answered Cobra dismissively.

Cobra grabbed a pair of binoculars that were hanging next to the clutch and panned across the forest and then out towards the expanse, up by some very tall termite mounds.

"What?"

Cobra flashed his lights on and off rapidly, and then resumed driving.

"Something wrong with your lights?"

"Thought I saw a black rhino. I've never seen one in this country before. Rhinos have very, very good eyesight," Cobra explained. "I thought I might announce our presence, give him a chance to move."

"This is no bloody safari, Cobra McCoors. I hope you're not having fun at our expense, or we'll be obliged to have our fun at yours."

"If you want to see a black rhino go through this car like popcorn, by all means, let's just go ahead and see what happens."

Cobra waited for a moment, looking not at the woodland but again at the very distant termite mounds, and then put the vehicle back in drive.

"I must have been wrong," said Cobra. "Can't be too careful out in the bush."

Cobra finally drove back to the place where he had left the group, near some sparse trees overlooking a shallow spot in the river. Xavier was on the ground holding Kevin, who had grown pale and weak, and was sweating profusely in the overcast heat. Mark, Hyacinth, and Susan each rose, taking a step backward. Andres climbed to his feet and stood behind a tree as Cobra disengaged the engine.

"I thought you said there were seven of them," said

Maiden.

"There are," said Cobra.

Everyone got out of the vehicle, and the two tough guys loosened their AR-15s from their shoulders.

"Delia's in the little girl's room," said Susan.

"She's taking a piss," translated Hyacinth.

"Don't worry," said Maiden. "We won't forget about her."

Susan and Hyacinth looked at each other nervously, guiltily. Cobra knew something was about to happen, and he hoped it wasn't what he thought it was.

"This has gone on long enough," said Andres, who marched straight for Cobra and Maiden.

"Andres," called out Hyacinth. "Don't."

"No, *you* don't. We don't all have to die out here," he said.

"What's going on?" asked Cobra, but Andres pushed him aside and addressed Maiden directly.

"What can I do for you, friend?" smiled Maiden threateningly.

"Delia has a weapon - an assault rifle, taken from your compatriot - and she means to ambush you," declared Andres.

"Andres!" yelled Mark, who took two steps forward until one of the tough guys swung his assault rifle in his direction.

"She's over there, lying behind those trees felled by the elephant earlier. Stand up, now, Delia," said Andres. "And drop it."

"You miserable piece of black mamba shit!" cursed the Professor, slowly standing, tossing the gun into the leaf litter.

"I suppose we have no agreement after all," said Maiden to Cobra.

"Maiden, I have no idea what's going on here," pleaded Cobra. "I swear to God I didn't know they were going to do this."

"Time for talking to God is over," said Andres. "Delia's weapon was only half-full anyway, and she was just as likely to hit any of us as you men. I figure if you were reasonable enough to come here in this vehicle, you might be persuaded to spare the one man in this movable psyche ward who tried to be reasonable with you."

"Clever fellow!" laughed Maiden, unholstering his own firearms. "I mean, at the least, we'll kill you last."

Andres looked at him sardonically, and Maiden said, "I'm joking, of course. Thank you for the courtesy. It goes without saying that everyone else will have to suffer for this indiscretion."

"If you must. But be quick with that one," Andres said, pointing to Susan. "I've grown rather fond of her."

"Whatever you say, friend."

Susan cried, "Andres, how could you?"

"Surprisingly easily," said Andres. "Am I so different from Michel Merle?"

"I thought so."

"Not so," said Andres. "In fact, we are both men who will kill for what we need. Like now."

Andres swiftly drew a gun - *Susan's gun* - from concealment under his shirt and peppered the first tough guy, nailing him with a solid grouping of three rounds in the center of his chest. He then fired all the remaining rounds at the second tough guy, who in turn opened fire on the group, but whom *in turn* was fired *upon* by the Professor, until Mark executed what could have passed for an Olympic-quality single-leg takedown and brought that sucker to the earth.

Cobra gifted Maiden with an explosive right cross to the jaw and then tried to secure Maiden's arms to his chest, locking them up in an X like a pharaoh in a sarcophagus. Maiden pushed backward with his legs and tumbled with Cobra down towards the riverbank, firing indiscriminately.

They splashed into the shallow waters. Maiden had dropped one of his guns somewhere along the way, and Cobra refused to free Maiden's remaining gun hand, clutching Maiden's right wrist for dear life. Maiden took advantage and pummeled

Cobra mercilessly with his free fist, knowing Cobra couldn't let go to defend himself.

The splashing and thrashing about stirred the interest of two crocodiles who had been waiting patiently for fish from upstream. Their reptilian brains ordered them to investigate what they perceived to be large prey in distress at the edge of the river.

Maiden got bitten first - by Cobra, in a frantic attempt to make him drop his weapon, which he didn't.

"Son of a bitch!" growled Maiden, who hammered his elbow down onto the top of Cobra's skull, hoping to get him off his arm.

With a powerful lateral stroke of its tail, the first crocodile cut through the water perpendicularly against the current.

Cobra knew he had a knife, but he couldn't get to it, and he felt his hold on Maiden's wrist loosening with the water. Going for broke, Cobra stepped in and turned, rolling Maiden off his back and jujitsu-throwing him towards the bank. They were separated. Cobra brandished the knife and ran through the mud to catch up to Maiden, who was now on the sandy bank.

But Maiden righted himself quickly and pointed the gun at Cobra, who froze.

"Not bad, for a Yank. But I ain't gonna shoot you!" laughed Maiden, blood dripping from the bite mark on his arm. "I'm gonna let my friends make half a snack of you instead!"

Cobra turned and saw the crocodiles behind him, but they suddenly stopped moving.

"I like that. But I want you to remember, I never implied that you were half a man for having a name like Maiden," said Cobra. "But I guess I didn't miss that opportunity after all. Because you're about to *be* half a man."

A gigantic, gray beast with a mouth like a steam shovel rocketed through Maiden from behind on the bank. It locked its jaws shut on Maiden, who had stood between it and the water, and powered on through to the river. Hippo. Maiden's torso, this way;

his legs, that way.

Cobra gave the hippo a very wide berth and climbed back to the bank. Picking up his hat, he said, "Circle of life."

From above, Hyacinth screamed shrilly, and Cobra ran back up to the forest's edge.


Hyacinth had Mark in her arms, with Andres, Susan, and the Professor surrounding them. Mark was bleeding freely from three, four, five bullet wounds in the torso.

Tears streaming from her eyes, Hyacinth begged, "Do something, Cobra!"

Cobra quickly knelt beside them and tried to apply pressure to the worst of the wounds. "Anyone got any water? Someone get some water!"

"God, fuck, no…" whimpered Mark.

"Get something to stop the bleeding, Professor!" commanded Cobra, who himself, was shaking.

"Get what?" Professor cried.

"Something like bandages! Strips of cloth. I don't know. Anything!"

"No, God, please, it…" gasped Mark.

Cobra was shaking, frightened, and looked at the Professor, who was also terrified. They both knew.

"It's… please…" said Mark, and his demeanor changed suddenly, for now, he also knew and accepted it as well.

"No," said Hyacinth, looking directly at Mark, commanding him not to give up. "I said no, Mark. I said no!"

"Cobra," said Mark, trembling. "Would you mind terribly… if I had a moment alone… with Hyacinth?"

Cobra looked at the Professor, and the two of them rose. The Professor gently took Susan's hand and brought her away. Andres nodded and walked off alone in another direction, saying nothing.

"Listen to me, hon," said Mark quietly.

"Please, Mark," she cried.

"I love you."

"I love you, Mark, I love you."

"I know you do. But this is it for me," he said, fading. "Listen to me, please, listen."

"I'm listening, hon."

"I don't regret a goddamn thing, not even this vacation. These were the best two days of my whole goddamn life. You know I mean it. The only regret I have is not marrying you sooner."

"You can't, hon, you can't. Please."

"It's better like this. I was like a superhero. Did you see me take that guy down?"

"I saw it," she laughed, tears rolling freely.

"And I'm going on Christmas Eve! What are the odds? Oh look," he said, fading, seeing and hearing things. "Oh, hon, can't you hear him? Can't you hear him barking? My little buddy's come for me."

Hyacinth knew who it was that her husband saw as the lights faded.

"I hear him," she smiled.

"It's better like this," he kept repeating.

"God, what will I tell Mara? She'll blame me. She'll never forgive me."

"Tell her I love her," whispered Mark. "Tell her I died on my favorite day of the year in my favorite place in the whole world holding hands with my favorite person on the entire planet. Who ever lived who was as lucky as me?"

And they said some more things, words that were important to be said out loud that meant something to the two of them alone, and then he was gone.

# CHAPTER 21:
# KRUGER'S GOLD

Cobra and Andres, not wanting the lions to develop a taste for human flesh, threw the bodies of the two mercenaries to the crocodiles, who would pretty much eat anything already anyway. Kevin was a real trooper and agreed, even with the venom working its way through his leg, to allow Mark to be put to earth. Cobra insisted on digging Mark's grave alone, which was just as well, as there was only one shovel in the vehicle. Hyacinth picked a spot near the open grasslands where Mark could forever remain under the vast, wild African skies that had so called to him in his dreams. They all said a few kind words; Susan wept openly, and then they all left Hyacinth to have a moment alone.

Hat off, Cobra leaned against a tree and watched Hyacinth kneeling at her husband's grave, not hearing whatever she was saying to him. The Professor, never seeing Cobra so shaken, took his arm.

"I know. Don't say it. It's not my fault," said Cobra.

"I wasn't going to say that," she said. "Although it isn't."

"Logically, I think I know that. I can do the math in my head, look back at all the things in play and say that I did the best I could for everyone. That in the trial in my head, I'm exonerated on all charges," he said.

"But you don't really believe it."

"No," he said, turning to her. "I don't really believe it."

"*We* fucked this up.  I was going to try dis-arm anyone who came back with you.  I wasn't really prepared to shoot at them.  I had no idea Andres had Susan's gun, or that he was planning on doing that."

"At least someone had a plan," said Cobra.  "I could have come up with some plan for this.  I just didn't think far enough ahead.  I knew it was a longshot they'd have given me a car, and it was even less likely that they'd give me one unescorted.  I should have told you all what to do."

"We're not children, Cobra.  Not even Susan."

"It was my job to get everyone home safe.  I held the truth from everyone, because I thought I knew better, that this was my wilderness.  Black Tiger is someone I knew from the army.  He and the people he works with steal valuable things, and they ice anyone who gets in their way.  Now he's here with a well-funded, well-outfitted unit of soldiers and mercenaries, and they're committed to finding this lost gold, and here I am, trying to keep them from deep-sixing some people who just wanted to see a few lions on an exotic vacation.  You were right.  I am in way over my head; I'm not even a soldier.  I'm just a guy who thought for a moment that if he acted the part, with some effort, he'd be the part.  It's stupid."

"Cobra McCoors, I was wrong before.  You're three-parts bravado, one-part experience," she said, "and three-parts heart."

Hyacinth finished saying whatever she had to say and returned to Cobra and the Professor.

"Hyacinth, I don't have the words to say how sorry…"

She stopped him, holding up a finger.

"He was sick," said Hyacinth.  "The oncologist gave him a half a year, maybe more.  It would have been a slow, painful decline, for both him, and for me and our daughter.  Instead, he died in a fistfight near crocs and hippos, and he's laid to rest where he can be with the animals he loved so much.  Did he ever tell you why we've been on safari so many times?"

Cobra and the Professor shook their heads.

"He was a decent teacher, and he helped a lot of kids learn to shoot three points and climb ropes, but it was never really his calling. Mark never fit in as an academic. He always wished he had chosen a different life, and even though he never said so, I knew it was really his biggest regret."

"What kind of life?"

"Your kind. He wanted to believe that there were still wild places, where lions still roamed the savannahs, where you could sit and feel their untamed beauty and then sip a scotch by the fire at night. Safari trips were the closest he could come to living that other life, even though he knew he was always safe in the car and never in any real danger. Until yesterday, that is. God bless him, he did more living in the last two days than in all his years put together. He wanted to make sure I told you that. He wanted me to thank you for that."

Cobra nodded, and not knowing how to properly respond, he said, "Let's get you all in the car and get you back to the lodge."

Susan and Andres were with Xavier and Kevin, who had vomited a little.

"How are you feeling, Kevin?"

"Well," he shivered, "Between you and me, I'm kind of having a rough day."

"I was wrong about you, Cobra," said Xavier. "You got us a vehicle. Now get us home."

"If you've got the anti-venom at the lodge, he's going to make it," said the Professor. "But we've got to leave now."

"No," said Cobra. "*You've* got to leave now."

"Wait," said Susan. "You're not coming with us?"

"They still have Kotani, and any minute now, they're going to discover I haven't been completely truthful with them. I can't let him die on that torture rack. It's shallow enough that in this four-by-four, you can fjord here. Once you're on the other side, get about twenty feet from the riverbank. The ground should be solid enough. Use the winch and cable in the front if you get stuck.

Keep going south until you connect with the dirt road, and then follow it west until you get to the lodge."

"What if there are elephants?" asked Susan.

"Or lions? Or rhinos?" asked Xavier.

"Well, stop and let them pass, obviously," said Cobra. You've still got plenty of daylight."

"Who's going to drive?" asked Susan.

"I was thinking of letting the Professor here take a crack at it."

"Big surprise," groaned Kevin.

"Cobra, I can't drive stick," said the Professor.

"Really? Even out in the desert?"

"Not even in a Toyota showroom, Cobra. I can't drive stick, only automatic."

"Well, what about you, Hyacinth?"

"Why, because I'm the old bag?"

"Can you?"

"No, Cobra, I can't, all right? They had automatic transmissions when I was a teenager," she said.

"I can drive manual transmission," spoke up Andres.

Cobra shrugged. "You're hired, Andres. Get these people back home. And maybe I had you wrong too; you've got some balls, and I owe you."

"Don't try to flatter me, Cobra. I still expect my camera to be fully reimbursed."

"Well, anything's possible," said Cobra. Everyone loaded up into the vehicle. Cobra picked up the radio speaker and spoke into it. "Black Tiger, this is Cobra. Are you there? Over."

A few moments of static, and then:

"Mr. McCoors, we were just about to call. Put Maiden on."

"He's not going to be much for conversation, Black Tiger. Neither half of him is."

A few moments of static, and then:

"I take it the others are no longer on this mortal coil as well?"

"They are both, in fact, extra dead. Over."

"You know what I'm about to say, don't you? Over."

"You are disappointed at the lack of gold in the location I provided. Over."

"Disappointed is understatement. That I will increase your friend's suffering a hundredfold is not hyperbole. Over."

"That's because you weren't listening carefully enough to my instructions. I'll be at the south-western edge of the miombo forest, where it meets the grassland. Come and get me, and I'll take you there personally. Over."

A few moments of static, and then:

"We'll be there. Over."

Cobra hung up the radio and Andres started the car. "Don't forget to light up the Christmas tree and save me a little whiskey, please."

"We haven't got all afternoon," said Andres. "Let's go."

As they slowly made their way through the forest, Hyacinth looked back at the grasslands, at her husband's final resting place, and the expression on her face changed from grief to something more resembling a quiet fury.

\*\*\*

It was looking cloudy again, and Cobra wondered if there'd be another afternoon storm as he sat down and leaned back against a termite mound. He had an AR-15 in each hand, one from each of the tough guys, although he knew he couldn't out-Rambo Black Tiger and his personal army. It felt good to have them, though.

"Is this seat taken?" asked the Professor, sneaking up behind the termite mound and scaring the shit out of Cobra.

"What the hell are you doing here?"

"You said you were in over your head, didn't you?"

"I said for you to go with everyone back to the lodge."

"No, you didn't. When did you say that?"

"I…" thought Cobra, trying to remember their conversation. "I think I strongly implied it, at least."

"I can't drive the car anyway," she said.

"I needed you to lead them, not chauffer them."

"They'll be fine. Andres surprised me as being half-way competent," said the Professor.

They sat there in silence for a moment, listening to the cape doves beginning to call.

"I'm happy to have you here, Professor."

"Have me here? You wish," she said.

Finally, they saw the windshields of three Land Cruisers shimmering in the waning sun, streaking across the grasslands from the North. They were a few miles away but driving rapidly, ejecting trails of dust behind them.

"What's the plan, Cobra? If we're going out guns blazing, I need one of your guns. I don't think this one has anything left in it."

"We're going to intentionally let ourselves be captured so we can show them where the treasure's located and so we can then free Kotani."

"That's a terrible plan. You want to begin with another conversation?"

"I thought we might," said Cobra.

The cars stopped about fifty yards away; Cobra saw Black Tiger in the passenger seat of the one in the middle, and he tightened his grip on his weapon. Cobra stood and walked forward a few paces and then threw his AR-15s as far as he could towards them.

"I know you were in the army once, but I don't think that's how guns work, Cobra," said the Professor.

"Do it. I want them to see that we're not going to fight."

The Professor tossed her weapon too, and after she did, the

cars resumed driving towards them, cutting through the grass and scrub until they were only ten yards away. Cobra raised his hands in surrender, and following along, so did the professor.

Two men got out of each flanking Cruiser, training their assault rifles on Cobra and the Professor. Black Tiger got out and put on a pair of gloves, pulling them tightly.

"I was almost certain you were playing with me," Black Tiger began. "The chances that you knew where the gold was hidden were remote, and it was even less likely that you'd be truthful even if you did know, but like you said, what did I have to lose?"

"Not a damn thing," Cobra said.

"I had a source in Zimbabwe, not far from where Maiden came from, that gave me convincing anecdotal evidence that the gold was hidden in this general area. Again, longshot, but he gave me enough detail that I thought it was worth financing this endeavor."

"Why don't you give him another call?"

"It amuses me that you think he's still alive. Either way, what did I have to lose by humoring you? I still had your friend as leverage."

"Just your car," said Cobra. "And, I guess, Maiden, and two of your goon squad, but you don't look like the sort who gets attached to people."

"The vehicle? I didn't mind lending it to you at all. Since we found our way to the colorfully-named Rhino Horn Ranch sometime last night, we've made ourselves at home there. It's my alternate command center on this expedition now; if your friends can manage to drive straight, they'll be returning it to my men in the next few hours and resigning themselves to their custody."

"If we get you the treasure, you don't hurt them," declared the Professor. "That's the deal."

"I don't think so. You didn't honor the last deal. And what do I call you?"

"Professor."

"Really? What is your Ph.D. in?"

"I haven't officially defended my thesis yet…"

"I did," said Black Tiger, approaching her. "Archaeology with a concentration in Near Eastern History, if you can believe that."

He punched her hard in the gut and she dropped to her knees, gasping for air.

"I don't have a degree in dispensing pain; that's more like a personal passion of mine."

Cobra took a step towards Black Tiger, and all four of the men fired by his feet, effectively freezing him out.

"You hurt her, you get nothing!" Cobra threatened.

"That again? I've already got your tracker friend to pressure you with, so I don't really need her. I barely need you, McCoors."

He kicked her in the ribs, and she stifled herself from crying out.

"She is Crow, Black Tiger," declared Cobra. "Descended from a proud warrior race. She can take whatever you've got; she's tougher than you on your best day, and today ain't it."

"Now you're an anthropologist?" wheezed the Professor. "Please shut up! I don't want to get kicked!"

"Let's see if she's tougher than you on yours," said Black Tiger, and he went to work on Cobra, striking him repeatedly in the midsection until he, too, dropped to his knees. Now, some people vent their frustration by doing yoga, talking it out with a trusted friend, or taking long walks on the beach. Black Tiger vented his by listening for that celery-snapping crunch of his knuckles tenderizing some poor bastard's ribs, in this case, Cobra's, and today he really indulged. However, if this were the most painful thing that were going to happen to Cobra before this night was done, it would have been a kind of mercy.

"Now," said Black Tiger. "You said something about

taking me to the actual treasure's location."

***

They drove in silence, the windows down. As the heat waned, the bush began to free itself from the sun's grip and came to life once more. The three Land Cruisers moved through the grasslands at disrespectful velocities, and the antelopes and zebra seemed to stop and stare with disdain.

"I was paying you a compliment," said Cobra.

"Do me a favor," said the Professor. "Don't do me any more favors."

They drove to the edge of the river until a tall escarpment rose up from the ground, and then they turned east, away from the sun, for a very short distance before stopping. At the base of the escarpment there was evidence of a man-made depression and some displaced rock and dirt scattered haphazardly on the adjacent ground.

"Go to where the river meets the hills and then move fifty paces east," repeated Black Tiger. "The flashbang grenades you hid here blinded and deafened one of my geologists. He's still disoriented."

"I wasn't the one who hid them here, actually. They're just a non-lethal deterrent to discourage any people like you from doing exactly what you're doing. When I told you about the decoy site, I assumed you would be the one doing the digging. Leaders lead, after all."

"We don't discourage easily," retorted Black Tiger. "Now let me encourage you." He pointed a gun at the Professor.

"I said I'd take you, personally," said Cobra. "When I said fifty paces east, I meant fifty paces… elephant paces. Keep driving along the escarpment."

"Cobra…" said the Professor.

"I'm telling the truth. No more games."

Black Tiger nodded to the driver, and they crawled along the ridge.

"Where are you from, Mr. McCoors?"

"Tampa," he said quickly.

"It's funny. You don't sound like you're from Tampa," said Black Tiger, his mind wrestling with the familiarity of Cobra's voice.

After a few moments, Cobra tapped the back of the driver's seat. They had arrived at a spot not unlike the one they had just left, an innocuous wall of grass and dirt at the base of the escarpment. This one, however, looked slightly discolored, and there was a subtle indentation in the steep hill.

"Congratulations, Black Tiger. This's the location of Kruger's Gold. You're about to be famous."

"You go first. Somebody has to…"

"…take the first hit. I got it."

"That's right," said Black Tiger, and his mind once again felt the echoes of another moment in time. "I'm sure you've planned no other surprises."

They got out, although the Professor was forced to stay in the car with two of the men.

"I don't even get to see the treasure?" she complained.

"You'd be disappointed."

Black Tiger thrust a shovel into Cobra's hands and pushed him along towards the escarpment; he followed with an AK-47 in his hands. Cobra hoisted the shovel upwards as if he were about to take a mighty swing, but then just tapped the dirt about four feet up. It was actually just a curtain of lightly packed sand which crumbled to reveal a sheet of aluminum attached to a hinge.

Black Tiger's eyes widened; upon closer inspection, there was some faded German writing on the metal door.

"What's it say?"

"Merry Christmas? I don't know. I don't speak German. Do you have a PhD in German, Black Tiger?"

"Open it," he commanded, and one of his men tossed him a large flashlight.

Black Tiger prodded Cobra down what appeared to be a man-made tunnel. It was dark and hot, the air difficult to breathe, and the farther they went, the more it tapered.

"Can I have the flashlight?" asked Cobra.

"No."

"Well, you'll have to watch out for scorpions on your own, then. It's really the snakes that you have to worry about."

"The least of your worries, McCoors."

The tunnel became so narrow that they had to crawl (which was tough for Cobra, who still held the shovel), until it led them into a large, open chamber. Cobra stood and stretched.

"Got a match?"

"If there's methane…"

"There isn't," said Cobra. "Or sulfur."

Black Tiger tossed a lighter to Cobra, who lit a small oil lamp hanging from the ceiling.

"I give you: Kruger's Lost Gold."

The lamp illuminated a room with some aluminum shelves on the walls that were sporadically holding old documents and files, the edges weathered away by time. In a corner were stacked eight dusty bars of gold.

"Congratulations, Black Tiger. You're rich!"

Even in the dim light, Cobra saw Black Tiger's face contort, and it gave him at least some small degree of satisfaction.

"That's it? That's Kruger's Gold?" he stammered.

"Yup. What's left of it, I guess."

"That's the fortune?"

"Black Tiger, sir, that's got to be ninety, maybe even a hundred thousand dollars' worth of authentic, genuine gold, all yours. If you invested it properly, think what you could do with it in ten years. Maybe put it into CDs."

"That can't be all of it. There must be a secret chamber. A hidden compartment!"

"Come on, man. You could buy a small house with that! Well, not on Long Island, I suppose."

And that was it; the switch had been flipped. Black Tiger touched the scar on his head... 'taking the first hit,' being alone with Cobra in a claustrophobic tomb, and now, the mention of Long Island.

"Motherfucker!" roared Black Tiger, and he ducked just in time to avoid the shovel Cobra swung at his skull. He pulled the trigger on his AK, and blood sprang forth from Cobra's arm like a ruptured water balloon, spinning him around.

"Specialist Campbell McConnors," spat Black Tiger. "I can't believe I didn't see it. I never believed you could have made it through the desert alive."

Panting, Cobra said, "I guess it's both our lucky days."

"Bad luck for you!"

Black Tiger squeezed Cobra's shoulder and thrust the AK-47's barrel into Cobra's ear.

"All this time! You've been out here getting rich, hiding from society! I didn't believe in God before today, but surely, *He* must exist if you fell back into my lap!"

"I hope you at least buy me dinner before I end up in your lap, Santana," said Cobra. "Although I must admit, that scar I gave you does make you look prettier."

"I was going to just seal *Cobra McCoors* in this cave and let you asphyxiate and starve to death, but that now that I have *Campbell McConnors*, I'll have to do much better than that."

"Don't go to any trouble on my account."

Black Tiger suddenly froze as an epiphany came to him: "The Lamassu!"

***

Cobra emerged from the cave first, blood flowing freely from his shoulder but with the eight gold bars in his arms. Black Tiger burst out, nearly knocking the aluminum door off the hinges, and he kicked Cobra's back, knocking him forward and spilling the gold bars everywhere.

One of his men was now sporting a shiner and said, "The girl tried to escape three times, so we *suggested* she take a nap."

"She's still alive?" demanded Black Tiger.

"Yes. We have her in the back seat."

"Let's go. We're almost done with this fifth-world country."

***

Night had fallen, and Cobra's and the Professor's arms were secured with copper wire to one of the metal drying racks, in between two halves of an enormous eland carcass. The wire bit sharply into their skin, with their arms spread wide as if crucified, and with their feet dangling twenty-four inches above the ground. Their own weight pulled their flesh deeper into the metal wire, and any attempt to struggle sliced even more severely. In spite of herself, the Professor wept.

"Proud warrior race, are you?" asked Black Tiger, looking up at two of them as though in a butcher shop.

"You ball-less son of a bitch," she cried.

He punched Cobra in his exposed groin; not too hard, but just enough to elicit some vomit.

"Me? Ball-less? I came from nothing, from the South Bronx. I defied the gangs, my abusive father, the poverty. I educated myself, traveled the world to make myself a better man. Campbell here is a deserter, a boy who watched his friend die and

305

did nothing, who sided with terrorists instead of facing us like a man, who stole from us and ran."

Cobra stiffened.

"You, Santana? You're a better man when you have the upper hand, when you can intimidate someone smaller and weaker, but you're still just a glorified errand boy. What did Red Scorpion say when you crawled out of that hole I left you in? When you botched that entire miserable operation and got outplayed by an army translator with one year of college? Did he give you the respect you were begging him for? He knew that you were not just a boy playing at being a man... you were a piece of shit playing at being a human fucking being worthy of respect," said Cobra. "And on top of that, a Yankees fan!"

"You still have it, don't you? The lamassu?"

"Long gone, asshole. It's probably sitting on the top shelf at some dive in Zanzibar now."

"I doubt that. That would have been your only remaining piece of leverage. It's at the lodge, isn't it?"

"Heh. I'll take you there, personally," Cobra smiled.

"I think I'll go myself this time, take that place apart, piece by piece. Why don't you just hang here?"

Black Tiger wheeled around and left Cobra and the Professor suspended on the rack, their limp bodies facing outward toward the vast grasslands. Blood trickled down both of their arms as they shivered from the pain. In the distance, the last vestiges of the sun, now set, painted a purple and orange line across the horizon.

"When you're in Africa," wheezed Cobra, "never miss a sunset."

"What's wrong with the Yankees?" trembled the Professor.

"Nothing. I guess they're actually a pretty good team."

"I don't know how much longer I can take this," she said. "I think we're going to die up here."

"No. We'll be out of this pretty soon. Trust me."

"He's going to kill everyone at the lodge. They're all going to die."

"Don't give up yet, Professor. I know it hurts. But we're going to get through this."

"You," she panted, "wish. How could he be so cold? So indifferent to human life?"

"Because it's all he knows."

"Do you think what he said was true? That he just one day decided to become a ruthless killer, and he decided to make it happen?"

"Believe it or not, Professor, and you have proven this to me, I think if you put your mind to it, you can become almost anything you want."

# CHAPTER 22:
# SUMMER PROJECT
# 2003

A sandy beach in Senegal facing the crystal blue Atlantic Ocean:

"You're skin and bones, Campbell," said Wyatt, enjoying the sun on his face and smelling coconut-scented sunblock. "Can you even do a push-up?"

"To be fair, I did just spend weeks in the desert with like, no food or water," answered Cambell, walking right behind Wyatt. "I don't want to sound like a complainer, but this sand is starting to get hot."

"I thought you just spent weeks in the freaking desert, mate! This is a resort!"

Wyatt brought Campbell to what looked like a state-of-the-art, outdoor gymnasium: benches, Universal machines, cables attached to cables attached to cables, inclined this, declined that, with rows upon rows of dumbbells.

"We're going to have to work on your conditioning, Campbell. You've shown that you've got some grit to you, but you need a little muscle before you're ready to fit in here. And here's the one to help you. Heidi!"

A beautiful Senegalese woman with short hair and an insane pair of guns (talking about her arms!) finished deadlifting a

SNAKE IN THE GRASS

barbell with enough plates on either end to have the bar bend at both sides. She dropped the barbell and sprinted over to Wyatt, embracing him in a deep hug. The sun shone off of her dark skin.

"Wyatt! You look great!" she said with a French accent.

"Me? What about you? Is it me, or did you put a few inches on your delts?"

"You always know the right things to say to a girl! Is this the guy?"

"This is my new pal, Campbell McConnors, from Long Island, U.S.A. Campbell, this is my good friend Adelheid Switzerland, who only settled for fourth in last year's Ms. Olympia because she blew out her knee on the leg extension the week before and could barely stand."

She shook Campbell's hand.

"Come on! You can grip harder than that!" she teased.

"You squeezed before my fingers got all the way in," said Campbell.

"Now where have I heard that complaint before..." she laughed, slapping Wyatt on the shoulder.

"When I said it, it wasn't a complaint!" Wyatt said, slapping her back.

"Um, do you two need a moment?" asked Campbell.

Adelheid looked Campbell up and down. "You've got a solid frame, and good proportions."

"We need to butch this man up, Heidi," said Wyatt. "Can you help him?"

"For you, Wyatt? Of course. We're going to get this guy on a program. We're going to blast his pecs and detonate his delts. We're going to energize his calves and nuclearize his quads. We're going to give him lats so big he'll fly, and you're going to have to call me Michelangelo, because I'm going to chisel his abs and obliques."

"But will he be ripped?"

"He'll be stacked!"

"But will he be cut?"

"He'll be shredded! It's going to take three hours a day, and it's going to be painful - he's going to hate me by the time we've finished warming up."

"No!" exaggerated Wyatt.

"But I'll give him the tools to be as lean, mean, a total scene and everything in between as he wants. That, I promise."

"I can do this," said Campbell, taking a deep breath.

"You can do this!" reassured Wyatt, walking away.

"Where the hell are you going, Wyatt?" asked Campbell.

"I'm going to go to the hotel bar and eat a bunch of cheeseburgers. Have a good lift, bro!"

Campbell turned to Adelheid. "All right. Let's begin. What do I do?"

"First, go grab a pair of those dumbbells, forty-fivers."

"What's a dumbbell?"

\*\*\*

Oktoberfest in Munich, Germany... *I mean*, a German beer hall in Windhoek, Namibia:

Wyatt and Campbell sat on benches at a long, wooden table, elbow-to-elbow with complete strangers, clanking liter-sized mugs of golden beer before guzzling them down.

"Now, that's *Namibian* for beer, mate!" Wyatt declared over the riotous German singalong that the polka band was leading.

"It's delishhhhus," slurred Campbell.

"I know it is! It's not like that swill you drink in your homeland. The Germans may have colonized this country and ruled it like despots, but they did give the Namibians the gift of a great lager."

"Heeeeeeeeeeey," protested Campbell.

"Oh, don't start with the craft beer revolution again."

"Don't be a beer snob," hiccupped Campbell, and if he

were in a cartoon, little bubbles would have floated out of his mouth. "I'm not ashamed to drink what I like. I'm not much of a drinker, but back in school, they called me Campbell McCoors!"

"Good on you, mate. Actually, McCoors has a nice ring to it. If you're gonna make it out here, we've got to build your liver as much as your biceps, get me?"

"Why?"

"Why? Half of what you'll be doing on this continent is drinking, McCoors! Now down the hatch!"

"Whatever you slay, Wyatt," slurred Campbell again, upending one of his mugs and getting at least half of it in his mouth.

"Atta boy. Now come with me. There are some people I'd like you to meet."

Wyatt helped Campbell to his feet and brought him to a staircase that led down to a cellar.

"Are we going to the baaathroom? Good. I've got to pee."

It turns out that it was indeed the cellar, with dozens of kegs stacked up along the walls, but it was also (wouldn't you know) the site of a *literally* underground fight club. Men and women of all shapes and sizes stood in a circle, exchanging Namibian dollars and cans of cold beer.

"Who are all these people? Are we going to see a show?"

"They are, McCoors."

"I hope it's *Wicked*. That's supposed to be really good."

"Curious choice of words, mate!"

In the center of the circle was a large, bald slab of humanity with a handlebar mustache, the kind of guy who looked like he should be a little more careful working on propeller planes on a World War II airfield, if you get the reference.

"*Jetzt stirbst du!*" he snarled.

"Wait," said Campbell. "I have to fight him, don't I?"

"Yes, you do. This kind of hands-on training beats the bejesus out of some stupid karate class. And since you'll probably be drinking half the time you get in fights, I figured getting you loaded beforehand was a good simulation. We'll follow this routine every day for two weeks until you get it right. Ready?"

"You really should have let me pee first."

"Yes. I really should have."

\*\*\*

Outside a traditional coffee bar on a hilltop, near Addis Ababa, Ethiopia:

"If you want to be a man of the world, you've got to know some men of the world," said Wyatt, sipping on some black Ethiopian coffee. They had a view of patches of little farms as far as the eye could see broken up by a large, Christian monastery. The sky was a bright, cloudless blue.

"But I've only been to Iraq, and here," said Campbell. "Cancun for Spring Break."

"That's not a bad run for someone your age. But in your travels, you can encounter anyone from anywhere, and it gives you common ground if you can guess where they're from. You pegged this Orange Tiger from the Bronx just by hearing him speak; we're only expanding on that talent."

"Black Tiger, Wyatt."

"I keep forgetting that, because there's no such damn thing as a black tiger. And here's our first guest."

A tall man in a brown blazer and jeans shook hands with Wyatt and sat down.

Wyatt said, "Try to guess where he's from, McCoors. If you miss, you owe him six hundred birr."

"Good afternoon, sir. My name is Nigel Greenmeadow. I export coffee beans from Ethiopia to markets in Europe. In my free time, I enjoy skiing. I like a small bar of chocolate after sex."

"Wow! What the fuck, man?" said Campbell.

"Did I say something offensive?"

"All right," reasoned Campbell. "I feel like there's some German, or maybe even Italian in the way you talk. Nobody outside of the UK is named Nigel Greenmeadow, though. I'm going to say that you're Welsh, but with Italian parents."

"Pay the man, Campbell!" said Wyatt, taking another sip.

"The reverse, sir," said Nigel. "My father is from London, but I was born and raised in Lucerne."

Later:

"Call me Charity Smoekhaus," said a *smoeking*-hot brunette. "I design sets for the opera back home. I used to club seals for fun, but I haven't done it in years."

"Because it's cruel and against international law?" asked Campbell.

"Carpel tunnel syndrome," she replied.

"You're from Greenland, off the coast."

"Pay the woman!" said Wyatt.

"I am from Argentina. We used to vacation near Antarctica. My family is originally from Norway."

"Wyatt, I don't think this game is fair."

"Don't be a sore loser. Pay the woman," he repeated.

Still later:

"I'm Gibson LaPaz."

"You're from Bora Bora," said Campbell, forking over the money without waiting.

"Pretty close; Hong Kong," said Gibson.

"You really are terrible at this," laughed Wyatt. "Are you broke yet?"

"Wyatt, I've been broke since I came to Africa. This is all *your* money, remember?"

"I think we've played enough today, don't you?" Wyatt said.

\*\*\*

The vast, green Liuwa Plain, Zambia:

Sahara O'Hara had waited patiently for the female to wander far enough from the pride to dart her, and as usual, she never missed a shot.

"How long before the tranquilizer takes effect?" whispered Campbell from the back seat of the roofless Land Rover, holding onto a clipboard with charts of hand-written data on the lions they'd been studying in the humid heat.

"Should be quick, any minute now," she whispered back.

Her husband, Mikey Kalahari, sat at the wheel, binoculars to his face.

"They've made a kill last night; they seem content and aren't following. Now's as good a time as any," Kalahari said, turning the ignition to move a little closer.

"Yeah," agreed Campbell as though he were contributing anything to this conversation.

"She's down," O'Hara said. "Let's go."

Kalahari put the vehicle between the darted lioness and her pride.

"No better way to study animals than by being there in the grass with them," said Kalahari. "Why don't you go help Sahara put a collar on her?"

"Oh, I don't know," stammered Campbell. "You've been living with them for months; you probably ought to…"

"Nonsense! Nothing to it, McCoors."

"You don't have to call me that, Mr. Kalahari."

"Wyatt insisted that we do," he said. "I'll keep an eye on her sisters. Now go after Sahara, and whatever you do, don't run!"

Campbell tip-toed through the grass after Sahara, who was carrying a leather strap with a small radio attached, as well as a kit with some measuring tape and needles for drawing blood.

"In a few weeks with us, you'll know the bush as well as any safari guide," said O'Hara. "We'll measure her paws and examine her teeth, draw a blood sample, and we'll attach the radio collar so we can track her for the study."

"Will she be all right?"

"Poaching is always an issue, everywhere in Africa. It would be in America, too, except that we've already eradicated most of our big wildlife. Habitat is shrinking, human-wildlife conflict escalating… it's hard out here for this girl."

"I mean, from the drug," he clarified.

"She'll wake up with a mild hangover and be no worse for it. I assume you know a thing or two about hangovers with a name like *Coors*."

"I'm actually not much of a drinker, but I am working on it."

Campbell was transfixed by the drowsy lioness. He'd never been this close to a lion before, not even at the Bronx Zoo. From so close, he saw the muscles beneath her coat, even relaxed. She was in good condition. He hadn't realized how much he was drawn to wildlife until this moment and wondered if maybe one day he might work with them in some capacity, like Mikey Kalahari and Sahara O'Hara.

He tentatively reached out to her, frightened and yet compelled.

"Is it safe to touch her?"

The lioness sprang to life, swinging her front paws at him at blinding speed; Campbell fell backwards and was glad he had used the bathroom before coming out for the morning's research.

"I might wait a minute or two," said Sahara.

\*\*\*

A dirt road thirty miles outside Alexandria, Egypt:

Wyatt drove the car, trying to avoid as many rocks and as much detritus as he reasonably could.

"I can't tell if the speedometer is in kilometers or miles per hour.  What do they use in Egypt?" he called out the window to Campbell, whom he was dragging by a cable hooked up to the rear bumper.  Campbell sported a hockey mask to protect his handsome mug, but what he really wished he had was a groin protector.

"What's this for, again?" yelled Campbell, terrified, to Wyatt.

"In case you're ever suspended from a moving vehicle!  It *could* happen," mused Wyatt.  "And, I don't know, core strength?"

\*\*\*

Ten p.m. at the upscale Milima Restaurant in the Serena Hotel in Kigali, Rwanda:

"I'd like to introduce you to my friends, Kiana, Pilar, and Linh.  Classy Sheilas, this is my new mate, Campbell McCoors."

"It's nice to meet you, Sheilas," said Campbell, extending his hand.

"Are we closing the deal on some municipal building permits, or are we going to have a little fun?" smiled Pilar at Cobra's extended hand.

The Milima showcased one of the most extravagant bars in all Kigali, which made it a fitting locale for these striking Sheilas, er, ladies...

"A little fun," answered Wyatt.  "I get distinct the impression that our young McCoors has never, shall we say, known the pleasures of a lady."

"I never said that!" gasped Campbell.

"We might be able to help with that," said Linh.  "We are, after all, ladies."

"Wyatt, are these..." Campbell said awkwardly, "...working girls?"

"How dare you!  They work, all right.  Kiana handles

booking and scheduling for Safarilink Air in all of East Africa. Pilar is a VP at Royal Bank of Scotland, Dar es Salaam branch, and Linh works in marketing for Carnivore, the ubiquitous Nairobi restaurant," said Wyatt, sipping his martini. "They also *occasionally* have sex for money."

"I never charge," said Kiana. "It's just that men are so impressed that they feel it's only right to provide a little thank-you afterward."

"Sheilas," stuttered Campbell. "I mean, ladies…"

"We're messing with you, McCoors!" laughed Wyatt. "That's why we're here. McCoors needs to build up a little confidence around the opposite sex. Can you just talk to him for a little while, loosen him up?"

"Go ahead, McCoors," said Linh. "Loosen us up."

"Uhhhhhhh…"

"Say something, you dummy!" said Wyatt.

"Come here often?"

"Swing and a miss!" said Wyatt.

"Forget lines, McCoors," said Pilar. "Women pick up on confidence. Just relax and try again."

"Hello, ladies," said McCoors, an octave lower. "You look lovely tonight."

"Better," admitted Kiana, "but still not genuine. What are you passionate about? What do you love more than anything?"

Campbell thought about it earnestly. "I don't know. I've been just getting by for so long, I haven't really thought about something like that in ages."

"That's a fair answer," said Kiana. "I want respect, to be treated the way I want to be treated."

"I want a B.M.W., and to drive it all the way down the Pacific Coast Highway one day," said Pilar.

"I want to be free to be myself, I guess," said Campbell. "And I want a clear conscience."

"Then you better stay away from us," laughed Linh, and

they clinked glasses.

"It sounds stupid. I was lying in the sand in the Arabian desert looking up at the moon rising a few weeks ago. I felt really alone, and I thought I was dying, but I also felt kind of at peace, you know?"

"What were you doing in the Arabian desert?" asked Pilar, legitimately curious.

"Running away from the army, from these guys who were trying to kill me. Just running from everyone and everything," he admitted.

Wyatt signaled to the bartender for another round and then quietly slipped away to go meander by the pool outside.

\*\*\*

A mile off-shore on the surface of the translucent, aquamarine Indian Ocean, the Seychelles:

Campbell splashed to the surface, spitting out his regulator and bobbing like a cork.

"Jesus! Where's the boat?"

Next to him surfaced Sammy Whitetip, renowned oceanographer.

"You've got to be more careful, Campbell. You could be looking at the bends after rising so quickly. How do you feel?"

"Scared shitless! Those were like, twenty sand tiger sharks!"

"Sand tiger sharks are generally harmless. There hasn't been one recorded human fatality attributable to sand tigers. We've got to change people's outlooks from fearing sharks to respecting them."

"Oh. Well, then. I'm sorry," panted Campbell.

"Yeah. Those were *actual* tiger sharks, responsible for plenty of bites a year worldwide."

Wyatt surfaced. "Ooh! I think I saw a turtle!"

***

A small Samburu manyatta, Kenya's semi-arid north:

The sun was setting, and it had been an incredibly hot, dry day, but if you've been on your own in the Arabian desert for a week, this was Disneyland. A thin layer of dust coated Campbell's face as he held the small cup that Adrian Gtuku, Samburu elder, had asked him to hold. Small huts held together with cattle dung dotted the enclosed settlement, and a group of curious women and children, along with Wyatt, had gathered to watch. The women wore colorful tunics and intricately beaded necklaces.

"This looks bad, but it doesn't hurt," said Adrian, and by the way, an elder in Samburu culture really just means an adult who has accomplished the prescribed rites of passage and is now no longer a warrior or a child, not necessarily a gray-faced Gandalf-wizard. Adrian's short beard was gray, but that's just coincidence.

A boy grabbed the steer's head and pulled just enough to provide a little tension, and with an arrowhead, Adrian nicked its exposed neck vein, causing blood to flow as if from a water fountain.

"*That* doesn't hurt?" asked Campbell.

"Quickly, McCoors," urged Adrian, and Campbell captured some of the blood in the cup. Adrian then applied a thick, organic paste to the vein and plugged up the wound as if putting a rubber stopper on an open bottle. Released and indignant, the steer shuffled off.

Another elder applied some milk to the blood-cup, and Campbell knew that there was no electric refrigerator in this traditional village.

"Bottoms up, McCoors," smiled Adrian.

When Cobra brought the cup to his face, it smelled as though someone poured the warm liquid from the bottom of an uncooked London broil into frothy buttermilk. Not wanting to

319

offend, he swirled the cup around as if it were a glass of pinot noir. Jesus, did it have legs...

"Down the hatch," he said, and then took a mouthful, swishing it around his teeth. He knew he would eventually swallow, but he just hadn't gotten around to it yet.

"You like it, then? It is a staple of our diet," said Adrian.

"Oh, yes," said Campbell, faking a big smile. "It's delicious."

"I'm surprised. Wyatt told me you were lactose intolerant, and if that were bottled, lactose would be the second ingredient."

"Oh, that Wyatt," said Campbell. "I'm not lactose intolerant, I just don't like milk, even souring milk like this, but I really really like blood, so it takes the edge off really nicely."

"You can spit that out."

Campbell sprayed the pink liquid from his lips, not being able to swallow or contain it any longer, and the women, children and spectators laughed heartily, including and especially Wyatt.

"I'm so sorry. I'll try it again. I think I had a hair from one of your goats tickling my throat."

"Here. Have this other staple of our diet," he said, handing Campbell a cold Tusker lager from a cooler, its iconic elephant head prominent on the label, which he gratefully accepted and gulped down. "And this staple of yours..." continued Adrian, handing him a Nestle Crunch bar.


Campbell and Wyatt sat next to Adrian with seven other elders arranged in a circle with a round boma of thorny bushes enclosing them. They each had a beer, and Adrian read from last week's *New York Times*.

"I think the Maple Leafs will be a formidable squad this year," pronounced Adrian thoughtfully, and many of the other elders nodded heavily.

"You follow hockey?" asked Campbell.

"I was educated in Canada," said Adrian. "I suppose you support the Islanders. Good luck with that."

Although somewhat spartan and desperately poor compared to the extravagant wealth of even middle-class Westerners, there was an undeniable beauty and elegance to this Samburu village. Young people yearned to be educated in Nairobi, wear current fashions and use cell phones, but the pull of the traditional life was not so easily extinguished.

Wyatt said, "Did you know that the Samburu and their Maasai cousins to the south don't really honor the concept of '*my*' in their languages? Everything is '*our*.' *Our* cattle, *our* children, *our* village."

"Is it fair to call that *our* Mustang we drove through Mozambique?" asked Campbell.

"No," he said decisively. "McCoors, I wanted you to spend time with these people to understand that you should be as comfortable drinking milk and blood with cattle-raising pastoralists as you would be sipping champagne with dignitaries in an embassy in London. Cultures are different, but not superior and inferior, and you've got to experience all that you can."

As the sun set behind the mountains, Campbell thought that anyone who could witness that dazzling splash of orange and purple each night could be considered both wealthy and privileged, despite the many earthly uncertainties the Samburu dealt with on a daily basis.

"The other thing is that nobody is only the sum of their culture. Adrian here leads a traditional life in an isolated village, but he also plays the stock market and watches ice hockey when the bars in the city carry it. Never assume a Samburu only drinks blood and milk. The same goes for you. Be all cultures, or some of each, or none. Only you limit yourself, not others' notions of whom you should be."

\*\*\*

A stream in dense rainforest, Democratic Republic of Congo:

The rain was teeming down in sheets, but it did little to stifle the heat. Campbell kept his grip on the Glock, which he pointed at Benchley Zulu's chest from five feet away. Benchley's hands hung limply at his side. Strokes of lightning lit up his dark eyes.

"Shoot him," said Wyatt.

"Wyatt..."

"This man killed five people - boys - and didn't even stop to bury them."

"He was probably some conscripted child soldier. I don't want to do this."

"He's thinking of killing you. He's waiting for you to lower the gun, to show mercy, and then he's gonna rush us and murder us both."

Benchley stepped forward, ankle deep in the mud, and Campbell steadied the gun.

"How can you be a man if you're unwilling to kill those who would hurt and destroy innocent lives? What would you do if it were Black Tiger?"

Campbell looked into Benchley's eyes and wiped the water out of his own face.

"Do it."

Campbell lowered the gun.

Benchley made his move. He rushed up to Campbell and then stuck a wad of cash into Wyatt's hand. Wyatt threw his arms around Benchley and said, "Did I fucking tell you, or what?"

"Well the joke's on you, because now you're buying dinner in Kinshasa," said Benchley.

"What the fuck's going on?" screamed Campbell, blood pounding in his temples, hoping there weren't too many parasites on his legs by now.

"Benchley's an old mate of mine! He studies gorillas out here, works with the game wardens on conservation," said Wyatt.

"I would have blown his ass to Kingdom Come for nothing!"

"I was so confident you wouldn't that I put money on it. I bet you thought this summer project just took a really dark turn, didn't you? We even had rain and lightning and shit!"

"Have *you* ever killed anyone?" demanded Campbell.

"Fuck, no!" he exclaimed.

"I used to have to take the fish off his line for him whenever he caught one," laughed Benchley.

"But there weren't really bullets in this, were there?"

"I honestly don't know!" said Wyatt. "I guess from now on whenever someone hands you a gun, you should check."

"But Benchley, this means that if you had won the bet, you'd have been shot!" said Campbell.

"Yes, but I would have won!"

\*\*\*

An outdoor braai in the suburbs of the safari hub, Maun, Botswana:

They drank whiskey, but only because they were out of beer, and they drank straight from the bottle, in spite of the fact that they had plenty of glasses.

Wyatt was like, *five* sheets to the wind, and all the other guests weren't too far behind, sitting around the fire and eating pieces of fatty, salty lamb that had been slaughtered a few hours ago.

"That's why you can't drive out onto those salt pans," said Wyatt, punctuating some harrowing yarn he spun to the rapt attention of his guests, which included Campbell, Mikey Kalahari and his wife, Sahara O'Hara, and a thoughtful old San Bushman named Kotani. "You never know if they're solid in the center, or if you'll break right through like ice. You could be stuck out there for weeks without seeing another person. You'd be *F*ucked with a capital *F*."

That particular idiom struck Campbell as an amusing turn of phrase; he'd make it part of his *l*exicon, with a lowercase *l*. Wyatt handed him the bottle, and knowing that he was already drunk enough, Cobra only took a *moderate* swig before passing it to Sahara, who took a long one.

"That's Makgadikgadi for you," she said. "Me and Mikey had a scrape there once; we were chasing brown hyenas - no, that's not a euphemism for anything - and we didn't realize that our engine block had cracked and was overheating. It was only a hundred and five degrees that afternoon."

"We had to keep pouring what little drinking water we had onto it every mile and a half until we got back to camp," said Mikey Kalahari. "I thought we were going to cash out on those pans, I really did. When we finally made it back, the skies opened up and it deluged for two straight days."

"Hey, Kotani," said Campbell. "I bet you've seen some crazy things out here in the bush."

"You people are all fucking crazy," he said. "God invented air conditioning for a reason."

Wyatt said, "Kotani is the greatest survivalist I've ever met. He could live out in the desert for three months with no food and no water and put on weight. He can read the trees like some people read the funny papers. He could tell a knock-knock joke to a gemsbok and have the gemsbok laughing at it."

"I can also type ninety words a minute, but you don't see anyone sucking my dick over that," Kotani said matter-of-factly, eliciting riotous laughter from everyone.

As he watched this unlikely assortment of people passing a bottle around the fire pit, Campbell felt a genuine sense of companionship both for and from them. It occurred to him that he felt at peace with himself and with the world around him. The visceral pleasure of licking the greasy meat off his fingers, the smoke of the fire, the laughter of friends… this was a life he could never have conjectured a few years ago.

It was a life that would come to a sudden end if *that snake* slithering up behind Wyatt sank its teeth into his exposed skin. Campbell sprang to his feet and knocked Wyatt off the tree stump he was sitting on, and the reptile snapped up at his arm as though a cracked whip.

"Night Adder!" Campbell screamed, throwing the snake backwards where it slithered into the grass.

Wyatt pulled himself back up and smiled. "McCoors, you've got guts!"

"Am I bit?" Campbell asked frantically, looking for the wound on his arm as the terror drained away his intoxication.

"No, mate!" said Wyatt. "That was a rhombic egg eater. It doesn't have teeth, let alone venom."

"They mimic night adders," said Sahara. "Discourages predators."

"Well," said Campbell. "Don't I feel stupid."

"You have courage," said Kotani. "You thought you were trading your life for my friend's."

"Let's not get carried away here," said Wyatt.

"If you are ever in the bush where I live in South Africa and need help, signal my people."

"From now on," said Wyatt, "I dub thee, Rhombic Egg Eater McCoors!"

"Can we maybe take a little liberty with that, Wyatt?" asked Rhombic Egg Eater McCoors. "Doesn't really roll off the tongue."

"Asp McCoors! Asps are very deadly," said Mikey.

"Sounds like Ass. Ass McCoors," said Sahara.

"Let's just split the difference and say it was a Mozambique Spitting *Cobra*," said Wyatt. "Can you live with that?"

A smile grew on Cobra's face.

"I mean, if *you all* can…"

"To Cobra McCoors!" toasted Wyatt, and they passed the bottle around until it was empty.

\*\*\*

Uhuru Peak, 19,000 feet up Mount Kilimanjaro, Tanzania:

The vastness of the Serengeti plains below the clouds at his feet, Cobra nearly cried at seeing the world through God's eyes. The sun had only begun to rise as he summited Kili. Despite coughing up a little blood from time to time onto the sleeve of his thick, Polartec coat, he was in pretty good shape after the week's ascent.

Behind him, Wyatt retrieved a small flask from his coat.

"They don't call Machame the Whiskey Route for nothing," said Wyatt, and he gave the first swig to Cobra, and the next one to the hired porter following a few steps back.

"Wyatt, thank you," said Cobra, overcome with emotion. "For this, and for all of it."

"You've done a lot of living in the last three months, Cobra McCoors," said Wyatt. "And to tell you the truth, so have I. I was going to drop you off in the desert, leave you for dead, make it a survival exercise or something, but I felt like you've already proven yourself capable in that kind of situation, and I always wanted to make this climb myself."

Cobra simply nodded, watching the sun's light move over the infinite grasslands like a slow tide.

"The Lamassu," said Wyatt. "Keep it."

"No, a deal's a deal."

"I don't need the stupid thing. Listen, I've got a place in South Africa, real rugged country. Why don't you come to work for me there? We'll get loaded every night, have the chicks flown in, have a blast. What do you say, mate?"

"I think I'd like to see what other trouble I can get into on this continent first, maybe have an adventure or two on my own. Hold the Lamassu for me. Can I take you up on it in a year or two?"

"Cobra McCoors, you son of a bitch," smiled Wyatt. "You come on down whenever you're ready. I'll take good care of your baby. I'll hide it under my bed. Who would ever look for it there?"

# CHAPTER 23:
# BOOTLICKER

"And that's how we climbed Kilimanjaro," said Cobra, sliding lower, his arms purple and bleeding.

"What's the point of that story? That Black Tiger is just an evil *you*?" groaned the Professor in agonizing pain. "I'm glad you learned how to tranquilize lions and dive with sharks and mix drinks and all. But how does any of that help us here and now?"

"Well, it took your mind off the pain for a while, didn't it?"

"In no way did your rambling story do that for me."

"Not even a little?"

"Negative."

"None?"

"Nope."

"Well, if you're so awesome, why don't you tell me how you became the Professor, and I'll let you know if it distracts me from this suffering."

"You started calling me that, literally a few hours ago. The end."

"Wait, shut up," shushed Cobra. "You hear that? I think the cavalry's arrived."

There was a padding sound coming from the grasslands, like people walking quietly through the African night.

"And now, we're free," said Cobra. "Oh, wait. My mistake. We're gonna die."

Unfortunately, it was not people walking quietly through the African night, but three adult female lionesses striding through the darkness. Their eyes shone in the moonlight, and they licked their chops like dogs in anticipation.

"Damnit, Cobra, do you ever get tired of being wrong?"

"They're just curious about us. Lions don't usually hunt people."

"We're dripping blood and hanging off a meat rack between two sides of beef! This isn't hunting; it's like going into their refrigerator for a burrito!"

The first lioness sauntered up to the Professor's boots and started sniffing them. The professor tried to scurry her feet up higher, but when she bent her knees it only dropped her arms deeper into the slicing copper wire. The lioness continued to investigate curiously.

"What should I do?"

"Scream real loud!"

The Professor obliged with one of those shrill, Friday-the-Thirteenth, air-raid siren screams that would have made Fay Wray proud. The lioness cocked her head as though she were a Staffordshire terrier whose master asked if she were ready for dinner and then pawed the Professor's feet back down. The other two lionesses went to work on the adjacent (and quieter) eland halves.

"Oh my God, I'm gonna kick her."

"Don't kick her," warned Cobra.

The Professor thrust her foot down and just barely tagged the lioness' nose with the tip of her heel. The lioness immediately growled, baring the four huge canines that framed the rest of her very sharp choppers. She tested the Professor's boot with her teeth.

"That seemed effective; why don't you try that again?" asked Cobra.

"I guess I have to, because your advice has been so useful!"

she yelled back at him.

One of the lionesses managed to drag an eland half down off the hook, the meat hitting the blood-soaked earth with a dull thud. The other lioness gave up on her carcass and pulled at the one that had been dislodged in a macabre tug-of-war.

And yet, even with this free venison, the Professor's lioness would not leave her alone. She nibbled at the Professor's feet, tugging backward. The copper wire wrenched against her arms.

"Are you wearing perfume?" asked Cobra.

"I haven't put on deodorant in two days, Cobra! I smell like a Port Authority bathroom!"

"I'm just saying, sometimes animals go for perfumes and colognes."

"And if I were wearing perfume," said the Professor, kicking with her free boot, "what could I then do to rectify the situation?"

"Um," mused Cobra. "Nothing, I suppose. But we would know!"

The lioness fit most of the Professor's foot in her mouth, sucking on the leather like a frozen fruit pop. The other two lions tucked into their prize.

"Didn't Mikey Kalahari and Sahara O'Hara teach you anything about lions?"

"Of course, they did. I'm not wearing cologne!"

"Neither am I, you moron!"

Blood-curdling roars from just beyond the darkness.

Two young male lions pounced onto the eland carcass, sending the two lionesses into temporary retreat. The Professor's lioness quickly abandoned the Professor's boot and rolled onto her back, swiping upward defensively with all four sets of claws.

"It's them!" yelled Cobra. "It's our boys!"

Tweed and Magua circled the carcass and faced down the lionesses, who were not about to relinquish their meal to two barely adult males they'd never met before. The lionesses tested them, snapping and roaring, and the males held their ground.

"The females are in a state of tension and uncertainty; their pride male was killed today," said Cobra. "These are the earliest stages of negotiation."

"Negotiation for what?"

"Regime change," said Cobra. "Our boys will have to prove that they're formidable. If the lionesses make them fold, they'll know that they won't be able to defend their offspring and they'll reject them."

A gunshot.

The lions all looked inwards toward the camp, where three armed men were approaching. They each fired into the air again, and the lions retreated a few feet to the edge of the grasslands before turning again to face them.

"Get away from that, you," yelled the man in the middle. "That's eland's breakfast."

"You just saved yourselves some nasty cleanup!" said Cobra. "Thanks for the help."

"Just got the call from Mr. Hernandez Santana," said the one in the middle. "We can kill the girl; you have to hang until you bleed out."

"Grim," said Cobra. "But I actually wasn't talking to you."

Something cut through the thick, humid air, though it was only perceptible by the quick, nearly silent *whoosh*.

"Glurg…" said the soldier on the right, an arrow embedded in his windpipe.

The soldier on the left drew his gun just as the first soldier dropped to the bloody ground, drowning in his own fluids, but he was rewarded with one arrow to the ribs and one to the lung. He grabbed at the soldier in the middle to remain upright, dragging down his weapon arm.

It was enough for three San to emerge from the darkness, bows drawn at the last remaining soldier, who dropped his weapon immediately.

"Please don't kill me!" he begged.

From behind the three San emerged Kotani, still naked, supported by a fourth.

"Be silent, first of all," he said, and the soldier complied immediately. "Our poison is from the larvae of leaf beetles and works slowly. You have put me in a position here. I do not like to kill people, but…"

"I don't mind at all," said Hyacinth, pushing past the San like the Angel of Death and shoving one of the AR-15s Cobra abandoned in the grasslands into the soldier's face.

"What the fuck?" mouthed the Professor to Cobra.

"Please, please, don't shoot me…" whimpered the soldier, his hands folded in prayer as he saw the vengeance burning in Hyacinth's eyes.

She stood still for a moment, weighing options in her head, and said, "I won't shoot you. Go walk out there into the plains."

"Bbbut…" he stuttered.

"Put one in his arm!" she directed, and a San shot an arrow right in front of the elbow.

"I *said*, take a walk."

"No. Please, have mercy…" he cried.

"Other arm!"

A second arrow embedded itself into the soldier's opposite shoulder, and he saw he had no choice but to do as Hyacinth commanded. He took about ten steps outside the light of camp when the growling started. Cobra expected there to be more screaming, but he figured the lionesses must have gotten to his throat sooner rather than later. He thought it was atypical, because lions are usually confused by the posture of bipedal targets, or at least, that's what he'd read. Either way, at least it was quick.

"How's it hanging, Cobra?" asked Kotani quietly.

"I'd ask you," laughed Cobra, "but I already know!"

"Can someone get us down and tell me what the hell is going on?" asked the Professor.

***

What followed was a silent campaign of stealth assassination tactics as Kotani led his San brothers through the camp *straight up murdering* anyone unfortunate enough to be in their way. Sleeping soldier? Hand over the face, knife through the heart. Drunk soldier? Knife across the throat. Geologist, logistician, scientist of some kind? Arrow, arrow, arrow. Soldier on guard? One-way guided hike to the grasslands at gunpoint, as per Hyacinth's very specific request. They cleaned out this camp like the creeping death extinguishing all the first-born sons of Egypt (I don't mean like in the Bible, again, but like in that old movie).

Cobra insisted that they spare who they could, and after some argument from Hyacinth who was a proponent of the *kill-em-all* approach, they secured those who surrendered and posed the least threat to the meat-drying racks. They didn't hang them, and they didn't use copper wire, but the prisoners would be very uncomfortable tied up and standing until *some kind of authorities* might get around to them later. It was lucky that the camp was largely understaffed at the moment, and the San only had to dispatch a handful of people. Most of those they captured were not disciplined soldiers but local men for hire.

"How did you find us?" the Professor asked.

"I signaled the San when I realized they had been following us," said Cobra. "I stopped and flashed the high-beams of the Land Cruiser when I was driving back to the miombo forest."

"We were watching for most of the afternoon," said one of the San. "We could see you with our spotting scopes. Who was the asshole who drank our water?"

"Where did you get a spotting scope?" asked the Professor.

"Mister Northside provides us with this and that to help us get by," said another. "Like the old car we sometimes use to cover great distances."

"It's a Volkswagon Beetle," said Kotani. "Totally inappropriate for life in the Bush, but fuck, it beats walking."

"Kotani once told me that his people would help if I asked," said Cobra. "So, in a way, since I signaled them, *I* actually rescued *you*."

"Don't get carried away," said Kotani.

"But where did you come from, Hyacinth?" asked the Professor. "I saw you in the Land Cruiser. I saw you cross the river."

"I swam back over."

"With the crocs?"

"With the crocs," Hyacinth said. "They killed my husband. Now I have to sanction all of them."

"*Sanction* them?" asked the Professor. "Hyacinth, when Cobra asked you if you were a spy, you said *no*."

"Isn't that what a spy *would* say?" asked Cobra. "Hyacinth…"

"No, I'm not a spy, but I did pick up a trick or two around the office. And Mark always said that if he were ever murdered, he would want to be avenged, like in some old kung fu movie. Kotani's friends found me wandering through the grasslands and picked me up in their crappy car, and now we're all caught up."

"Black Tiger took over the lodge, and he probably has all our friends," said Cobra. "We're going to have to move our asses if we're going to save them. What time is it?"

One of the San looked at his watch (not a traditional Bushman item but still very nice) and said, "Three twenty-five."

"If we borrow one of their cars, we can be there before sunrise. Wheels-up in twenty minutes, people," said Cobra.

"I think that only applies to flying, Cobra," said Kotani.

"Not the way I drive."

\*\*\*

334

One thing Black Tiger's camp had in abundance was medical supplies. They taped up Hyacinth's ankle very tightly and gave her about five Advils, which Cobra said wasn't very healthy for the liver, to which Hyacinth replied, "Neither are your G&Ts." They treated the cuts on Cobra's and Hyacinth's arms with antiseptic solutions and cleaned out Cobra's various boo-boos (from leopards, baboons, etc...) and just like that, it was decided that the three of them had clean bills of health.

Kotani, however, was in a much worse state. Everyone agreed that he and the San would stay there and occupy the camp, keeping watch over the prisoners and convalescing as best as possible until they returned. They were to stay off the radio until Cobra contacted them, and then hopefully they'd arrange for a plane to make it to the airstrip for evacuation.

Cobra loaded a Land Cruiser with an obscene amount of guns and ammo, as if he could fire more than two at a time. He went into one of the tents to look for the keys, or this mission would be sort of a non-starter. Sure enough, Black Tiger's men had organized well and there was a box of vehicle keys easily accessible.

The Professor followed him into the tent.

"Looks like we're in business," he said, holding up four sets of keys. "One of these has to work."

"I love that your plan was to get captured and have someone *else* rescue us," she said.

"My goodness, Professor. You followed me in here to rip on me again?"

"I came in here to wish you a merry Christmas."

"What?"

"It's Christmas Day, Cobra," she said. "Merry Christmas."

"Holy shit, it is!"

She kissed him, and he didn't expect it, but boy did he

335

enjoy it, until she stopped.

"Jesus, Cobra, you taste like throw-up."

"Well, I did just vomit a few hours ago," he said. "But it was very little."

"I thought you learned how to act around women at that hotel bar in Rwanda," she said, wiping the taste from her mouth.

"I learned *lots* of stuff from those women in Rwanda," he said. "I can't figure you out, Professor. One minute I can't do anything right, and the next, I could swear you're flirting with me. Maybe that's what I like so much about you."

"You know, that's acacia above this tent, not mistletoe," she said, looking around the room and finding an open bottle of *mezcal*, of all things. "But here, take a swig."

"I'm going to have to drive in a few minutes…"

"Are you worried about getting pulled over? Just a swig."

"Uh, OK…"

He took a big mouthful, finally figured it out, and swished it around like mouthwash before spitting it out on the floor.

"Good enough?" he asked.

"You wish," she said, and she leaned in and kissed him again, and she explored the inside of his shirt with her fingertips. Cobra thought it was so wonderful that he ignored the stinging pain of her hands on the leopard scratches. After all, he had just been tortured on an *actual* rack, and this was definitely *not* torture. He leaned into her, kissing her deeply and flexing the muscles in his chest and arms to try to impress her.

A sudden sound, like intruders outside the tent sneaking about. They broke off abruptly and grabbed their guns, pointing them outside.

A big warthog shuffled by, occasionally walking on his wrists to help get lower to the dirt to root for buried food. He looked in the tent curiously but decided that he was not interested and continued about his business in no particular hurry. Cobra and the Professor let out a sigh.

"That take you out of it?" he asked.

"Not really, no."

"Good," he said, going back in for some more tonsil-wrestling, until Hyacinth honked the horn from the Land Rover outside.

"Aaaaaand we're done."

# CHAPTER 24:
# PRIDE

The sun still wouldn't rise for a while, but the clouds had dissipated and pulled back the curtain of night just enough to showcase some brilliant, lingering starlight onto the grasslands. The three lionesses had dragged both eland halves more than a hundred yards away from where they had requisitioned them, and when you consider that a whole eland can weigh up to half a ton, that's a feat that probably makes you wish you spent a few extra minutes at the gym each day.

Tweed and Magua lay prone, facing them, a healthy fifteen yards away, and the lionesses, in turn, looked back. The males didn't have enough experience to fully interpret the signals. Were the females challenging them? Daring them to come closer? Warning them to stay away? Inviting them to display their strength?

The males couldn't smell any cubs, not even any subadults. They had passed the carcass of the male that had been shot and detected his scent on grasses and trees but didn't find the presence of any other males that might already have claim to this small pride. Tweed curled his lips back around his canines in what looked like a snarl but was actually what wildlife biologists called *flehmen*… using pits in the roof of his mouth to scan for pheromones and other useful olfactory information that might be in the air. He was testing the waters.

Magua looked to Tweed for assurance, and then got up and rubbed his body laterally against him to confirm and strengthen their bond. Confounded, Tweed seemed to shrug, *I don't know*. He resumed his study of the females on the eland carcasses and licked his lips.

Tweed rose to his feet and strode confidently towards the females, his head held high and his burgeoning mane fluffed out widely like a peacock in display. Backing him up, Magua followed. The lionesses immediately stood and growled, their ears pinned down angrily against their heads in defiance.

Tweed stopped and let the lionesses growl it out for a few minutes, hoping they'd get it out of their systems. They seemed to want him to back off, but if he did, would he be showing weakness, and thus, *unsuitability* as a pride male? Maybe they *wanted* him to try and take the eland carcass.

He advanced, and Magua padded behind him, emboldened by his audacity. The first lioness roared and swiped at Tweed, clipping him several times around the ears, but he held his ground and pounced on one of the carcasses, swinging back and scattering the three of them. Carcass acquired, Magua also leapt on it, emphasizing the takeover.

Tweed sunk his teeth into the meat outside the ribcage and tugged, tearing it from the bone, and Magua went to work on the leg. The lionesses circled them, looking for openings to come back to the eland, but with two pairs of eyes watching them, it was difficult to surprise them from the rear.

One tried anyway, and Tweed punished her for it, assertively running her off with snapping jaws and thick saliva. He returned to the carcass and continued crunching the tips of bones, and the lionesses begrudgingly retreated a few yards away, their eyes locked onto Tweed and Magua and instinctively hoping they hadn't made enough noise to attract hyenas.

After twenty minutes of eating, Tweed abruptly stopped and walked away, flopping down on the grass nearby, and taking

Tweed's lead, Magua did the same. The lionesses tentatively approached the carcass. There was still plenty of meat on the one Tweed and Magua had started on, and the other carcass was more or less untouched. They each sat down and tucked back in, with Tweed's apparent blessing.

It was still dark but the stars were beginning to fade into the deep blue. Tweed understood that this exercise might have to be repeated a dozen times or more if they were to be accepted as the pride's new patriarchs, but at least for now, they were fed, and at least for now, they had a home. It was a start.

# CHAPTER 25:
# THE MERRIEST OF CHRISTMASES

It didn't seem like a very good idea to cross the river in the dark, but Cobra figured he'd been running on so many bad ideas over the past three days, why stop now? He killed the engine at the edge of the water and listened to the sound of the current flowing by, and then he turned to the Professor and to Hyacinth, both carrying a staggering array of deadly weaponry for which neither of them were licensed nor trained.

"Buckle up, ladies."

"Don't you at least want to get out and check the water to see how deep it is here?" asked the Professor.

"Totally not necessary!" replied Cobra. "I listened. I can tell by the sound that it can't be more than a foot, maybe a foot and a half deep at this point. No problem!"

"What could it hurt to get out and check?" she protested.

"Well, it's cold."

"...which would mean that the crocs would still be torpid now, so it'd be safe."

"Come on, Delia," said Hyacinth. "Cobra's probably crossed here a hundred times. Right?"

"Sure, why not?" sort of confirmed Cobra. "And this is a top-of-the-line Land Cruiser. Black Tiger didn't cheap out when he outfitted these turkeys. It's made specifically for this kind of application."

"If I had a hundred dollars on me right now, I would feel completely confident betting you that we're about to get stuck in the middle of this river. Like, no doubt. Easy money," the Professor said, folding her arms.

"You can just add that to my tip," said Cobra, turning the engine over again, putting the Cruiser into gear and slowly coaxing the vehicle into the opaque, black river. "I would hang onto something, though."

The Professor was already counting that money in her head when the flowing water immediately came up to the tops of the hubcaps only a few feet into the river. She felt its constant force pushing perpendicularly against the side of the car.

"Cobra, this is not going to work," she warned.

"Two hundred dollars," he said, concentrating.

Water seeped into the car now, soaking the bottoms of their boots and making the car feel more like a guided boat ride at Pirates of the Caribbean.

"Deal," said the Professor, angrily, as water welled up to her ankles. They progressed to almost halfway across the river, and they were slowing down as the tires sunk into the mud. Hyacinth reached out the window and touched the water.

The engine stalled, and the cruiser stopped. They were at least fifteen yards from the shore, but it was hard to tell in the darkness. With the engine off, they could hear the early birds calling to one another over the sound of the rushing water.

"God damn it, Cobra!" yelled the Professor.

Hyacinth squinted as she looked upriver. "Is that a..."

"Three hundred clams!" offered Cobra, jamming on the clutch and working with the stick as water came up to his ankles.

"Of course, I'll take that!" the Professor yelled back. "I don't know how I'll collect it when we all *drown*, but if I see you in Hell, you better have my money!"

"We won't drown in this," he replied, twisting the key in the ignition but hearing nothing in return. "You might want to quiet down a little, though. Crocs might be torpid, being ectothermic, but the hippos aren't."

"I knew that's what I saw," said Hyacinth, watching the enormous swimming boulders making their way downstream towards their stalled vehicle. There was just enough light to see the sprays of water ejecting from their nostrils as if from the blowholes of whales.

The water was nearly up to their knees now, but as if by some miracle, Cobra got the engine to turn over. He gave it some gas, and even the Professor and Hyacinth felt the tires spinning beneath them, digging deeper into the mud.

"Might need the winch," Cobra mused. "You know, Professor, maybe we should have gotten out and checked the water first. Next time, remind me to listen to you."

"Gee, you think?"

The wheels spun faster as Cobra tried another gear, but unless one of those gears was a hovercraft setting, they weren't going anywhere. Who knows what miracle kept the engine from stalling?

Cobra turned to the Professor and said, "Um, maybe we should abandon ship."

"Hippos hippos hippos..." said Hyacinth, watching the hippos submerge a few yards away from them.

"On second thought, keep your arms inside the vehicle at all times!"

They felt a powerful collision, like three torpedoes slamming into the side of the Cruiser. They spun ninety degrees and were now almost facing completely upriver, against the current. The impact knocked Hyacinth onto the adjacent seat, and the Professor white-knuckled the dash. The current now pushed against them head-on.

But, the hippos had dislodged them from the mud.

Cobra quickly shifted into reverse and, with the current pushing them backwards, turned the car around so that the rear was now pointed towards the bank they needed to climb. He gunned it, driving backwards as fast as he could, hoping that there were no hippos behind them.

All three lurched forward with a jerk when the tires made contact with dry land, the car reversing up the bank and climbing until the river was behind, er, in front of them. Cobra pulled a U-turn, crushing some bushes and stinging Hyacinth and the Professor with some branches. He shut off the engine.

They opened the doors, draining the vehicle and half-expecting a fish to swim out. Hyacinth's side of the car had three huge dents in it, impressions each two and a half feet wide. Cobra folded his arms and smiled smugly, but the Professor was quick to point out:

"We never shook on it."

\*\*\*

They drove as quickly as possible, given the circumstances, but with only the headlights to illuminate their way, it was pretty treacherous. Cobra managed to hit just about every rock and bush that happened to be on the game reserve, and he was happy to point out the geology and Linnean classification of each, respectively, as he did so. Hyacinth felt as though she were in a 1930s wooden rollercoaster that battered her against the metal of both sides of the car. It was a very good thing that all the guns had safeties on them.

Avoiding the roads, they passed the hyenas that had tangled with Tweed and Magua two days ago; their clan had killed a few hartebeests and were in the process of crunching down the bones. Cobra, the Professor, and Hyacinth had also seen the lion pride they encountered, which had by now cooperatively cleaned the buffalo carcass they'd been working on into an almost museum-quality display skeleton. A lonesome giraffe, a zebra stallion, a secretary bird, and then there they were, in thick bush about half a mile from the lodge.

Cobra shut off the headlights and killed the engine; dawn was just breaking.

"From here on out, we go on foot," he said.

"All right," said the Professor. "I assume you have a plan."

"We're about a ten-minute hike from the lodge. That's plenty of time to think of one," he said.

"We're going to waste every one of those miserable fucks down to the last man," said Hyacinth grimly.

"That's a good start," said Cobra, "but do you have any specifics?"

"No," she said sheepishly. "I'm sure these will be involved."

Each of them was now carrying an AR-15 in each hand. You read that right - each hand, so make sure you picture septuagenarian Hyacinth wielding double sub-machine guns. Cobra also had two sticks of dynamite that Black Tiger's crew must have brought for unearthing all those heaping piles of gold they were supposed to find. Only the Professor had the foresight to remember to find a lighter to go with that dynamite.

"OK, team. Let's put it on the back burner for now. Single-file, please."

They marched through the dense bush, careful to be as quiet as they could but crunching on deadfall with nearly every step. Up in the trees, a large troop of vervet monkeys followed them from branch to branch like a gang of miniature Tarzans, curious about these clumsy, noisy, upright apes.

"Don't these things ever sleep?" asked Hyacinth.

"They're generally diurnal," answered Cobra. "Always pay attention to them. They'll usually spot a leopard long before we will. Look ahead, please."

The Professor continued walking, keeping her eyes up on the mischievous vervets.

"You think they're looking for fruits?" she asked.

"With these crazy little guys, it could be anything."

345

"They look so FUCK!" she suddenly exclaimed, inhaling sharply and falling forward. She bit her lip to keep from screaming.

Cobra and Hyacinth dropped to her side, holding her by the torso. "What? What is it?"

Grinding the words through her teeth, the Professor uttered, "My foot."

She had stepped on an acacia thorn, and it had punctured straight through the sole of her boot and impaled her foot in the center of the arch. The three-inch spike had gone in so deeply that only a tiny piece of it still protruded from her boot like a golf tee that had been pressed too deeply on the green. The vervets stopped and looked at her from the safety of their branches.

"Vervets," she hissed.

"I did just say to watch where you were going," said Cobra, regretting those words the nano-second they left his larynx.

"Up yours," she growled. "You said look ahead. Ahead doesn't specify a direction!"

Cobra disagreed with her semantics but knew better than to argue.

"We've got to get this boot off her," said Cobra.

"How are we going to do that without breaking it?" asked Hyacinth.

"The shoe'll be fine, except for the little hole, but I don't know why we should be concerned about..."

"The thorn, Cobra, breaking the thorn," said Hyacinth. "How are we going to get the boot off without breaking the thorn and leaving it stuck in her foot?"

"Oh," said Cobra. "Right. Do you think you can do it?"
"No."

"Just take all the time you need, people," said the Professor.

"You have longer nails, Hyacinth. Maybe you can grip it between your nails and sort of yank it out."

"I don't know," she said, doubtful. "I'll try. Sweetie, this is going to hurt."

"It is? Really? No way," growled the Professor.

"Hey, I'm only trying to help. You don't have to be a jerk about it." said Hyacinth.

"No, but you do have to be a little quieter about it," said Cobra. "If they didn't hear that F-bomb you just broadcast at maximum volume, we don't want to alert any scouts or sentries they might have posted near the lodge. Bite down on this."

Cobra handed her a thin branch that had fallen nearby. She took it and yelped.

"There's a thorn on this too!" she grunted, breaking off the much smaller thorn and tossing it away.

"OK, well now you're just being a baby," said Cobra, and she looked at him as though he were lower than worm shit. She bit down on the stick and nodded.

"Here we go," said Hyacinth. She took the edges of the nails on her pointer finger and thumb and attempted to dig into the rubber of the Professor's boot to gain some purchase on the thorn. The Professor bit down hard and tried not to squirm as Hyacinth kept clipping her nails together like dull scissors, just grazing the tip of the thorn. After thirty excruciating seconds, Hyacinth stopped.

"Did you get it?" panted the Professor, spitting out the stick. "It feels like it's still in there."

"It is. I'm sorry. I wish I hadn't gotten that manicure last week," said Hyacinth.

Cobra picked up the thorn that the Professor had discarded and looked at her apologetically. "This is not going to hurt at all. Not one bit. Barely a mosquito bite."

The professor, exhausted, said, "Just get it over with."

Cobra used the other thorn as a wedge to help lever out the tip of the one stuck within her foot. He jammed it down, poking through and widening the hole, cutting through the flesh as he attempted to pry the first thorn out without breaking it. The

Professor squeezed her eyes tightly but tears still escaped.

"What are you doing, playing Q-bert with that thorn?" she yelped.

Applying more pressure, Cobra managed to gain just enough traction to wrench the thorn up a quarter of an inch. He sat backward.

"Want to close her up for me, nurse?"

Using her nails again, Hyacinth clamped down on the protruding thorn and pulled, sliding it out with blood dripping from the boot hole like a leaky faucet. The Professor immediately took her boot off and clutched her foot, her sock completely saturated with blood and dirty water from the river.

"Here. Have a souvenir," said Hyacinth, handing her the bloody thorn.

"I know that hurt, Professor, but I think we're out of the woods," said Cobra, taking his hat off and clearing the sweat from his forehead.

"Drop your weapons and throw those hands up nice and slow!" commanded a voice from behind.

"Aw, shit," said Cobra, surrendering his assault rifles and turning to see a woman wearing a sports bra and a headband; the rest of her face was war-painted with mud. In her hands was a long, thick tree branch sharpened into a spear point. She looked as if she had lived alone in the jungle for twenty years, surviving on wild boars and fish that she'd speared out of a river; Cobra checked to make sure she wasn't wearing a necklace made of ears or something.

"Delia?"

"Annie?"

"Whoa!" exclaimed Annie, tossing her spear aside and tackling Delia back down to the ground, hugging her tightly. "The Wildhorse is free!"

Cobra stood up and smiled, because he knew who must have been with her.

"Come on out, Wyatt. And don't say you could have killed me three dozen ways. I knew you were there the whole time," he lied.

"I won't, but only because Annie would have already killed you thirty-five ways herself," said Wyatt, emerging from the foliage as though the light had been bending around him supernaturally. He threw his arms around Cobra and gave him a genuine, un-self-conscious hug, picking him up off the ground. "When we saw the car drive in without you, we thought those assholes might have gotten you."

Katy was there too, not looking too worse for wear. "Where's Kotani?"

"He's safe now," said Cobra. "He's at their original camp north-east of the river with the other San. He needs some medical attention, but he's all right."

"These army guys came in and took over the lodge," said Annie. "If Wyatt hadn't brought me out on a walking safari a few hours after you'd all left, they'd have captured us too."

"I managed to slip out myself when they pulled in. I assumed they were ivory hunters, the bastards," said Katy. "Wyatt and Annie found me, and we've been living out here for the last two days, watching."

"Mrs. Sarasota!" said Wyatt. "I'm glad you're alive! I hope you won't hold this experience against the sterling reputation of our humble Rhino Horn Ranch. But where's..."

Wyatt stopped speaking as Cobra slowly shook his head. Wyatt went to Hyacinth and gave her a long hug, even though he barely knew her.

"I am so sorry," said Wyatt. "We're going to get these fuckers, I solemnly promise."

"Wyatt," said Cobra. "It's him."

"Him? Him who?"

"Hernandez Santana."

"No."

"Yes, Wyatt. Black Tiger."

"No fucking way," he said in disbelief. "Did he track you here?"

"Not originally. They're here for Kruger's gold. They've been digging and surveying all over the reserve; they set off your flashbang grenades when I gave them the decoy site, and I took them to the Germans' bunker," explained Cobra.

"Did you tell them about me?" asked Wyatt.

"No, but I'm sure they've figured it out," said Cobra.

"Wait a minute, I haven't figured it out," said Annie.

"I found Kruger's gold here five years ago, chasing after some crazy story this lunatic in Zim told me. It's a ton of South African gold lost here on this property by the government. This wilderness wasn't suitable for farming or cattle. When I discovered the treasure, I used the money to buy all this land, and we converted the hunting lodge into Rhino Horn."

"Wyatt re-stocks the bunker with a few gold bars every time some treasure hunter gets lucky and finds it, so they'll go away thinking they're rich and that they've found the gold, generally leaving us alone and not making a pain in the ass of themselves," said Cobra.

"So why is your Black Tiger still making a pain in the ass of himself?" asked Wyatt.

"Because he figured out that someone, you, already liquidated most of the treasure, making his expedition an extravagant failure, and he can't go back to his boss empty-handed. To recoup his losses, he's gone after the Lamassu, which he knows must be hidden in the lodge."

"It's under my bloody bed!" said Wyatt.

"What's a Lamassu?" asked Annie.

"It's a unique, ancient Assyrian relic that I stole from him. It's priceless," said Cobra.

"Hell," said Katy. "Let him have it and be done with it."

"We can't," said Wyatt. "He's going to kill everyone in

there once he's done."

"And go back to his first camp and slaughter Kotani and the San," said Cobra.

"A car came in late last night. That must have been Black Tiger," said Katy.

"He could have the lammy sue already," said Annie. "We've got to move quickly. The sun's almost up."

"All right, then. What's the plan?" asked Wyatt.

"Now that we've found you, I figured you'd come up with a plan," said Cobra.

"Me? My plan was to wait them out until they've gone. Live off the land, throw sticks at antelopes, that kind of thing," said Wyatt. "I mean, what's the best thing you've got?"

"We have six assault rifles, and there are six of us," said the Professor. "Maybe that's a sign."

"I have a wooden spear!" said Annie.

"She made that herself, by the way," said Wyatt.

"I was wrong, Wildhorse," said Annie. "This has been the best vacation. I'm having a hell of a time."

"I'm glad. And you can call me Professor now."

"You defended your thesis out there in the bush?" asked Annie.

"Back to topic," said Wyatt. "Cobra, I thought you said that this Tiger guy was dangerous, talented in every survival and combat art. That he built himself up from poverty in some shitty neighborhood and self-educated himself in the sports of murder, torture, and violence. Now he's got the lodge secured with what must be fifteen men - all of them armed, even the pencil-pushing nimrod scientists - and you guys are telling me that you think the six of us should just Rambo our way to victory?"

"Well, when you say it like that, it just sounds stupid," admitted Cobra.

"Little bit, mate," said Wyatt. "And you've never even killed anyone before."

"You're still holding that over my head..."

"Not even in DRC, which is like the Wild Fucking West but with gorillas and deadly river parasites, when the rain was pouring down on us and there was thunder and lightning and that guy..."

"...who turned out to be your friend, who paid you money," interrupted Cobra.

"...thunder and lightning! It was so dark and dramatic! Any grandmother would have shot that guy with all that moody atmosphere going on."

"Cobra shot some guy just two nights ago," said the Professor. "Although, to be fair, he lived. He also watched as another guy got bitten in half by a hippopotamus."

"Well, let's just contract the hippo, then," said Katy.

"I don't have any problem sanctioning anyone. None," said Hyacinth.

"That's true," said Cobra. "Hyacinth just killed, like, five people just a few hours ago. She tortured them first with poison arrows and then fed them to the lions!"

"Again, those kills really belong to the lions, then, don't they?" said Katy.

"I have a spear," repeated Annie.

Silence, except for the birds and the insects.

Cobra said, "We also have two sticks of dynamite."

\*\*\*

I don't think it's hyperbole to suggest that not since Washington himself crossed the Delaware has there ever been a more daring military raid on Christmas Day than the one Cobra and his compatriots attempted that morning. All they had going for them was some guts and the element of surprise, and they were about to cash them in at the start.

Just on the periphery of the lodge grounds were a few warthogs and a kori bustard, which, if you don't know, is the largest bird still capable of powered flight. They were nosing around by the four vehicles that had been parked there intermittently over the past few days, finding crumbs left by the men and absorbing some of the early morning sun.

"Shoo," whispered Annie, holding her AR-15 up and gently swinging her makeshift spear at the wildlife, who more or less ignored her.

"I think you can be a little more forceful," whispered Wyatt, who had just lit the fuse to a stick of dynamite.

"Aren't they endangered?"

"I don't think so," said Wyatt. "Maybe the bird?"

Annie kept swinging, slapping a warthog on the ass with the blunt side of the spear. He turned indignantly and then sauntered off into the savanna, entourage in tow.

"I think we're clear now," she said.

"Marvelous," he replied, tossing the dynamite underneath the vehicle in the middle, taking her by the arm and running behind a huge, nearby baobab tree.

Black Tiger must not have liked to wait for his demolitions, because that fuse was set so short that it disappeared faster than a small popcorn before a Saturday Matinee. The car jolted up as though it had been parked on top of an active volcano, flaming tires bouncing up and down the dirt path, black smoke billowing up to the sky.

"Now what?" asked Annie.

"What do you mean, now what?" replied Wyatt. "Now we shoot everyone."

"I thought we were just supposed to provide a distraction."

"We are! We're going to distract their heads from their bodies," said Wyatt.

"Well, as long as I won't have to answer for this in a court of law."

"What kind of court would you prefer?" he laughed.

"I don't know. Tennis? Basketball? Kangaroo?"

\*\*\*

In the visitor's center, soldiers ran through the lounge and indoor dining room, grabbing their guns and responding to the loud boom they just heard outside in their impromptu parking lot.

"You two, stay with them," commanded a guy with aviator sunglasses to a pair of men wearing camo t-shirts. Sunglasses dashed out the door, leaving the soldiers with Susan, Andres, Xavier and Kevin, each securely tied up on the couch. Kevin looked like he had a severe flu, his skin drained of all color. He shook as though he were covered with ants.

"What is going on?" demanded Andres in a typically demeaning tone.

"You are being tortured, that's what," said Camo Number One, slapping him hard across the cheek.

They heard gunfire from outside now.

Camo Number Two turned to his comrade and said, "Let him go out there and get killed if he wants to."

"Right?" said Hyacinth, who snuck in amid the chaos, Katy behind her. "You can die right here."

Hyacinth squeezed the trigger until both the gun ceased spitting out bullets and Camo Number Two was no longer standing. Katy dispatched Camo Number One with a single shot through the eye.

"Jesus, Hyacinth!" screamed Susan. "I think you got him!"

"You shoot like an American, Hyacinth," said Andres.

"Is that an insult?" she asked.

"Right now, it's a compliment," he answered with his thick, German accent.

"Give us a second," said Katy, working on their bindings.

"Can you all walk?" asked Hyacinth.

"Kevin's dying," cried Xavier. "They wouldn't allow him

the anti-venom. Please, help him!"

Katy turned to Hyacinth, who said, "He was bitten yesterday afternoon."

"Antivenom's in the kitchen fridge," Katy said. "Let's go."


Outside, Wyatt had a gun under each arm, blasting them both from the hip. Annie clutched her spear tightly, hiding with him behind the massive tree as he periodically swung out to fire. She heard the rounds being fired at her snapping through the air, digging into the wood. Soldiers poured out of the visitor's center, firing wildly at them.

"Did you get any yet?" she asked.

"Yeah, I think I got three or four of them," he answered. "You sure you don't want your rifle back? Just for a few minutes?"

"Yeah, I'm comfortable. If someone tries to sneak around the tree, I'll just jab them with my stick," she said.

"I knew I could count on you!" he said, swinging out and shooting.


Black Tiger heard the explosion and the shooting, and he knew his time was almost at an end here. He figured someone must have fucked up at camp and allowed Cobra to get to a radio and call the South African Special Forces, or perhaps he was just unlucky and a low-flying plane spotted their operation. He could still get away on a motorcycle, drive north. He had people in Botswana and Namibia.

But he couldn't leave with nothing, not again, not this time. He knew it would not be tolerated, especially with the expense he'd incurred and the mess of bodies he'd left in his wake. There was nothing he could have done about Kruger' Gold; they'd have to accept that. If he could bring them the lamassu, well, then that would do a lot to rewrite their shared history.

Black Tiger had spent all night personally ransacking this whole lodge, overturning every brick and board, becoming wilder and more frustrated with each cleared rondavel. Kitchen, visitor's center, hut by hut by hut. He had only a few more rooms to check, although it occurred to him that Cobra could have buried it anywhere on this property. He cursed himself for letting his anger get the better of him, leaving Cobra to suffer on that rack instead of bringing him here to the lodge to interrogate and torture as necessary. Now it might be too late.

Black Tiger kicked down the door to one of the last little buildings left. It was lined on all sides with shelves stacked with books from floor to ceiling, and a small weight bench sat innocuously with a pair of army dog tags hanging from them. He knew right away whose quarters these were.

"Long Island fucking punk-ass!" he howled, his refined speech patterns dissolving in the heat of his own rage. He grabbed the dog tags and kicked over the bench, insanely throwing each book he could get his hands on off the shelves. He rifled through the closet, hurling khaki shirt after khaki shirt over his head, until he found what looked like a spiraled piece of tapering bone.

"That, Jeter, is a lesser kudu horn given to me by a Samburu elder," said Cobra, standing in the entrance, helping to support the Professor. "You better clean up all my shit."

"Specialist McConnors!" he roared, eyes lit up like fire. "You're going to tell me where..."

"Looking for this?" taunted Cobra, producing the lamassu in all its bejeweled radiance. "You can't have it, but if you'd like me to smash another gem off into your face, I think we can work something out."

Black Tiger touched the scar on his forehead and then the jewel that hung around his neck. He reached for his gun, but the Professor pointed her AR-15 at him first, freezing him in place.

"Uh uh," she scolded. "You defended your thesis, did you? Let's see you defend your ass from some steel!"

"Lead," whispered Cobra. "Bullets are made of lead."

"Really?" she asked.

"McConnors, listen for a minute. Just listen!" Tiger scowled.

Cobra lit the fuse on his stick of dynamite.

"On second thought, don't worry about cleaning up my room," he said. "I'll take care of it myself."

"You can't! That's mine! That's mine!" he howled as the fuse burned down.

"You educated yourself, but you didn't finish learning. Now I'm going to take you back to school to..."

Before Cobra could finish whatever extremely cool and callous thing he was about to say before blowing Black Tiger to Kingdom Come, the dynamite stick was whisked out of his hand.

"What the hell?"

A vervet monkey had landed on his arm and pilfered the dynamite right from his hand! It jumped off and scampered up the tree next to Cobra's room. Deciding the sparkly thing wasn't as interesting as he first considered, the vervet dropped it down onto the top of the roof.

"Oh shit," said Cobra.

Black Tiger threw himself through the window.

Cobra tackled the Professor away and rolled as far from the building as he could before it blew like Mount Vesuvius, scattering every earthly possession he had to the Four Winds in a blizzard of fiery detritus.

Ears ringing and stained black with ash, the Professor was lying prone on top of Cobra, her full weight upon him. "I told you we should have just shot him!"

"Yeah," coughed Cobra. "Next time, we'll just fill him full of steel."


Dead bodies festooned the lawn like plastic Christmas

decorations, but none of them were Wyatt and Annie, who were running-and-gunning across the dry grass as bullets snapped over their heads. They had a clear path to Katy's office, and it was now or never, or so determined Wyatt. Annie didn't know why it couldn't have been now or some undetermined time in the future, but she didn't communicate that properly to Wyatt, so they went for it.

"Cover me!" yelled Wyatt as he swung his size twelve boot against the locked door to the office.

"OK!" roared Annie, still not carrying either gun but instead pointing her wooden stick at their attackers menacingly, bullets slapping into the wood behind her.

Wyatt splintered the door with his third kick. He grabbed Annie by the shoulder and yanked her inside. The office looked like a hurricane had blown through it, with Katy's once-meticulously arranged papers and folders now carelessly crumpled at each corner of the room. Black Tiger had no doubt thoroughly searched it... but he left the radio alone and fully operational.

"Annie, do you know how to operate a radio?" he asked, turning back to the door.

"I mostly just listen to the CD player in my car!" she responded.

"I love ya, you brilliant Sheila!" he laughed. "I'll have to do it. You have to cover me then." He took her spear and traded it for an AR-15.

"I have to shoot this?"

"Yes! At this point, you can call it coercion, so I'd take the rap for you in court if it came to it, assuming we live through this."

"All right; what do I do?"

"If someone shows up and you don't know him, squeeze the trigger 'til it's empty!" he said.

"Then what?"

"Then take this other gun and do the same thing!"

Rounds pounded against the door from outside.

"And then what do I do?" Annie asked, steadying the rifle.

"I don't know! Throw stuff, I guess!" he said as he sat at the desk, picked up the microphone and adjusted the dial.


It was Xavier who lead the charge into the kitchen, where a scientist wearing headphones was making coffee, impossibly oblivious to all the Rambo-ing going on around him. He turned around just in time for Xavier to smash a blender across his face, breaking it in three pieces. The guy was pretty lucky the blades didn't cut his throat.

"Guess we're not having daquiris later," said Susan, watching Xavier kick the unconscious scientist in the guts a few times.

"Hyacinth, hold the door," said Katy, and Hyacinth dropped to one knee, endorphins silencing the pain in her ankle as she prepared to sanction anyone following them. Katy gave her AR-15 to Andres.

"You have to cover the other door. Do you know how to use this?" she asked.

"I can figure it out. If Hyacinth can do it," he said arrogantly, and he covered the other door.

Katy retrieved a box of anti-venom vials from the refrigerator, syringes included, as Xavier propped Kevin up on a chair.

"Hold on, Kev," said Xavier, and Kevin, shivering, said nothing.

"You're going to have to help me, Xavier," said Katy.

"Whatever you need," he replied. "Let's just do it."

Susan grabbed eggs, bacon, and some diced peppers and onion from the refrigerator. Katy asked, "What the hell are you doing?"

Susan replied, "Making an omelet, obviously."

\*\*\*

Black Tiger crawled across the boma on his hands and knees, disoriented and looking for his weapon.  His ears rang painfully, and it was hard to find his balance and right himself. The embers of last night's fire were still smoldering in the fire pit, the sweet smell of charring wood wafting up and out around the wall of thorns that discouraged the wildlife from entering this space.

"Boom!" yelled Cobra, pointing his AR-15 at Black Tiger and holding the Professor up under her shoulder to keep the weight off her injured foot.  "You.  Are.  Dead."

"That's it," cursed Black Tiger, struggling to his feet. "Shoot me from ten meters away, like the gutless, heartless coward you are.  You haven't changed a bit."

"Shoot you from ten meters?" challenged Cobra.  "Let's be fair.  It's more like five, and I'm a pretty mediocre shot."

"You have no heart," spat Black Tiger.  "Campbell McConnors, the boy who runs.  Who cheats.  Who lets others take the hit for him.  Who hides in the armpit of the world, unable to face the consequences for the things he's done.  For the things he's failed to do."

"I see what you're trying to do, appealing to my machismo, hoping I'll put the gun down and give you a chance," said Cobra. "Because you've lost.  All your men are dead or captured.  There is no gold; not anymore.  And I have the lamassu, the thing you've probably obsessed about for the last four years.  You'd be lucky if I killed you, you fuck, because if I take you alive, Red Scorpion's going to find you sooner or later.  And he knows that my very existence is your failure.  All that training, all that education you put yourself through, and you're just a scared little child now. Choke on that, asshole."

"I don't get it," said the Professor.  "Didn't we learn anything from before?  Let's just shoot him!"

"At least she has some balls!" laughed Black Tiger. "So did your friend Christian. It's too bad they never found them, buried beneath the Iraqi sand. Now you choke on that, Specialist McConnors!"

Cobra paused for a moment, and the Professor knew. She just fucking knew.

"Oh shit," she grumbled. "Here we go."

Cobra gently set her on the ground. He said, "If I lose, ventilate him. If you can't get a shot," he said, "then ventilate us both."

"No problem," she said.

"Really?" he asked. "None at all?"

"Nope."

Cobra then turned to Black Tiger, who was smiling from ear to ear. Black Tiger said, "You really have learned nothing. Biggest mistake of your life."

"Like I told your henchman Priest, we take wildlife crime pretty seriously in these parts. You did just poach that magnificent lion yesterday. Now I'm going to poach your goddamn nuts. It's Christmas morning, and I told you that I would finally get what I wanted for the last four years: your ass lying in a puddle of blood under a Douglas fucking Fir!"

"No Douglas Firs in Africa," corrected the Professor from the ground. "Just *acacia tortillis*."

"Thanks, Professor," he replied, cracking his knuckles, "but I'll just have to make this work anyway."

Cobra ran to Black Tiger and greeted him with a predictable, wide-swinging right with all his momentum behind it, which, of course, Black Tiger easily parried. Almost gently, Tiger pushed Cobra backward two feet and then nailed him with a full-on, dragon-whips-his-tail, spinning hook kick to the head. Cobra spun horizontally through the air as if he were in some hi-octane Hong Kong action movie, crashing unceremoniously to the dirt below.

Clutching his head in his hands, Cobra said, "Recovered your balance pretty good, didn't you?"

"Learned that in Myanmar," smiled Black Tiger, swinging his foot straight up in the air and then bringing his heel down like an axe upon Cobra's head. Cobra rolled out of the way, missing the blow by inches.

"South Korea," Black Tiger boasted, pivoting on the ball of his foot and driving his instep into Cobra's jaw, a textbook roundhouse. Cobra spat blood, dizzy.

"Brazil," he said, grabbing Cobra by the neck and slamming him down again on the hard ground. Without slowing down, Black Tiger drove his knee into Cobra's solar plexus, making him gasp for air. "Tel Aviv."

Cobra struggled to his feet, and if he were in a cartoon, there would have been little birdies floating around in circles above his head. At least he was standing, or more accurately, wobbling.

"South Bronx, bitch!" cursed Black Tiger, swinging his foot towards Cobra's groin. But Cobra angled his shin just enough to solidly block Tiger's boot, something he'd learned in...

"Tangiers," Cobra smiled, teeth bloody, before thrusting his skull into Tiger's nose, shattering it like a water balloon filled with fruit punch. "Mineola, Long Island. Church parking lot!"

Cobra unloaded. Left, right, left, right, left... huge right hand to Black Tiger's eye. Tiger staggered backward, feet unsteady and eyes watering.

"Don't feel badly," taunted Cobra. "Even A-Rod strikes out sometimes."

Black Tiger didn't like that. He dashed towards Cobra and took to the air, leaping a full four feet off the ground and planting his foot into Cobra's chest - almost through Cobra's chest, with all the momentum - sending Cobra rolling backward and off his feet.

Black Tiger kept moving forward, and he grabbed Cobra by the scruff of his neck and by the back of his belt and threw him out like garbage on recycling day into the smoldering embers in the fire pit. Cobra screamed like a ten-year-old girl, his hands and face stinging, his clothes black with ash and soot. He rolled out of the pit, just a foot or so away from it, and dusted the hot embers away from his skin.

Pleased with himself, Black Tiger marched over to Cobra to dispense further harm but was rewarded by Cobra smashing a still-burning log into his ribs, doubling him over. Cobra leapt to his feet and tackled Black Tiger to the ground, but he was having none of it and clutched Cobra's arm and tried to swing his legs up around his head, attempting a punishing jiu-jitsu maneuver popularly referred to in MMA as a triangle.

Bullets snapped into the ground around them, and Black Tiger quickly released Cobra's arm. They both rolled to their feet.

"What the fuck are you doing? Stop it!" yelled Cobra to the Professor, whose rifle barrel was smoking.

"Oh, come on," she said plaintively. "Like you were getting out of that."

"He didn't have it locked in! I was about to make a move!"

"Yeah, OK," she said. "You wish."

Distraction over, Black Tiger slid in and kicked Cobra in the guts. Cobra tried the wide, arching right again, to which Tiger put his hand up to parry, not realizing that Cobra had learned from his mistake and was only feinting this time. Cobra got under Black Tiger's chin with a left uppercut, lifting him right off the ground.

"You may have mastered the art of fighting," said Cobra, "but I have a degree in the refined science of brawling."

"Fuck you," gnashed out Black Tiger, dazed and barely standing.

"I'm blushing! Now, I'm even going to tell you the punch I'm about to throw, because I'm just that confident that there's nothing you can do to stop it. That's how badly I've beaten you. I want you to remember this feeling of helplessness. Ready?"

"Go to Hell."

"Right cross to left eye," said Cobra, and he delivered on his promise, finally connecting with that big right hand, turning Black Tiger around into the thick thorn bushes encircling the boma. Cobra snatched Black Tiger by his ponytail and yanked him back into a headlock from behind, squeezing both carotid arteries, feeling the life draining from his opponent.

With his last ounce of strength, Black Tiger managed to tap Cobra's arm in submission. Cobra pushed Black Tiger down into the thorn bushes, and air flowed back into Santana's lungs.

Cobra tore the tiger-claw bracelets from both of Tiger's arms.

"Look at you, Campbell McConnors," wheezed Black Tiger, bleeding into the dirt where his assault rifle lay under the thorns, visible only to him. "Looks like you got your Christmas wish after all."

"It's Cobra McCoors, and you're not Black Tiger anymore. You're on your knees; that's good practice for when Red Scorpion finds you."

"Cobra!" screamed the Professor, noticing the gun by Tiger's hand. Cobra was in her way; she had no shot.

In a flash, Tiger raised the assault rifle and fired; Cobra fell to the ground in a cloud of dust and blood.

"You stupid, arrogant..." laughed Black Tiger, but he was suddenly grabbed around the throat and pulled *through* the thorny wall of the boma with such force it seemed impossible that his head didn't pop off like a dandelion.

It was an elephant - Attenborough - and he remembered. He remembered Black Tiger, he remembered what guns do, and he remembered the female lying dead in the riverbed before the rains washed over her.

Attenborough thrashed Black Tiger about as though he were a rag doll. He smashed him on the ground and pinned him in place, a tusk on either side, and crushed him under the weight of his head, oblivious to Tiger's choking shrieks. He stood up, took two steps backward, and trampled on Tiger's body, before finally picking him up again with his trunk and tossing him back through the thorns into the boma.

The mighty elephant trumpeted so loudly that all the other sounds of the bush stopped, each creature paying respect to his proclamation, and then he continued off into the bush.

The Professor ran over to Cobra, lying face-down and turning the dirt beneath him into mud with his leaking body. She didn't see any exit wounds; she quickly turned him around.

"Cobra," she cried. "Are you alive?"

"Pretty sure," he said. "Because I'm in a shit-load of pain."

"I don't see any new holes," she said, checking him over. "I think he missed you. You're bleeding from all your old ones."

"I thought you said you'd shoot us both if you couldn't get a shot," he said.

"I didn't," she laughed, "because I knew I wouldn't miss you."

"You wish," he laughed back, and she kissed him, but quickly stopped because of all the blood in his mouth.

"Gross," she said, and then, "Jesus, look..."

They both saw Black Tiger's hand, or what was left of it, twitching. His chest undulated as he took short, sporadic breaths. The son of a bitch was still alive.

\*\*\*

Later that night, Katy had prepared a complete Christmas dinner for Wyatt, Cobra, the guests and for about two dozen South African tactical commandos who had remained on the property after they came in to clean up the mess. They had airlifted many of the wounded out and had apprehended most of Black Tiger's force at both the lodge and his main camp out by the grasslands. Priest was not among them.

When last Cobra saw Black Tiger, he was still breathing,

clinging to life as if by sheer will alone. Cobra wondered if he had taken classes on not dying. They strapped him tightly to a chopper headed for some medical center in Joburg and had given him fifty-fifty odds of survival at best, and frankly, Cobra thought those odds were higher than he was comfortable with.

But it was a merry Christmas after all, with guests and soldiers alike drinking and singing Andy Williams' classic "Happy Holidays" outside in the boma around a roaring fire. And everyone tipped Cobra very high. Well. Almost everybody.

Kevin and Xavier sat together by the fire, a blanket around Kevin and fresh bandages around Xavier's head. The medic said both were expected to make full recoveries; despite how much time had transpired, Kevin's flesh was only a little necrotic, which meant his future of playing league soccer was not in jeopardy. Xavier would require a brain scan just to be sure, but he seemed OK, and the medic exonerated most of his erratic behavior, saying that traumatic brain injuries often make people coo-coo for Cocoa Puffs.

"Merry Christmas, Xavier," said Kevin.

"Merry Christmas, Kev," replied Xavier.

"You saved my life out there," said Kevin.

"You saved mine too, Kev," said Xavier.

A moment passed, and they heard the hyenas caroling to the lions out in the bush over the revelry.

"I think we should see other people," said Kevin, and Xavier burst out laughing.


"You're hired," said Katy, freshening up people's wine glasses.

"Really? Even though I threatened your staff with a loaded gun?" asked Susan.

"You showed initiative. And your omelet wasn't half bad."

"It's like the ones they serve in the restaurant in Rome's..."

"Conditional upon you stopping that bullshit. You're scrubbing toilets, chopping onions, and cleaning zebra shit off the walkway. We'll pay you in room and board and no questions asked, seeing as how you have a wad of money in that purse of yours anyway. Deal?"

"Deal," Susan said. "Thank you for your kindness."

"This is a good place to hide yourself," said Katy, remembering some story she's obviously never shared, "or to find yourself."


"May the merry bells keep bringing," sang Wyatt, totally hammered, "happy holidays to yoooooooou!"

"Ringing!" corrected Kotani, bandaged like Imhotep, "merry bells keep *ringing* happy holidays to you!"

"No, no, no! The bells *bring* you happy holidays. That's the point of the friggin' song!"

One of Kotani's San companions said, "Bells ring. That's what bells do! How can a bell bring you something?"

On the other side of the fire, Annie gave the Professor the warmest hug she'd ever given her.

"I love you, Wildhorse," she gushed. "Thank you, thank you, thank you for bringing me to this place. I know it wasn't my first choice, but it was one of the most unbelievable experiences of my life. Real *Eat Pray Love* shit. It changed my life in a profound way."

"I think Wyatt touched your," said the Professor, "life in a profound way."

"Ha! There's no denying that."

"So, you and Wyatt?"

"No, I don't think so. He was a lot of fun, but I think it's best if we keep the memories and move on. I will ride him like a Harley on a bad stretch of road tonight, if he doesn't pass out first," she admitted. "So, you and Cobra?"

"You know, I don't really know," said the Professor, watching Cobra with Andres (who, as you may have guessed, withheld gratuity). "I have to finish my Ph.D., and then I've got to do some work on the Reservation. I owe them that much, at least."

"Of course," said Annie. "But don't forget to live your own life, Wildhorse. You owe yourself that much, at least. I mean, Professor."


"When can I expect my compensation?" asked Andres.

"After all that, you're still harping about that fucking camera, Andres?" asked Cobra, guzzling a Castle. "We've been through life and death together!"

"That was our arrangement. Are you not fulfilling your promise?"

"Wyatt says he'll match whatever the cost is, plus another five hundred for your troubles. Katy will wire it to a bank of your choice once you provide a routing number, and I guess after we share a flight to Cape Town tomorrow, our transaction is complete," said Cobra.

"Good," said Andres. "The sooner, the better. Northside will care for Susan, I trust?"

"She'll be safer here than anywhere on earth," said Cobra.

"Ha. That's what you said about all of us three days ago. I will check up on her, from time to time."

"She's important to you," said Cobra.

"Not really. The only thing that matters to me is that my camera is replaced and this debacle is far behind me."

Cobra nodded and took another swig of beer.

Andres said, "I wanted to put together a book - a book of photography - that might raise money for African wildlife."

"Really?"

"They have so few voices, so few people to speak for them,

for conservation," said Andres, looking out into the bush, wondering what wild things were roaming in the magical darkness, doing as they had done for untold thousands of years. "I like animals. You don't have to be self-conscious in front of them, don't have to watch what you say, don't have to pick up on subtle social cues constructed by society. It's the only honesty left on this planet, the relationship between the camera and the subject."

"You don't strike me as a self-conscious guy at all," said Cobra, only beginning to understand. "You'll just have to visit us again."

"I doubt that," said Andres. He noticed that Cobra was watching Hyacinth, who was by herself at the entrance to the boma, gazing out at the endless sky over the savanna. "I tire of your prattle, Cobra McCoors. Why don't you go bother her?"

"You're all right, Andres," said Cobra, slapping him lightly on the back.

---

Cobra took Hyacinth's hand, seeing her face wet with tears as she kept her vigil, scanning the heavens.

"Merry Christmas, Hyacinth," said Cobra, offering her a beer.

She took the beer and sank it, handing him back an empty bottle. "Merry Christmas, Cobra."

"You kicked a lot of ass today. You were like Desert Storm Commando Warriors with that AR-15."

"I keep expecting Mark to show up in the clouds, like Mufasa or something," she said. "He loved Christmas. It was always his favorite time of year."

"Well, you really honored his memory today."

"Yeah. Imagine that," she said, wiping tears from her eyes. "He's home now. And it's a beautiful home, a place where his soul can be forever at peace. That does not a goddamn thing for me right now, but it'll be a comforting thought later."

Cobra said, "Andres reminded me of a German man whose son had loved the bush, who died in the Serengeti, who's buried out there. I think he was trying to tell me something."

"What about you, Cobra? Do you ever want to go home?"

"I can't," said Cobra. "That part of my life is done now."

"You can't? Why not?"

"I've done some things I've been running from for years now. When I was a soldier, a big mess."

"What did you do?"

"It's blurry, now that I look back on it. I trusted the wrong people, let myself get used, didn't act soon enough, and then ran for my life. A lot of people got hurt. I'm a deserter."

"That's awful, Cobra. It's a terrible thing to never be able to go home."

"Africa's my real home now, and it's one I'll never take for granted, and I'm proud that I spent years trying to make myself into someone I respected, instead of what others expected of me. But in some ways, I've never faced up to what I've done," said Cobra, taking a swig of his beer. "When I say it like that, it makes me sound like kind of a coward."

"You took responsibility for all of us these last three days," said Hyacinth.

"Yeah. I guess so."

Cobra looked out into the bush, drinking in the wonder of this amazing place.

"If you had the chance to take responsibility for what you had done in the past, would you take it?"

# CHAPTER 26:
# COBRA McCOORS, I PRESUME

If you're ever in Cape Town and have the opportunity to go to the top of Table Mountain, you should do it. Assuming it's not too windy, you have to ride a large, circular funicular all the way up to the top as it gently spins. Once you're up there, you're treated to what feels like another world, a secret wonderland of paths criss-crossing through green gardens and offering a spectacular vista of the whole city and surrounding waters. It's not Kilimanjaro; in fact, it's more like a tall, flat, table-shaped plateau than an alpine peak, but the air is definitely quite a bit cooler up there, and it's one of those tourist experiences that actually is worth braving all the other tourists.

Cobra had spent the morning at Mitchell's Pub, and he would have gladly spent the afternoon there as well, but he had an almost tangible sensation that this was the right thing to do. He stood, bracing against one of the mossy rocks, and felt the moisture of a low-hanging cloud against his skin. He watched the V&A Waterfront from here, boats docking at the piers, even as the hyraxes (or dassies, in South African parlance) curiously peeked out from under their little hiding spots to view him. You'll recall that while dassies look like large groundhogs, they're more closely related to elephants. They seemed to wonder too what Cobra had brought in his large, canvas sack.

He saw Hyacinth, dressed more formally than the last time

he'd seen her, coming out through the mist from the little restaurant that receives visitors. Behind her was an older man with white hair, eyes permanently frozen in mid-squint, and skin that looked tougher than microwaved steak.

Cobra and Hyacinth embraced.

"How're you holding up, Hyacinth?"

"I'm having a tough time, Cobra. I'm having a real tough time."

"Take it slowly," said Cobra. "Talk to him, out loud, as often as you want."

"I have been, Cobra," said Hyacinth. "Anyway, I'd like to introduce you to Jeff Devonshire. Jeff, Cobra; Cobra, Jeff."

As they shook hands, Cobra was taken aback by how powerful his grip was; although he had a few years under his belt, his age disguised an efficient, off-the-charts strength. There was something very sullen about Jeff, as if he had faced many demons, personal and otherwise.

"Let's sit, Mr. McConnors," said Jeff, escorting Hyacinth to a bench and waiting for Cobra to do the same.

"Please call me Cobra," said Cobra, but when Jeff gave him a wilting glare, he added, "Campbell is fine."

"Hyacinth tells me you had yourselves a little adventure," started Jeff.

"That's not typical for a safari at Rhino Horn. I hope you won't judge our hard-working staff by this incident."

"What can you tell me about Hernandez Santana?" asked Jeff bluntly.

"Did he make it? Is he alive?"

"He is. We have him in a secure facility. He hasn't come back to a state where he can communicate with us. We'd like to know more about him," said Jeff.

"*We* would?" asked Cobra. "Could you clarify who *we* is, please?"

"Some people interested in the security of our nation, and

that of the world at large."

"Mm, nope. Gonna have to do better than that. I've already seen the movie where the naive idiot trusts someone they don't know claiming to be an authority figure. It's how this mess started in the first place. NSA? CIA? FBI? IRS? Give me an acronym, at least."

"I'm not a very patient man, McConnors. If I were to tell you that I represent any of those organizations, would you even know how to verify it anyway? Pick one, for fuck's sake."

"CIA."

"Fine, you guessed it. CIA."

"Cobra, I've known Jeff for a long time. You can trust him," said Hyacinth.

"All right, then. Santana went by the name Black Tiger for most of the time I've known him. He's from New York, from a rough part of the Bronx. He felt like his options were limited as a teenager and decided to expand his horizons by learning how to kill, maim, and torture by traveling the world looking for conflict; he also picked up social skills like masking his native accent by finding the right teachers. Allegedly killed a tiger with his bare hands. Likes the Yankees, not the Mets, if that helps you out at all."

"And you first encountered him when you were an Arabic translator for the army in Iraq," nodded Jeff, his voice gruff.

"He was taking some associates of his out into the dessert to find some rare artifact, a priceless statue of a woman with a few animal parts thrown in, forged in gold and adorned with gems," said Cobra. "I was young and stupid, and I was complicit in helping Black Tiger and his friends try to acquire this thing. I thought I was following orders."

"And people died, including the vehicle driver, one Kurt Christian, is that right?" cut in Jeff.

Cobra took a deep breath. "Yes. That's right. Black Tiger's people then tried to kill me, but I escaped into the desert. I never returned to the base, since I knew I would be court-martialed and probably executed, if I weren't killed by Black Tiger's friends or insurgents along the way. I've been in Africa ever since."

"And what about his friends?"

"There were three of them. A woman with short hair that went by Grey Shark. A big guy named Blue Viper. You can see they had fun with the handles; we've got kind of a pattern going here."

"And?"

"The final boss. Red Scorpion; they sometimes called him the Baron. Had an eastern European accent of some kind. They all deferred to him; he's the one you really need to look out for."

"No," said Jeff. "He's the one *you* need to look out for."

"Come again?"

"You have a unique knowledge of this small cadre that we'd like to exploit. You are in a very elite group of people who've interacted with them and are still breathing. We hope to interrogate Black Tiger should his condition improve, but besides him, you're really the only one we can use to lure them out into the open."

"As bait," said Cobra, not thrilled with this idea.

"As an agent of the United States of America paying off his debt to society. You are still a traitor to the nation, and we have every right to take you into custody and see you hang for that fiasco in the Middle East," said Jeff.

"Hey, I came here in good faith."

"So did I; that's why you're not in handcuffs, but Christmas is over."

"You know it wasn't my fault. I had no choice," protested Cobra.

"We all shoulder responsibility for our choices," said Jeff. "Me more than anyone. But if you agree to work for us..."

"...with you..." corrected Cobra.

"...with us, we'd exonerate you on the charge of treason and the army would grant you an honorable discharge. We'd clear your name. That's more than most get, Cobra. You'd be stupid not to take this deal."

Cobra looked out across the bay, watching some gulls ascend on thermal updrafts as though they were riding invisible elevators.

"I may be stupid anyway, but I'll take the deal. I'm not wearing a tie, though," he finally said.

"I won't either," said Jeff. "I'll be your handler, and since she's decided she now has somewhat of a personal stake in this affair, Hyacinth will be your contact."

Hyacinth said, "Make sure you tip me high."

Jeff said, "We know very little about these terrorists, not even their real names. We're not sure why they go after these artifacts, stealing the world's heritage, except perhaps to sell them and finance whatever their real agenda might be. And speaking of, there's one more matter to take care of, before our transaction is ratified."

Cobra nodded, both disappointed and relieved. He retrieved the lamassu from his burlap sack and handed it over to Jeff. Above the clouds, the sun reflected sharply off its golden finish.

"We'll arrange for this to be on display at a university museum in the Middle East until the people of Baghdad are ready to receive her. It's theirs, after all."

"Careful with her," said Cobra. "I hear she's cursed."

\*\*\*

A field of endless cornstalks. White picket fence. A few chickens running around the house from the barn. A windmill standing guard over the farm, with a bright blue sky above and an old, worn American flag below.

Cobra pulled the rental car up the dirt driveway and killed

the engine.

"Well," he said. "Here we are."

"We are here," said the Professor. "Want me to come in?"

Cobra took a very deep breath. "I don't think so. Not at first, anyway. Need a magazine or something?"

The Professor smiled. "I have data to look at."

"Maybe I should have worn a suit. A sport coat, at least."

She took his chin in her hands and gently turned his head to look her in the eyes. "It's going to be fine. You'll see."

"I know. What do you think she'll say?"

"Probably nothing, at first."

"Probably nothing," echoed Cobra.

"Only one way to find out," she said.

Cobra nodded, took the folded American flag with the dog tags draped over it, and got out of the car. He touched the mailbox, the N missing from the name CHRISTIA in hardware-store, adhesive letters, and went to the doorstep, where he paused, his heart still heavy.

Cobra knocked at the door and waited, knowing that until he went through this door, there was really no other place else he could go.

# EPILOGUE:
# MANY YEARS FROM NOW, PLUS A
# COUPLE OF HOURS

There, you see?  That wasn't a terrible way to burn through a few hours, was it?  I don't know if you noticed, but that bruiser must have gotten bored and left Dodge, although I haven't checked the floor.  I'm sure I'm not the only one who's passed out on the hardwood in this place.

How is it possible we still have whiskey in this bottle?  You haven't been keeping up your end, my friend, because I know I've been keeping up mine.  Yes, that story is true, more or less, and the names have not been changed to protect anyone, mostly because I don't really give a fuck.  I love telling it, though. Fires like this one just beg for these kinds of tales.

Finally, I see the one I'm meeting here over at the door. You're welcome to stay, of course, unless you want to get some shut-eye before you climb the ninth circle of frozen hell tomorrow. Not for me, I don't think, but I'd never judge what someone wants to do for a little adventure.  I mean, when it all boils down, nobody on their death bed wishes they'd spent more time at the office, unless you work for *Hustler* or something, I guess.

You know, I'm getting on in years a little, but now that you mention it, maybe looking for a little adventure tonight is not the worst idea after all.

# COBRA'S G&T RECIPE

1) Squeeze the juice of a ½ lime into a large, frozen beer mug (larger than a pint). Leave the fruit in the bottom of the mug.

2) Squeeze the juice of a ¼ lemon into the mug. Leave the fruit in the bottom of the mug with the lime; don't worry about the seeds.

3) Fill the mug to the brim with ice.

4) Pour (at least) 2 full shots of gin over the ice. Hopefully, you've had the foresight to chill the bottle. Don't over-spend on gin; Cobra prefers Gordon's Extra Dry, but he's not picky.

5) Fill the remainder of the mug with diet (or regular, if you prefer) tonic water and stir gently.

# COBRA'S SCOTCH RECIPE

1) Open bottle.

2) Drink (pour in shot glass/tumbler if you're feeling fancy; one ice cube or a splash of water is not unacceptable, if you must).

# AUTHOR'S NOTE

The landscape of the (fictional) Rhino Horn Ranch is a gestalt of several real wildlife parks and reserves. Geographically, it would appear somewhere near Kgalagadi Transfrontier Park in the northwest corner of South Africa. In creating Rhino Horn, I've borrowed elements from the savannahs of the Timbavati and Sabi Sands, the desert thirstlands of Central Kalahari Game Reserve in Botswana, and bits and pieces of Tsavo West, Samburu and the Mara Triangle in Kenya.

There is nothing like an African wildlife safari; please do not let the outrageous and improbable events described in this work of fiction discourage you from exploring the wonderful parks of East and Southern Africa.

I'd like to thank Linda Friedman, Kathy Obbish, David Nganga, Nancy Karanja, James Morinte, Joseph Ngige, John Ngure and the entire staff of Custom Safaris for making our safari dreams come true again and again.

# RESOURCES

Linda Friedman
Custom Safaris (book an amazing wildlife safari)
9504 Starmont Road
Bethesda, MD 20817 USA
1 (301) 530-1982
1 (866) 530-1982
info@customsafaris.com

Panthera (support big cat conservation)
8 West 40th Street
18th Floor
New York, NY 10018
1 (646) 786-0400
panthera.org

Save the Elephants (support elephant conservation)
Marula Manor, Marula Lane, Karen
P.O. Box 54667
Nairobi 00200
254 720 441 178
savetheelephants.org

Daphne Sheldrick (support orphaned wildlife of Kenya)
25283 Cabot Road
Suite 101
Laguna Hills, CA 92653
1 (949) 305-3785
sheldrickwildlifetrust.org

# ABOUT THE AUTHOR

Michael Tumminio has a BFA in Dramatic Writing from NYU and an MFA in English and Education from Hunter College. He teaches English/Language Arts in Brooklyn, where he lives with his wife and dog. At the time of this writing, he has been on five African safaris and is currently planning his sixth. He prefers Johnnie Walker Black Label and Laphroig 10-Year, but like Cobra, he's not picky.

Made in the USA
Monee, IL
11 June 2021

70957206R00226